The Enchanted Wanderer
Selected Tales

Christina 1990

Ben

Nikolai Leskov

The Enchanted Wanderer
Selected Tales

Nikolai Leskov

Translated by David Magarshak

Farrar Straus and Giroux
New York

Contents

Translator's Preface

⁜⁜⁜⁜
⁜⁜⁜⁜ Nikolai Leskov was born in the village of Gorokhovo, Oryol Province, on February 16, 1831. He was the son of a poor civil servant. As a child, he came in close contact with the common people, his grandmother, Alexandra Alferyev, taking him with her to the different monasteries she used to visit regularly (these early memories of Russian ecclesiastical life he was to use later with telling effect in *Cathedral Folk*, the most famous of his novels). His nurse, Anna Kalandin, also helped to instill in him a love for the colloquial Russian speech and a regard for the illiterate and often inarticulate peasant. Many years later he acknowledged it himself by declaring that, unlike many another Russian writer, he did not learn to know the Russian people "from conversations with Petersburg cabbies," but that he had grown up among the common people who accepted him as one of them.

"I have still many personal friends among them," he declared, "and I have therefore no need either to raise them on stilts or trample them underfoot."

At the age of ten Leskov was sent to the Oryol secondary school, but he left it five years later without finishing the eight-year course. Instead of doing his homework, he spent most of his free time in the large library of Prince Mossalsky, to which he had access. He read, as he later declared, almost every book in that library. In 1847 he joined the civil service and became a junior clerk in the Oryol criminal court. (Reference to these two far from successful events of his early life will be found in his story *The White Eagle*.) Three years later he got himself transferred to Kiev, where his uncle, S. P. Alferyev, was professor of medicine at the University. There, among his uncle's friends and students, he had many opportunities to fill the gaps in his education. But the stigma of lacking a university education clung to him all through his life and the question, "Aren't you a graduate of Kiev University?" was always certain to make him flush with anger. The fact remains, however, that it was just because he was practically a self-taught man that his writings are marvelously free from any "literary" taint and his language is so amazingly rich and idiomatic.

Another factor that helped to shape Leskov's art was that, on leaving the Civil Service in 1857, he joined the English firm of Wilkins and Scott, one of the directors of which, Alexander Scott, a "Russified" Englishman, was his uncle by marriage. As a member of this firm, Leskov had to travel all over Russia, and it was during these travels that he obtained the raw material for his novels and stories.

Leskov began his writing career as a journalist. His articles dealing with different aspects of Russian social and economic life began to appear in 1860. His first stories were published in 1862 and for the next thirty-three years (he died on March 8, 1895) he devoted himself entirely to literary work. "I love literature," he wrote, "as something that enables me to express what I regard as truth and what I esteem to be good for humanity at large. I do not look upon literature as an art pure and simple. The term 'art for art's sake' is entirely incomprehensible to me. Art must be of benefit to mankind, for it is only then that it acquires a definite meaning. The same is true of literature. If a writer cannot serve truth and goodness by it he might as well give up his profession and do something else. I cannot imagine," he concludes, "any more than I can imagine myself as a tall man, how any writer can sit down and write a novel if he does not know why he is writing it. I cannot, of course, tell beforehand whether my story will turn out as well as I should like, but I do know *why* I am writing this story or novel and what I want to say by it."

The five stories in the present volume cover every period of his writing career and show his profound knowledge of the human heart and his great wisdom and humanity, qualities that assured him a large reading public in his lifetime and secured him his unique position among the Russian writers of the first rank.

Lady Macbeth of the Mtsensk District, published in 1865 in the January number of Dostoevsky's periodical *Epoch*, is Leskov's first major work. "I wrote it," Leskov declared twenty-three years later in a letter to a friend, "without any firsthand knowledge of the world of convicts, but the late Dostoevsky found that I had reproduced it remarkably well." The story was finished in November 1864, in Kiev. To be able to concentrate on it Leskov used to lock himself in the punishment cells of Kiev University at the end of a long and gloomy corridor and spent hours there, his nerves, as he recalled many years later, "so highly strung" that it nearly drove him "into a delirium." As he conjured up the dreadful events of that terrible story, his hair stood on end and he grew cold with terror at the movement of his leg or a turn of his head. "Those painful moments," Leskov declared, "I shall never forget and since then I have avoided the description of such horrors." And, indeed, the effect of the story is quite hair-raising in its stark realism. The story, incidentally, has been turned into an opera by Shostakovich and was first performed in Leningrad in 1934.

Quite different is the effect of Leskov's magnificent picaresque tale of *The Enchanted Wanderer*, one of his most famous short novels. Leskov visited the monastery islands of Korela, Konevetz, and Valaam on Lake Ladoga in the summer of 1872. He described the impressions of his visit in a series of articles which appeared in the newspaper *Russian World* from August 8 to September 19, 1873, and he published *The Enchanted Wanderer* in the same paper in October and November 1873.

The Left-handed Craftsman, published in the monthly periodical *Russia* in October 1881, is written more in the manner of the traditional Russian folk tale or *skaz* than *The Enchanted Wanderer*, but actually it is based, according to Leskov himself, on nothing more than the jocular saying: "The English made a flea out of steel, but our Tula craftsmen shod it and sent it back." "This," Leskov wrote in *New Times* on June 11, 1882, "is the only 'folk' element about the 'flea' and the 'left-handed craftsman.' I must confess that I invented the whole story myself in May of last year and the left-handed craftsman is a completely fictitious character." The moral of the story, however, is real enough, as recent events have all too clearly shown.

The Sentry belongs to the last period of Leskov's authorship. It is one of his best historical sketches based on ascertainable fact. It was first published in the monthly periodical *Russian Thought* in April 1887. Leskov was told of the incident of the saving of a drowning man by a sentry outside the Winter Palace by General Nikolai Ivanovich Miller, former director of the Alexandrovsk Lycée, who was the Captain Miller of the story. The bishop in the last chapter of the story is the celebrated Moscow Archbishop Filaret Drozdov, who is also mentioned in the first chapter of *The Enchanted Wanderer*.

Russian literature has no tradition of spooky ghost stories and Leskov's *White Eagle* is a unique example in this genre. It is more of a psychological study than a blood-curdler, and a delightful example of Leskov's light satirical vein.

D.M.

Lady Macbeth of the Mtsensk District

It's only the first song that brings a blush to the cheek. [RUSSIAN PROVERB]

1.

In our part of the country you occasionally come across characters some of whom you can never remember without an inward shudder however many years may have passed since you first met them. Such a character was Katerina Lvovna Izmaylov, a merchant's wife, who some time ago played the chief part in so terrible a tragedy that the gentlemen of our neighborhood began calling her the Lady Macbeth of the Mtsensk District, a name first invented for her on the spur of the moment by someone or other.

Katerina was not a beauty in the strict sense of the word, but she was a very attractive woman all the same. She was about twenty-four, not very tall, but slim, with a neck that was like chiselled marble, fine round shoulders, firm breasts, a straight, thin little nose, a pair of sparkling black eyes, a high white forehead, and black, almost raven black hair. She was given in marriage to Zinovy Izmaylov, a merchant of our district, by her parents, who lived at Tuskar in the Kursk province, not because she was in love with him, but simply because Izmaylov had made a proposal of marriage and, being a poor girl, she could not be very particular about the choice of a husband.

The Izmaylov business was one of the most important in our town: they dealt in the best quality wheat flour, leased a large mill in our district, owned a profitable orchard on the outskirts of our town and a fine house in the town. They were, in fact, wealthy merchants. Their family, besides, was quite small—it consisted of her father-in-law, Boris Timofeyevich Izmaylov, a man of nearly eighty who had long been a widower, his son Zinovy, Katerina's husband, and Katerina herself. Katerina had no children, though she had been married for five years. Zinovy had no children by his first wife, with whom he had lived for twenty years before he became a widower and married Katerina. He had thought and hoped that God would at least give him by his second wife an heir to whom he could leave his fortune and business, but he was unlucky also in his second marriage.

Not having children grieved Zinovy very much, and not only Zinovy, but also his old father Boris, and indeed it made even Katerina very sad. For one thing, living in the locked and bolted merchant's great house with its high fence and its unleashed watchdogs made the young woman feel so bored sometimes that she was nearly driven out of her mind, and she would have been only too glad—God only knows how glad—to have had a child to nurse and fuss over. Besides, she was tired of hearing such constant reproaches as: "Why did you get married? What for? Why have you, a barren woman, ruined a man's life?" Just as though she had committed a crime against her husband, against her father-in-law, and against their entire family of honest merchants.

In spite of all the wealth and prosperity, Katrina's life in her father-in-law's house was very dull. She rarely went out of the house, and if she did go out with her husband to visit some of his merchant friends, she did not enjoy it very much. His friends were all so strict: they watched how she sat down, how she walked across the room, and how she got up. Katerina had a passionate nature and, having been brought up in poverty, she was accustomed to simplicity and freedom: running down to the river with pails, bathing under the pier in a shift, or scattering husks of sunflower seeds over the gate on any young fellow who happened to pass by. Here everything was different. Her husband and father-in-law got up very early, had their tea at six o'clock, and then went out to attend to their business, while she was left alone in the house, to walk aimlessly about from one room to another. Everywhere it was clean, everywhere it was quiet and empty, the lamps glimmering before the icons and not a living sound, not a human voice, in the whole house.

Katerina walked about the empty rooms, yawned out of sheer boredom, and at last went upstairs to the bedroom she and her husband shared in the high, small attic. There, too, she sat for hours at the window, looking at the men weighing hemp or filling sacks with white flour, and again she would begin to yawn and she was glad when she felt sleepy; she would take a nap for an hour or two, and when she woke, there was again the same Russian boredom, the boredom of a merchant's house, the sort of boredom that, people say, would make one glad even to hang oneself. Katerina was not very keen on reading and, besides, there were no books in the house except the Kiev *Lives of the Fathers*.

It was a dull existence Katerina had led in the house of her rich father-in-law all the five years of her married life with her indifferent husband; but, as usual, nobody took the slightest notice of that!

2.

In the spring of the sixth year of Katerina's marriage the dam of the Izmaylovs' mill burst. As it happened, a great deal of work had been brought to the mill just at that time and the breach in the dam made by the water was quite enormous: the water had flowed under the lower beam of the millrace and it had been impossible to stop it in time. Zinovy had brought workmen from all over the district to the mill and he himself spent all his time there; his old father carried on with the business in town, and his old father carried on with the business in town, and Katerina languished at home for days on end. At first she was even more bored without her husband, but soon she felt much better: she was freer when alone. She had never particularly liked her husband and without him there was at any rate one man less to order her about.

One day Katerina was sitting at the small window of her attic bedroom, yawning for all she was worth and without a thought of anything in particular. At last she became ashamed of yawning. The weather was lovely: warm, bright, gay, and through the green trellis of the garden fence she could see the busy birds in the trees fluttering from branch to branch.

"Why am I yawning?" thought Katerina. "Why shouldn't I get up and walk in the yard or stroll in the garden?"

Katerina threw an old wool and fur cloak over her shoulders and went out.

It was bright and sunny in the yard. She could breathe freely and could hear laughter coming from the steps near the barns.

"What's so amusing?" Katerina asked her father-in-law's clerks.

"Why, ma'am," an old clerk answered, "they've been weighing a live sow."

"Oh? What sow?"

"Remember Aksinya, who gave birth to a son, Vassily, and never invited us to his christening?" a young fellow replied boldly and gaily; he had an impudent, handsome face, framed in curly, coal-black hair, and a little beard that was just beginning to sprout.

At that moment the fat, red face of the cook Aksinya peeped out of the flour vat attached to the beam of the weighing machine.

"Oh, you devils, you sleek-faced sons of the evil one," the cook swore, trying to catch hold of the iron beam and scramble out of the swaying vat.

"Weighs ten stone before dinner, but when she's eaten a bagful of hay there won't be enough weight left unless we skin her," the handsome young fellow explained again and, turning the vat over, flung the cook out on some sacks that were heaped up in a corner.

The peasant woman, swearing at them good-naturedly, began to put herself in order.

"Well, and how much do you think I weigh?" Katerina asked jokingly and, taking hold of the rope, she stepped on to the plank of the weighing machine.

"Seven stone, fifteen pounds," Sergey, the handsome young fellow, answered at once, throwing the weights on to the weighing machine. "Good Lord!"

"What's the matter?"

"Why, you weigh only seven stone, seven, ma'am. One could carry you about all day in one's arms, I imagine, and not get tired—it would be nothing but pleasure."

"I'm a human being and not a bundle. I don't doubt you'd get tired," Katerina answered, blushing slightly and feeling a sudden desire to talk and banter.

"Not a bit! Why, good heavens, I'd carry you to Araby the blest," Sergey said in answer to her remark.

"You're wrong, you know, young man," said a peasant who was filling the sacks. "Now, what do you think weight is? You see, it's not our body that weighs. Our body, my dear man, counts for nothing on the scales. It's our strength that weighs, not our body."

"Yes, I was terribly strong when I was a girl," Katerina said, again unable to restrain herself. "Stronger than a good many men."

"Oh well, ma'am, if that's so, give me your hand," said the handsome young clerk.

Katerina looked embarrassed, but she held out her hand.

"Let go of my ring, it hurts!" Katerina cried when Sergey squeezed her hand in his, and with her free hand she hit him on the chest.

The young fellow let go of the mistress' hand and staggered back two paces from the blow.

"Well, I'm damned," cried the little peasant in surprise, "who would have thought that of a woman!"

"Oh, no," Sergey, tossing back his curls, protested. "If you want to see who's stronger, try wrestling with me."

"All right, come on!" Katerina answered gaily, lifting up her elbows.

Sergey put his arms round the young mistress and pressed her firm breasts to his red shirt. The moment Katerina moved her shoulders, Sergey raised her from the floor, held her up in his arms, pressed her tightly to his breast and set her down gently on the overturned vat.

Katerina had not even time to show off her boasted strength. She flushed crimson, pulled her fur cloak back over her shoulders as she sat on the vat, and quietly walked out of the barn. Sergey cleared his throat with an air of bravado and shouted: "Come on, you imbeciles of the heavenly king, fill the sacks and, mind, keep the strickle level, anything over and we're in clover!"

It was just as though he were paying no heed to what had just taken place.

"He's always after the girls, that damned Sergey!" said the cook Aksinya as she waddled after Katerina. "The dirty thief has everything—tall, dark, and handsome. He's the kind of scoundrel who'll seduce any woman he takes a fancy to. The rogue will tell her how beautiful she is, and then get her into trouble. But no, of course, he's not fickle—he's as fickle as they come!"

"And how about you, Aksinya?" the young mistress said, walking in front. "I mean is . . . er . . . your boy still alive?"

"Of course he's alive, ma'am. Why shouldn't he be? You see, when they're not wanted they always live."

"And do you know who his father is?"

"Good gracious, no, ma'am. He's illegitimate, that's what he is. You live among such a crowd of people, you see. How can you tell who his father is?"

"Has he been long with us, that young fellow, I mean?"

"Which one? Sergey?"

"Yes."

"About a month. Had a job at Konchonov's before, but the master kicked him out." Aksinya lowered her voice and went on:

"They say he had an affair with the mistress. They were in love, it seems. Bold as brass he is, damn his soul!"

3.

A warm, milky twilight hung over the town. Zinovy had not yet returned from the dam. Katerina's father-in-law, Boris Timofeyevich, was not at home either; he had gone to an old friend's name-day party and had said that she should not wait supper for him. Having nothing to do, Katerina had had her supper early, and opening the little window of her attic, leaned against the window post and cracked sunflower seeds. The servants had finished their supper in the kitchen and had all walked across the yard on their way to bed: some to the barns, some to the granaries, and some to the sweet-scented haylofts. Sergey was the last to leave the kitchen. He walked round the yard, unchained the watchdogs, whistled, and as he passed under Katerina's window, looked up at her and greeted her with a low bow.

"Good night," said Katerina to him softly from her attic window, and a dead silence fell over the yard just as if it were a desert.

"Madam!" someone called two minutes later at Katerina's locked door.

"Who is it?" Katerina asked, frightened.

"Don't be afraid," answered the clerk. "It's me, Sergey."

"What do you want, Sergey?"

"I have something to ask you, ma'am. Oh, a little business matter. May I come in for a moment?"

Katerina turned the key and let Sergey in.

"What do you want?" she said, moving away to the window.

"I've come to ask if you have some book I could read, ma'am. I'm bored stiff."

"I'm afraid I have no books, Sergey: I don't read them," replied Katerina.

"Oh, I'm so bored!"

"Why should you be bored?"

"Why should I? I'm a young man, it's like living in a monastery here, and so far as I can see I'm doomed to this solitary life till my dying day. It makes me despair sometimes. It really does."

"Why don't you get married?"

"Married? That's easily said, ma'am. Who can I marry here? I'm not a great catch, am I? I can't expect a master's daughter to marry me. And as for anyone else, you know very well, ma'am, that the girls here are too poor and have had no education. How can you expect them to know anything about love? Why, ma'am, you know yourself the sort of idea even the rich among them have about it. Now you, if you don't mind my saying so, ma'am, would have been a comfort to any man who had any feelings, but they just keep you in a cage like a canary."

"Yes," Katerina could not help confessing, "I am bored."

"How can you help being bored, ma'am, with this sort of life? Even if you had, as others have, a lover on the side, you would have found it impossible to see him."

"I'm afraid you—you're talking nonsense. Now, you see, if I'd had a child I'd have been happy with him."

"But, ma'am, a child, too, if you don't mind my saying so, does not just happen to come along without some reason. Don't you think that having lived so many years with different masters and having seen the sort of life women lead among merchants, I've learned a thing or two? As the song has it: *Without my love my heart's breaking,* and let me tell you, ma'am, I'm so sad and heartbroken that I could take a sharp knife and cut my heart out and throw it at your little feet. I'd feel much better then, a hundred times better . . ."

Sergey's voice shook.

"What are you talking to me about your heart for? It's no business of mine. You'd better go . . ."

"No, please, ma'am," said Sergey, trembling all over and taking a step towards Katerina, "I know, I see, I feel, and I understand very well that your lot in the world is no better than mine. But now," he went on in a barely audible whisper, "now at this moment all this is in your hands and in your power."

"What are you talking about? What do you mean? What have you come here for? I shall throw myself out of the window," said Katerina, and suddenly overcome by indescribable panic, she caught hold of the window sill.

"Oh, my dearest darling, why should you throw yourself out of the window?" Sergey whispered and, tearing the young mistress away from the window, he caught her in a tight embrace.

"Oh, let me go!" Katerina moaned softly, weakening under his passionate kisses and against her own will pressing closer to his powerful body.

Sergey lifted his mistress up in his arms like a child and carried her to a dark corner.

A hush fell over the room, broken only by the regular ticking of Katerina's husband's watch, which hung over the head of the bed; but this did not interfere with anything.

"Go, please," said Katerina half an hour later, without looking at Sergey, as she arranged her dishevelled hair before a small looking glass.

"Why should I go away from here now?" replied Sergey in a happy voice.

"My father-in-law will lock the front door."

"The people you have known must have been a strange lot, my sweet, if they really thought a door the only way to a woman. Either coming or going—there are doors everywhere for me," the young fellow said, pointing to the pillars that supported the gallery.

4.

Katerina's husband Zinovy did not come back home for a whole week and during that time Katerina spent every night until daybreak with Sergey.

A great deal of wine from her father-in-law's cellar was drunk during these nights in Zinovy's bedroom; many a tasty titbit was eaten and many a kiss lavished on the mistress' sugared lips, and many a time her black tresses were toyed with on the soft pillows.

But no road runs smooth forever; here and there, there are ruts in every road.

Katerina's father-in-law could not sleep: in his multicolored print shirt, the old man wandered about the silent house; he first went to one window, then another, looked out and saw Sergey in his red shirt sliding very quietly down the pillar beneath his daughter-in-law's window. There's a fine piece of news for you. The old man rushed out of the house and grabbed the young fellow by the legs.

"Just where have you been, you dirty thief?" the old man said.

"Wherever it was," replied Sergey, "I'm not there any longer."

"Spent the night with my daughter-in-law, have you?"

"Well, sir, of course I know where I've spent the night, but the wise thing for you is to listen: you can't undo what's done, so don't disgrace your house. What do you want? Satisfaction?"

"I'll skin you alive, you dirty scoundrel," the old man replied.

"Very well," the young fellow agreed, "it's my fault; do you as you wish. Tell me where to go and you have your fun. Drink my blood."

The old man took Sergey to his little stone storeroom and lashed him with a leather thong until he was exhausted. Sergey did not so much as let out a moan, but he did chew away half of his sleeve.

The old man left Sergey in the storeroom until his back which was covered with black and blue bruises should heal; he gave him an earthen jug of water, locked the door with a great padlock, and sent for his son.

But even today you cannot drive very swiftly over Russian country roads, and as for Katerina, she could no longer live a single hour without Sergey. Her nature, hitherto dormant, suddenly awakened and she became so willful that it was impossible to restrain her. She found out where Sergey was, talked with him through the iron door, and rushed off to look for the keys.

"Let Sergey out, Father," she begged her father-in-law.

The old man turned green with anger. He had never expected such brazen impudence from his daughter-in-law who, though now erring, had always, up to this time, been obedient.

"Oh, you impudent slut, you . . ." and he began to call her all sorts of shameful names.

"Let him go," she said. "We haven't done anything wrong."

"Nothing wrong!" he exclaimed, gritting his teeth. "And what were you doing with him at night in your bedroom? Restuffing your husband's pillows?"

But she kept on begging him: "Let him out! Let him out!"

"If it's as bad as that," the old man said, "let me tell you what I'm going to do: as soon as your husband gets back, we'll take you, honest woman that you are, to the stable and give you a good whipping—as for him, I'll have that rascal off to prison tomorrow."

This was what the old man decided to do; but he was not given the chance to carry out this decision.

5.

The old man had mushrooms with buckwheat porridge for supper and this gave him heartburn; suddenly he was seized with a cramp in the pit of his stomach, began vomiting, and died towards morning, just like the rats in his granaries. Katerina, to take care of the rats, had always prepared with her own hands a special kind of meal mixed with a dangerous white powder that had been entrusted to her.

Katerina released Sergey from the old man's stone storeroom and, not caring two pins for what people might think, put him in her husband's bed to recover from the whipping her father-in-law had given him. As for her father-in-law, he was buried according to the rites of the Christian church and no one was in the least suspicious. Oddly enough, it never occurred to anyone to ask questions: the old man was dead and that was that. He had died as many people have after eating mushrooms. He was buried in haste without waiting for his son's arrival as the weather was very hot and the man who had been sent to fetch Zinovy did not find him at the mill. Zinovy, as it happened, had heard of a wood that was for sale very cheap about a hundred miles away and had gone to inspect it without telling anyone where it was.

Having settled this business, Katerina became utterly uncontrollable. She was not timid by nature anyway, but now it was impossible to say what she would do next. She walked about with her nose in the air, giving orders to everybody in the house and not letting Sergey out of her sight for a moment. The people in the yard were very surprised at first, but Katerina knew how to win them over with a bountiful hand, and suddenly their surprise ceased. "The mistress," they thought, "is having an affair with Sergey, and that's all there is to it. It's her business, and no doubt she will have to answer for it."

By this time Sergey had recovered; once more erect, he became again the same handsome fellow as before, stepping proudly round Katerina like a falcon round his mate, and once again they lived happily together. But time was passing not only for them: after his long absence, Zinovy, the wronged husband, was hurrying home.

6.

It was a scorching afternoon and the ubiquitous flies were becoming unbearable. Katerina had closed the shutters and had also hung a woolen shawl across her bedroom window before lying down with Sergey to rest on the merchant's high bed. Katerina did not know whether she was asleep or not, so exhausted was she from the heat; perspiration poured from her face; her breath came hot and labored. It seemed to her it was time to wake, time to go into the garden to have tea, but she felt unable to rise. Finally the cook came to the door and knocked: "The samovar is getting cold," she said. "It's under the apple tree." Katerina turned over with an effort and began to caress the cat, which was rubbing itself against her and Sergey, such a lovely tabby, large and fat, and with whiskers like a quitrent bailiff's. Katerina began to stroke his thick fur and he pushed his face into her body, thrusting his blunt snout against her firm breasts, while softly singing a song as though he were telling her about his love. "What is this enormous cat doing here?" Katerina thought. "I remember putting some cream on the window sill; this nasty creature will most certainly lap it up. I'd better put him out," she decided and was about to seize the cat, but the creature slipped through her fingers like mist. "Where did the cat come from?" Katerina asked herself in her nightmarish dream. "We've never had a cat in our bedroom, and now look what a huge one is here!" She again tried to catch the cat, but once more it disappeared. "What can it be?" Katerina thought. "Is it really a cat?" She suddenly felt panicky and both sleep and dream vanished. She looked round the bedroom—there was no trace of a cat anywhere, only her handsome Sergey lay there, pressing her breasts with his strong hand to his burning face.

Katerina rose and sat down on the bed, kissing Sergey. Then she kissed and caressed him again and again. Finally, after straightening out the crumpled featherbed, she went down to the garden to drink tea. By this time the sun had set and a wonderful, enchanting evening had fallen upon the hot earth.

"I'm sorry that I overslept," Katerina said to Aksinya, as she sat down on a rug beneath the flowering apple tree to drink tea. "Tell me what this means," she inquired of the cook who was wiping a saucer with a tea cloth.

"What, dear?"

"As I slept, a cat kept rubbing himself against me, and it was so real, it didn't seem like a dream. Now what do you think that means?"

"You're sure it happened that way?"

"Of course!"

Katerina again told how the cat had rubbed against her.

"But why did you stroke him?"

"I don't know. I just couldn't help it."

"That is strange!"

"Yes, I couldn't help being surprised myself."

"It must mean someone is going to cling to you very tightly—anyway, something like that."

"Like what exactly?"

"Dear, no one can tell exactly, but something of the kind is sure to happen."

"First I kept dreaming of the moon and then of this cat," Katerina went on.

"The moon—well that means a baby."

Katerina blushed.

"Shall I ask Sergey to come and have tea with you?" Aksinya asked, trying to please her mistress since she was anxious to become her confidante.

"Yes, do," Katerina said. "Go ask him. He may as well have tea with me."

"I thought you'd want me to call him," Aksinya declared, waddling off like a duck towards the garden gate.

Katerina also told Sergey about the cat.

"Just a silly dream," Sergey said.

"But why did I never have a silly dream like that before, darling?"

"Well, what if you never did. Until now I could only look at you longingly. But now your whole body is mine."

Sergey caught Katerina in his arms, swung her round, and threw her down playfully on the thick rug.

"Oh, I'm dizzy!" Katerina said. "Come here Sergey, darling. Sit beside me," she called to him rapturously, stretching herself luxuriously.

The handsome young fellow bent down so as to get under the low branches of the apple tree which were covered with white blossoms, and sat down on the rug at Katerina's feet.

"So you longed for me, darling?"

"How could I help it?"

"How did you long for me? Tell me how."

"How can I tell you? A man can't explain something like that. I felt miserable."

"Well, why didn't I feel your suffering, darling? I'm told one does."

Sergey didn't answer.

"And why did you sing if you were so unhappy about me? Why? You see, I did hear you singing under the balcony."

Katerina continued to question him, caressing him at the same time.

"Suppose I did sing! What about gnats? They sing all their lives, but it's not for joy," Sergey replied dryly.

There was a pause. Katerina was delighted with Sergey's confessions.

She wanted to talk, but Sergey frowned and was silent.

"Look, Sergey! Oh my darling! What a paradise, what a paradise!" Katerina cried, looking up through the thick branches of the blossoming apple tree into the clear, blue sky where the full moon shone serenely.

She lay on her back under the tree and the moonlight, streaming through the leaves and blossoms, drifted across her face and body forming bizarre spots. The air was still; only a light, warm breeze slightly stirred the sleepy leaves, scattering the faint fragrance of blossoming herbs and leaves. Every breath she drew filled her with languor, laziness, and dark voluptuous desires.

Getting no reply, Katerina was again silent and kept gazing at the sky through the pale pink blossoms of the apple tree. Sergey, too, said nothing, but it was not the sky which interested him. Clasping his knees with both arms, he gazed intently at his boots.

A lovely night! Stillness, light, scented air, and beneficent life-giving warmth. Far away, beyond the ravine, on the other side of the garden, someone began singing loudly; in the bird-cherry thicket near the fence a nightingale trilled once and then burst into song; a sleepy quail in a cage set on a long pole uttered a few shrill calls, and a fat horse sighed languorously behind the stable wall, while a pack of excited dogs ran noiselessly across the common behind the garden fence and disappeared into the hideous black shadows of the ancient, almost dilapidated, salt warehouses.

Katerina raised herself on an elbow and looked at the tall garden grass. It seemed to her that the grass was playing games with the moonbeams which broke into flickers of light as they fell on the flowers and the leaves of the trees; everything was gilded with capricious, bright spots of light that twinkled and trembled like fireflies; it was as if the grass under the trees had been scooped up in a net of moonbeams and moved from side to side.

"Oh, how lovely it is, darling," Katerina cried, looking about her.

Sergey looked without enthusiasm.

"Why are you so gloomy, Sergey? Are you tired of me already?"

"Don't talk nonsense," Sergey replied dryly and, bending down, kissed Katerina lazily.

"You're not to be trusted, Sergey," Katerina said in a fit of jealousy. "You're fickle."

"I refuse to take what you say seriously," Sergey said calmly.

"Then why do you kiss me like that?"

Sergey didn't answer.

"Only husbands and wives," Katerina went on, playing with his curls, "brush each other's lips so casually. I want to be kissed so that the blossoms of the apple tree fall to the ground."

"Like this, like this," Katerina whispered, hugging her lover and kissing him passionately.

"Listen, dearest," Katerina began a little later, "tell me why everyone says you are false."

"Who's been telling such foolish lies about me?"

"It's what people say."

"Anyone I was unfaithful to wasn't worth loving."

"Why did you have anything to do with such women? One shouldn't love that sort."

"That's all very fine for you to say. But you don't reason about such things. You're tempted; you break the commandment. You haven't any serious intentions, but the girl throws herself around your neck! Love!"

"Dear, I don't want to know what the others were like, nor anything about them. But let me tell you this: it was you who coaxed and cajoled me, and your cunning drove me into your arms; I didn't want to love you. Sergey, I must warn you that if you are unfaithful to me, that if you leave me for someone else, no matter whom, I will not—and I am sorry to have to say this to you—part from you alive."

Sergey started violently.

"But, Katerina, darling," he said, "you can see for yourself how things are. You've just mentioned how gloomy I am today. But what do you expect? I am heartsick."

"What is it, darling? Tell me."

"What's there to tell? There's your husband, first of all. He'll be back any day now, the Lord be praised, and what will happen to me? Why, Sergey, dear fellow, you'll go back to the yard, to the musicians, and you'll watch the candle burn in the mistress' bedroom from behind the barn, you'll see her shaking the feather-bed and then getting into bed with her lawful husband, Zinovy!"

"No, that will never happen!" Katerina exclaimed gaily with a wave of the hand.

"Never? Well, as far as I can see, there's nothing to stop it. And, my dear, I too have a heart. I can see what suffering awaits me."

"Oh, do stop worrying, darling!"

Katerina was pleased at this expression of Sergey's jealousy and she laughed and began kissing him again.

"And let me tell you once more," Sergey went on, quietly disengaging his head from Katerina's arms, which were bare to the shoulders, "let me repeat that my wretched condition has made me consider the outcome of all this not once but a dozen times. If I were your equal, if I were a gentleman or a merchant, I would never leave you, Katerina—never! But you can see what I am compared to you. How do you think I'll feel when I see you grasped by your lovely hands and led into your bedroom? I'll have to grin and bear it, and most likely, I'll end up despising myself. I'm not one of those men, Katerina, who care about nothing but getting pleasure from a woman. I know what love is, and how, like a snake, it sucks your blood."

"Why are you telling me all this, Sergey?" Katerina interrupted. She felt sorry for him.

"How can I help telling you, Katerina? I must talk about it. Your husband has probably been told everything already. And if he knows, it isn't a matter of days or weeks; tomorrow Sergey won't be here any longer. There won't be a trace of him within miles."

"No, no, don't talk that way, darling. That won't happen. I can't live without you," Katerina declared, comforting him as best she could with her caresses. "If it ever comes to that, then either he or I won't be alive—you'll still be with me, darling."

"No, that's not the way it will be," said Sergey, shaking his head mournfully. "It's too bad that this has happened. I should have fallen in love with someone like myself. Then I would have been happy. How can I expect you to love me forever? What honor is there in being my mistress? If only we were married, I should still be your servant, but the whole world would see how much my wife esteems me because of the respect I have for her . . . ."

Katerina was overcome by Sergey's words, by his jealousy, by his desire to marry her, which desire always pleases a woman, however intimate her relations with the man have been before marriage. Katerina was now ready to go through fire and water for Sergey, to go to prison or to the cross for him. He had made her so much in love with him that there was no limit to her devotion. She was mad with happiness; her blood was on fire and she could not listen to anything more. She quickly covered Sergey's mouth with the palm of her hand and, pressing his head to her bosom, said:

"Don't worry, darling. I know how to make a merchant of you and have us live together properly. But please don't hurt me needlessly while things are still unsettled."

And again she showered kisses and caresses on him.

The old clerk, asleep in the barn, heard in the stillness of the night through his slumber whispering and low laughter, as if naughty children plotted tricks to play on decrepit old age, and then, loud, gay laughter, as if the water nixies from the lake were tickling someone. But it was only Katerina gamboling in the moonlight, rolling on the soft rug, making love to her husband's young clerk. The leafy apple tree shed fresh, white blossoms on them until at last no further blossoms fell. The short white night was passing away; the moon hid itself behind the steep roof of the high barns, and as it grew dimmer and dimmer gazed slantingly down on the earth. From the roof of the kitchen came the piercing sounds of a cats' duet, followed by angry spittings and splutterings, after which two or three of the animals, losing their foothold, rolled noisily down some planks that were propped up against the roof.

"Let's go to bed," Katerina said, rising slowly from the rug as though utterly exhausted. She walked across the quiet, the deathly quiet, of the yard while Sergey followed her, carrying the rug as well as her blouse, which she had thrown off during their love-making.

7.

No sooner had Katerina blown out the candle, undressed, and lain down on the soft featherbed than she fell asleep. After her antics and love-making, she slept so soundly that even her arms and legs were asleep; but, once more, through her sleep she heard the door open and again the cat she had dreamed of dropped on the bed like a heavy old boot.

"What a nuisance this cat is," Katerina reflected. She still felt very tired. "I purposely locked the door with my own hands, and I know the window is shut, but here he is again. I'll throw him out immediately," Katerina thought, preparing to get up, but her weary arms and legs refused to obey her, and the cat continued to walk over her, purring strangely, as if it were uttering human words. A cold shiver ran down Katerina's spine.

"No," she thought, "there's nothing else to be done. Tomorrow I must get some holy water and sprinkle the bed with it, for this is surely a strange sort of cat."

But the cat started purring and mewing close to her ear, and thrust its muzzle forward, and said distinctly: "What sort of cat do you think I am? It's very smart of you, Katerina dear, to take me for a cat at all. Actually I'm Boris Timofeyevich, a highly esteemed merchant of this town and your father-in-law. Only one thing is wrong with me; my bowels have burst because of the fine treatment my dear daughter-in-law gave me. That's why I mew. You see, I've shrunk and look like a cat to those who have no idea who I really am. Well, and how are you getting on now, Katerina dear? How faithfully you keep your vows! I've come from the churchyard just to find out how warm you and Sergey are keeping your husband's bed. Prrr-prrr . . . I can see nothing, you know. Don't be afraid of me. Even my eyes have fallen out from the good things you gave me. Look at my eyes, dear, don't be afraid."

Katerina looked and screamed at the top of her voice. The cat was once more lying between her and Sergey and its head was that of Boris Timofeyevich, full-sized, looking just as it had on his corpse, but instead of eyes, fiery circles whirled round and round.

Sergey woke and calmed Katerina, then fell asleep again; but her sleep had gone completely, and it was good that it had.

She lay with eyes open and suddenly heard a sound as if someone had climbed the gate into the yard. A moment later the dogs rushed at the intruder, but suddenly ceased barking— probably fawning on whomever it was. Another minute passed and she heard the iron lock click downstairs and the door open. "Either I'm dreaming or that's Zinovy; the door has been opened with his spare key," Katerina thought and hastily nudged Sergey.

"Darling, listen," she said, raising herself on her elbow and listening intently herself.

And, indeed, someone was softly mounting the stairs, carefully placing one foot after another on the steps, and coming nearer and nearer to the locked bedroom door.

Katerina quickly jumped out of the bed in her nightdress and opened the window. At the same moment Sergey, barefooted, leaped onto the gallery, and with his legs clasped the pillar by which he had many times descended from the mistress' bedroom.

"No, don't, don't! Lie down here—don't go too far," whispered Katerina, throwing his boots and clothes out of the window to Sergey. Then she again slipped under the blanket and waited.

Sergey obeyed Katerina: he did not slide down the pillar but hid under a shelf in the gallery.

Meanwhile Katerina heard how her husband came to the door and listened, holding his breath. She could even hear his jealous heart beating very fast; but it was not pity that filled Katerina but wicked laughter.

"You're wasting your time," she thought to herself, smiling and breathing like an innocent child.

This went on for about ten minutes; but at last Zinovy got tired of standing behind the door and listening to his wife's breathing: he knocked.

"Who's there?" Katerina called after a short pause in a sleepy voice.

"It's me," replied Zinovy.

"You, Zinovy?"

"Yes, me! Can't you hear?" replied Zinovy.

Katerina jumped out of bed and, as she was in her nightdress, opened the bedroom door and dived back into the warm bed.

"Now that it's near dawn, it's getting awfully cold," she said, wrapping herself in the quilt.

Zinovy came in, looked round, said a prayer, lit a candle, and looked round again.

"How are you?" he asked his wife.

"I'm all right," answered Katerina and, sitting up, began putting on a loose cotton blouse.

"Shall I put on the samovar?" she asked.

"Don't trouble. Call Aksinya and let her do it."

Katerina put her bare feet down, slipped into her shoes, and ran out of the room. She was away for about half an hour. During that time she had blown on the red hot charcoal in the samovar and had quietly rushed out to Sergey in the gallery.

"Stay here," she whispered.

"How long?" asked Sergey also in a whisper.

"Oh, don't be a fool! Stay here, till I call you."

And Katerina made him sit down again in the same place.

Sergey could hear everything that went on in the bedroom from where he was in the gallery. He heard the door slam again when Katerina went back to her husband. He could hear every word they uttered.

"What have you been doing out there all this time?" Zinovy asked his wife.

"Been putting on the samovar," she replied calmly.

There was a pause. Sergey could hear Zinovy hang up his coat on the clothes tree. Now he washed, snorting, and splashing the water about; then he asked for a towel. They began to talk again.

"Well, how did you come to bury Father?" inquired her husband.

"Oh," she replied, "he died and so he was buried."

"That's very odd!"

"I don't know," answered Katerina and began rattling the cups. Zinovy paced the room mournfully.

"Well, and how have you been passing the time here?" Zinovy asked his wife again.

"Everyone knows the life of pleasure we lead—we don't go to balls, do we? Nor to the theatre?"

"You don't show any particular pleasure in seeing your husband, either, do you?" Zinovy remarked, looking sideways at her.

"We're not young any more—are we?—we don't lose our senses every time we meet. Of course, I'm pleased. Don't you see me bustling and running about doing things to please you?"

Katerina ran out again to fetch the samovar and again she rushed to Sergey, pulled him by the sleeve and said: "Look sharp, Sergey!"

Sergey had no idea what it was all about, but he got ready for any emergency.

When Katerina returned to the bedroom she saw her husband kneeling on the bed and hanging up his silver watch and beadwork chain on the wall at the head of the bed.

"Why did you make up the bed for two when you were alone, Katerina?" he suddenly asked his wife rather strangely.

"I've been expecting you constantly," Katerina replied, gazing calmly at him.

"I'm much obliged to you for that, I'm sure. But tell me where did you get this thing from? I found it on your featherbed."

Zinovy picked up Sergey's little woolen girdle from the sheet and held it up by the end before his wife's eyes.

Katerina did not hesitate for a moment.

"I found it in the garden," she said, "and tied my petticoat with it."

"I see!" said Zinovy with special emphasis. "I've also heard a thing or two about your petticoats."

"Oh? What did you hear?"

"About all the splendid things you've done."

"I've done nothing."

"Well, we'll get to the bottom of that," said Zinovy, pushing his empty cup towards his wife. "We'll get to the bottom of everything."

Katerina made no answer.

"We'll drag everything you've been doing into the light of day, dear Katerina," said Zinovy again after a long pause, frowning at his wife.

"Your dear Katerina is not easily frightened," she said. "She isn't at all afraid."

"What? What?" cried Zinovy, raising his voice.

"Nothing—nothing!" replied his wife.

"Well, you'd better look out! You're talking a little too much!"

"And why shouldn't I talk as much as I like?" cried Katerina.

"You should have been more careful."

"There's nothing I have to be careful about. If some gossip told you some stupid tale about me, that's no reason why I should put up with all sorts of abuse, is it? I like that!"

"No one told me anything. Everyone here knows the way you've been carrying on."

"Oh?" cried Katerina, flaring up in earnest. "And just how have I been carrying on?"

"I know."

"Well, if you know, you'd better tell me about it."

Zinovy didn't answer and again pushed his empty cup towards his wife.

"I can see there's nothing to tell," Katerina cried with contempt, throwing a teaspoon on her husband's saucer. "Well, tell me who they say it is. Who's the lover I've been unfaithful with?"

"You'll find out. Don't be in such a hurry."

"Has anyone by any chance been telling you stories about Sergey?"

"We'll find out, we'll find out, Katerina. Nobody can deprive us of our authority over you and no one will . . . You'll confess everything yourself . . ."

"Shall I, indeed?" cried Katerina, gritting her teeth. "That's as much as I can stand," she went on, and turning white as a sheet, she suddenly rushed out of the room.

"Well, here he is!" she declared a few seconds later, leading Sergey by the sleeve into the room. "You can question him and me too about what you know. Perhaps you'll learn more than you bargain for."

Zinovy was completely taken aback. He looked at Sergey, who stood leaning against the lintel of the door, and at his wife, who had sat calmly down with folded arms on the edge of the bed, and he could not for the life of him understand what all this was leading to.

"What are you up to, you snake?" he muttered with an effort without getting up from his chair.

"Question us about what you appear to know so well," Katerina answered impudently. "You thought you could frighten me by threatening to beat me," she went on, with a significant flash of her eyes. "Well, that is not going to happen. But I'm going to do what I knew I would do even before your threats."

"What? Get out!" Zinovy shouted at Sergey.

"Indeed!" Katerina mimicked him.

She quickly locked the door, put the key in her pocket and again sat down on the edge of the bed in her loose blouse.

"Come here, Sergey dear, come here, darling, sit beside me," she said, beckoning to the clerk.

Sergey tossed back his locks and sat down boldly near the mistress.

"Good Lord, what's all this? What are you doing, you savages?" cried Zinovy, going purple in the face and rising from his chair.

"What's wrong? Don't you like it? Look, look, my darling husband, isn't this beautiful?"

Katerina laughed and kissed Sergey passionately before her husband's eyes.

At that very moment she received a deafening slap on her cheek and Zinovy rushed to the open window.

8.

"A-ah, so that's how it is!" cried Katerina. "Well, my dear friend, thank you very much. I was only waiting for that. Now it will be neither your way nor my way . . ."

With a quick movement she pushed Sergey away from her, rushed quickly at her husband, and before Zinovy had time to reach the window, seized him from behind round the throat with her thin fingers and flung him on the floor like a sheaf of damp hemp.

Falling heavily and striking the back of his neck against the floor, Zinovy became frantic with rage. He had not expected such a quick ending. His wife's first act of violence proved to him that she would stop at nothing to get rid of him and that his present position was one of great danger. Zinovy realized it all in a flash at the moment of his fall, and he did not cry out because he knew that his voice could not reach anybody's ears but would merely hasten his end. He rolled his eyes in silence and rested them with an expression of anger, reproach, and suffering on his wife, whose thin fingers were tightening round his throat.

Zinovy did not defend himself; his arms with tightly clenched fists lay stretched out twitching spasmodically. One of them was quite free; the other Katerina pressed to the floor with her knee.

"Hold him," she whispered in an indifferent tone of voice to Sergey, while turning to her husband herself.

Sergey knelt on the master, pinning his two arms down with his knees, and was about to seize him by the throat under Katerina's hands, but at that instant he himself uttered a frenzied scream. At the sight of the man who had wronged him a violent desire for revenge aroused in Zinovy all his remaining strength and with a tremendous jerk he wrenched his pinned arms from under Sergey's knees and catching hold of Sergey's black locks bit his throat like a wild beast. But this did not go on for long: almost immediately Zinovy uttered a groan and dropped his head.

Katerina, pale and scarcely breathing, stood over her husband and her lover; in her right hand she held a heavy cast-iron candlestick, which she gripped by the top with the heavy part downwards. A thin trickle of red blood ran down Zinovy's temple and cheek.

"A priest . . ." Zinovy moaned weakly, throwing his head back with loathing as far as he could from Sergey who was kneeling on him. "To confess . . ." he said still more indistinctly, shivering and looking sideways at the warm blood that was coagulating under his hair.

"You'll be all right without it," whispered Katerina.

"We've wasted enough time with him," she said to Sergey. "Put your hands around his throat properly."

Zinovy began to wheeze.

Katerina stooped down, pressed Sergey's hands, which were round her husband's throat, with her own and put her ear to his breast. After five quiet minutes she got up and said: "That'll do. You can leave him now."

Sergey, too, got up and drew a long breath. Zinovy lay dead—strangled and with a deep cut on his temple. Under his head on the left side was a small pool of blood, which had flowed from the small wound now clotted and matted with hair.

Sergey carried Zinovy into the cellar under the floor of the stone storeroom in which the late Boris Timofeyevich had so recently locked up Sergey himself, and then returned to the attic. During this time Katerina, rolling up the sleeves of her loose blouse and tucking up the hem of her skirt, had carefully washed away with a bast sponge and soap the bloodstain left by Zinovy on the floor of his bedroom. The water had not as yet gone cold in the samovar out of which Zinovy had warmed his heart with poisoned tea, and the stain washed away without leaving any trace.

Katerina took a copper slop basin and a soaped bast sponge.

"Come on, give me a light," she said to Sergey, going towards the door. "Put the light down lower, lower," she went on, carefully examining all the floorboards over which Sergey had had to drag Zinovy to the cellar.

Only in two places on the painted floor were two tiny bloodstains the size of a cherry. Katerina rubbed them with the bast sponge and they disappeared.

"That will teach you not to creep up to your wife like a thief and spy on her," declared Katerina, straightening herself and looking towards the storeroom.

"Now it's all over," said Sergey, starting at the sound of his own voice.

When they returned to the bedroom a thin red streak of sunrise cut across the sky in the east and, lightly gilding the blossoms of the apple tree, peered through the green trellis bars into Katerina's room.

The old clerk, a short sheepskin thrown over his shoulders, walked slowly across the yard, yawning and crossing himself.

Katerina carefully pulled the shutters up by their strings and scrutinized Sergey carefully, as though wishing to look into his heart.

"Well, now you too are a merchant," she said, laying her white hands on his shoulders.

Sergey made no answer.

Sergey's lips trembled and he shook all over as though in a fever. Katerina's lips were cold.

Two days later Sergey's hands became calloused from the use of a heavy spade and a crowbar, but then Zinovy was so well stowed away in his cellar that without the help of his widow or her lover nobody would have been able to find him till the general resurrection.

9.

Sergey went about with a crimson kerchief wrapped round his neck, complaining of a pain in his throat. Meanwhile, even before the marks left by Zinovy's teeth on Sergey's throat had healed, the disappearance of Katerina's husband was discovered. Sergey himself began commenting on the fact more often than anyone else. He would sit down on the bench near the gate with the other young fellows and say: "I wonder, boys, what can have happened to the master, why he hasn't returned yet."

The young men were surprised also.

Then the news came from the mill that the master had hired horses and had long since started for home. The coachman who had driven him declared that Zinovy had seemed to be very upset and had dismissed him rather strangely: about three miles from the town he had got off the cart near the monastery, taken his bag, and walked off. Hearing this story, people were even more dumbfounded.

Zinovy had disappeared and that was all there was to it.

A search was made for him, but nothing could be discovered: the merchant appeared to have vanished into thin air. From the statement made by the coachman, who was arrested, they merely learned that the merchant had got off the cart near the monastery by the river and walked off. The matter was not cleared up and meanwhile Katerina in her widowed state went on living with Sergey quite freely. Now and again the rumor spread that Zinovy had been seen in one place or another, but he still did not come back and Katerina knew better than anyone that it was quite impossible for him to do so.

In this way one month passed, then another and a third, and Katerina felt herself with child.

"The property will be ours, darling: I shall have an heir," she said to Sergey, and she went to petition the town council, declaring that she was pregnant and there being no one to carry on the business, she demanded that she should be put in charge of it.

And how, indeed, could a commercial undertaking be allowed to go to ruin? Katerina was the lawful wife of her husband, there were no visible debts, and there was therefore no reason why she should not take possession of the business. And so she was given possession of it.

Katerina was now established as the sole owner of her husband's estate and she assumed full authority over it, and in view of her position, Sergey was no longer addressed by his Christian name but by his name and patronymic—Sergey Philippych. Then, suddenly, like a bolt from the blue, a new calamity befell Katerina. A letter came from Liven to the mayor of the town informing him that a large share in Boris Timofeyevich's business belonged to his nephew Fyodor Lyamin, a minor, and that the thing had to be looked into and the business must not be left entirely in Katerina's hands. As soon as this news arrived, the mayor had a talk with Katerina and a week later an old woman and a small boy arrived from Liven.

"I am Boris Timofeyevich's cousin," said the old woman, "and this is my nephew, Fyodor Lyamin."

Katerina asked them into the house.

Watching their arrival from the yard and observing the reception Katerina gave them, Sergey went as white as a sheet.

"What's the matter with you?" asked the mistress, noticing his deathly pallor as he followed the visitors into the house and stopped in the front room to examine them.

"Nothing," he replied, turning round and going from the front room into the passage. "I'm just thinking how extraordinary these people from Liven are," he said with a sigh, closing the front door behind him.

"Well, and what is going to happen now?" Sergey asked Katerina as they sat together that night at the tea table. "Now everything we hoped for is going to rack and ruin."

"Why to rack and ruin, darling?"

"Because it will all be divided now. What's the use of carrying on with a small business?"

"Why? Will it be too small for you?"

"That's not the point. I'm not thinking of myself. All I'm thinking of is that we won't be as happy as before."

"Why not? Why won't we be as happy, darling?"

"Because loving you as I do I should like to see you a real lady and not living as you have been until now," replied Sergey. "For everything will be reversed now: with the decrease of capital you'll sink much lower than before."

"But what do I care if I do, darling?"

"Well, of course, Katerina, you may not be interested in such things but I respect you too much to see that happen; and then, considering your position in the eyes of the world, mean and envious as everybody is, it will be very painful. You can please yourself, of course, but I'm afraid I'll never be happy under such circumstances."

Sergey went on improvising on the same theme to Katerina, insisting that Fedya Lyamin had made him the most unhappy of men, for he had been deprived of the power to raise her, Katerina, above all the merchants in the town. Sergey kept impressing on her that if this Fedya had not existed the whole of the fortune would have been hers, for she would give birth to a child before nine months had elapsed since her husband's disappearance, and then there would have been no end to their happiness.

10.

Suddenly Sergey stopped talking about the heir altogether. As soon as Sergey ceased mentioning him, Katerina could not get Fedya Lyamin out of her heart or mind. She grew pensive and even less affectionate to Sergey. Asleep or looking after the business or saying her prayers, she could think only of one thing: "Why so? Why should I really lose all that money through him? Think of what I have suffered, think of the sin I have taken on my soul," reflected Katerina, "and here he comes along and without any trouble takes it away from me . . . If at least he were a man, but he's only a child, a boy . . ."

The first autumn frosts set in. No news, of course, of Zinovy came from anywhere. Katerina was becoming bigger and went about always looking pensive and self-absorbed. In the town the gossip about her never ceased, people wondering what was the real reason why the young Mrs. Izmaylov, who had been barren for such a long time, always growing thinner and pining away, now suddenly began to swell out in front. And the young co-heir, Fedya Lyamin, wandered about the yard in his light squirrel-fur coat breaking the thin ice in the ruts.

"Well, really, young master!" the cook Aksinya shouted at him as she ran across the yard. "Is it proper for a merchant's son like you to play about in puddles?"

But the co-heir, who was such an embarrassment to Katerina and her lover, just went on playing as serenely as a young kid and he slept even more serenely opposite his fond great-aunt without dreaming or suspecting that he stood in anybody's way or decreased anybody's happiness.

At last Fedya caught the chicken pox and, in addition, a cold and a pain in the chest. The boy was put to bed. At first he was treated with herbs and simples, but at last they sent for a doctor.

The doctor began paying regular visits, gave prescriptions, and the medicines were given to the boy at certain hours by his great-aunt, who sometimes asked Katerina to do it.

"Please, Katerina dear," she would say, "you'll soon be a mother yourself, you are waiting for God's judgment yourself, please . . ."

Katerina did not refuse the old woman. Whenever she went to evening Mass to say a prayer "for the boy Fyodor lying on his sickbed" or to early Mass to get him consecrated bread, Katerina would sit by the patient, giving him his medicine at the appropriate time.

So the old woman went to the evening service and to vespers on the eve of the Entry of the Holy Virgin into the Church and she asked "dear" Katerina to look after little Fedya. At that time the boy was already recovering.

Katerina went into Fedya's room. The boy was sitting up in bed in his squirrel coat, reading the *Lives of the Fathers*.

"What are you reading, Fedya?" she asked, sitting down in an armchair.

"The *Lives*, Auntie."

"Interesting?"

"Very interesting, Auntie."

Katerina leaned on her hand and began watching Fedya as he moved his lips, and suddenly it was as if demons had slipped their chains and she was all at once overwhelmed by her former thoughts of all the evil the boy was causing her and how wonderful it would be if he were dead.

"But then," thought Katerina, "he is ill, he has to be given medicine—anything might happen during an illness . . . One has only to say that the doctor has made a mistake in his prescription."

"Isn't it time for your medicine, Fedya?"

"Yes, Auntie," replied the boy, and emptying the spoon he added: "These stories of the saints are very interesting, Auntie."

"Well, go on reading," Katerina remarked and looking coldly round the room, she stared for some time at the frost patterns on the window panes.

"I must order the shutters to be closed," she said and went out into the drawing room, and from there into the hall, and then upstairs into her own room where she sat down.

Five minutes later Sergey, in a bargeman's sheepskin coat trimmed with thick sealskin, came into the room.

"Have the shutters been closed?" Katerina asked him.

"Yes," Sergey replied abruptly, snuffing the candle with snuffers, and stopped near the stove.

There was a long pause.

"Evening Mass won't be over so soon tonight, will it?" asked Katerina.

"It's a great holiday tomorrow; the service will be long," replied Sergey.

Again there was a pause.

"I shall have to go down to Fedya; he's alone there," said Katerina, rising.

"Alone?" Sergey asked, giving her a sidelong glance.

"Alone," she replied in a whisper. "Why?"

Their eyes seemed to flash messages like forked lightning to each other, but neither of them so much as uttered a word.

Katerina went downstairs and walked through the empty rooms; it was quiet everywhere; the lamps glimmered peacefully before the icons; her own shadow went scampering along the walls; the shuttered windows began to thaw and weep. Fedya was sitting up and reading. When he saw Katerina, he only said:

"Auntie, please, put this book back and give me that one from the icon shelf."

Katerina carried out her nephew's request and gave him the book.

"Don't you think you'd better go to sleep, Fedya?"

"No, Auntie, I'd like to wait for Granny."

"Why wait for her?"

"She promised to bring me some consecrated bread from vespers."

Katerina suddenly turned pale, her own child for the first time moved under her heart, and a cold shiver went through her. She stood for some time in the middle of the room and then went out, rubbing her hands, which had gone cold.

"Well!" she whispered, quietly entering her bedroom and finding Sergey still in the same position near the stove.

"What?" Sergey asked scarcely audibly and swallowed hard.

"He's alone."

Sergey knit his brows and began breathing heavily.

"Come on," said Katerina, turning abruptly to the door.

Sergey hastily took off his boots and asked:

"Shall I take anything?"

"No, nothing," answered Katerina in a soft whisper and, taking him by the hand, she led him quietly out of the room.

11.

The sick boy gave a start and let the book drop on his knees when Katerina entered his room for the third time.

"What's the matter, Fedya?"

"I don't know, Auntie, I got frightened," he replied, smiling uneasily and cowering in the corner of the bed.

"What are you frightened of?"

"Who came with you, Auntie?"

"Where? Nobody came with me, darling."

"Nobody?"

The boy bent forward to the foot of the bed and, screwing up his eyes, gazed in the direction of the door through which his aunt had come in, and calmed down.

"I suppose I must have imagined it," he said.

Katerina stood still, leaning against the head of her nephew's bed.

Fedya looked at his aunt and observed that she had turned quite pale for some reason.

In answer to this remark Katerina deliberately coughed and glanced expectantly at the door of the sitting room. But only a floorboard creaked quietly there.

"I'm reading the life of my guardian angel, St. Fyodor Stratilates, Auntie. How well he served God!"

Katerina stood there without uttering a word.

"Won't you sit down, Auntie, and I'll read to you again?" asked her nephew coaxingly.

"Wait, I'll be back in a minute. Let me just trim the lamp before the icon in the drawing room," said Katerina and went out hurriedly.

There was a faint whispering in the drawing room but it reached the sharp ears of the child in the dead silence.

"Auntie, what's all this? Who are you whispering to there?" the boy cried with tears in his voice. "Come here, Auntie, I'm afraid," he called still more tearfully a second later, and he thought he could hear his aunt say in the drawing room, "Well!" which he thought was addressed to him.

"What are you afraid of?" asked Katerina in a somewhat hoarse voice, coming in with a bold and resolute step and stopping before his bed in such a position that her body hid the door of the drawing room from the sick boy. "Lie down," she went on.

"I don't want to, Auntie."

"You listen to me, Fedya, and lie down—it's time—lie down," repeated Katerina.

"But why, Auntie? I don't want to at all."

"Lie down, lie down!" Katerina repeated again in a changed, shaky voice and, lifting the child in her arms, she put him down at the head of the bed.

At that moment Fedya uttered a piercing cry: he had caught sight of Sergey, pale and barefoot, entering the room.

Katerina put her hand over the mouth the frightened child

had opened in his horror. "Come on, be quick!" she shouted. "Hold him straight and see he doesn't struggle!"

Sergey seized Fedya by his arms and legs, while Katerina with one movement covered the childish face of the sufferer with a large down pillow and lay on it herself with her firm, resilient bosom.

For four minutes there was a sepulchral silence in the room.

"He's dead," Katerina whispered and had only just raised herself with the intention of putting everything in order when the walls of the quiet house that had concealed so many crimes were shaken by deafening blows: the windows rattled, the floors shook, the chains of the hanging lamps before the icons quivered and flitted round the walls in fantastic shadows.

Sergey trembled all over and ran off as fast as his legs would carry him; Katerina ran after him, and the noise and uproar followed them. It seemed as though some unearthly power were shaking the sin-ridden house to its foundations.

Katerina was afraid that in his panic Sergey might run into the yard and betray himself by his fright; but he rushed straight to the attic.

At the top of the stairs Sergey struck his forehead in the darkness against the half-opened door and fell headlong down the stairs, completely out of his wits with superstitious fear.

"Zinovy Borisovich! Zinovy Borisovich!" he mumbled, as he fell down the stairs head foremost, knocking Katerina off her feet and dragging her down with him.

"Where?" she asked.

"He just flew over us with a sheet of iron. There, there he is again! Oh, oh!" cried Sergey. "He thunders! He thunders again!

Now it was quite plain that hundreds of hands were knocking at all the windows from outside, and that someone was trying to break in through the door.

"You fool, get up! Get up, you fool!" cried Katerina, and with these words she rushed back to Fedya, arranged his dead head in the most natural sleeping position on the pillows, and with a firm hand opened the door through which a crowd of people tried to get into the house. It was a terrible sight. Katerina looked over the heads of the crowd that was besieging the front steps and saw rows upon rows of strangers climbing over the high wooden fence into the yard and heard the hubbub of thousands of voices in the street.

Before Katerina had time to find out what was happening, the crowd surrounding the front steps knocked her off her feet and flung her back into the house.

12.

All this uproar had arisen in this way: there were immense crowds at vespers on the eve of one of the twelve great church festivals in all the churches of the town where Katerina Izmaylov lived, for though it was only a district town, it was a rather large industrial center, and in the church where the image of the Virgin was to be brought the next day there was not enough room even in the courtyard for an apple to drop. It was in that church that a special choir composed of young men selected from the merchant class, led by a special precentor who was also a lover of the vocal art, used to sing on an occasion like this.

Our townspeople are pious, devoted churchgoers, and for that reason to a certain extent artistic as well: ecclesiastical magnificence and harmonious, "organ-like" singing are one of their chief and purest enjoyments. Where a choir sings nearly half the town gathers to hear it, especially the young men belonging to the mercantile classes: shop assistants, errand boys, merchants' sons, the hands from the factories and workshops, and the manufacturers themselves with their better halves—all crowd together in the same church; everyone is anxious to be there even if only to stand in the porch or under a window in the noonday heat or hard frost, to hear how the octaves swell like an organ while the impudent tenor executes the most intricate grace notes.

In the parish church of the Izmaylov household was placed the throne for the Entry into the Church of the Holy Virgin and therefore on the eve of the festival, at the very time that the murder of Fedya took place, the youth of the whole town was gathered there and, as they left in a noisy crowd, they were discussing the merits of a well-known tenor and the accidental blunders of a now less well-known bass.

But not everyone was interested in these musical questions; there were people in the crowds who were interested in quite different subjects.

"I say, fellows, have you heard the strange stories about young Mrs. Izmaylov?" asked a young mechanic who had been brought from Petersburg by one of the local merchants, as he approached the Izmaylov house. "I'm told," he went on, "that she's having an affair with their clerk Sergey. Making love all the time!"

"That's an old story," replied a man in a sheepskin coat covered with blue nankeen cloth. "She wasn't in church tonight, was she?"

"In church? Why that young slut has become so vile she fears neither God, nor conscience, nor the eye of man."

"Look, there's a light in that room," observed the mechanic, pointing to a bright streak of light between the shutters.

"Have a look through the chink—see what they are up to," called a few voices.

The mechanic climbed on to the shoulders of two of his comrades and had no sooner put his eye to the opening in the shutters than he shouted at the top of his voice: "Good Lord, they're smothering someone there, smothering someone!" And the mechanic began to knock desperately at the shutters. About a dozen people followed his example and, rushing up to the windows, began hammering at them with their fists.

The crowd increased in numbers every minute and that is how the siege of the Izmaylov house began.

"I saw it myself, saw it with my own eyes," the mechanic told the police before the dead body of Fedya. "The child was lying on the bed and the two of them were smothering him."

Sergey was taken to the police station that very evening and Katerina was led to her attic room and two guards were stationed over her.

It was unbearably cold in the Izmaylovs' house; the stoves were not heated, the front door was never closed; one large crowd of curious people followed another without interruption. All came to look at Fedya lying in his coffin and at another large coffin covered with a wide shroud. On Fedya's forehead was a white satin band which covered the red scar left after the skull had been opened. The post-mortem revealed that Fedya's death had been caused by suffocation, and Sergey, when confronted with the corpse, burst into tears at the first words of the priest who told him of the Last Judgment and the punishment awaiting the unrepentant, and frankly confessed not only to the murder of Fedya, but also asked that Zinovy, who had been buried by him without a funeral service, should be disinterred. The body of Katerina's husband, buried in dry sand, was not as yet entirely decomposed: it was taken out and laid in a large coffin. As his accomplice in both these crimes, Sergey, to the general horror, named the young mistress. To all the questions put to her Katerina merely replied: "I know nothing about it." They made Sergey repeat his accusation against her to her face. Having heard his confession, Katerina looked at him in mute surprise but without anger, and then said without emotion: "If he wants to confess, I won't deny it: I killed them."

"Why did you do it?" she was asked.

"I did it for him," she replied, pointing at Sergey, who hung his head.

The criminals were taken to prison, and the terrible case, which had attracted universal attention and aroused general indignation, was soon settled. At the end of February, Sergey and the widow of the third guild merchant, Katerina Izmaylov, were sentenced in the criminal court to be flogged in the market place and to be sent to penal servitude. At the beginning of March, on a cold frosty morning, the executioner counted out the appointed number of black and blue wales on Katerina's bare white back and then administered the allotted portion of strokes on Sergey's shoulders, too, and branded his handsome face with the three marks of a convict.

During all that time Sergey for some reason aroused more general sympathy than Katerina. Dirty and bloodstained, he stumbled as he came down the black scaffold, while Katerina came down quietly, merely taking care that the thick shirt and coarse convict coat she wore did not stick to her lacerated back.

Even in the prison hospital, when they handed her child to her, she only said: "Oh, take him away!" and, turning to the wall, fell with her bosom on the hard bed without uttering a moan or a word of complaint.

13.

The gang of convicts to which Sergey and Katerina found themselves attached left when spring had begun only according to the calendar, and the sun, as the proverb has it, "shone brightly but warmed lightly."

Katerina's child was given to Boris Izmaylov's old cousin to be brought up, for legally he was the legitimate son of the husband of the murderess and the sole heir to the entire Izmaylov property. Katerina was completely satisfied with this and gave up the baby without any sign of emotion. Her love for the baby's father, like the love of many very passionate women, was not transmitted in any degree to the child. However, neither light nor darkness, neither sorrow nor joy, existed for her. She understood nothing, she loved no one, not even herself. She only waited impatiently for the departure of the gang of convicts, for she hoped to see her darling Sergey again on the road; as for her child, she even forgot to think of him.

Katerina's hopes were not disappointed: heavily shackled with chains and branded, Sergey came out of the prison gates in the same party as she.

Man gets used, as far as possible, to any horrible situation, and in every situation he retains, as far as possible, the ability to pursue his own scanty pleasures; but Katerina had nothing to adjust herself to: she saw Sergey again and with him even the road to Siberia was bright with happiness.

Katerina took but a few valuable things with her in her coarse, variegated cotton bag and even less money. But long before they had reached Nizhny she had distributed all this among the non-commissioned officers in charge of the transported convicts for permission to walk beside Sergey on the way or to stand with him and embrace him for an hour in a secluded corner of the narrow corridor of the cold halting stations.

But for some reason Katerina's branded lover became far less affectionate: he spoke in an abrupt, harsh way to her, nor did he particularly value their secret meetings, for which she went without food and drink and gave away twenty-five-copeck pieces from her lean purse, money she needed so badly herself. Indeed, more than once he said to her: "Instead of coming out to rub against the corners of the corridor with me, you'd do better to let me have the money you gave to the guards."

"I only gave him twenty-five copecks, darling," Katerina replied in an attempt to justify herself.

"Well, isn't a twenty-five-copeck piece money? You must have picked up lots of alms on the road, and shoved the money into different pockets, I shouldn't wonder."

"But we've seen each other, haven't we, darling?"

"And what's the good of that? Some joy to see each other after such torture! Oh, to hell with this life and these meetings!"

"But I don't mind, darling, so long as I see you."

"That's nonsense," Sergey replied.

Sometimes during their nocturnal meetings Katerina bit her lips till they bled at such answers and sometimes in the darkness tears of anger and vexation came to those eyes which had never known tears before; but she put up with it all, was always silent, and tried to deceive herself.

In this way, with their relationship so newly altered, they reached Nizhny-Novgorod. There, their party was joined by another gang of convicts which had marched to Siberia along the Moscow highroad.

Among a great number of people in the women's division in this vast gang, there were two very interesting personalities: one of them, Fiona, was the wife of a soldier from Yaroslav, a handsome, magnificent woman, tall, with a thick plait of black hair and a pair of languorous brown eyes, over which long lashes hung like a mysterious veil. The other, a pretty girl of seventeen with a sharp face, a delicate, rosy skin, a tiny mouth, dimples in her fresh cheeks, and fair golden locks that strayed capriciously on to her forehead from under her striped convict kerchief, was called Sonetka.

The beautiful Fiona had a soft and lazy disposition. In her party all knew her and none of the men was particularly gratified to gain her favors or particularly upset to see that she bestowed the same favors on anybody else who sought them.

"Auntie Fiona," the convicts said jestingly in one voice, "is the kindest of creatures—she never refuses anyone."

But Sonetka was quite a different kind of woman.

About her they said: "She is as slippery as an eel: slips round your fingers, you can never lay hands on her."

Sonetka had taste, was particular about her choice of lover, perhaps a little too particular. She wanted passion to be offered to her not as if it were a common or garden mushroom, but one with a highly spiced, piquant sauce, with sufferings and sacrifices; Fiona, on the other hand, was the personification of the simplicity of the typical Russian woman who is too lazy to say "Go away" to a man, and who only knows that she is a woman. Such women are highly thought of in convict gangs and robber bands and in the Petersburg social-democratic communes.

The appearance of these two women in the combined convict party ended tragically for Katerina.

14.

From the very first days of the march of the united party of convicts from Nizhny to Kazan, Sergey tried in no uncertain manner to wheedle himself into the favor of the soldier's wife, Fiona, and not without success. The languid beauty did not break Sergey's heart as, indeed, owing to her good nature, she broke no one's heart. At the third or fourth halting station Katerina, by bribing the guard, arranged a meeting with her darling Sergey at an early hour of the night. She lay awake waiting for the non-commissioned officer on duty to come up and quietly nudge her, whispering: "Run quickly!" The door opened once and some woman dashed into the corridor; the door opened again and another woman convict jumped quickly down from her bunk and also disappeared after the guard; at last someone pulled the coat with which Katerina was covered. The young woman jumped quickly down from the bunk so many convicts had polished with their sides, threw the coat over her shoulders, and hustled the guard who was standing in front of her.

When Katerina went along the corridor, which was lighted only in one place by a dimly burning lampion, she stumbled over two or three couples who could not be seen at a distance. When she passed the door of the men's barracks she heard suppressed laughter coming through the little window cut in it.

"Enjoying themselves!" Katerina's guard muttered with sudden irritation and, taking hold of her shoulders, pushed her into a corner and went away.

Katerina felt with her hand a coat and a beard; her other hand touched a woman's hot face.

"Who's that?" Sergey asked in an undertone.

"And what are you doing here? Who are you with?"

Katerina pulled her rival's kerchief off in the darkness. The strange woman darted away and, as she ran, stumbled against someone and fell.

A burst of loud laughter came from the men's barracks.

"Villain!" whispered Katerina and hit Sergey across the face with the end of the kerchief she had torn from his new friend's head.

Sergey raised a hand, but Katerina shot quickly down the corridor and regained her own door. The laughter that followed her from the men's barracks became so loud that the sentry, who was standing apathetically near the lampion, spitting at the toes of his boots, raised his head and roared: "Quiet there!"

Katerina lay down in silence and remained so till morning. She tried to say to herself: "I don't love him," but the love she felt was more passionate than ever. She could see before her eyes his hand trembling under *her* head and how his other hand embraced her hot shoulders.

The poor woman wept and against her will, prayed that that same hand should be under her own head and the other embracing her hysterically quivering shoulders.

"How about giving me back my kerchief?" the soldier's wife, Fiona, said, waking her the next morning.

"Oh, so you were the one!"

"Now come on, let's have it!"

"Why have you come between us?"

"Come between you? Listen to that! Do you think that kind of love is worth getting angry about?"

Katerina thought about that for a moment and then she took the kerchief she had torn off Fiona's head from under her pillow and threw it at the soldier's wife. She turned to the wall.

She felt better.

"What am I doing?" she said to herself. "Am I really jealous of this painted washtub? To hell with her! Even comparing her to myself makes me sick!"

"Now, look here, Katerina," Sergey said the next day as he marched alongside her on the road, "please understand that, in the first place, I am not Zinovy and, secondly, that you're no longer a rich merchant's wife and a fine lady. So do me a favor: don't give yourself airs! You can't make a silk purse out of a sow's ear—understand?"

Katerina didn't reply to that and for a whole week she marched beside Sergey without exchanging either a word or a look with him. She was the one who had been treated badly and she obstinately refused to take the first step towards a reconciliation.

During this period, while Katerina was angry, Sergey began parading himself before pretty little Sonetka and flirting with her. Sometimes he would bow to her with a sort of exaggerated politeness, or he would smile at her, or, when meeting her, try to embrace and hug her. Katerina saw all this and her blood boiled the more.

"Shouldn't I make up with him?" Katerina wondered, staggering, unable to see the ground under her feet.

But now more than ever her pride would not permit her to take the first step. Sergey pursued Sonetka more persistently and it seemed to everyone there that Sonetka, the unapproachable, she who was as slippery as an eel, had suddenly become tamer.

"Well, you were furious with me," Fiona said to Katerina one day, "but what did I ever do to you? I had my chance and it's gone. Now you'd better watch Sonetka!"

"To hell with pride: I'll make up with him today," Katerina decided, thinking only of how best to bring this about.

It was Sergey himself who helped her out of this predicament.

He called to her at one of the halting places: "Tonight come to see me, Katerina. I've something to ask you."

Katerina remained silent.

"You're not still angry? Will you come?"

Katerina still said nothing.

But everyone who was interested in Katerina, including Sergey, noticed that she got nearer and nearer to the guard as they approached the halting place, finally shoving into his hand the seventeen copecks she had received as alms from the people on the way.

"I'll give you ten copecks more as soon as I collect them," Katerina entreated him.

The guard hid the money in his cuff.

"All right," he said.

At the end of these negotiations, Sergey cleared his throat and winked at Sonetka.

"What a wonder you are, Katerina," he said, embracing her as he mounted the steps of the halting station. "Men, there's not a woman in the world who can compare to her."

Katerina flushed, breathless with happiness.

At night, as soon as the door opened quietly, she rushed out and groped for Sergey with trembling hands in the dark corridor.

"Katya, my darling!" Sergey said, embracing her.

"Oh, you wretch!" said Katerina through tears, and pressed her lips to his.

The sentry walked up and down the corridor and, stopping, spat at his boots, then proceeded; on the opposite side of the doors the tired convicts snored, a mouse gnawed at a feather under the stove, the crickets chirped lustily as though vying with each other, and Katerina was blissfully happy.

But one wearies of raptures and becomes aware of the inevitable prose of life.

"My legs hurt awfully," Sergey complained as he sat with Katerina on the floor of the corridor. "My bones ache from the ankle right up to the knee."

"What can we do about it, darling?" she asked, nestling under the skirts of his coat.

"I don't know. Maybe I should ask to be put in a hospital at Kazan."

"How can you say that, darling?"

"What else can I do! It just hurts terribly."

"But how can you stay behind and have me go on?"

"Then what? It's terribly chafed, I tell you. It's chafed so much the chain is eating into the bone. Of course, if I had some woolen stockings . . ."

"Stockings? Why, darling, I have a new pair."

"Oh no, I couldn't take your stockings!" Sergey said.

Without saying another word, Katerina slipped into the barracks, emptied the things from her bag onto her bunk, and then hurried back to Sergey with a pair of thick blue woolen stockings which had bright red clocks on the sides.

"Thanks," Sergey said, as he parted from Katerina, taking with him her last stockings. "I'm sure it will be all right now."

Happy, Katerina returned to her bunk and fell fast asleep.

She heard neither Sonetka's departure nor her silent return just before daybreak.

This happened only a two days' march from Kazan.

A cold rainy day, wind-blown and sleety, gave a gruff welcome to the party of convicts as they marched out of the gates of the airless halting station. Katerina was in fairly good spirits until she took her place in line and then she trembled and turned green. Blackness swam before her eyes and her aching limbs went limp. There stood Sonetka and she had on the pair of blue woolen stockings with bright red clocks.

Katerina began the march more dead than alive; but her eyes were fixed on Sergey in a terrible stare and she did not remove them from him for an instant.

At the first resting place she calmly went up to Sergey, whispered "Pig!" and quite unexpectedly spat in his face.

Sergey was about to strike her, but was restrained.

"Just wait!" he said, wiping his face.

"Not afraid of you, is she?" the convicts jeered at Sergey; and Sonetka burst out into particularly gay laughter.

The cheap little love affair in which Sonetka had got herself involved was quite to her taste.

"You'll suffer for this," Sergey threatened Katerina.

Exhausted by the long march and the bad weather, that night Katerina tossed restlessly on her bunk at the halting station, yet she did not hear two men enter the women's barracks.

As they entered Sonetka rose from her bunk and silently pointed to Katerina; then she lay down again and wrapped herself in her coat.

That moment Katerina's coat was thrown over her head and the thick end of a doubly twisted cord came down with all the strength of a peasant's arm on her back, which was only covered by a coarse shirt.

Katerina cried out but her voice could not be heard under the coat in which her head was wrapped. She made a violent effort to jump from her bunk, but again without success, for a burly convict was sitting on her shoulders and pinning down her arms.

"Fifty," a voice finally counted, a voice which no one would have found it difficult to recognize as Sergey's, and the nocturnal visitors at once disappeared behind the door.

Katerina uncovered her head and sat up, but there was nobody there; only somewhere near at hand someone tittered malevolently under a coat. Katerina recognized Sonetka's laugh.

There was no limit to the injuries Katerina had suffered, nor was there any limit to the feeling of anger which boiled up at that moment in her heart. She rushed forward without thinking and fell unconscious into the arms of Fiona, who caught her just in time.

It was on Fiona's full bosom, which had only so recently gratified her unfaithful lover's lust, that Katerina now cried out her
unbearable sorrow and, as a child clings to its mother, so she
clung desperately to her stupid, plump rival. They were both
equal now: of equal price and jilted.

Both equal—Fiona, who could not resist the call of love from
whomever it might come, and Katerina, who was now acting the
last scene in the drama of love!

Still, Katerina was no longer capable of feeling pain. Having
shed her tears, she hardened herself and prepared to go out for
roll call with a wooden calmness.

The drum beat: tra-ta-ta-ta, and the convicts, chained and unchained, tumbled into the yard, Sergey, Fiona, Sonetka, Katerina,
a sectarian chained to a Jew, a Pole on the same chain as a Tartar.

They all crowded together, then formed into some sort of order
and marched off.

A most cheerless picture: a handful of people torn from the
world of men and deprived of every shadow of hope, their feet
sinking into the cold black mud of the highroad. Everything
about them was hideous: endless mud, gray skies, a wet leafless
tree, a crow with ruffled feathers on a spreading branch. The wind
moaned, raged, howled, and roared.

In these hellish, heart-rending sounds, which put the finishing
touches to this picture, one could catch the voice of the wife of
the Biblical Job: "Cursed be the day wherein you were born."

He who does not wish to hear these words, he who is not
tempted by the thought of death even in such mournful circumstances, but is frightened by it, must try to drown these howl-
ing voices by something still more hideous. The ordinary man
knows this very well: he gives free play to his animal simplicity,
he begins to play the fool, to jeer at himself, at other people, at
human feelings. Not particularly tenderhearted, he becomes
doubly spiteful.

"And how is your ladyship? Are you still in good health?"
Sergey asked Katerina insolently, as soon as the village in which

the caravan had passed the night disappeared behind a wet hill-ock.

Having said these words, he immediately turned to Sonetka and, covering her with his coat, began to sing in a high falsetto voice:

> A *fair pretty head in the shade behind a window hides,*
> You're not *asleep, my sweet tormentor, you're not asleep, my rogue,*
> With *my coat I shall cover you, so none shall see.*

Having sung these words, Sergey embraced Sonetka before everyone and gave her a loud kiss . . .

Katerina saw it and yet did not appear to see: she walked like a lifeless person. But her companions began nudging her to draw her attention to the way Sergey was acting with Sonetka. She had become an object of mockery and derision.

"Leave her alone," Fiona cried, taking her part each time one of the party laughed at Katerina as she stumbled blindly along.

"Must have wet feet, poor thing," a young convict joked.

"Why, of course," Sergey responded, "she comes from a merchant's family, you see. Had a delicate upbringing."

"Now," he went on, "if she only had a pair of warm stockings, it wouldn't be so bad."

Katerina came to life for a moment. Unable to restrain herself, she cried out, "Laugh at me, serpent, go ahead, laugh."

"Why, not at all, great lady, not at all! I'm not laughing at you. It's just that Sonetka is selling a pair of fine stockings, and I was just wondering whether a merchant's wife like you might not want them."

Many of the convicts laughed. Katerina walked on like a mechanical doll.

The weather was getting worse. Snow descended in wet flakes from the gray clouds that covered the sky, and melted as soon as it reached the ground, adding to the deep mire. At last a dark leaden line appeared in the distance beyond which nothing could be seen. It was the Volga. There was a strong breeze blowing on the river, driving the slowly forming dark waves backwards and forwards.

The caravan of wet, shivering convicts marched slowly to the river bank and stopped to wait for the ferry.

The dark, wet boat arrived and the guards began herding the convicts on board.

"They say someone's selling vodka on this boat," one of the convicts observed when the ferry, covered with flakes of wet snow, had put out from the bank and was tossing on the waves of the choppy river.

"Yes, it wouldn't be bad to have a drop or two," Sergey declared and, baiting Katerina for the amusement of Sonetka, he went on: "I say, great lady, how about offering me a drop of vodka for old time's sake? Don't be stingy. Don't forget, my darling, how we used to pass the long autumn nights together making love and hurrying off your family to eternal peace without the help of a priest or deacon."

Katerina shivered with the cold. Nor was it only the cold which penetrated through her drenched clothes to her very bones; something else was taking place inside of her. Her head burned as though it were on fire; the pupils of her eyes were dilated and shone brightly with a distraught, sharp look which fixed itself on the rolling waves.

"Well, I'd certainly take a drop or two of vodka, it's freezing cold," Sonetka said in a loud, ringing voice.

"Come on, great lady, treat us to a drink," Sergey went on imploring her in mockery.

"Don't you have a conscience?" Fiona said, shaking her head reproachfully.

"That's no way to act," the little convict Gordey said, backing up the soldier's wife.

"You ought to be ashamed of yourself, if not for her sake, then for ours," Fiona continued.

"Oh, shut up, you overused snuffbox, you!" Sergey shouted at Fiona. "Ashamed of myself, indeed! What do I have to be ashamed of, tell me. I don't believe I ever loved her. Sonetka's old shoe is dearer to me now than her ugly face—the draggle-tailed cat! What do you say to that? Let her love Gordey here with his twisted mouth, or," he added, glancing at the small seedy-looking guard, who was sitting on his horse in his long felt cloak and military cap with its cockade, "perhaps she'd better make eyes at that guard: under his cloak she'd at least be out of the rain."

"And everyone would call her the officer's lady," Sonetka called out in her ringing voice.

"And so we should!" Sergey agreed. "And she'd have no trouble getting herself a pair of fine stockings, either!"

Katerina said nothing in her own defense: she gazed more intently at the waves, moving her lips. Between Sergey's ugly remarks she heard the moan and roar of the rising and breaking waters. Suddenly out of one of the breakers rolled the blue head of her father-in-law, Boris Timofeyevich, and out of another came her husband, and he clasped the drooping head of Fedya. Katerina tried to remember a prayer, but her lips only whispered: "How we used to make love together in the long autumn nights, and hurry people out of this world."

Katerina shuddered. Her errant gaze had become fixed and wild. Aimlessly once or twice she stretched her arms into space and let them fall. Another minute—then suddenly she swayed and without removing her gaze from the dark waters bent forward and, seizing Sonetka by the legs, with one lunge pulled her overboard.

Everyone froze in astonishment.

Katerina appeared on the top of a wave and then dived beneath it; Sonetka was borne aloft on another wave.

"A boat hook! Throw them a boat hook!" the convicts on the ferry shouted.

A heavy boat hook attached to a long rope rose in the air and fell to the water. Sonetka disappeared again. Two seconds later, carried away from the ferry by the current, she raised her arms once more, but Katerina broke from another wave, emerging almost to the waist, and threw herself on Sonetka like a strong pike on a soft little perch, and neither appeared again.

The Enchanted Wanderer

1.

Leaving the island of Konevetz, we sailed on Lake Ladoga bound for the island of Valaam and on the way we entered the harbor of Korela, having stopped there on ship's business. Many of us were glad to go ashore and we rode on sturdy Finnish ponies to the desolate little town. On our return, our captain was ready to resume the journey and we sailed off again.

After our visit to Korela it was very natural that a discussion should have arisen about that poor, though rather ancient, Russian settlement, than which nothing drearier could be imagined. On our boat everybody was of the same opinion and one of the passengers, a man given to philosophic generalizations who fancied himself as a political wag, observed that he could not for the life of him understand why the authorities in St. Petersburg found it expedient to send undesirable characters to more or less remote places, which of course entailed an expense to the Exchequer for the cost of their transportation, when just there near the capital there was on the shore of Lake Ladoga such a wonderful place as Korela, where no freethinking, nor indeed any inclination towards independence of mind, could stand up against the apathy of the population and the terrible boredom induced by surroundings so bleak and depressing.

"I'm certain," this passenger said, "it is red tape which is chiefly responsible for this state of affairs or, if not that, then perhaps lack of proper information."

Someone, evidently a man who was familiar with those parts, replied that all sorts of exiles had lived there at different times, but that it seemed they had not lasted long.

"One young man, a student of a religious seminary, was exiled here as a junior deacon (an exile which was to me quite inexplicable). On his arrival here the poor man did his best to keep his spirits up for a time in the hope of a turn for the better in his fortunes, but later, having sought solace in drink, he began to drink so steadily that he went off his head completely and petitioned the authorities to order him 'to be shot, or to send him to the army as a private, or to condemn him to be hanged for general incapacity.'"

"What was the decision?"

"Well, I really don't know. You see, he didn't wait for any decision: he hanged himself of his own accord."

"He did right," said the philosopher.

"Right?" exclaimed the man who had related the story, by the look of him a merchant who was, besides, a man of substance and religion.

"Why not?" queried the philosopher. "At least, once dead there was an end to his suffering!"

"How do you mean there was an end to his suffering? What do you suppose will happen to him in the next world? Suicides, you know, are condemned to eternal torment. People are not even allowed to pray for them."

The philosopher smiled sardonically and said nothing, but at this point a new disputant entered the lists against him and the merchant, a man who to our surprise took the part of the unfortunate deacon who had executed his own death warrant without waiting for permission from the authorities.

This was a new passenger who had come on board at Konevetz unnoticed by any of us. He had kept silent till now and nobody had taken any notice of him. But now we all turned to him and everyone was clearly puzzled at how on earth we had failed to notice him before. He was a man of enormous size, swarthy and open of countenance, with thick, curly hair of the color of lead: very striking indeed did his grizzled head appear! He wore the short cassock of a novice of a monastery with a wide monastic leather belt and a high, black, cotton ecclesiastical hat. Whether he was only a novice or a full-fledged monk who had taken his vows, it was difficult to say; for the monks on the Ladoga Islands do not always wear skullcaps either when travelling or when going about their business on the islands, but in their rural simplicity prefer to wear tall ecclesiastical hats. Our new passenger, who later appeared to be a man of quite unusual fascination, seemed to be a man of some fifty years, but he was in every sense of the word a real giant of a man, and, moreover, a typical Russian giant, simple-minded and good-natured, who reminded you of the legendary figure of Ilya Murometz in Vereshchagin's beautiful painting or in the poem of Count Alexey Tolstoy. You could not help feeling that he ought not to be walking about in a cassock at all, but riding on "a dappled-gray steed" in bast shoes of enormous size, roaming through the forests and inhaling "the scents of resin and wild strawberry in the dark pinewood."

But in spite of his undoubted good nature it did not require much observation to divine in him a man who had seen many things in his lifetime, a man who, as the saying goes, "had been around." He bore himself bravely, with self-confidence though not with any objectionable bravado, and he spoke in a pleasant bass voice in the manner of a man who was in the habit of addressing audiences.

"All that means nothing," he began, letting each word fall lazily and softly from beneath his thick, gray mustache, which, Hussarlike, was curled upwards. "I do not agree with your views about the fate which is in store for suicides in the next world, I mean that they will apparently, according to you, never be forgiven. As for there being no one to pray for them, that, too, is nonsense, for there is a man who can improve their unhappy lot very simply and without much trouble."

Asked who the man was who had so intimate an acquaintance with the circumstances attending suicides after death and who was capable of mending them, "The man in question, gentlemen," the giant clad in the black monastic garb answered, "is a lowly village priest in the Moscow diocese, a hard drinker, who himself was very nearly unfrocked, and it is he who is exerting himself on their behalf."

"How do you happen to know about it?"

"Why, bless my soul, gentlemen, I am not the only one who knows about it: everybody in the Moscow district knows about it! For it is a matter with which no less a person than his Grace the Archbishop Filaret personally concerned himself."

A short pause ensued during which someone was heard to say that the whole affair seemed rather dubious.

The black-robed novice or monk did not seem in the least put out by that remark. "To be sure," he said, "it does seem a bit dubious at first. Nor is it surprising that it should appear dubious to us when even his Grace himself would not believe it for a long time, but afterwards, having obtained all the necessary evidence, he realized that it was impossible not to believe it and he believed it."

The passengers besought the novice to tell them this amazing story. He was, indeed, very willing to do so, and he began thus:

The story goes that one day an archdeacon wrote to his Grace the archbishop to say that the village priest, your Grace, was a terrible drunkard, drank vodka day and night, and was no good in his parish. And that, his report I mean, was in point of fact quite justified. So his Grace ordered that the humble priest should be summoned to appear before him in Moscow. One look at the priest was quite enough to convince his Grace that he was indeed a confirmed drunkard, and the archbishop therefore decided that the priest should be deprived of his incumbency. The poor priest was much aggrieved, so much so that he even stopped drinking. He spent all his time bewailing his unhappy lot, weeping disconsolately. "What a sorry pass have I come to," he said to himself, "and what is there left for me to do but lay violent hands upon myself? That is all that remains for me to do," he said, "for then his Grace will at least take pity upon my poor family and find a husband for my daughter to take my place as breadwinner and provide sustenance for my wife and children." Well, so he made up his mind without any more ado to end his wretched life and even appointed the day on which he was to do it, but, being by nature a good man, he thought to himself, "All right, suppose I do die, but what will happen to my soul then? I am not a beast of the field, I am not without a soul, so where will my soul go to after I have done away with myself?" And thereupon he was even more cruelly distressed in his mind. Well, while he grieved and grieved, his Grace, who had decided to deprive him of his incumbency on account of his drunkenness, one day after a meal lay down on a couch with a book to rest and fell asleep. Well, so he fell asleep or just dropped off into a doze when suddenly he saw that the door of his cell seemed to open. He naturally called out, "Who's there?" thinking that it was probably his attendant who wanted to announce somebody's arrival, but lo! instead of his attendant, who should walk in but a venerable old man, whose face bespoke infinite goodness and in whom his Grace immediately recognized one of the saints of the Church, no other than the Right Reverend Sergius himself.

So his Grace said: "Is it thou, holy father in God Sergius?"

And the saint replied: "It is I, Filaret, servant of the Lord."

His Grace then asked: "What dost thou, who art pure in heart, desire of me, thy unworthy servant?"

And St. Sergius replied: "I crave mercy."

"To whom dost thou want me to show mercy?"

So the saint there and then named that same humble priest who had been deprived of his place because of drunkenness and, after that, withdrew. But his Grace woke up and said to himself, "What can it all mean? Was it an ordinary dream, or just an idle fancy, or a supernatural vision?" And he began to think it over and, being a man famed throughout the world for his great intellect, he came to the conclusion that it was just an ordinary dream; for, indeed, was it possible that St. Sergius, who had spent all his life in fasting and who was so strict an advocate of the good life, should intercede on behalf of an ecclesiastic of a notoriously weak character who was so shockingly careless of the pitfalls with which human life is beset? All right. So, having come to this conclusion, his Grace left the whole business to take its natural course as had been arranged from the very beginning, and he himself carried on as usual and, at the appointed hour, went to bed again. But no sooner did he fall into a slumber than again he saw a vision, and such a vision that the great spirit of his Grace was sore afflicted. Just imagine, gentlemen: a rumbling noise, such a strange noise . . . so strange that it is quite impossible to describe it. . . . Horses galloping . . . knights without number . . . tearing along, all attired in green coats of mail, breastplates, and feathers, and horses like so many black lions, and in front of them their proud captain, wearing the same attire, and in whichever direction he waves his black banner, there all of them gallop, and on the banner is a dragon. . . . His Grace knew not what that procession might signify, but that proud captain roared out an order. "Tear them to pieces," he shouted, "for they have no one now to pray for them!" And after that he galloped away, and after the captain his warriors also galloped away, and after them, like a flock of lean geese in springtime, there passed a whole procession of dismal spirits, and all of them nodded their heads sorrowfully to his Grace and besought him pitifully, moaning quietly through their sobs, "Let him go! He alone prays for us!" As soon as he got up, his Grace sent for the drunken little priest and began asking him what kind of prayers he was in the habit of saying and who he was praying for. The priest, weak in spirit as he was, was greatly perplexed in the presence of the archbishop and he said, "I do everything according to the rules laid down by the Church, your Grace." It was with great difficulty that his Grace succeeded in getting him to confess. "I confess," he said, "to being guilty of one transgression. For, being weak in spirit myself and in my despair thinking that it were better to take my own life, I always during the service of the Holy Communion say a special prayer for those who die without absolution and lay violent hands upon themselves. . . ." Well, his Grace then understood what those spirits were who in his vision had sailed past him like lean geese and, not wishing to give joy to those demons who had sped before them bent on destruction, he gave his blessing to the humble priest. "Go," said his Grace, "and sin no more, and for whomsoever thou hast been praying, continue praying for them," and he sent the priest back to his parish. So he, this lowly priest, can always be useful to people who find life's struggles too great a burden to bear, for he isn't likely to prove untrue to his calling, presumptuous though it may appear, but he will go on importuning the Creator for them and He will have to forgive them.

"Why 'have to'?"

"Because 'knock, and it shall be opened unto you.' That was what He Himself commanded and that, sir, cannot be altered."

"But tell me, please: is there nobody else besides that Moscow priest who prays for suicides?"

"I really don't know what to say to that, sir. People will tell you that you shouldn't pray to God for them because they have taken the law into their own hands, but I shouldn't be surprised if there are people who, not understanding it, do pray for them. I believe that on Trinity Sunday—or is it on Whit Monday?—everybody is allowed to pray for them. They say special prayers for them on that day, wonderful prayers, so moving that I could listen to them forever!"

"Can't you say those prayers on any other day?"

"Don't know, sir. You'd better ask those who have read a lot about such things. I expect they ought to know. You see, as I am not really interested in this matter, I haven't discussed it with anybody."

"But haven't you noticed whether those prayers are ever repeated in any church service?"

"No, I haven't, but do not take my word for it, for I don't go to church very often."

"Oh? Why not?"

"Well, you see, I'm pretty busy and I can't spare the time for it."

"Are you a monk or a deacon?"

"I'm neither. At present I'm just wearing a monk's habit."

"But that surely means that you're at least a novice, doesn't it?"

"Well . . . I suppose so. At least people regard me as one."

"They may regard you as one," the merchant remarked, "but I've known cases where men wearing cassocks have been pressed into the army."

The giant clad in the black garb of a monk was not in the least offended by that remark. He just considered it for a little while and said:

"I daresay you're right, sir. I, too, have heard of such cases, but, you see, I'm a bit too old for the army, I'm in my fifty-third year, and, besides, I'm not a stranger to army life."

"Why? Have you served in the army?"

"I have."

"As a non-commissioned officer, I presume?" the merchant asked him again.

"No, not as a non-commissioned officer."

"What were you then? A private, a quartermaster-sergeant, or what? Neither fish, flesh, nor fowl?"

"No, sir, you're quite wrong. I was a real army man. In fact I have been busy with regimental affairs almost since childhood."

"I see, you're the son of a regular soldier and therefore liable to military service. Is that it?" The merchant, who was beginning to lose his temper, seemed quite determined to get to the bottom of it.

"Wrong again."

"Well, blast you, who are you then?"

"I'm a connoisseur."

"A wha–a–at?"

"A connoisseur, sir, a connoisseur, or, to put it in plain language, a good judge of horseflesh. I was employed as assistant to army officers purchasing horses. Acted as their adviser, I did."

"Oh, so that's it!"

"Yes, sir. I've selected and trained thousands of horses in my time. I used to break in wild horses which, for instance, used to rear up and fall backwards with all their might and, like as not, fracture the rider's chest with the saddle bow, but no horse ever did that to me."

"But how did you tame such horses?"

"Me? Why, it's very simple really, for, you see, gentlemen, nature has endowed me with a special gift for that sort of thing. As soon as I'd jump on the back of such a wild horse, I'd give it no time to collect its wits. With my left hand I'd get hold of its ear and give it a mighty pull to one side, while at the same time I'd deal it a terrific blow with my right fist between the ears and I'd grind my teeth in a most terrifying way, so that many a poor beast would start bleeding at the nostrils and it really looked sometimes as if its brains came out with the blood. Well, of course, after that it would become as meek as a lamb."

"Well, and then?"

"Then I'd dismount, look it all over, give it a chance to have a good look at me so that it should retain a good impression of me and I'd mount it again and ride off."

"And the horse would behave itself after that?"

"Yes, it would behave itself all right, for a horse is a clever animal; it scents the kind of man it is dealing with and it knows what he thinks about it. So far as I'm concerned, for instance, every horse formed an excellent opinion of me and, indeed, loved and regarded me. In a riding school in Moscow there was a horse which got completely out of hand. No rider could do anything with it, and, in addition, the brute had learnt a dastardly trick of biting through a rider's knee. The devil would seize the rider's knee with its huge teeth and bite right through the knee-cap. That horse was responsible for the deaths of many people. At that time an American by the name of Rarey was visiting Moscow. Called himself the world champion tamer of wild animals, he did. But this mean horse nearly ate him up, too. Put him to shame, anyway. He only saved himself because, so I heard it said, he wore a steel knee guard, so that although the horse bit his leg, it couldn't bite through it and threw him instead. But for that it would have killed him. However, I put it right."

"How did you do that?"

"I did it with God's help, for, I repeat, I'm gifted that way. That Mr. Rarey, he who called himself 'the world champion tamer of wild animals,' and the rest of them who had tried to break in that horse thought that the whole art of subduing its vicious temper consisted in the right way of manipulating the reins so that it couldn't move its head either one way or the other. As soon as that American, Rarey, refused to have anything to do with it, I said, 'Nonsense,' I said, 'there's nothing to it, for all that's wrong with the horse is that it is possessed of a devil. The American can't grasp that, but I can and I'm quite willing to help you.' The authorities agreed. So I said, 'Take him out behind the Dragomilov tollgate!' They took him out. All right. We led him by the halter to a gully in Fily where the gentry spend their summer holidays. I saw that the place was just what I wanted, quite big enough for my purpose, and I lost no time in getting to work. I jumped on the back of that man-eating horse, without a shirt to my back, barefooted, in nothing but a pair of wide breeches and a cap. The only thing I wore round my naked body was a braided cotton belt dedicated to the memory of the brave and saintly Prince Vsevolod-Gabriel of Novgorod whom I had greatly admired for his valorous deeds and in whose protection I had great faith; and the belt had this inscription woven into it: *My honor I shall yield to no one.* In my hands I had no special implements of any kind, save, in one, a heavy Tartar riding whip with a lead head of no more than two pounds in weight, and in the other an ordinary crock of thin dough. Well, so there I was, sitting on the back of that savage horse, while four men were pulling his muzzle for all they were worth in different directions, so that he shouldn't assault any one of them with his teeth. And he, that demon of a horse, seeing that we were about to take up arms against him, started to neigh and to whinny, and he broke out into a sweat and shook all over with rage, quite intent on eating me up. I saw it plainly, so I shouted to the stablemen, 'Hurry up,' I said, 'take the bridle off the rascal!' They couldn't believe their own ears, for they never expected me to give them such an order, so they just stood there, staring at me, with their eyes popping out of their heads. I said to them, 'What are you standing about for? Come on, do what I tell you! Didn't you hear me? If I give you an order, you have to carry it out immediately!' And they replied, 'Good heavens, Ivan Severyanych'—they used to call me Ivan Severyanych in the world, Flyagin was my family name—'do you really want us to take the bridle off?' I couldn't help losing my temper with them, for I could see and I could feel with my legs that the horse was getting mad with rage. So I squeezed him tightly between my knees and I bawled at them, 'Take it off!' They were going to say something, but I got so mad that I started grinding my teeth at them and they pulled off the bridle in no time and took to their heels, running off helter-skelter in all directions. Well, as soon as they had pulled off the bridle, I straightway did something that the horse did not expect: banged the crock on his head! The crock broke and the dough began to run into his eyes and nostrils. The poor beast got scared properly, for he thought, 'What's all this?' But I took my cap off quickly with my left hand and started spreading the dough into his eyes with it, while with my right I slashed him across the side with my riding whip. . . . He just went off at a gallop, and I kept on rubbing the dough into his eyes with my cap to dim his eyesight and hitting him with the whip on the other side. . . . So I went on trouncing him merci- lessly. I did not give him any time to get his breath or look round him, kept on rubbing the dough all over his face, blinding him, grinding my teeth to put the fear of God into him, frightening him, hitting him hard on both his sides with my riding whip, so that he should understand that this was no joke. . . . He did understand it all right, for he did not remain obstinately in one place, but went on galloping for all he was worth. Well, so the poor rascal kept on carrying me on his back, while I kept on thrashing him, and the quicker he ran, the more zealously did I belabor him with my whip and in the end both of us began to tire of this work: my shoulder began to ache and my arm became too limp to lift, and he, too, I could see, had stopped looking sideways at me and his tongue was lolling out of his mouth. It was clear that he was on the point of capitulating, so I got off his back, wiped his eyes, took him by the forelock, and said to him, 'Have you had enough, you cur, you hellhound, you?' And I gave him such a pull that he fell down on his knees before me, and from that time he became so tractable that one couldn't ask for anything better: he would let any man mount him and any man could ride him to his heart's content, only he soon gave up the ghost."

"So he gave up the ghost after all, did he?"

"Yes, he died. You see, he was too proud a creature. Became gentle in his behavior, but couldn't subdue his character, it seems. But Mr. Rarey, when he heard how I had tamed that horse, offered me a job with him."

"Did you work for him?"

"No, sir."

"Why not?"

"Well, how am I to explain it to you? You see, in the first place, I was a connoisseur and was more used to that branch of the business. My job was to select horses and not to break them in, and he, of course, wanted me to help him with the taming of wild animals. Secondly, I didn't think his offer was quite genuine. I rather suspected him of a dark design against me."

"What kind of dark design?"

"He wanted to get my secret."

"Would you have sold it to him?"

"Oh, yes, I should have sold it to him."

"So what was the trouble?"

"I don't know. . . . I suppose he must have got frightened of me."

"Frightened of you? What kind of a story is that? Tell us about it!"

"It isn't much of a story really, except that he said to me, 'Tell me your secret, my dear fellow, and I'll not only give you a lot of money, but I'll also give you a job as my expert on horses.' But as I could never bring myself to cheat anyone, I said to him, 'What secret are you talking about? There's nothing in it!' But he wouldn't believe me, for, being an American, he naturally thought that there must be some scientific explanation to everything. 'Well,' he said, 'if you don't want to reveal your secret to me when sober, let's have some rum first!' So after that we drank so much rum that he got red in the face and said, not knowing any better, 'Well, now,' he said, 'out with it! Tell me what you did to that horse!' And I replied, 'That's what . . .' and I looked at him as fiercely as I could and ground my teeth and, not having the crock with the dough with me at the time, I (just for the sake of demonstration, you understand) grabbed a glass from the table and made as if I was going to hit him with it, but he, of course, seeing that, just dived under the table and then bounded for the door in double-quick time and that was the last I saw of him. Since then he kept out of my sight and we never met again."

"So that's why you didn't take the job he offered you?"

"Yes, sir. For I couldn't very well take a job with him if he was afraid to meet me, could I? Mind you, not that I didn't want the job! As a matter of fact, I wanted it badly, for I got to like him very much while we were having that rum-drinking competition, but, it seems, no man can run away from his fate, and I had to follow a different calling. . . ."

"And what do you consider your calling?"

"I'm afraid I don't quite know how to put it. . . . I wandered far and wide, on horses and under horses, in captivity and in battle, fought against many people and was crippled so badly that I daresay not every man would have survived it."

"But when did you enter the monastery?"

"Oh, that was quite recently, only a few years after the adventurous part of my life had come to an end."

"And, no doubt, you also felt a calling for it?"

"Well, I really don't know how to explain it to you. . . . However, I suppose I must have."

"But . . . er . . . why aren't you sure about it?"

"Because I can't be sure about it, for my past life is still a great mystery to me."

"Why so?"

"Because much that I did, I didn't do of my own free will."

"Whose will did you obey, then?"

"Well, it was all really due to a vow taken by my parents."

"And what happened to you as a result of that vow?"

"All my life I hovered on the very brink of perdition, but I did not perish in spite of everything."

"Do you really mean it?"

"Yes, I do."

"Won't you tell us the story of your life?"

"All right, I'll do my best to tell you what I can remember, but you'll have to listen to my story from the very beginning, for I can't tell it any other way."

"By all means, that should be all the more interesting."

"I'm afraid I can't say whether you'll find it interesting or not, but if you're willing to listen to me, I shall be glad to tell you everything."

2.

Ivan Severyanych Flyagin began the story of his life in these words:

I was born a serf and my parents were the personal servants of Count K., who owned estates in the province of Oryol. These estates have now fallen into the hands of the young masters and have been divided up and sold, but in the lifetime of the old count they were very large indeed. The count himself lived in the village of G. in a big mansion with separate wings for guests, a theatre, a special skittle alley, dog kennels, bear pits where bears were chained to poles and gardens; concerts were given by the count's own choir and all sorts of plays were performed by the count's own actors; the count had his own weaving sheds and other workshops, but his lordship's chief concern was his stud farm. Each separate establishment had its own special people attached to it, but most particular attention was paid to the stables and, as in the army in the old days every regular soldier was made to send his sons into it, so at our place a coachman's son in due course became a coachman, and a groom's son became a stableboy and was obliged to look after the horses, and a peasant whose duty it was to supply fodder for the stables had his sons assigned to the same task of bringing oats straight from the threshing floor to the stalls.

My father was the coachman Severyan, and although he did not count as one of the head coachmen, for we had a great number of them, he nevertheless drove a carriage and six, and once, on the occasion of the Czar's visit, he was seventh in the rank of coachmen and was graciously presented with an ancient blue banknote.

My mother died while I was a baby and I do not remember her, for I was her *prayed-for* son, which meant that, being without children for many years, she had spent a long time praying to the Lord for a child and, when her prayer was granted, she died as soon as I was born, for I came into the world with an unusually large head, so that for that reason I was never known by my name of Ivan Flyagin, but was called Golovan, being nicknamed thus from *golova*, a head.

While living with my father in the coachmen's establishment, I spent all my time in the stables and it was there that I was initiated into the mystery of understanding an animal and that, I might say, I learnt to love the horse. For even as a baby I used to crawl on all fours between the feet of horses and they did me no injury, and when I grew up I became thoroughly familiar with them.

The stud farm on our estate was quite a separate establishment and the stables, too, were separate from it, and we, the stablemen, had no truck with the men of the stud farm, but received from them the horses for training and we trained them. Every one of our coachmen and his outrider had six horses and all of them were of different breeds: there were Vyatka horses, Kazan horses, Kalmuk horses, Bityutzk horses, and Don horses, and all of them had been acquired from outside, bought at different fairs. Most of our horses would naturally come from our own stud farm, but it is hardly worth while talking about them, since stud horses are, as a rule, gentle and possess neither strength of character, nor liveliness of imagination. The others, however, the wild horses that is, were a real terror. His lordship used to buy them wholesale, a whole drove at a time, cheap, too, about eight or ten roubles a horse, and directly we brought them home, we began to train them. We had the devil of a time of it on account of the stiff fight they would offer. Half of them sometimes preferred to die rather than to submit. They would be standing in the yard unable to accustom themselves to their new surroundings and they would shy away even from the walls and all the time they would be squinting at the sky, like birds. I couldn't help being overcome by pity sometimes as I looked at one of those horses; for I could see that the poor beast would gladly have flown away, if only he had wings. . . . Such a horse would at first neither eat oats nor drink water from the trough, but would just waste away until his heart broke and he fell dead. Quite often it happened that we'd lose half the horses we bought that way, particularly if they were Kirghiz horses, for they were terribly fond of their free life in the steppes. On the other hand, many of those horses which remained alive and became domesticated would be crippled in the course of their training; for there is only one way of getting the better of a horse's wildness and that is by severity. But the horses which survived all their schooling and training would turn out such capital horses that no stud horse in the world could compare with them in prowess between the shafts.

My father, Severyan Ivanych, drove six Kirghiz horses and when I grew up I was appointed outrider to his six horses. They were ferocious animals, not at all like our present cavalry horses which are ridden by officers. We used to call those officers' horses "court chamberlains" because there was no pleasure at all in riding them, since even officers could ride them; but my father's horses were just brutes: beast, serpent, and basilisk all rolled into one. One look at their faces, or teeth, or legs, or manes was enough to . . . well . . . make you die of fright. They never knew what it meant to be tired: a drive of fifty, or seventy-five, or a hundred miles from our village to Oryol and back again without a stop was nothing to them. Let them get into their stride and you'd have to look out or they'd leave you miles behind.

Now, at the time when I was put into the outrider's saddle I was only eleven years old, but I already had the right kind of voice for my job, a voice which according to the manners of those days was quite indispensable to an outrider of a nobleman: a most loud and piercing voice and so drawn out that I could sustain that "hi-ee-ee-o-oh!" on a high note at the top of my voice for half an hour. But I was not yet sufficiently strong in body to be able to stay in the saddle unaided on the long journeys and they used to tie me to the horse, that is to say, to the saddle and the girth; they would strap me with leather thongs to everything that would hold, and contrive it so that I could not possibly fall off. Every bone in my body would be aching horribly and quite often I'd feel so faint that I would lose consciousness for a time, but, of course, I'd go on riding in the same position and, shaken up in the saddle, I'd come round again. When I got back home, they would hoist me out of the saddle as if I were dead and they'd put me down and give me grated horseradish to smell. But I got used to it in time and took it all in my stride; and sometimes I'd even ride along and pray for a peasant to come walking on the road so that I could lay him out with a well-directed blow of my riding whip across his shoulders. That was one of the time-honored pastimes of an outrider.

Once we were driving the count on a visit. It was a beautiful summer day and his lordship was sitting in the open carriage with his dog, my father was driving the four horses, and I was streaking on ahead. We had to turn off the highroad and for about fifteen miles follow a lane leading to a monastery known as the P. hermitage. This lane was made by the monks, who were anxious to attract visitors by making the way to their monastery as pleasant as possible, and that was natural enough, for while the highway was covered with all kinds of filth and the willows on either side of it stuck out of the ground like so many crooked wands, the lane leading to the monks' hermitage was kept beautifully clean, swept from end to end of all dirt and dung, and shaded at the sides by large, hand-planted birch trees, a lovely avenue of green leaves spreading a delicious odor, and at the end of it there opened up a wide prospect of fields. . . . In a word, it looked so delight-

ful that out of sheer gladness of heart I nearly yelled at the top
of my voice, which, of course, I was strictly forbidden to do without any reason. So I kept on riding along at a gallop, but three or
four miles before the monastery gates the road took a sudden
plunge downhill and then all of a sudden I spied in front of me
a black speck. . . . Somebody was crawling along the road just
like a hedgehog. I jumped at the chance and uttered a prolonged
"hi–ee–ee–o–oh!" at the top of my voice and kept it up for a
whole mile and I got so excited that as soon as we began to overtake a farm cart drawn by two horses, at which I had been yelling,
I rose in the stirrups, and I saw that a man was lying on top of the
hay in the cart. The man, no doubt warmed pleasantly by the sun
in the gentle breeze, had fallen fast asleep, without a care in the
world. He lay with his face buried in the hay and his arms were
thrown wide apart, and it looked as if he were embracing the cart. I
could see that he would not give way, so I hugged the side of the
road and, as I came up to the cart, I raised myself in the stirrups
and, grinding my teeth for the first time in my life, I gave him a terrific blow across the back with my whip. His horses just bolted
with the cart down the hill and he gave a jump, such a wizened
old man he was, wearing the same kind of clerical hat as myself
now, and his face looked so woebegone, like the face of an old
peasant woman. Frightened to death he seemed to be and tears
were streaming down his cheeks, and he was writhing on the hay
just like a gudgeon in a frying pan, and then, probably failing to
perceive where the edge of the cart was, for he was still half-asleep,
he tumbled off the cart and fell under the wheels and began to be
dragged along in the dust . . . his feet entangled in the reins.
. . . At first the way he went head over heels seemed very funny
to me as well as to my father and to his lordship, but then I
saw that at the bottom of the hill by the bridge a wheel caught
on a projecting strip of wood and the horses stopped, but the old
monk did not get up, neither did he move. . . . When we drove
up, I noticed that he was all gray from the dust and that there
was not even a trace of a nose left on his face, but just one big
gash with blood pouring out of it. . . . His lordship ordered us
to stop, alighted from his carriage, took a look at the monk, and

said, "Killed." He threatened to have me flogged when we came back home and ordered me to ride quickly to the monastery. From there some people were sent to the bridge and the count himself had a long talk with the abbot in the monastery and for the next few months, till the autumn, gifts were sent from our estate to the monastery, a whole train of farm carts loaded with oats and flour and dried carp, and father gave me a thrashing behind a shed in the monastery with a whip across my trousers, but it wasn't a real flogging, for I had my duties to perform and had to get straight back into the saddle.

That was the end of the affair except that the same night the monk whom I had whipped to death appeared to me in a dream and again began crying like a silly old woman. I said to him:

"What do you want of me? Clear out!"

But he replied:

"You took my life without giving me a chance of repentance."

"Well," I replied, "it's tough luck and I'm very sorry, but what do you expect me to do about it now? I didn't do it on purpose, did I? Besides," I said, "what have you got to grumble about? You're dead and that's that."

"Aye," he said, "that's that all right and, mind, I'm grateful to you for it, but now I've come from your own mother to ask you whether you know that you're her *prayed-for* son?"

"Of course I know that," I said. "My granny Fedossya has told me about it lots of times."

"But do you also know," he said, "that you're a *promised* son?"

"What do you mean?"

"I mean," he said, "that you were promised to God."

"Who promised me to Him?"

"Your mother."

"Well," I said, "why doesn't she come herself and tell me that? How do I know that you've not invented it all?"

"No," said he, "I haven't invented it. You see, the trouble is your mother can't come herself."

"Why not?"

"Because," he said, "things are quite different with us here from what they are with you on earth: here not everybody speaks, nor does everybody return, for only he who has been given the gift of doing certain things can do them. But if you wish," he said, "I'll give you a sign to show you that I am speaking the truth."

"All right," I said, "but what kind of a sign is it?"

"This sign I give you," he said, "that you will suffer many hardships and adversities, but you will not die until the day appointed for your doom, and then you'll remember your mother's promise and you'll become a monk."

"That's fine," I replied. "I consent and I shall be ready."

So he disappeared and I woke up and forgot all about it, nor did I even suspect that all those hardships and adversities were going to befall me immediately one after another.

A short time after that we went with the count and countess to Voronezh (to cure their little daughter of her deformed toes they were taking her to the recently discovered relics of a saint) and we stopped in the district of Yelets in the village of Krutoy to feed the horses, and I fell asleep under the trough and again I saw that wizened old monk whom I had sent to his last account coming along and saying:

"Look here, Golovan," he said, "I'm very sorry for you. Ask your master at once to let you enter a monastery and he will let you go."

I replied: "Whatever for?"

But he said: "I warn you, if you don't, you'll suffer many hardships."

I thought, "All right, I suppose I can hardly blame you for croaking, seeing that it was I who killed you," and with that I got up, helped my father to harness the horses, and we drove off.

Now the road at that place was going downhill and the hill was exceedingly steep and on one side of it was a sheer drop into a deep ravine where hundreds of people had been killed in accidents at one time or another. His lordship said to me, "Mind, Golovan, be careful!" I was a good hand at handling situations like that. While it was, of course, the coachman who held the reins of the shaft horses which had to be used in going down that precipitous hill, I knew how to be useful to my father in many

ways. My father's shaft horses were strong and very reliable when
it came to getting a firm foothold on the road: they had a way of
taking the carriage down by just sitting on their tails in the roadway. One of them, however, was a real villain of a horse with a
predilection for astronomy: it was enough for his reins to be pulled
in with some force for him to throw up his head at once, and
confound his eyes if he wouldn't start scanning the skies! These
astronomers are truly the worst kind of horses you can get, and especially between the shafts they are a real danger! An outrider
must be constantly on his guard against a horse with such a habit,
for an astronomer, of course, does not look where he's putting his
feet down and he usually gets himself and everybody else in a terrible mess. All this, of course, I knew about my astronomer, and
I'd always try to assist my father in any emergency. I would, for
instance, steady my own saddle horse and the horse next to it by
grasping their reins in the crook of the elbow of my left hand, and
get them into such a position that they would press against the
muzzles of the shaft horses with their tails and have the shafts
themselves between their cruppers, while I had my whip always
poised in front of the astronomer's eyes and the moment I saw
that he had begun to climb a bit too high into the sky, I'd hit him
across the muzzle and he'd instantly put his head down and we
would drive down the hill in fine style. So now, too, I kept my
eye on the astronomer as soon as we had started taking the carriage down the hill, turning round in the saddle and steadying him
with my whip. Then I became suddenly aware that the horse was
no longer paying the slightest attention either to my father's reins
or to my own whip. I could see that his mouth was covered with
blood from the bit and his eyes were turned up, and I had hardly
time to take in the situation when I suddenly heard something
creak behind me and—bang!—the whole carriage lurched forward
and went full tilt down the hill. . . . The brake had snapped
off. . . . I bellowed to my father, "Hold on! Hold on!" and he
bellowed back to me, "Hold on! Hold on!" but there was nothing
to hold on to any more, for all the six horses had bolted and were
tearing down the hill like mad, without looking where they were
going. Something flashed past my eyes and, looking up, I was just

in time to see my father flung off the box: a rein had broken! And in front of us was that terrible precipice! . . . I don't know whether it was for my masters or for myself that I was sorry, but, seeing utter ruin staring me in the face, I jumped from the saddle horse straight on to the shafts and hung on to the ends by the skin of my teeth. . . . I'm afraid I can't say how much I weighed at the time, but whatever my weight was I must have weighed much more in the overbalance. Anyway, I pressed the necks of the shaft horses together with such force that their breath began to rattle in their throats and when I had summoned enough courage to look up I saw that the front horses were gone, as if somebody had cut them clean off, and that I myself was hanging over the precipice and that the carriage had stopped, having come to rest in a good position against the shaft horses which I had almost smothered between the shafts.

It was only then that I came to my senses and I got frightened and let go my hold of the shafts and dropped into the ravine and I remembered nothing more. I don't know how long I was unconscious, but when I came to I saw that I was in a peasant's cottage, and a big peasant said to me:

"Hullo, are you really alive, sonny?"

I replied: "I suppose I must be."

"Do you remember what happened to you?" he said.

I began to recall what had happened and I remembered how the horses had bolted and how I had jumped on to the ends of the shafts and had hung suspended over the precipice, but I couldn't remember what happened after that.

But the peasant smiled and said:

"I reckon you can hardly be expected to remember," he said, "since those horses of yours never reached the bottom of that precipice alive, got smashed up long before, they did, and you yourself was only saved by a miracle, for, you see, as you hit a lump of clay you fell down on it and slid as if you were on a toboggan. We thought you were dead as a doornail, but since you were still breathing, we thought you must have fainted on account of the rush of air when you fell. And now, my lad," he said, "get up if you're feeling well enough and hurry to the saint: his lordship left money to bury you if you were to die or to send you to him to Voronezh if you recovered."

So off I went to Voronezh and I didn't speak a word, but only listened to the peasant who was driving me and who played "Mistress Mine" on his accordion all the way to the town.

When we arrived in Voronezh, his lordship summoned me to his rooms and said to her ladyship:

"Well," he said, "your ladyship, we owe our lives to this boy!"

Her ladyship just nodded her head, but his lordship said:

"Ask me anything you like, Golovan, and it shall be done."

I said:

"I don't know what to ask, sir."

And he said:

"Well, what do you want?"

So I thought and thought and then I said:

"An accordion, if you please, sir."

His lordship laughed and said:

"Well, you're a little fool, but that is neither here nor there: when the time comes, I shall keep you in mind and in the meantime," he said, "an accordion shall be bought for you immediately!"

One of the footmen was sent to a shop and he brought me the accordion in the stables.

"Here you are," he said, "now you can play it!"

I took it and tried to play, but I soon discovered that I didn't know how to, so I chucked it away at once and later it was stolen from me by some women pilgrims, who fished it out from under the shed the next day.

I should have made use of the occasion of his lordship's kindness to me and asked him, as the monk had advised, to let me enter a monastery; but instead I had, without knowing myself why, asked for an accordion and thereby renounced my first true calling, and was destined for that reason to suffer one calamity after another, undergoing greater and still greater trials, but always escaping with my life, until everything the monk had foretold in my dream had been fulfilled in my present life as a punishment for my lack of faith.

3.

After this proof of my master's singular benevolence towards me, I returned home with his lordship and his family in a
carriage drawn by six horses, all of which had been newly pur-
chased in Voronezh, and no sooner was I installed in my old quarters in the stables than I took it into my head to get myself a pair
of crested doves, a cock and a hen, which I kept on a shelf. The
cock had clay-colored feathers, but the hen was a white one and
with such lovely red feet, a real beauty she was! I liked them very
much, especially when the cock pigeon would start cooing at
night, which I found very pleasant to listen to, and in the daytime they would fly about between the horses and sit on the man-
ger, pecking the grain and exchanging kisses with each other.
. . . It is a sight that to a child is a joy to behold!
And after all that billing and cooing, they started rearing a family; they would hatch out one pair and they would grow up, and
then they would again start billing and cooing and hatch out some
more. . . . The pigeon chicks were so tiny, and they were covered with a kind of woolly down, with no feathers at all, and so
yellow, like mallow seeds you find in the grass, which children
call "cheeses," but with huge beaks, not a whit worse than on the
faces of Circassian princes. . . . One day I started examining
those chicks and, so as not to hurt them between my fingers, I
took one by his beak and could not tear my eyes away from him,
such a sweet little thing he was, while the pigeon was all the time
trying to get him out of my hands. So I had my fun with him,
teasing him with his baby pigeon, but when I took the dear little
mite back to his nest, I saw that he wasn't breathing any more. I
was mad at myself! I warmed him in my cupped hands for a long
time, breathed on him, all the time trying to bring him back to
life, but it was no use at all—he was dead and that was that! I got
angry, picked him up and threw him out of the window. All right.
There was another one left in the nest; a white cat, which seemed
to have appeared from nowhere, picked up the dead one as she

ran past the stables and carried him off. I marked the cat well. I saw that she was all white except for a black spot, just like a little hat, on her forehead. Well, I thought to myself, to blazes with her, let her eat the dead chick up. But at night, as I was asleep, I suddenly heard how on the shelf above my bed the pigeon was having a ferocious fight with someone. I jumped up and looked round. It was a moonlit night and I saw the same white cat, which was now carrying off my other chick, the live one.

"Well," I thought, "that is a bit thick! Why do that?" So I threw one of my boots after the cat, but I missed her, and so she carried off my poor little pigeon and, I suppose, must have eaten him somewhere. My poor pair of doves lost their children and at first they grieved for a little while, but soon they started their billing and cooing again and once more a pair of chicks were in the nest, and that confounded cat came back again. . . . The devil alone knows how she got to know about it, must have been keeping the stables under regular observation, but, anyway, there she was dragging away another of my chicks, in broad daylight, too, and so neatly that I hadn't time to throw anything after her. But this time I decided to teach her a lesson and I contrived such a trap on the window that as soon as she showed her face again at night, she was caught in it, and there she sat, looking very sorry for herself and miaowing. I took her out of the trap at once, thrust her face and forelegs into the top of one of my high boots, so that she shouldn't scratch me, and, taking her hindlegs and tail in my left hand, I took down a whip from the wall with my right, sat down on my bed and began to give her a good thrashing. I reckon I must have given her about a hundred and fifty strokes, with all my strength, too, until she even left off struggling. Then I took her out of my boot and I was thinking to myself, Is she alive or not? How, thought I, was I to find out whether she was dead or not? So I put her across the threshold and with my little axe I chopped off her tail. Crumpled up as she was, she gave a start and, turning over and over about ten times, ran off.

All right, I thought, now I bet you won't come stealing my pigeons again; and to frighten her off in case she did come, I went and took her tail next morning and nailed it outside my window, and I felt very pleased with myself for having done that. But an hour and certainly no more than two hours after that who did I see rushing into the stables but her ladyship's maid, who had never shown her nose in our stables before, and she was brandishing an umbrella in her hand and shouting:

"Oh, so that's who it was! So that's who it was!"

I said:

"What's the matter?"

"Was it you," she said, "who mutilated poor Zozinka? You'd better confess at once, for I can see her little tail nailed over your window!"

I said:

"Fancy making such a fuss because a cat's tail is nailed over my window!"

"How did you dare to do a thing like that?" she said.

"How did she dare to eat my pigeons?" I said.

"Who cares about your pigeons?"

"Well, if it comes to that," I said, "your cat isn't such a great lady herself!"

I was already, you understand, of an age when I was beginning to use strong language.

"Who cares," said I, "for that damned cat of yours?"

Well, she just went at me hammer and tongs. "How dare you speak to me like that? Don't you know that it is my cat and that her ladyship herself used to stroke her?" And having said that, she slapped me across the face with her hand and I, who have since my childhood been rather quick with my hands, got hold of a dirty broom from behind the doors and, without further ado, hit her with it across the waist. . . .

Lord, what a to-do there was! They took me to the manager's office to be tried, and the manager, a German, sentenced me to be soundly flogged and then to be dismissed from the stables and to be sent to the English gardens to knock stones into the paths with a mallet. . . . They gave me a terrible flogging, so that I could not even stand on my feet afterwards, and they carried me to my father on a piece of straw matting, but I didn't mind that very much; what I did mind was the last part of my sentence, which condemned me to go down on my knees and knock stones into a garden path. . . . I felt so bad about it that after vainly casting about in my mind how to find a way out of my trouble I decided to do away with myself. I got myself a strong white rope, which I had obtained from one of the footmen, had a bath in the evening, and went to the aspen wood behind the threshing floor, knelt down, said a prayer for all good Christians, fastened the rope to a bough, made a noose, and put my head in it. All that was left for me to do was to jump off, and that was only a matter of a second or so. . . . My character being what it is, I should have done it all, but no sooner did I take a flying leap off the tree, jump off the bough, and drop, than I found myself lying on the ground and in front of me stood a gypsy with a knife in his hand, laughing: I could see his snow-white teeth gleaming in the darkness of the night in that dark-skinned face of his.

"What are you up to, mate?" he said.

"Mind your own business," I said.

"Do you find life so terrible?" he kept on pestering me.

"As you see," I said, "it isn't all beer and skittles."

"Well," he said, "sooner than hang yourself by your own hand, you'd better come and live with us; perhaps you'll hang a different way then."

"And who are you and what kind of living do you make? I bet you're just thieves."

"Thieves?" he said. "Why, of course, we're thieves *and* rogues."

"I thought so," I said, "and sometimes I daresay you don't stop at cutting a man's throat, do you?"

"That, too, has happened," he said. "We don't stop at doing that, either."

Well, I thought it over in my mind and . . . what could I do? At home—tomorrow and the day after—the same old thing was in store for me: down on my knees and knock, knock, knock, all day long knocking little stones with a mallet. Already my knees were covered with calluses from that kind of work, and, in addition, all I heard was how everybody was laughing at me, because a dastardly German had sentenced me to work through a whole mountain of stones and all for a cat's tail. All of them were laughing at me: "And you call yourself a life-saver," they were saying. "Saved your master's life, did you?" I just couldn't put up with that any longer and, realizing that if I didn't strangle myself, I'd have to return to that kind of life, I abandoned all hope and, crying a little, I decided to become a highwayman.

4.

But the cunning villain of a gypsy gave me no time to collect my wits and said:

"If you want me to believe you won't go back," he said, "you must first get me a pair of horses from your master's stable, and, mind, take only such horses as you know are the best so that we can ride fast and be as far away as possible from here by tomorrow morning."

This proposal made me greatly doubt whether I ought to go along with the man and cast in my lot with him, for I hated the idea of becoming a thief. However, one needs must go when the devil drives and, knowing all the ins and outs of the stables, I experienced no difficulty at all in bringing out on the threshing floor a pair of swift horses that did not know what it meant to be tired. Meanwhile the gypsy had taken out of his pocket some wolves' teeth threaded on strings and he hung them round the necks of the horses, and we mounted and rode off. Scenting the wolves' bones on themselves, the horses carried us at such a terrific speed that at daybreak we were a hundred miles away on the outskirts of the town of Karachev. There we had no trouble at all in selling the horses to some house porter, and we took the money and went to a little stream to divide it up. We received three hundred roubles for those horses, all of it, as was the custom in those days, in bank notes, but the gypsy gave me only one silver rouble and said:

"Here's your share."

That seemed unfair to me.

"Why," I said, "wasn't it I who stole those horses and, if

caught, should I not have suffered more than you? Why, then, should my share be so small?"

"Because," he replied, "it didn't happen to grow any bigger."

"Don't be silly," I said. "Why should you take such a lot?"

"That again," he said, "is because I'm the master and you're only my pupil."

"What are you talking about?" I said. "Pupil indeed!" And so one word followed another and we quarrelled. At length I said:

"I don't want to go along with you, because you're a rascal."

"All right," he said, "for Christ's sake don't, for you have no passport and I'll only get myself into trouble on account of you."

Thus we parted and I had half a mind to go to the justices and give myself up as a runaway serf, but first I told my story to their clerk and he said to me:

"You're a big fool, my boy. What do you want to give yourself up for? Have you got ten roubles?"

"No," I said, "I've got one silver rouble but I haven't got ten roubles."

"Well," he said, "haven't you got anything else on you? A silver cross round your neck, perhaps, or that thing in your ear. It's an earring, isn't it?"

"Yes," said I, "it is an earring."

"A silver one?"

"A silver one. And I've got a cross, too," I said. "Got it from Mitrofania. It is silver, too."

"Well, what are you waiting for?" he said. "Take them off quickly and give them to me and I'll write out a discharge for you and then you can go to Nikolayev. They want lots of people there and hundreds of our tramps have already run off there."

I gave him my silver rouble as well as my earring and my cross and he wrote out a certificate and put the justices' seal on it and said:

"There should really be an extra charge for the seal, for everybody has to pay extra for that, but I feel very sorry for you, seeing how poor you are, and I don't want any certificate issued by me not to be in order. So off with you," he said, "and if you meet anyone who wants a certificate, don't forget to send him to me."

"All right," thought I, "what a good Samaritan you are! Takes the cross off my neck and is sorry for me, if you please!" I didn't send anyone to him, but just trudged along, begging for alms in the name of Christ, not having a farthing to bless myself with.

I arrived in that city and went to the market place to see if anyone would hire me. As it happened there were very few people who put themselves up for hire that day: only three men, and they, too, I supposed, just tramps like myself. But there were hundreds of people anxious to hire us, and they just pounced on us, one man pulling one way and another man another way. I was pounced on by one gentleman, a big, burly man, much bigger than I. He just brushed the others unceremoniously aside and, grasping me by the arms, dragged me after him. While leading me thus, he kept on pushing the others out of the way with his fists, swearing villainously, but there were tears in his eyes. He took me to his house, put together hurriedly out of some junk, and said:

"Tell me the truth: you're a runaway, aren't you?"

I said: "Yes, sir. I'm a runaway."

"Are you," he said, "a thief, a murderer, or just a tramp?"

I replied: "What do you want to know that for?"

"Oh, just to see what kind of job you're fit for."

I told him why I had run away, without concealing anything, and he suddenly embraced me and said:

"You're just the man I want, just the man I want! If," he said, "you were sorry for those pigeon chicks of yours, you'll be able to look after my child: I'm engaging you as her nurse."

I was horrified.

"How do you mean as a nurse, sir? I'm quite unequal to such a task."

"Oh, that's nothing," he said, "nothing at all. I can see that you'll make an excellent nurse. For I don't mind telling you," he said, "that I'm in an awful fix: my wife got tired of me and ran off with a cavalry officer, an officer who buys horses for the army, and she left her baby girl with me and I can't feed her, for I have neither the time nor the food, so you'll have to nurse her and I'll give you two silver roubles a month as your wages."

"But, Lord, sir," I said, "it isn't a question of the two roubles! How shall I cope with such a job?"

"Why," he said, "that's just nothing. You're a Russian, aren't you? Well, a Russian can cope with anything!"

"Well, sir," I said, "it is quite true that I am a Russian, but I am a man and I haven't been gifted by nature with the things that are necessary for the nursing of a baby."

"Don't you worry about that," he said. "I'm going to buy you a goat from a Jew to help you out in this matter. All you'll have to do is milk the goat and feed my child on her milk."

I thought it over and said:

"Of course, sir, one could nurse a child with the help of a goat, but all the same," I said, "you really ought to get a woman for such a job."

"No," he said, "don't you ever mention women to me: they're the cause of all the trouble in the world. Besides, you can't get them, anyway, but if you refuse to nurse my child, I'll go and call the Cossacks and I'll tell them to bind you hand and foot and take you to the police station and from there they'll send you back to your master. Make up your mind now which you like better: to knock stones into the path of your count's garden or to bring up my child."

So I debated with myself and I decided: No, I shall certainly not go back—and I agreed to stay on as a nurse. The same day we bought from a Jew a nannygoat with her kid. I slaughtered the kid and made from it a soup with noodles in it which my new master and I ate, and I milked the goat and began to feed the child with her milk. The baby was very tiny and miserable and wretched, crying all the time. My master, her father, was a Pole, a civil servant, and he was never at home, the silly old fool. He spent all his time with his cronies, playing cards, and I was left alone with my charge, the baby girl, and I was getting terribly attached to her, for time hung heavy on my hands and, having nothing else to do, I busied myself with her. I would put the baby in a wooden tub and give her a good bath, and if a rash appeared on her skin I would sprinkle some flour over it, or I would comb her little head, or rock her on my knees, or, if I got very tired of sitting at home, I'd put on my coat and put her inside it and go to the beach to wash her diapers, and the goat got so used to us that she too would go out for a walk with us. In this way I lived there until the next summer, and my baby grew up a bit and began to crawl about and even to stand on her little legs, but I noticed, as she tripped along, that she was bowlegged. I pointed it out to my master, but he didn't seem to be worried about it, merely saying:

"What can I do about it? It isn't my fault, is it? Take her to the doctor; let him have a look at her."

So I took her to the doctor, and the doctor said:

"This is the English disease, rickets. You have to cover her legs with sand."

And I did. I chose a place on the beach where there was plenty of sand, and on a fine, warm day, I'd take the goat and the little girl and go there with them. I'd dig up the warm sand with my hands and bury the girl up to her waist in it and give her some sticks to play with and some pebbles, and our goat would walk round and round us, nibbling the grass, and I would sit and sit with my hands round my knees, until I'd fall into a doze and go to sleep.

We spent many days in this manner, the three of us, and passing the time like that was the best remedy for low spirits that I had discovered, for, I repeat, I felt terribly dejected; and especially at that time, in the spring, when I started to bury the baby girl in the sand and to fall asleep on the beach myself, I began to be troubled by all sorts of foolish dreams. As soon as I'd fall asleep with the thunder of the waves in my ears and a warm breeze from the steppe blowing over me, something would come over me with that wind, an enchantment of some kind, and I would fall under the spell of some horrible vision: I saw strange steppes and horses and all the time somebody would be calling me and luring me on and on; I could even hear him calling me by my name: "Ivan! Ivan! Come along, brother Ivan!" I'd give a start and wake up with a shudder and spit with vexation: "Damn you, can't you leave me alone? What are you calling me for?" I'd look around and see the same dreary sight before me: the goat would by then have wandered off a long way, roaming about, nibbling the grass, and the child was sitting there, buried in the sand, and that was all. . . . Ugh, how dismal! A desolate stretch of land, the sun, the estuary, and I'd fall asleep again and that strange enchantment would return with the warm breeze and again I'd hear the voice calling me, "Ivan! Let's go, Ivan! Let's go, brother Ivan!" I just couldn't help swearing. "Come on," I'd say, "show yourself for once, damn you! Who are you? What are you calling me for?" And on one occasion when I got angry like that I was sitting there half-asleep and looking at the sea and I saw a small cloud rising on the horizon and coming straight for me. I said, "Whoa! You there! What are you up to? Not going to drench me by any chance, are you?" And then who did I see standing before me but that monk with the wizened face whom I had whipped to death a long time ago when I was still an outrider. I said, "Curse thee! Go away!" But he replied in a very kind, ringing voice, "Come along, Ivan! Come along, brother Ivan! You've got to undergo many more trials and tribulations and only then will you achieve salvation!" I cursed him in my sleep and said, "Catch me coming with you! And what kind of salvation do you want me to achieve, anyway?" But he turned into a cloud again and, through himself, showed me a most extraordinary vision, but I couldn't make head or tail of it: a steppe . . . strange, savage people . . . Saracens . . . the kind of people one finds in fairy tales about Yeruslan and Bova the Crown Prince—in huge, shaggy hats, armed with bows and arrows and mounted on wild, terrible horses. And as I beheld all that, I heard a yelling, neighing, and wild laughter and suddenly . . . a sandstorm, the sand was swept up into a cloud and everything vanished, except that somewhere a bell was tolling faintly, and a big white monastery appeared on a high eminence, glowing red in the sunset, and on its walls winged angels with golden spears were walking and round about it was the sea, and every time an angel struck his shield with his spear the sea round the monastery would begin to boil and spume and from the great deep dreadful voices would set up the cry, "Holy!"

"Well," I thought to myself, "here goes that monkish business again!" And I woke up feeling greatly vexed and I was surprised to see a lady kneeling on the sand over my little girl in an attitude of great tenderness and crying as if her poor heart would break.

For a long time I gazed at that strange scene, for I naturally thought that it must still be part of my dream, but, seeing that the vision did not vanish, I rose to my feet and took a few steps towards the lady and imagine my surprise when I saw that she had dug the baby out of the sand and taken her in her arms and was kissing her, her face streaming with tears.

I asked her:

"What do you want?"

But she rushed towards me, holding the child tightly to her breast, and she whispered:

"This is my child, it's my daughter, my daughter!"

I said:

"Well, what about it?"

"Give her back to me," she said.

"Why do you suppose that I'd give her back to you?" I asked.

"Aren't you sorry for her?" she said, crying. "See how she clings to me!"

"Why shouldn't she cling to you? She's just a silly child; she clings to me, too. Anyway, I can't possibly give her to you."

"Why not?"

"Because," I said, "she has been entrusted to my care. There, you see, is our goat: she always comes with us on our walks. I have to take the child back to her father."

"Very well," she said, "if you don't want to give me my child, at least be kind enough not to tell your master—my husband, that is—that you saw me, and come here to this same place again tomorrow with my child, for," she said, "I want to hold her in my arms again."

"That," I said, "is quite a different proposition; that I promise you I'll do."

And so it was. I said not a word about it to my master, and next morning I took the goat and the baby and went with them to the beach again. The lady was already waiting for me. She was sitting in a sand pit, and as soon as she saw us, she jumped out and ran towards us, laughing and crying, thrusting toys into the baby's hands and even hanging a little bell on a red ribbon round the goat's neck, and she gave me a pipe, a pouch of tobacco, and a comb.

"Smoke this pipe, please," she said, "and I'll mind the baby."

In this manner we had many meetings on the beach. The lady was always busy with the child and I was asleep most of the time, but it also happened that sometimes she would start telling me about herself, well . . . that is . . . how she had been married to my master against her will by her wicked stepmother and how she had always disliked her husband. . . . "Could never bring myself to love him," she said. But it seemed that the other one, that blessed cavalry officer of hers, she loved dearly, and indeed she kept on bewailing her fate, for it appeared that she had tried hard to overcome her love for him, but couldn't. "I'm his forever," she said, "for my husband, as you know very well yourself, lives a disreputable life, while . . ." Well, the other one, it seemed, was a paragon of virtue, but above all he had a very beautiful mustache and I don't know what else. "He's a man of very clean habits," she said, "and he cherishes me dearly, but there again," she said, "that's not enough to make me happy, for I can't live without my child. . . . Now," she said, "I've come back to this city with him and we live at the house of one of his friends, but I'm in constant dread that my husband may get to know about it. But we shall be leaving soon and, I suppose, I shall be pining away for my darling baby again! . . ."

"Well," I said, "what's to be done about it? If, having violated the laws of God and man, you prefer to live in sin," I said, "then you just have to suffer for it."

But she would start crying and one day her crying became more pitiful than usual and I was beginning to get tired of her constant lamentations when, without any reason whatever, she began promising to give me a lot of money. Well, at last she came for the last time to bid us good-bye and she said:

"Look here, Ivan"—she knew my name already—"listen to me," she said, "listen carefully to what I'm going to tell you: today," she said, "*he* is coming here himself."

I asked her:

"Who's *he?*"

She replied:

"Why, the cavalry officer."

I said:

"What business is it of mine whether he comes or not?"

So she went on to tell me a whole story about how he had won a lot of money at cards the night before and how he had told her that, as he wished to please her, he had decided to give me a thousand roubles, if I, that is, would give her back her daughter.

"No, ma'am," I said, "that I shall never do."

"But why not? Why not, Ivan?" she started pestering me. "Aren't you sorry for me and for her that we should be separated?"

"Sorry or not," said I, "I've never sold myself either for big or little money and I never shall, so that your cavalry officer can keep his thousand roubles and I shall keep your daughter."

She started crying, but I said to her:

"You'd better stop crying, for it won't make any difference."

She said:

"You're a brute, you're made of stone."

But I replied:

"I'm not made of stone at all, I'm made of flesh and blood like the rest, only I know my duty and I shall remain true to it: I undertook to guard the child and I shall keep it under my protection."

She tried hard to persuade me to change my mind. "Can't you see that the child itself will be happier with me?" she said.

"That again," I replied, "is not my business."

"Do you mean," she exclaimed, "do you mean that I shall have to part with my child again?"

"Well," said I, "if, having . violated the laws of God and man . . ."

But I had no time to finish what I wanted to say, for at that moment I saw a sprightly Uhlan officer walking across the steppe towards us. In those days regimental officers used to walk with a swagger in a real military uniform, not at all like our present-day officers who are just indistinguishable from clerks. Well, so there that Uhlan officer was marching along, a fine figure of a man, hands pressed against his sides and greatcoat slung over his shoulders . . . not that there was any great strength in him, mind you, but plenty of dash. So I looked at that visitor of ours and I said to myself, "Why not have some fun with him? I'm bored to death and a little amusement won't do me any harm." And I made up my mind that if he said an uncivil word to me, I'd be as rude to him as possible, so that, God willing, we might have a good scrap. That, I said joyfully to myself, would be just fine, and I didn't even listen any more to what the lady was babbling with tears in her eyes, for all I wanted then was to have some sport with that officer.

5.

Having decided to provide myself with a little amusement, I began to cast about in my mind how best to provoke that officer so that he should attack me first. So I sat down, took out my comb, and pretended to be combing my hair. In the meantime the officer walked up and went straight to the lady, who started talking nineteen to the dozen to him: all about how I would not let her have the baby.

But he just stroked her head and said:

"Don't worry, darling, I'll find some way of persuading him. We'll show him the money and," he said, "his eyes will pop out of his head, but if that shouldn't work, we'll just take the child away from him," and with these words he walked up to me, handed me a roll of bank notes, and said:

"Look here, my man," he said, "there's exactly a thousand roubles here; give us the child and you can have the money and go where you like."

But I didn't reply to him at once, for I was trying to be as rude as possible to him on purpose: I first raised myself very slowly from the ground, next I hung my comb on my belt, cleared my throat, and then only did I say:

"No, sir, that won't do at all!" And I snatched the bank notes out of his hand, spat on them, and threw them on the ground, saying as if I were speaking to a dog, "Come on, Spotty, come on, sir, pick 'em up!"

He looked aggrieved, flushed a deep red, and let fly at me; but, as you can judge for yourselves, gentlemen, no army officer would stand much of a chance against a man of my physique: one little push from me and he was finished—sprawling on the ground, his spurs flying skywards and his saber wheeling sideways. I immediately stamped on that saber of his and said:

"That's how I tread your bravery under my foot!"

But although that little cavalry officer wasn't much to look at, he had plenty of guts. Seeing that he couldn't get his saber from me, he unbelted it and went for me with his fists. . . . Now he was asking for it and, of course, he got it good and proper. But I couldn't help admiring his spirit, which betokened a brave and honorable character: I refused to take his money, but neither did he pick it up himself.

After we had had enough of fighting, I shouted to him:

"Why don't you pick up your money? It'll come in useful to pay your lordship's fares!"

Did he pick it up? No, gentlemen, he didn't: instead he ran to the child, wishing to carry her off, but of course, as soon as he caught hold of one of her arms, I caught hold of the other.

"Come on," I said, "let's pull and see which of us gets the bigger half!"

He shouted:

"You dirty swine! You bully!" and, having said that, he spat in my face and let go of the child and was now only set on comforting the lady and persuading her to leave the beach with him, but she, in her despair, set up a most pathetic clamor, and although, pulled away by force, she followed him, her eyes were beseeching me and her hands were stretched out to the child and me. And I could clearly see and, indeed, I felt it inside me that the poor lady was torn in two; one half of her wanted to follow her lover and the other her child. . . . And at that very moment I saw my master, who came running from the town. He had a pistol in his hand and he kept on firing it and shouting:

"Ivan! Ivan! Stop them!"

"Stop them?" I thought to myself. "Not likely! Not for you, I shan't. Why shouldn't they go on loving each other?" So I caught up with the lady and the Uhlan officer and I gave them the child and said:

"Take your brat, but," I said, "now you'll have to take me, too, for if you don't he'll deliver me to the officers of the law, for I have a faked passport."

He said:

"Yes, come along with us, dear Ivan. We'll go away together and you'll live with us."

So we galloped off and we took the little girl, the child left in my keeping, with us, and the goat, the money, and my passport remained in the possession of my master.

All the way to Penza one thought kept on recurring to me as I sat on the box of the four-wheeler in which I was travelling with my new masters: had I done right in thrashing an army officer? After all, I said to myself, he had taken an oath of allegiance and in wartime he defended his country with his saber and the Emperor himself quite probably addressed him as "sir," as behooved his rank, and I, fool that I was, had treated him so dishonorably! And then another thought occurred to me: what did fate have in store for me now?

There was a fair in Penza at the time and the Uhlan officer said to me:

"Look here, Ivan, I'm awfully sorry, but it seems I can't possibly let you stay with us."

I said: "Why not?"

"Because," he said, "I am a servant of the State and you never had a passport."

"No, sir," I said, "it isn't quite correct to say that I never had a passport. I had a passport, only it was a fake."

"Well, you see, don't you?" he replied. "And now you haven't even got a faked one. Here, take two hundred roubles for your travelling expenses and good luck to you!"

Well, I don't mind confessing that I hated the very thought of leaving them, for, you see, I'd got so fond of the little girl, but I could see that there was nothing to be done about it, so I said:

"Well, good-bye, sir," I said, "and thank you very much for your kind reward, but I'm afraid there's something else that must be settled."

"What's that?" he asked.

"It's this, sir," I said. "I feel guilty because I've had a fight with you and been disrespectful to you."

He laughed and said:

"Oh, that's nothing. I like you: you're a nice fellow!"

"No, sir," I replied, "that has nothing to do with my being a nice fellow. It can't be left like that, for it would always remain a blot on my conscience. You're a defender of our country and I daresay the Emperor himself addresses you as 'sir.'"

"That's true enough," he said. "When we get our commission, we receive a paper on which is written, 'Sir, we confer upon you the rank of officer and we command our people to respect and honor you.'"

"Well, you see, sir," I said, "you can hardly expect me to forgive myself for having inflicted such a dishonor on you."

"But what's to be done about it now?" he said, "That you're stronger than I can't be helped—can it?—and you can't very well take back the blows you've given me."

"That I can't take back the blows is quite true," I said, "but at least to ease my conscience, sir, I'd be obliged to you if, whatever you yourself may feel about it, you'd hit me a few times yourself," and I blew out my cheeks and placed myself in front of him.

"But what for?" he said. "What shall I hit you for?"

"Just for no reason at all, sir," I said, "just for the sake of my conscience, so that I shouldn't have offended an officer of the Czar without proper punishment."

He laughed and I blew out my cheeks again, as much as there was breath in me, and again placed myself in front of him.

He asked me:

"What are you blowing out your cheeks for? What are you making faces for?"

And I replied:

"That's according to the army rules and regulations," I said.

"Please, do me a favor and hit me hard on both my cheeks," and I blew out my cheeks again.

But instead of striking me, he embraced me and began kissing me.

"Drop it, Ivan, for heaven's sake, drop it," he said. "I shan't hit you for anything in the world, only go away quickly now before Mary comes back with the child, for they're sure to start crying when they see that you're leaving us."

"Very well, sir," I said. "That, of course, is a different matter. Why make them feel sad on my account?"

And although I did not want to go without accepting my punishment for insulting an officer's uniform, there was nothing I could do about it, so I left the house quickly without taking leave, and as I went through the gates I stopped dead in my tracks, thinking, "Where shall I go now?"

And indeed I could not help reflecting that although a long time had passed since I left my masters, I could find no place to settle down. . . . "That's the end," I thought, "I'm going to give myself up! And yet," it occurred to me, "that isn't quite right, either, for I've got money now and at the police station they're sure to take it away from me: let me at least spend some of it, let me have some tea at a tavern and some white rolls and just a little pleasure for my money." So off I went to the fair and there I went into a tavern and asked for some tea and white rolls and I sat there drinking a long time. However, seeing that I couldn't very well sit there forever, I went out for a walk. I walked beyond the Sura River into the steppe where the horse fair was and where the Tartars had pitched their tents. All those tents looked alike except one which was gaily colored and round which a large number of gentlemen were occupying themselves in putting saddle horses through their paces. They were gentlemen of all sorts there, civilians, army officers, and landowners who had come specially to the fair, and all were standing round, smoking pipes, and in the center, on a beautiful rug of many colors, sat a tall, grave-looking Tartar, as thin as a reed, in a long patchwork robe and wearing a golden skullcap. I looked round and, observing a man who had drunk tea in the same tavern with me, I asked him who that important Tartar was who was the only man to sit in that crowd of people. And the man said to me:

"Don't you know him? It's Khan Jangar."

"Who," I asked, "is Khan Jangar?"

And the man said:

"Khan Jangar is the biggest breeder of horses in the steppe. His herds of horses are driven from the Volga to the Urals and all through the Rhyn-Sands, and he himself, this same Khan Jangar, is regarded in the steppe just like a Czar."

"Doesn't that steppe belong to us?" I asked.

"Why," he said, "of course it belongs to us, only that makes no difference because we can't do anything with it, for there's nothing there except salt marshes which stretch as far as the Caspian Sea, or else grass waving in the wind or birds flying under the heavens, and our civil servants in particular can't get a damn thing there and that's why," he said, "Khan Jangar lords it over everybody and, indeed, they say he has there, in the Rhyn-Sands, his own sheikhs and under-sheikhs and ulemas and imams and hajis and mullahs, and he orders them about as he pleases, every mother's son of them, and they are glad to do as he bids them."

While listening to my new acquaintance, I noticed a Tartar boy had driven a small white mare up to the Khan and started jabbering to him about something; the Khan got up, picked up a whip with a long handle, and, placing himself right in front of the mare's head, stood still, holding the whip stretched out vertically against her forehead. How can I describe to you the way that bandit-chief was standing? Just like a beautiful statue! Aye, he was a sight to marvel at, and one look at him told you that in his leisurely way he saw right through that mare. And as I myself had since the days of my childhood been accustomed to judge the points of a horse at a glance, I saw that the mare herself recognized an expert in him and she stood erect before him as if to say, "Come on, feast your eyes on me!" And it was thus that the grave-looking Tartar looked and looked at the mare, without walking round her as is the custom with our army officers, who always bustle about a horse, unable to stand still for a minute; he, on the other hand, just kept on looking at her from one point and then suddenly he let fall the whip and just kissed his finger tips without uttering a word: "A beauty!" so to speak; and he sat down again on the rug, crossing his legs, and the mare at once pricked up her ears and started to show off her high mettle.

The gentlemen who stood about now begun to outbid each other: one bid one hundred roubles, another one hundred and fifty, and so on, raising the bids against each other. The mare was, to be sure, a glorious animal, not too large in size, in shape somewhat like an Arabian horse, but well proportioned, with a small head, a full eye like an apple, and sharp ears; her sides were resonant, airy, her back like an arrow, and her legs light, beautifully turned, the swiftest you can imagine. I, a lover of such beauty, could not tear my eyes away from her. Khan Jangar, seeing that everybody was bewitched by her and that the gentlemen were raising the price for her like mad, nodded to the dirty-faced Tartar boy, who leapt on to the back of the little darling and started putting her through her paces: he sat on her, you know, in his own Tartar fashion, squeezing her sides with his knees, and she just flew under him, as though she were a bird, without rolling even once, and whenever he bent over her little neck and whooped at her, she would disappear in a whirlwind of sand. "Oh, you little hussy," I thought to myself, "you little bustard of the steppe, where, oh, where could you have been born, my beautiful one?" And I felt how my soul yearned for her, for that lovely horse, with a great passion. Presently the Tartar boy brought her back and she just gave one little snort with both her nostrils, blew the breath out, and shook off all weariness of body and not another breath could be heard from her, not a snort. "Oh, my darling," I thought. "Oh, my sweetheart!" Had that Tartar asked me to give up not only my soul, but my father and mother, for her, I should have gladly given them to him, but how could I hope to get such a winged courser when the gentlemen and the army buyers were just falling over each other and offering God knows what price for her! But even that was just nothing to what was to come, for before the bidding for her had come to an end and while she was still unsold, we saw a fast rider coming on a black horse from beyond the river Sura, from Selixa, and he was waving a wide-brimmed hat and, coming up like a hurricane, he jumped off his horse and made straight for the white mare and stopped dead in front of her, just like another statue, and said:

"The mare's mine!"

But the Khan replied:

"No, sir, she's not! These gentlemen here are offering me five hundred gold pieces for her."

But that rider, a huge Tartar with a big paunch, a sunburnt face with the skin peeling off it and looking as if it had been torn off in places, and with tiny eyes like little chunks, just shrieked:

"I'm offering a hundred pieces more than anybody else!"

But the gentlemen refused to give up and began raising their bids, and that dry-as-dust Khan Jangar just sat there, pursing his lips, and from the other side of the Sura River another Tartar came riding along on a horse with a long mane, a chestnut with a whitish tail and mane, and he was a terribly lean man, yellow, all skin and bone, but he seemed to be even keener than the one who came first. He just slid off his horse and stood like a post in front of the white mare and said:

"Listen to me, all of you, I've made up my mind to have the mare!"

I turned to my acquaintance and asked him how he thought it would all end, and he said:

"That depends entirely on what Khan Jangar himself decides. It isn't the first time," he said, "that he has played such a trick on the buyers. It is his custom at every fair to dispose first of the ordinary horses he brings for sale and to keep one or two horses up his sleeve for the last day, when—presto!—he produces them as if by magic, and the poor buyers just go off their heads in their eagerness to buy them. But he, cunning Tartar that he is, has a fine time and rakes in the money, too. Knowing this habit of his, everybody expects him to produce this last baby, and so it has also come to pass now: everybody expected the Khan to leave today and so he will, but not before nightfall, and now he comes out with such a mare. . . ."

"What a beauty of a horse!" I said.

"Yes, she's a beauty all right," he said. "He brought her to the fair in the middle of a whole herd of mares, and so cunningly did he contrive it that nobody could see her for the other horses and nobody knew anything about her except the two Tartars who have just arrived, and he told even them that his mare was not for sale and he sent her off to graze in a wood with a special herdsman and now he produces her just like that and offers her for sale, and you'd better watch out what wonders will come to pass on account of her and what money the cur will get for her, but if you like let's have a bet on who'll get her in the end."

"How do you mean?" I asked. "How in heaven's name are we to have a bet on that?"

"Well, you see," he replied, "that's not as difficult as you think, for, mark my words, these gentlemen here are sure to back out soon and the mare will be taken by one of those Asiatics."

"Why," I said, "are they so rich?"

"Rich?" he echoed. "Why, they're rolling in money, both of them, and they're keen sportsmen, too. They bring their own herds to the fair, and if they take a liking to a horse, they'll fight tooth and nail for it. Everybody knows them: that one, the one with the big belly, the one whose face is all peeling, is called Bakshey Otuchev, and the other one, the one who's all skin and bone, is Chepkun Yermucheyev, a real terror he is, but the fat one isn't a bit better. You just watch the fun that's coming. . . ."

I fell silent and saw that, indeed, the gentlemen who had been bidding for the mare had withdrawn from the sale and were just looking on, while the two Tartars kept on pushing each other out of the way and grasping Khan Jangar's hands, and both of them held fast to the mare, trembling with rage and screaming at the top of their voices.

One shouted:

"I'll give you five heads"—that is to say, horses—"in addition to the money!"

And the other one hollered:

"The devil you will, you ugly brute! I give ten!"

Bakshey Otuchev shrieked: "I'm giving fifteen!"

And Chepkun Yermucheyev: "Twenty!"

Bakshey: "Twenty-five!"

And Chepkun: "Thirty!"

Now more than that neither of them could bid, for it seemed they had no more horses to spare. . . . Chepkun shouted: "Thirty," and Bakshey, too, offered thirty, and no more. Thereupon Chepkun capped his offer by the addition of a saddle and Bakshey by a saddle and a robe; Chepkun also added a robe, and once more they hesitated, trying to think how to best each other. Then Chepkun shouted, "Listen to me, Khan Jangar, as soon as I return home I'll fetch you one of my daughters." So Bakshey, too, promised Khan Jangar one of his daughters, and again there was a deadlock, neither of them being able to outbid the other. Here the whole Tartar mob, who had been the silent onlookers of that contest, suddenly started to shout in their own lingo, raising one hell of a din. They tried to pull the two bidders for the mare apart in order to prevent them from ruining themselves entirely, pulling them—Chepkun and Bakshey—in opposite directions, poking them in the ribs, imploring them to reconsider.

I asked the man standing beside me:

"Tell me, what's all the row about now?"

"Well, you see," he said, "those Tartar princes who're trying to separate Chepkun and Bakshey are sorry for them; they think that they've gone far enough, so they're trying to separate them and bring them to their senses and, somehow or other, persuade one of the two to give up the mare to the other."

"But how can you expect either of them to give up the mare, if both like her so much?" I asked. "It seems to me," I added, "that they're wasting their time."

"Not at all," he replied. "The Asiatics are a sensible people and they like to do everything without any excitement: they'll decide that it isn't fair for either of them to ruin himself and they'll give Khan Jangar as much as he asks for his mare and then put the mare up as a prize in a flogging match."

"And what," I asked, "is a flogging match?"

And the man answered:

"Don't ask so many questions! Have patience and you'll find

out everything for yourself. It's something that has to be seen, and it's about to start any moment now."

So I looked and I saw that both Bakshey Otuchev and Chepkun Yermucheyev were beginning to calm down a little, and presently they broke loose from the Tartars who had been trying to make peace between them, ran up to each other, and began shaking hands. "All right," said one, "it's a bargain!" and the other one replied in the same words, "All right, it's a bargain!"

And both of them immediately threw off their robes and their long Caucasian tunics and their morocco-leather slippers, and they took off their cotton shirts and flopped down on the ground, sitting down opposite each other like two steppe sandpipers, and they stayed like that.

It was the first time in my life that I had seen such an extraordinary sight and I couldn't help wondering what was going to happen next. Well, they grasped each other by the left hand, holding on firmly, spread out their legs, and put their soles and heels together, one pair against the other, and shouted:

"Come on, let's have 'em!"

I couldn't even guess what it was they were demanding to "have," but they, the Tartars that is, shouted back to them from the crowd:

"Presently, gentlemen, presently!"

Then an old Tartar came out from that crowd, a fine, grave-looking old patriarch, and in his hands he held two mighty whips. He measured them carefully and, putting them together, showed them to the public and to Chepkun and Bakshey. "Look," he said, "they are of the same length."

"Aye," the Tartar mob shouted, "both are of equal length, we can see that, both are well made, everything's fair and aboveboard! Let them sit down and start!"

Bakshey and Chepkun nearly jumped out of their skins in their eagerness to get hold of those whips, but the grave old Tartar said to them, "Wait!" and then he himself handed the two whips to them, one to Chepkun and one to Bakshey, and he clapped his hands softly three times: one, two, three . . . And no sooner did he clap a third time than Bakshey struck Chepkun a mighty blow with the whip across the bare back over the shoulder and Chepkun replied in the same manner. So they went on regaling each other like that: looking straight into each other's eyes, the soles and heels of one pressed hard against the soles and heels of the other, left hands clasped firmly, and with their right hands flogging each other with leather thongs. Ugh! what a lovely fight that was! One would strike a real beauty of a blow and the other would fetch an even better one. So they went on flogging each other till there was a stunned look in their eyes and their left hands went stiff, but neither one nor the other would give in.

I asked my acquaintance:

"Do they fight one another like that just like our own gentlemen do at a duel?"

"Yes," he replied, "this is also a kind of single combat, but they don't fight to save their honor, but to save their money."

"Are they allowed to flog one another like that for a long time?" I asked.

"Just as long as they please," he said, "and as long as their strength holds out."

Meanwhile those two went on flogging each other and the people began to argue among themselves, some saying, "Chepkun will outflog Bakshey," and the others saying, "Bakshey will outflog Chepkun," and those who were of the sporting fraternity laid bets against each other, either for Chepkun or Bakshey, all depending on whom they pinned their hopes upon as the winner. They'd look into their eyes and examine their teeth with an expert air and they'd also glance at their backs and they seemed to be able to judge by certain signs who was the more likely winner, and that one they would back. The man with whom I had been talking was also one of these experts, and at first he was all for Bakshey, but later he changed his mind and said:

"Ah, well, I've lost my twenty copecks! Chepkun's sure to beat Bakshey!"

But I said:

"How do you know that? It's quite impossible to tell yet: both are sitting tight!"

But he answered:

"It's true that both are sitting firmly, but their methods are different."

"If it comes to that," I said, "Bakshey's strokes are much more vicious."

"That's the trouble," he said. "Yes, sir, my twenty copecks are as good as lost. Chepkun will flog him to a standstill."

"That's strange business," I thought. "My acquaintance seems to be all wrong, and yet," I said to myself, "he must be an old hand at this kind of fight or he wouldn't bet."

So my curiosity was rather aroused, you know, and I kept on worrying my friend:

"Please be so good as to explain to me," I said, "why you're so apprehensive about Bakshey?"

And he said:

"What a country simpleton you are! Just have a look at Bakshey's back!"

I looked and there seemed nothing wrong with his back: it was a lovely back, a strong back, big and plump as a cushion.

"But can't you see how he's hitting?" he said.

I looked again and I could see that he was hitting out viciously, so that his eyes were popping out, and every time he hit his opponent, he'd draw blood.

"Now just try to think what's happening inside him."

"How do you mean, inside him? All I can see is that he's sitting up straight and that his mouth is wide open and that he's taking in the air in quick gasps."

"Well, that's the trouble, you see. He has a large back and every blow across it goes home, he hits fast and he's therefore getting winded, he's breathing through an open mouth and that means that he'll burn up all his insides with the air."

"So you think that Chepkun is more likely to win?" I asked.

"Of course he's more likely to win," he replied. "Have a good look at him: there's not a drop of sweat on him and his bones have no fat on 'em, just skin and that's all, and that back of his is just like a scooped-out wooden spade, no blow can possibly fall on it fully, but it will strike him only in places, while he, you see, is hitting Bakshey steadily, not too fast, but with a pause between each blow, so that the whip doesn't descend with a crash, but just strongly enough to raise a weal on the skin. That's why that one's back, Bakshey's I mean, is all swollen and is as black as a kettle and there's not a drop of blood on it, which means that all the pain remains inside his body; but the skin on Chepkun's back is cracked like the skin of a roasted sucking pig, and it breaks, so that all the pain will go out with his blood and he's bound to give Bakshey the beating of his life. Do you see it now?"

"Yes," I said, "I see it now," and, indeed, now I grasped the whole secret of that Tartar sport and began to be greatly interested in it and particularly in the question of what was the best thing to do in such a contingency.

"And, mind, the most important thing," my acquaintance told me further, "is that that damned Chepkun keeps good time with that ugly face of his. Look! Do you see? He strikes, then he takes his punishment in his turn and each time he shuts or opens his eyes as the case may be. That's much easier than having your eyes popping out of your head all the time. Chepkun has clenched his teeth and bitten his lips and that, too, makes it easier for him, for by holding his mouth shut he prevents any unnecessary burning inside him."

I made a mental note of all those interesting points and, as I looked more and more closely at Chepkun and Bakshey, I began to see for myself that Bakshey was bound to collapse, for his eyes had already glazed over and his lips had distended into a thin line, baring all his teeth. . . . And so it was: Bakshey struck Chepkun about twenty more times and every time the force of his blow got weaker and weaker, then—wallop!—he suddenly swayed backwards, let go of Chepkun's left hand while still moving his right one up and down as if he were continuing to deal blows with it, but he was already unconscious and in another moment he passed right out. Well, then my acquaintance said, "It's all over! Goodbye to my twenty copecks!" Here all the Tartars started talking at once, congratulating Chepkun and shouting:

"A clever fellow, Chepkun Yermucheyev! Oh, what a brainy fellow! Knocked Bakshey right out! Now the mare's yours. Come on, get on her back!"

And Khan Jangar himself also got up from his rug, sucked his lips, and said:

"It's yours, it's yours, Chepkun. The mare's yours. Mount her and have a ride on her, you can have a rest on her back."

Well, so Chepkun got up. The blood was streaming down his back, but he showed no sign of feeling any pain. He put his robe and tunic over the mare's back and jumped on her, lying flat on his belly, and rode off like that, and I was beginning to feel depressed once more.

"Well," I thought, "now that's finished I'll start worrying about my position again," and I just hated to think about it.

But, luckily, that acquaintance of mine said to me:

"Wait, don't go. Something more's sure to happen."

I said: "What's going to happen now? It's all over."

"No," said he, "it isn't over. Look" he said, "do you notice Khan Jangar smoking his pipe? He keeps on puffing away at it; that's a sure sign that he's contemplating some other Asiatic trick!"

So I thought to myself, "If only something of the kind were to happen again and somebody were to back me by a promise to pay for the horse, I'd never let him down."

6.

And would you believe it? Everything came to pass exactly as I wished. Khan Jangar was blazing away at his pipe and from a nearby wood another Tartar boy came galloping towards him, but this time not on a mare like the one Chepkun had won from Bakshey in a public contest, but on a bay colt which defied all description. Have you ever watched a corn crake flying over the boundary between two fields? If you have, you must have noticed how he spreads out his wings while his tail—unlike that of other birds—is not spread out in the air at all, but hangs down, and his legs, too, he lets droop, as though he had no use for them, and you get the impression that he is riding on air. So did the new horse, like that bird, seem to tear along driven by some power not his own.

It is the honest truth I'm telling you when I say that the colt didn't even fly, but that it looked as if the earth was gaining on him. Never in my life had I seen such lightness, and I did not even know what price to set on such a horse, what treasure to give for him and who was the man worthy to own him, what Crown Prince he should belong to, and least of all did I dream that I myself might become his owner.

"Did you become his owner?" the surprised passengers interrupted the novice.

"Yes, he became mine, mine according to all the rules, but for one minute only, and how it all happened, gentlemen, you will hear, if you will be kind enough to give me your attention."

As was to be expected, the gentlemen began to haggle over the horse, and my cavalry officer, to whom I had given the child, also joined in the bidding; but against them all, as though he were their equal, a Tartar started bidding for the horse, a Tartar by the name of Savakirey, a stocky sort of fellow, a little man but of strong build, with the devil of a temper, his head shaven as if turned on a lathe and round like a firm cabbage fresh from the field, and a face like a red carrot, and altogether he looked like a fine, fresh vegetable. "Why waste money for nothing?" he hollered. "Let anybody who likes put down as much money as the Khan asks and let him have a flogging match with me and the winner takes the horse!"

Well, the gentlemen naturally would not accept such a challenge and they at once withdrew, for how, indeed, could they even think of entering a flogging contest against that damned Tartar, who was quite certain to flog the whole lot of them to death? And my cavalry officer was not exactly rolling in money at the time, for he had again lost a lot of money at cards in Penza, and I could see that he wanted that horse badly. So I pulled him by the sleeve from behind and said to him, "Don't offer any more money for the horse, but just give as much as the Khan asks and let me have a go at Savakirey at that flogging match of theirs." He would not hear of it at first, but I persuaded him to let me have a try, saying:

"Do me a favor, sir, I'd like to very much."

And so he did.

"And you and that Tartar . . . did you really flog each other?"

"Yes, we did flog each other according to their custom, in public, and I got the horse."

"Then you won?"

"Yes, I won. Mind you, it was no easy victory, but I did get the better of him in the end."

"But the pain must have been terrible."

"Well . . . how shall I put it? . . . At the beginning, yes, the pain was rather bad, especially as I wasn't used to it and, besides, he, that Savakirey fellow, also knew all about hitting your back so that it swelled up but did not bleed. However, I used a trick of my own against his clever art: every time he had a crack at me I'd pull up the skin on my back under the whip and I got so clever at it that I'd tear the skin and in that way I escaped the danger of a swollen back and I myself flogged that Savakirey to death."

"What do you mean? Actually to death?"

"That's right. You see, through his own pigheadedness and through what he thought was clever policy on his part, he brought things to such a pass that he departed this world for good and all," the novice replied quite good-humoredly and rather casually, but seeing that the passengers looked at him, if not in terror, then in mute bewilderment, he seemed to feel the need to add a gloss to his story.

"You see," he said, "that was his lookout, not mine, because he was famed far and wide throughout the Rhyn-Sands as one of their strongest men and, being naturally ambitious of his title, he would not give in to me for all the world. He wanted to bear his punishment honorably, so as not to be the means of discrediting the whole Asiatic nation, but, poor fellow, he just couldn't bear it, I suppose. Couldn't stand up against me, and I suspect, gentlemen, that was chiefly because I had a coin in my

mouth. You can't imagine what a great help it is! I kept on biting
on it so as not to feel the pain and to distract my thoughts I
counted the blows in my head so that I didn't mind it very much."

"And how many blows did you count?" one of the passengers
interrupted him.

"That I couldn't tell you for certain, sir. All I remember is that
I counted up to two hundred and eighty and then I seemed to
have had a kind of fainting fit and I got confused in my head for
a moment and lost count of the blows and didn't bother to count
any more and, anyway, soon after that Savakirey aimed his last
blow at me, but had not the strength to hit me and fell forward
like a doll on top of me. They looked him over, but he was
dead. . . . Oh, what a fool I was! To think what it was I had
stuck it out for! I nearly landed in jail on account of him. The
Tartars, mind you, didn't care a bit: if you've killed him, you've
killed him, for according to the rules he could have flogged me to
death, too. But our Russians were quite hopeless. Really, I was
terribly disappointed in them: they didn't seem to grasp the situation at all. Made such a fuss. I said:

" 'What do you want? What are you getting so worked up
about?'

" 'What do you mean?' they said. 'You killed an Asiatic, didn't
you?'

" 'What if I did kill him? Wasn't it done according to the rules?
Would it have been better if he had killed me?'

" 'He could have killed you,' they said, 'and gone scot free,
because he isn't a Christian; but you,' they said, 'are a Christian
and you'll therefore have to be put on trial according to the
Christian laws. Come on,' they said, 'to the police station with
you!'

" 'But I said to myself, Oh, no, my dear friends, you're as likely
to put the wind on trial as me,' and as in my opinion there can't
be anything less wholesome than the police, I just dodged behind
one Tartar and then behind another, and I whispered to them:

" 'Save me, princes! You saw yourselves how it all happened. It
was a fair fight. . . .'

"Well, they just closed up their ranks and pushed me from one to the other and so they concealed me."

"Forgive me, but how do you mean they *concealed* you?"

"I ran away with them to their steppe for good."

"To their steppe?"

"Yes, sir. As far as the Rhyn-Sands."

"And did you stay there long?"

"For ten whole years: I was twenty-three when I reached the Rhyn-Sands and I ran away from them in my thirty-third year."

"Did you like life in the steppe?"

"I didn't. What is there to like about it? I was terribly homesick all the time I was there, but I couldn't get away earlier."

"Why not? Did the Tartars keep you at the bottom of a well or did they mount guard over you?"

"Oh, no, nothing of the sort. They're a kindly folk and wouldn't permit anyone to treat me so dishonorably as to throw me into a well or put me into stocks, but they just said to me, 'We want you to be our friend, Ivan. We love you dearly,' they said, 'and we want you to live with us in the steppe and be a useful man, cure our horses and help the women.' "

"And did you cure their horses?"

"Yes, I did. As a matter of fact, I was their only doctor and I took care of their health as well as of the health of their cattle, their horses, and their sheep, but most of all I treated their wives, the Tartar ladies."

"And did you cure their illnesses?"

"Well, I don't rightly know what to say. . . . You see, there isn't much in it when you come to think of it, is there? If any of them took sick, I'd give them some aloes or the root of galanga and it would pass off. Luckily, they had plenty of aloes: a Tartar had found a sack full of them in Saratov and he had brought it home with him, but before I went to live with them they didn't know what to do with them."

"So you settled down among them?"

"No, I didn't. I was always trying to get back."

"And did you really find it so hard to get away from them?"

"No, I shouldn't have found it so hard if my feet had been in good shape. I should have gone back to my country long before."

"What was the matter with your feet?"

"I was bristled up after my first attempt."

"What's that? Pardon us, but we don't quite understand what you mean by saying you were *bristled up!*"

"Oh, that's one of their usual tricks: if they take a liking to a person and want to keep him and if that person is feeling down in the mouth and tries to escape, they do something to him to prevent him from running away. The same thing happened to me after I had tried to run away and lost my way in the steppe. They caught me and said, 'Look here, Ivan,' they said, 'we want you to be our friend, and to make sure that you won't run away again we're going to take the skin off your heels and shove some bristles in and then sew it up again.' Well, in this way they crippled my feet and I had to crawl on all fours all the time."

"How do they perform this terrible operation?"

"Very simple. About a dozen of them threw me to the ground and told me, 'Shout, Ivan, shout as loud as you can when we start cutting your flesh: you'll feel much better then.' And they sat on top of me and one of them, a past master in this art, cut away the skin of my heels in less than no time and put in some hair from a horse's mane which had been cut up very fine, and, putting back the skin on top of the bits of hair, he sewed it up with some gut. After that, I admit, they did keep me bound hand and foot for a few days, for they were afraid that I might interfere with my wounds and get rid of the bristles by matting them. But as soon as the skin healed up, they let me go, saying, 'Welcome to our tents, Ivan, for now you're our friend for better or for worse and you will never leave us again!' I tried to get up, but as soon as I stood on my feet, down I went again, for the cut-up hair under the skin of my heels hurt terribly because it pierced into the living flesh and I couldn't take a single step. However hard I tried, I couldn't think of a way of standing on my feet. I had never cried in my life before, but just then I couldn't help bawling at the top of my voice, and I said to them, 'What have you done to me, you damned Asiatics? I'd rather you'd killed me outright than crippled me for the rest of my days and made it impossible for me to stand on my feet!' But they said to me, 'Don't cry, Ivan, there's nothing to worry about. Why are you making such a fuss about nothing at all?' But I said, 'What are you talking about? Do you call crippling a man nothing and do you really expect me not to make a fuss about it?' And they said, 'Get used to it, don't step on your heels, but walk about in a bandy-legged way by stepping on your anklebones!' 'Oh, you rascals,' I thought to myself, and I turned away from them and spoke no more, but I made up my mind that I'd rather be dead than follow their advice and walk bandy-legged on my anklebones. However, after lying about for some time I felt as melancholy as a cat, and I started getting used to walking about bandy-legged and by and by I was hobbling on my ankles. They laughed at me a lot on account of that and they even had the effrontery to tell me, 'That's very nice, Ivan, you can walk beautifully now!' "

"What an awful thing to happen to you! Did you try to run away a second time and did they catch you again?"

"No, I didn't do anything of the kind. You see, it was quite impossible. The steppe is flat, there are no roads, and one has to eat. . . . The first time I had walked for three days and I had grown so weak that I could hardly drag my feet. I caught some bird with my hands and I ate her raw and then again hunger and thirst. . . . How was I to go on? . . . In the end I collapsed and they found me, brought me back, and bristled me."

One of the passengers remarked in regard to that "bristling" that it must have been very awkward walking on one's ankles.

"At first it is rather a bit of a nuisance," Ivan Severyanych replied, "and even later on when I got the knack of it, I found it quite impossible to walk very far. But to give them their due, those Tartars after that appreciated the awkwardness of my situation and they did their best to make life tolerable for me. They said to me, 'You can hardly manage for yourself now, Ivan: you can't fetch any water for yourself, nor can you cook yourself any food, so why don't you take a Natashka to help you? Choose any Natashka you like and we'll be glad to give her to you.' But I said to them, 'Why waste my time choosing, if there's only one thing they're good for, anyway. Let's have any one you like.' So without any more ado they married me."

"What? Do you mean they married you to a Tartar woman?"

"Well, of course they married me to a Tartar woman. First to one, the wife of Savakirey, whom I had flogged to death, but she, this Tartar woman, was not to my taste at all: a queer one she was, and she seemed to be scared of me and was no fun at all. I don't know whether it was that she was longing for her husband or whether it was something else that made her so broken-hearted, but as soon as the Tartars saw that she was more of a burden than a delight to me, they brought me another one, a little girl she was, no more than thirteen years old. They said to me, 'Take this Natashka for your second wife: she'll be more fun for you.' So I took her."

"And was she more fun?" the passengers asked Ivan Severyanych.

"Yes," he replied, "she was more fun, she'd amuse me a lot sometimes, but at other times she'd just get my goat with her naughty ways."

"What kind of naughty ways?"

"Well, all sorts. . . . Just as her fancy took her: she'd jump on my knees, for instance, or when I'd be asleep she'd scoop up my skullcap with her feet and send it flying all over the tent, laughing her head off. I'd start scolding her, but she'd go on laughing and running about like a blessed pixie and, crawling on all fours, I couldn't catch her and I'd slip and start laughing myself."

"And did you shave your head and wear a skullcap there in the steppe?"

"Yes, I shaved my head."

"But why did you do that? Did you want to please your wives?"

"I hardly think so, more for the sake of cleanliness, for, you see, they have no baths there."

"So that you had two wives at the same time?"

"Yes, two in one steppe, but afterwards when I lived with another Tartar chief, Khan Agashimola, who had carried me off from Yermucheyev, they gave me two more."

"But," one of the passengers could not help interjecting, "how did they manage to carry you off?"

"By a stratagem. From Penza I had run away with the Tartars of Chepkun Yermucheyev and for five years I lived with the Yermucheyev crowd, and it was there that all the Tartar princes and ulemas and sheikhs and under-sheikhs used to assemble in celebration of a feast, including even Khan Jangar and Bakshey Otuchev."

"Is that the one Chepkun flogged?"

"Yes, the same."

"But how's that? Didn't Bakshey bear a grudge against Chepkun?"

"Why should he? They never bear a grudge against each other for such a thing: the winner in a flogging match gets the prize and that's all there is to it. Khan Jangar, though, did say to me once, 'Oh, Ivan, Ivan, what a stupid idiot you are, Ivan, to have sat down to that flogging match with Savakirey when I was just going to enjoy a good laugh at your prince, watching his highness himself take off his shirt.' But I told him, 'You'd never have lived to see that.' So he asked me, 'Why not?' And I replied, 'Because our princes are cowards and have no pluck at all and their strength isn't anything to boast about, either.' He understood and he said to me, 'I could see that there were no real sportsmen among them and that if they wanted a thing, they expected to get it for money.' And I said, 'That's true enough: they can't do anything without money.' Anyway, that Khan Agashimola belonged to a distant Tartar tribe and his herds of horses grazed somewhere near the Caspian Sea. He liked to doctor himself, it was quite a hobby with him, and he asked me to come and see if I could cure his wife and promised many heads of cattle to Yermucheyev if he let me go. So Yermucheyev let me go with him. I took with me my aloes and the galanga root and went off with him. But once he got me, Khan Agashimola moved off with all his tribe to some other grazing grounds; for eight days we galloped before we came to them."

"Did you go on horseback?"

"Why, yes."

"And what about your feet?"

"What about them?"

"But didn't that chopped-up hair in your feet trouble you at all?"

"Not in the least. You see, they had thought it out very cleverly. They put the bristle under a man's heels so that he can't walk, but such a bristled man can ride a horse better than ever before, because he has got used to walking bandy-legged and he always holds his legs in a crooked position. He therefore finds it an easy matter to get a firm grip on the horse's sides like a hoop and no horse can throw him."

"Well, and what adventures did you have while living with Khan Agashimola?"

"I suffered worse and worse trials and tribulations."

"But you didn't perish."

"No, I did not perish."

"Won't you tell us what further trials you had to undergo with Khan Agashimola?"

"Gladly, gentlemen."

7.

"As soon as Agashimola's Tartars brought me to their tents, they broke camp and away they went to look for new pastures and they would not let me go back. They said to me, 'Why do you want to go back to Yermucheyev, Ivan. Yermucheyev is a thief. You'd better stay with us, we'll take you hunting with us and we'll give you lovely Natashkas. You had only two Natashkas there, but we'll give you more.' But I refused, saying, 'I don't want any more of them. What shall I do with more of them?' But they said, 'You don't understand, Ivan: the more Natashkas you have, the better it is for you, for they'll bear you more Kolkas who will all be calling you Daddy.' But I didn't consider the prospect of bringing up lots of Tartar children particularly inviting and I told them so. I said, 'If I could have baptized them and made sure that they received Holy Communion, it would be a different matter,' but in my present circumstances, however great a number of children I had they would still be theirs and they would not be Orthodox Christians and—who knows?—they might even grow up to cheat Russian peasants. So I only took two more wives and no more, for if there are too many women about, they start quarrelling among themselves, Tartar women though they be, and I'd have had my work cut out keeping them in order."

"Well, and did you love those new wives of yours?"

"How do you mean?"

"Did you love your new wives?"

"Love them? Oh, I see, you mean *that*? Well, there was one I got from Agashimola and she always tried to please me and . . . well . . . I did take pity on her."

"And that girl, the young one who had been your wife before, didn't you like her even more?"

"Yes, I guess I took pity on her, too."

"Didn't you miss her when they abducted you from one tribe to another?"

"No, I don't think I missed her particularly."

"But didn't you have any children by those first wives of yours?"

"Why, of course I had. Savakirey's wife bore me two Kolkas and one Natashka and the other one, the little one, bore me six in five years, for she brought me two Kolkas at the same time."

"Why, pray, do you always call them 'Kolkas' and 'Natashkas?' "

"That's a Tartar custom. They have only one name for Russians: a man they call *Ivan* and a woman *Natashka* and boys *Kolkas*, so my wives, although they were Tartar women, were considered by them to be Russians because I was a Russian, and they called the girls Natashkas, and the boys they called Kolkas. I am, mind you, talking of them as my children only in a manner of speaking, for as they had never received the sacraments of the Church, I, for one, never considered them as my children."

"Why didn't you consider them as your children? Whose children were they then?"

"I couldn't very well consider them as my own, if they had not been baptized and anointed with myrrh."

"But what about your parental feelings?"

"What would that be?"

"Didn't you love those children of yours? Didn't you ever fondle them?"

"How should I have fondled them? Sometimes when I was sitting alone and one would run up to me, I . . . well . . . I'd stroke his head or say to him, 'Go to your mother!' But that didn't happen very often, for I couldn't be bothered with them."

"But why not? Were you so very busy?"

"No, I wasn't busy, but I was always brooding, wanted to go home to Russia very badly."

"So even in ten years you couldn't get used to the steppes?"

"No, I couldn't. I wanted to go home. . . . I'd be overcome by melancholy thoughts, especially in the evenings, and sometimes even in the daytime when it happened to be a very fine day, very hot, and everything in the camp was quiet, for on a hot day the Tartars keep to their tents, going to sleep, but I would raise the flap of my tent and look out onto the steppe . . . one way and another . . . it was all the same. . . . A fiery furnace, pitiless . . . For miles and miles the horizon stretched without a break: grass everywhere, feather grass, white and tufted, waving like a silver sea and scenting the air on the breeze; there was a smell of sheep, and the sun would be blazing from a clear sky, burning, and wherever I looked there was no end to the steppe, just as there's no end to life's sorrows, and as there was no bottom to my heartache. . . . I looked without knowing myself where I was looking and suddenly I would behold a monastery or a church and I would remember my own Christian land and I would start shedding tears. . . ."

Ivan Severyanych stopped and, overcome by his memories, heaved a deep sigh; then he went on:

"It was much worse among the salt marshes close to the Caspian Sea: the sun glared, baked, and the salt marsh sparkled and the sea sparkled. . . . You'd get dizzier from that sparkling than from the feather grass and then you wouldn't know where, in what part of the world, I mean, you were, whether you were numbered among the living or you were among the dead and were being tormented in hell without hope of redemption. In the steppe, which is covered thickly with feather grass, it is, at any rate, more agreeable; occasionally in some ravine there you can at least catch a glimpse of the bluish mist of blossoming sage or else, now and then, small bushes of wormwood and savory dazzle the eye with a splash of whiteness! But here there is nothing but that sparkling. . . . There, the grass would sometimes be set ablaze and a trail of fire would pass across the steppe. A general hubbub would arise: great bustards would rise in the air, little bustards and steppe snipe, and we'd have some sport. The great bustards we'd overtake on our horses and start killing them with long whips; and, as likely as not, in the end we'd have to take to our heels ourselves, fleeing on our horses from the flames. . . . All that would, to some extent, break the monotony of our existence. And then wild strawberry would again begin to flower on the burnt-out patches of steppe; all kinds of birds would come flying there, mostly small birds, and there'd be a constant chirping in the air. . . . And then again, here and there, you'd come across some shrubs: meadowsweet, wild peach, Siberian pear trees. . . . And when at the rising of the sun the mist descended and covered the grass with dew, there'd be a lovely coolness in the air which would be full of the fragrance of plants. . . . No doubt even then one felt sick at heart, though all that would make life at least bearable, but God preserve any man from spending a long time among those salt marshes! The horse finds the life quite pleasant there for a time: he licks the salt and that makes him drink a lot and get fat, but no man can live there for long without perishing. There's no wild life of any kind there, except, funnily enough, one little bird, a redpoll, like our swallow, a most ordinary bird except for that red streak round its beak. Why she should go to the shores of that sea I don't know, but as there's nothing there on which she can alight, she just drops on the salt marsh and sits there on her rump and, lo! up she rises again and off she flies. But you can't even do that, for you have no wings, and you stay there and there's neither life, nor death, nor repentance for you, and if you die, they'll put you, like mutton, in salt and you'll lie there till the end of the world like a piece of salted meat.

But, if anything, it is even worse to spend a winter on those dismal grazing grounds. There isn't much snow about, just enough to cover the grass and then it hardens. The Tartars spend all their time in their tents over a fire, smoking, and out of sheer boredom they often flog each other. If you leave your tent, there is nothing to look at: the horses walk about with their heads hanging down, shrivelled up and with their ribs showing, their tails and manes alone streaming in the wind. They can hardly drag their feet, they rake up the frozen snow with their hoofs and swallow the frozen grass, which is the only fodder they get. It's enough to drive you crazy. . . . The only distraction you get is when a horse is seen to be getting too weak to rake up the snow with his hoofs and nibble the frozen grass, for then they stick a knife into his throat, take off his hide, and eat his flesh. It's rotten meat, though: sweet, just like a cow's udder, except that it is tough. You eat it, of course, but that's only because you have to, for it just turns your stomach. One of my wives, fortunately, knew how to smoke a horse's ribs: she'd take a rib just as it was, with the meat clinging to the bone on both sides, put it inside a large gut, and smoke it over the hearth. That wasn't so bad; you could eat it with some relish, for the smell at least reminded you of smoked ham; but it turned your stomach all the same. Well, I'd be chewing that bit of carrion and, suddenly, the thought would cross my mind: Oh, to be at home now in my village! Christmas would be coming soon and everybody would be plucking ducks and geese, slaughtering pigs, cooking cabbage soup with stuffed birds' necks, as fat as anything! And Father Ilya, our priest, such a dear old soul, would soon be leading a procession to glorify Christ the Lord and with him in that procession would be his deacons, the priests' ladies, and the deacons' ladies, walking side by side with the seminary students, and all of them a bit tipsy. . . . Father Ilya himself can't hold much drink: at the hall the butler would offer him a glass of vodka on a tray and at the office the manager would send out the old nurse with another, so Father Ilya would get a bit fuddled and he'd totter along to the servants' quarters, hardly able to drag his feet, drunk as a lord, poor soul! In the first cottage, at the edge of the yard, he'd somehow manage to sip another glass, but that would be his last, and every other glass offered to him he would empty into a bottle which he carried under his chasuble. Being a most devoted family man even where food was concerned, Father Ilya, if he should happen to see a tasty morsel lying about, would never miss the chance of begging for it. 'Wrap it up in a newspaper,' he'd say, 'and I'll take it home with me!' Generally, such a request would bring forth the reply, 'We have no newspaper, father!' But he wouldn't get angry and would take it as it was, without bothering to wrap it up, and hand it to his wife just as it was, and continue on his way, as serenely as ever. . . . Oh, gentlemen, when all those happy memories of my childhood would come crowding into my head and oppress my soul and weigh heavily upon my liver, I'd say to myself, What a dog's life you're leading now, far away from all that happiness, bereft of spiritual consolation for so many years, you live unwedded and you'll die unmourned! . . . And I'd be overcome by such melancholy that, as soon as night came, I'd steal quietly out of the camp, away from the sight of my wives and children and all the other heathens, and I'd start to pray . . . and I'd pray and pray and I wouldn't even notice that the snow under my knees had melted, and where my tears had dropped I could see the grass next morning. . . .''

The novice fell silent and sank his head. No one disturbed him, for all felt deeply moved by the sacred sorrow of his last memories; but after a short time Ivan Severyanych heaved a sigh, with which he seemed to dismiss the whole thing, took off his monastic hat, and, crossing himself, said:

"Well, everything passed off all right, the Lord be praised!"

We gave him time to rest a little and then ventured to ask more questions about how he, our enchanted hero, managed to get rid of the bristles in his crippled heels and how he succeeded in fleeing from the Tartar steppe, from his Natashkas and Kolkas, and entering a monastery.

Ivan Severyanych satisfied our curiosity with great frankness, from which, indeed, he was quite incapable of departing.

8.

As we set great store on consecutive order in the development of the story of Ivan Severyanych, which we had found so fascinating, we asked him to tell us first of all by what unusual means he had rid himself of the bristles and how he had managed to flee from his captivity. He gave us the following account of his adventures:

I completely despaired of ever returning home and seeing my native land again. The very thought of it seemed a waste of time to me and my homesickness gradually began to die down. I went on living like some lifeless statue and that was that. But sometimes the thought would occur to me that in our church at home the same Father Ilya who used to ask for newspaper in which to wrap up some delicacy would pray during the divine service for "all that travel by land, or by water, and all sick persons and *captives*," and that I, hearing that prayer, would always wonder: "Why? Are we at war now that he should be praying for captives?" Now I understood why those prayers were said in church, but what I could not understand was why those prayers were not of the slightest use to me, and, to tell the truth, although I am not an unbeliever I am sometimes perplexed, and so I stopped saying any prayers.

"What's the use of praying," I said to myself, "when nothing comes of it anyway?"

In the meantime I suddenly noticed one day that the Tartars were in a state of great excitement.

I said:

"What's the matter?"

"Oh, nothing much," they said, "except that two mullahs have arrived from your country with a safe conduct from the White Czar and they're going on a long journey to spread their gospel."

I just gasped and I said:

"Where are they?"

They pointed out a tent to me and I went there. When I entered the tent I saw that a large number of sheikhs and under-sheikhs had gathered there, as well as imams and dervishes, and all of them were sitting cross-legged on rugs and among them were two strangers who, though dressed in travelling clothes, were obviously men of the cloth. Both of them were standing in the midst of that mob preaching the gospel to the Tartars.

As I beheld them, I greatly rejoiced to see two of my fellow countrymen and my heart leapt within me and I fell down at their feet and wept. They, too, rejoiced to see me prostrate myself before them, and both exclaimed:

"Well, brethren, do you see how wonderfully the grace of God works? Behold, one of your own kith and kin has already become converted and renounced Mohammed!"

But the Tartars replied that it did not seem to have worked at all, for that man, they said, was just one of their own Ivans who lived as a captive among them.

The missionaries were greatly displeased with that. They would not believe that I was a Russian, so I roused myself and said:

"Yes, I am truly a Russian! Fathers," I said, "servants of the Church, have mercy upon me, save me, help me to escape from here! I've been held captive here for over ten years and you can see for yourselves that I've been crippled and cannot walk on my feet."

But they paid little heed to my words and turned away and carried on with their business: they went right on preaching!

So I thought to myself, "I have no right to murmur against them, for they are on an official mission and perhaps they find it a bit awkward to treat me otherwise in the presence of the Tartars." I therefore left the tent and chose a more auspicious time when they were alone in a tent, and I went to them and told them frankly all about myself, what a cruel fate had befallen me, and I besought them:

"Dear fathers," I said, "put the fear of our great White Czar into them, tell them that he has forbidden the Asiatics to keep one of his own subjects in captivity, or, what would be more to the point, offer them a ransom for me, and I will follow you and become your servant. Living among them," I said, "I have learned to speak their language like a native and I could be very useful to you."

But they replied:

"We are very sorry for you, my son, but we have no ransom to offer and," they said, "we are strictly forbidden to threaten the infidels, for they are, as it happens, a cunning and treacherous people, and as for our being civil to them, it is just politics."

"Do you mean," I said, "that I have to perish utterly here by remaining with them all my life because of those politics of yours?"

"Well, my son," they said, "it matters little where a man perishes. What we'd advise you to do is to pray: our Lord is a Lord of mercy. He will, perhaps, devise some way of delivering you."

"I have prayed," I said, "but my strength is at an end and I've given up all hope."

"You must not despair," they said, "for that is a grievous sin."

"I do not despair," I said, "but . . . how can you treat me like this? . . . I'm deeply grieved that you, Russians and fellow countrymen of mine, should refuse to stretch out a helping hand to me."

"No, my son," they said, "do not try to involve us in this business. We are one body in Christ, and in Christ there are neither Jews nor Gentiles: our fellow countrymen all obey the law of Christ. To us all are alike, all are equal."

"All?" I said.

"Yes," they replied, "all. That is the teaching we have received from St. Paul the Apostle. Wherever we go, we avoid trouble . . . it doesn't become us to be mixed up in any trouble. You are a servant of the Most High and you just have to suffer, for," they said, "according to St. Paul the Apostle, servants must be obedient. You have to remember that you are a Christian and that therefore we have no further business with you, for the pearly gates are even without our help open to admit your soul, but these people here will abide in darkness if we do not convert them, so it is with them that our business lies."

And they showed me a book.

"Do you see how many people are put down in this register?" they said. "All of them have been converted to the true faith by us."

I did not waste any more words on them, nor did I see them again, except one of them, and that too by mere accident. One day one of my sons came running from somewhere and said to me:

"There's a man lying by our lake, Daddy!"

I went to have a look. I saw that the socks were torn off from his knees downwards and the gloves taken off from his hands and arms up to the elbows: the Tartars are past masters at that sort of thing—they make a cut round the arm or leg and tear the skin off. The head of the man was lying a few paces away and on his forehead a cross was cut.

"Oh," thought I, "you refused to do anything for me, fellow countryman of mine, and I blamed you for it, but now you have been thought worthy of a martyr's crown and you have sealed the testimony of your faith with your blood. Forgive me, I pray, for Christ's sake! "

And I made the sign of the cross over his body, put his poor head near his trunk, and, making a low obeisance, I buried him and said the Lord's Prayer over his grave; but what had happened to his companion I never could find out. I suppose he too must have ended up by winning a martyr's crown, for afterwards the Tartar women in our camp had a large number of holy icons to amuse themselves with, the same icons which those two missionaries had brought with them.

"But do missionaries usually go as far as the Rhyn-Sands?"

"Of course they do, but it doesn't make much difference."

"Why not?"

"They don't know how to deal with them. An Asiatic can be converted to the faith by fear, he must be made to tremble with fear, and those missionaries preach to them about a God of love. That spoils everything from the start, for an Asiatic will never respect a meek God who doesn't threaten and they will kill those who preach His gospel."

"What a band of cutthroats!"

"Yes, sir. The same thing happened to a Jew while I was still living with them. One day a Jew appeared from heaven knows where, and he too started preaching his faith. He was a good man, and evidently a great believer in his religion, and he was dressed in such rags that you could see his naked flesh through them. He began preaching his faith with such fervor that I could have listened to him forever. At first I tried to argue with him. I said to him, 'What kind of religion is yours if you have no saints?' But he said, 'We do have saints,' and he began to read from the Talmud all about the kind of saints they had, very interesting it was, and the Talmud, he said, was written by Rabbi Joash ben Levi, who was such a learned man that sinful men could not look at him, for one look at him and they would fall dead and that was why God called him before Him and said, Listen to me, O, Joash ben Levi, it is a good thing to be as learned as you are, but it is neither good nor proper that all my Jews should die because of you, for it wasn't for that that I led them through the desert with Moses and helped them to cross the sea: you must therefore leave your native country and live in a place where no man can see you! So Rabbi ben Levi went and wandered about till he came to the very place where Paradise had been and there he buried himself up to his neck in sand and spent thirteen years in the sand, but every Saturday he would prepare a lamb for himself which was roasted by a fire that descended from heaven. And if a gnat or a fly would alight on his nose to feed on his blood, it was also instantly devoured by a fire from heaven. . . . The Asiatics liked the story about the learned Rabbi very much and they listened a long time to the Jewish preacher, but afterwards they set about finding out where he had buried his money. The Jew called heaven and earth to witness that he had no money, and he asserted that God had sent him to them with his wisdom only, but they did not believe him and, raking out the coals, they put a horse's hide on the burning embers and began to toss him about on it. Again and again they demanded that he tell them where he had hidden his money, and when they saw that he had gone black all over and had stopped screaming, they said, 'Stop, let's bury him up to the neck in sand, perhaps that will make him change his mind.' And so they buried him, but the poor Jew died, buried like that, and for a long time his blackened head remained sticking out of the ground; as the children, however, were rather frightened of it, they cut it off and threw it into an empty well."

"So that's what comes of preaching to them!"

"Yes, it is a very difficult job, but the Jew, you know, did have money after all."

"Did he?"

"Yes. You see, after a time the wolves and jackals began to pull him about and they dragged him out of the sand bit by bit until at last they came to his boots. When they started pulling those to bits, seven silver coins fell out of the soles. They were picked up later."

"Well, and how did you escape from them?"

"I was saved by a miracle."

"Who performed this miracle for you?"

"Talafa."

"And who's Talafa? Is he also a Tartar?"

"No, he belongs to quite a different race, an Indian, and he isn't just any Indian, either, but one of their gods who descended to earth."

In compliance with the entreaties of the passengers, Ivan Severyanych Flyagin told the following story about this new act in the tragicomedy of his life.

9.

About a year had passed since the Tartars had gotten rid of the missionaries and it was winter again, and we drove our horses to new grazing grounds, in a southerly direction, nearer to the Caspian Sea. It was there that one day towards evening two men—if indeed one could call them men—suddenly appeared in our camp. Nobody knew what kind of men they were, or where they came from, or to what tribe they belonged, or what their calling was. They couldn't even make themselves understood properly either in Russian or in Tartar, but spoke one word in our own tongue and another in the Tartar tongue, and to each other they spoke in a lingo of their own which neither the Tartars nor I could understand. Neither of them was old. One of them had black hair and a big beard and he wore a long robe, rather like a Tartar, except that his robe was not of many colors but all red, and on his head he wore a pointed Persian hat; the other one was redheaded and he also wore a long robe, but he seemed to be a tricky customer; he had all sorts of boxes with him, and whenever he found himself alone and nobody was looking, he would immediately take off his robe and remain in a short coat and trousers of the style worn by the Germans employed in the factories in Russia. He would keep on sorting and turning over the articles in his boxes, but what those articles were only the devil and himself knew. It was rumored that they had come from Khiva to buy horses and that they were contemplating going to war against somebody or other in their own country, but who they wanted to go to war against they did not say, and all the time they were inciting the Tartars against the Russians. The redheaded one —so I was told—didn't say much (he wasn't much of a linguist), but every time he pronounced the Russian word for governor, he'd spit: but they brought no money with them, for, being Asiatics themselves, they knew perfectly well that anyone who came to the steppe with money took his life in his hands and that it was a hundred to one that he would not come out of it alive; they were trying to persuade the Tartars to drive their herds of horses to the river Darya and they promised to settle their accounts there. The Tartars were in two minds about it, not knowing whether to accept their offer or not. They thought and they thought, taking their time like people searching for gold in the sand, but it was clear that they were afraid of something.

At first those two tried to persuade the Tartars by saying that, being men of honor, they'd never let them down, but later they changed their tune and tried to scare them.

"You'd better get a move on," they said, "or something terrible will happen to you: for our god Talafa has sent his fire with us and heaven forbid that he should get angry."

The Tartars had never heard of that god and they doubted that he could do anything to them in the steppe in winter, but the man with the black beard who had come from Khiva in a red robe said, "If you're still in doubt, then Talafa will reveal to you the glory of his power even tonight, but I warn you," he said, "don't run out of your tents whatever you may see or hear, or he'll burn you to ashes." Now all that sounded very exciting to us, for we were badly in need of some distraction from the monotony of our life in the steppe in winter, and while we were also a little afraid of the terrible things that might happen, we were no less pleased by the opportunity of finding out what that Indian god could really do: how and by what kind of a miracle he would reveal himself.

We went to our tents early with our wives and children and waited. . . . Everything was quiet and dark as on any other night, but no sooner had I fallen asleep than I suddenly heard a high wind rising with a hiss in the steppe and then something exploding with a bang and through my sleep it seemed to me as if sparks were falling from the skies.

I roused myself and I saw that my wives were all in a flutter and the children began to howl.

I said:

"Hush! Shut up, the lot of you! Nurse them and don't let me hear a sound from them! "

So the little ones sucked away and everything became quiet again, but presently a ball of fire went up with a hiss in the dark steppe . . . and again there was a bang. . . .

"Well," I thought, "it seems Talafa means business! "

A little later he began to hiss again, though in a different manner, and he flew upwards like a fiery bird with a tail, which was also fiery, and the fire was such an unusual one, red as blood, and when it burst everything turned yellow and then blue.

Everything in the camp, I noticed, had grown as still as a grave. For anybody not to have heard that racket was, of course, impossible, but all of them, I could only suppose, must have been terrified and were lying huddled up under their sheepskins. All one could hear now was how the ground would suddenly tremble and shake and then everything would be quiet again. That, I surmised, must have been the horses shying and crowding together in a panic. Then I heard those Khiva men or Indians rush somewhere and again a fire swept over the steppe like a dragon. . . . The horses just gave one terrified neigh and bolted, whereupon the Tartars forgot their terror, scampered out of their tents, jerking their heads about and bellowing, "Allah! Allah!" and away they went in pursuit of the horses. As for the men of Khiva, they just disappeared, vanished without a trace, leaving one of their boxes behind as a memento. . . . So, as all our able-bodied men had gone after the herd and left only the women and old men in the camp, I went to have a look at the box: what, I wondered, did they have in it? I began to investigate and I found that it contained different kinds of earths and medicines and paper tubes. I was examining one of those tubes at the campfire and, as I brought it a little too close to the fire, it suddenly exploded, nearly burning my eyes, and up it went into the sky and there— bang!—burst into a shower of stars. . . . "Oho," I thought to myself, "so it isn't a god after all, but only the common garden variety of fireworks which we used to let off in our public parks!" So I let off another and, lo and behold, the Tartars, the old men who had stayed behind, all fell down on their faces and lay flat on the ground, every man where he fell, wriggling like eels. . . . At first I almost got frightened myself, but when I saw them writhing on the ground I felt quite differently inclined and, for the first time since my captivity, I ground my teeth and began roaring a string of meaningless words at them:

"Parlez-bien-comme-ça-chirez-mir-verfluchtur-min-adieu-m'sieu!"

And I let off another firework, a Catherine wheel this time. . . . Now when they saw the Catherine wheel scouring along and leaving a fiery trail behind, they all seemed to give up the ghost. . . . The fire went out, but they continued to lie on the ground, and then one of them raised his head a little, but immediately bobbed down again, and kept on beckoning to me with a finger, indicating that he wished to talk to me. I went up to him and said:

"You damned scoundrel, which do you prefer—life or death?" for I saw that they were mortally afraid of me.

"Have mercy on me, Ivan," he said, "don't kill me! Please, let me live! "

And from all over the place they started beckoning to me in the same way and all implored me to forgive them and spare their lives.

I could see that my affairs had taken a favorable turn at last: I must have atoned for all my sins by my sufferings, so I prayed:

"Holy Mother of God and you, St. Nicholas, take pity on me, oh, my adored ones, stretch out a helping hand to me, oh, my benefactors! "

And, turning to the Tartars, I asked them in a stern voice:

"What do you want me to forgive you for and why do you ask me to spare your lives?"

"We want you to forgive us," they said, "for not believing in your God."

"Aha," thought I, "so that's how scared you are of me now!" and I said, "Oh, no, my dear people, this time you won't get off so easily: I shall never forgive you for your hostility to the true faith!" and I ground my teeth again and set off another firework.

This time it was a rocket: there was a terrific explosion and a huge flame.

Then I yelled at the Tartars:

"I give you one more minute to make up your minds: if you still refuse to believe in my God, I shall destroy the whole lot of you! "

"Don't destroy us, please," they replied. "We all agree to submit ourselves to your God."

So I stopped setting off more fireworks and baptized them in a nearby brook.

"Do you mean you baptized them there and then?"

"Yes, sir, on the spot! You see, I didn't want to waste much time, for I was afraid they might change their minds. I sprinkled their heads with water over a hole in the ice; said, In the name of the Father and the Son; put round their necks the crosses left by the missionaries; told them to honor the murdered missionary as a martyr and pray for him; and I showed them his grave."

"And did they pray?"

"They did."

"But they did not know any Christian prayers, did they? Did you teach them some?"

"No, I had no time to teach them any prayers, for I saw that now was my chance to escape. All I did was to tell them: 'Carry on as before, say your old prayers, but don't you dare to call upon Allah in future, but address yourselves only to Jesus Christ!' And it was this profession of faith that they accepted."

"But how did you afterwards manage to run away from those newly converted Christians in spite of your crippled feet, and how did you cure yourself?"

"Afterwards I found in that box with the fireworks a kind of corrosive earth: as soon as you applied it to your body, it would begin to burn you terribly. I applied it to my heels and pretended to be ill, and while lying under the rug, I kept on applying it to my heels and during the next two weeks I had applied it with such good effect that the flesh on my feet was covered with festering sores and the bristles which the Tartars had put there ten years ago were carried away with the pus. I got well as speedily as I possibly could, but I didn't tell anybody about it but pretended to be feeling worse and told the women and the old men to pray as hard as they could for me, for, I said, I was dying. In addition, I imposed a fast upon them as a kind of penance and ordered them not to leave their tents for three days and, to make doubly sure, I let off one of the biggest fireworks in the box and went away. . . ."

"And they didn't catch you?"

"No, they couldn't very well catch me, for I had so scared them and so weakened them by the fast that I imagine they were only too glad not to put their noses out of their tents for three days and when they did go out afterwards I was gone too far for them to overtake me. My feet, after I had got rid of the bristles, healed up completely and they were so light that, having started to run, I ran and ran till I had run from one end of the steppe to the other."

"And all on foot?"

"Naturally! How else? There are no roads there and you don't meet anyone on the way and if you do happen to meet someone, you aren't always pleased with the companion you have acquired. On the fourth day of my journey I came across a Chuvash tribesman who was driving five horses. He said to me, 'Get on one of my horses!' But I thought it over carefully in my mind and decided that it would be much safer not to."

I wasn't afraid of anything in particular. . . . He just didn't look trustworthy to me, and, besides, I couldn't find out what his religion was, and unless you know that, it isn't safe in the steppe. He kept on shouting like a fool:

"Get on," he shouted, "it'll be merrier to ride along together!"

But I said:

"Who are you? Have you a god or not?"

"Of course I have," he said. "The Tartar has no god, he eats horseflesh, but I have a god."

"Who's your god?" I asked.

"Why," he replied, "everything is a god to me. The sun's my god and the moon's my god and the stars are my god . . . everything's my god. What do you mean: have I got a god?"

"Everything? Hmmm . . . Everything you say? And what about Jesus Christ," I said, "isn't He your god?"

"Why, yes," he said. "He, too, is my god and the Holy Virgin is my god and Nicholas is my god. . . ."

"Which Nicholas?" I asked him.

"Why," he said, "the one who lives in summer and the one who lives in winter!"

I could not help congratulating him upon his respect for the Russian saint, Nicholas the Miracle-Worker.

"Honor him always," I said, "because he is a Russian," and I was about to declare myself completely satisfied with his religion and to accept his invitation to go along with him, but, luckily, he went on talking and revealed himself in his true colors.

"Indeed," he said, "I honor Nicholas. I may not kneel to him in summer, but in winter I always give him a twenty-copeck piece to keep an eye on my cows. Not that I put my entire trust in him alone! No, sir! I also offer up a bullock to Keremetee."

I just couldn't help getting angry at that.

"How dare you not put your trust in St. Nicholas the Miracle-Worker and give him, a Russian, only a twenty-copeck piece, while you give a whole bullock to that heathen goddess of yours, the thrice-accursed Keremetee! On your way," I said, "I won't go with a man who shows so little respect for St. Nicholas the Miracle-Worker!"

And I didn't go with him; I took to my heels and, before I knew it, towards the evening of the third day after my meeting with the Chuvash, I saw water in the distance and some people. I hid myself in the long grass as a precaution and looked out to see what kind of people they were, for I was afraid of falling into worse captivity, but I saw that they were cooking a meal: They must be Christians, I thought to myself, and I crawled a little nearer and then I saw that they were crossing themselves and drinking vodka, and that settled it: they were Russians all right! So I jumped out of the grass and I revealed myself. I discovered that they were fishermen: they were casting nets into the river. They gave me a great welcome, as behooved fellow countrymen of mine, and said:

"Have a drink of vodka!"

I replied:

"Thank you, dear friends, but I've spent many years with the Tartars and I've quite lost my taste for it!"

"No matter," they replied, "you're among your own folk now, your own nation, and you'll soon get used to it again. Come on, have a drink!"

I poured myself out a glass, thinking, "Now then, praise the Lord for your safe return!" and drank it, but the fishermen—what splendid fellows they were!—insisted on my having another glass.

"Have another drink," they said; "see how weak you've grown without it."

I permitted myself another glass and I became very talkative and told them everything. I went on talking to them throughout the night, sitting at the campfire drinking vodka and feeling so happy because I was in Holy Russia again, but towards morning, when the campfire began to go out and almost all who had been listening to me were asleep, one of them, a member of the team of fishermen, said to me:

"But have you got a passport?"

I said:

"No, I haven't."

"If," he said, "a passport you can't show, it's to jail you're sure to go."

"If that's so," I said, "I shan't leave you. I daresay one can live with you without a passport, can't one?"

And he repled:

"To be sure, you can live with us without a passport, but you can't die without one."

I said:

"Why's that?"

"That," he said, "is very simple, for how can you expect the priest to register your death if you have no passport?"

"What will happen to me in that case?" I asked.

"Oh," he said, "we'll throw you into the river to feed the fish."

"Without a priest?"

"Without a priest."

Being a little tipsy, I got terribly frightened of that and I began to weep and bewail my fate, but the fisherman laughed:

"I was only pulling your leg," he said. "Don't be afraid to die: we shall bury you in good old mother earth."

But I was very cross with him and I said:

"Some joke! If you go on cracking jokes like that I won't live to see another spring!"

No sooner had the last fisherman fallen asleep than I got up quickly and made off and I came to Astrakhan, where I earned a rouble as a day laborer and immediately took to drink and drank so heartily that I couldn't remember how I got to another town, where I found myself in jail, and from there they sent me under police guard to my own part of the country. They brought me to our town, gave me a good flogging at the police station, and sent me to our estate. Her ladyship the countess who had ordered me to be flogged for the cat's tail had died, and the count alone remained, but he had grown very old and had become a devout churchman and given up hunting altogether. When my arrival was announced to him, his lordship remembered me and he ordered that I should be flogged again at home and that I should then go to Father Ilya for confession. Well, they gave me a good, old-fashioned sort of flogging at the records office and I went to Father Ilya and he started to hear my confession and, having heard it, refused to grant me absolution for the next three years. . . .

I said to him:

"Oh, dear," I said, "what am I to do now, Father? I haven't partaken of the sacrament for so many years and . . . I had thought that . . . having waited so long . . ."

"That you've waited so long," he said, "is neither here nor there. You'd better tell me," he said, "why you've kept so many Tartar women as wives? You must understand," he said, "that I'm really doing you a great favor in refusing you the sacrament, for if you were to be dealt with properly according to the rules laid down by the Holy Fathers of the Church, you should have been set on fire alive and your clothes burnt off you, but," he said, "you needn't be afraid of that because that is no longer permitted by our penal code."

"Well," I said to myself, "as I can't do anything about it, I'll have to do without the sacrament, stay at home a little, and have a rest after my captivity." But his lordship wouldn't allow that. His lordship was so good as to say:

"I cannot allow a man who has been refused absolution by the Church to live near me."

So he ordered the manager to give me another thrashing, this time in public as an example to the world at large, and then let me go a free man provided I paid a certain sum each year as a tax. And so it was done: they administered another flogging to me, but in quite a new way, on the top of the steps in front of the office and in the presence of all his lordship's servants, and they gave me a passport. I felt very happy to be a free man at last after so many years and to be in possession of a legal paper, and so I went away. I had no definite plans for my future, but the Lord soon provided me with a job.

"What sort of job?"

"In my old line again: horses. I started from the bottom, without a penny, but very soon I found a very good job and I could have done still better for myself were it not for one thing."

"And may we ask what that thing was?"

"I became greatly possessed with evil spirits and evil passions and with one more unseemly thing."

"What was that?"

"Magnetism, gentlemen."

"Wha-at? Magnetism?"

"Yes, gentlemen. The magnetic influence of one person."

"How did that influence manifest itself over you?"

"A stranger's will had the whip hand over me and I was made the stalking-horse of another man's destiny."

"So it was there that your *own* doom overtook you, after which you realized that you had to fulfill your mother's promise and you entered a monastery?"

"Oh, no, all that came later. Before that many other adventures befell me; before, that is, I was granted perfect understanding."

"You wouldn't mind telling us your adventures, would you?"

"Why, not at all, gentlemen! With great pleasure!"

"Please do."

10.

Taking my passport, I went off without any definite plans for my future, and I came to a fair and there I saw a gypsy exchanging a horse with a Russian peasant and deceiving him disgracefully. He began to show off his horse's strength and he harnessed it to a cart loaded with oats, while the peasant's horse was sweating because it was overcome by the smell of apples, for there is nothing more disagreeable to a horse than that smell; besides, I also saw that the gypsy's horse was subject to fits, for it had a certain mark on its forehead showing that it had been branded with fire, but the gypsy said it was a mole. Well, of course I was sorry for the peasant because he would not be able to do his farm work with a horse suffering from fainting fits, for it might collapse and that would be the end of it. And, besides, I developed a great hatred for gypsies at that time, seeing that it was a gypsy who first gave me a taste for the life of a tramp, and I must, I suppose, have also had a premonition of something else which indeed came to pass. So I revealed the fraud about that horse to the peasant, and when the gypsy started arguing with me, insisting that the mark on the horse's head was not due to branding but was a mole, I, to prove my point, prodded the horse in the kidney with an awl and it immediately fell to the ground in one of its convulsive fits. So I went and chose a good horse for the peasant, in accordance with the knowledge of such things that I had acquired, and they treated me to vodka and to a fine spread and they also gave me money, twenty copecks in silver coins, and we all had a good time. That, gentlemen, was the beginning of it: my capital began to grow and so did my addiction to drink, and barely a month had passed when I realized that I was making good; I hung all sorts of metal plates over myself as well as the various appurtenances of a horse doctor, and I went tramping from one horse fair to another, giving the word to poor and ignorant people everywhere, making a reputation for myself and being only too glad to allow my clients to stand me to drinks, as is the custom at horse fairs; in the meantime I became an absolute anathema to all the gypsies who were eager to defraud, beguile, and cheat the people into buying horses, and I had been tipped off that they were plotting to give me a beating. I began to avoid them, for I was one and they were many, and since they could never find me alone they couldn't beat me up, because they didn't dare do so in the presence of the peasants, who always stood up for me, being highly appreciative of my virtues. Instead, the gypsies spread an evil rumor about to the effect that I was a sorcerer and was such a good judge of horse-flesh only because I was assisted by the devil; but of course all that did not matter in the least since, as I have already told you, gentle-men, I have a way with a horse, having been gifted by nature in that respect, and I was always ready to share my secret with any man, except that it would not have been of any use to him what-soever.

"Why wouldn't it have been of any use?"

"Because nobody could grasp it, since for that sort of thing one must be gifted by nature, and there were many cases where I revealed my secret and all in vain—but with your permission, gentlemen, I shall tell you about that later."

Well (the novice went on), when my fame had spread far and wide through all the fairs in the land and I had become known as a man who could see right through a horse, one purchaser of horses for the army—a prince—came and offered me a hundred roubles.

"Tell me your secret, my dear fellow," he said, "your secret about understanding the way of a horse, for such a secret is worth a lot of money to me."

And I replied:

"I have no secret, my lord. It is just a natural gift."

But he wouldn't leave me alone.

"Tell me," he said, "how you go about it, and so that you don't think that I want to get your knowledge from you for nothing, here's a hundred roubles for you."

What was I to do? I shrugged my shoulders, tied the money up in a rag, and said:

"I'll tell you all I know with pleasure, but you, sir, would do well to give me all your attention and apply your mind to what I'm going to tell you, for I must warn you that if, having learned all I can teach you, you still derive no profit whatever from it, I, for one, shall not hold myself responsible for it."

However, he was satisfied with that, saying:

"It isn't your fault if I'm slow to learn. All I ask is for you to tell me all you know."

"The very first thing," I said, "a man must bear in mind if he really wants to know what sort of a horse he's buying is what is the best way of examining a horse and, above all, he must never shirk such an examination. The first thing to do is to look at its head, and not just anyhow, but with understanding; the next thing is to cast a quick glance all over the horse, from head to tail, and one must never paw the horse as army officers usually do. An army officer as a rule begins his examination of a horse by touching its crest, its forelock, its muzzle, its windpipe, its chest, and, indeed anything else, but all to no purpose. That's why a horse dealer is so fond of cavalry officers: it is their habit of running their fingers all over the horse that pleases him. As soon as a horse dealer notices this kind of pawing by military men, he starts to turn the horse around, keeping it constantly on the move, but you can be sure that if there's any blemish he doesn't want to show, he won't reveal it for anything in the world, and it is in the part he conceals that the fraud lies, and there is no end to such frauds. Say, if a horse is lop-eared, they'll cut an inch of hide out of its neck, pull it together, sew it up, and smear it over, and that's why the horse keeps its ears straight, but not for long, for the skin will soon stretch and its ears will hang down again. Or, if a horse's ears are too long, they'll cut them and to make them stand upright they'll insert bits of horn into them. Should a man be anxious to purchase a well-matched pair of horses, and supposing only one of the horses has a star on its forehead, the dealers will do their best to provide the other one with a similar star: they'll rub the hair with pumice stone, or apply a hot baked turnip where necessary to make white hair grow, and it does grow, but anybody who takes the pains to examine such hair closely will find that it is always longer than the natural hair and that it curls like a beard. The dealers deceive the public even more shamefully about a horse's eyes: one horse may have little cavities above its eyes which spoil its looks, but the dealer will prick the skin with a pin, apply his lips to the place, and blow for all he's worth, and to such good effect that the skin will lift up and the eye will immediately look fresh and beautiful. This can be done easily, for a horse enjoys the sensation of warmth such breathing gives it and it will stand stock-still, but the air is bound to escape sooner or later and the horse will again have cavities over its eyes. There's only one way of detecting such a fraud: feel near the bone to see whether there's any air under the skin! But even funnier is the way horse dealers sell blind horses: it's a real treat, that is. The cavalry officer waves a straw in front of the horse's eyes to find out if the horse can see it, but what he himself doesn't see is that when the horse might be expected to shake its head the dealer gives it a prod with his fist under the belly or in its side; and even if he strokes it gently, he has a nail hidden in his glove and only pretends to stroke it, but in reality pricks it."

I told the prince ten times as much as I have told you here, but for all the good it did him I might as well have saved my breath. Next day when I saw him again he had bought some horses I should have been ashamed to be seen with: one jade worse than the other, and he actually called me to come and admire them, saying:

"Well, my dear fellow, aren't I clever to have learned to know a good horse so quickly!"

I just glanced at them and laughed, and replied that there was nothing, so to speak, to look at.

"That one's shoulders," I said, "are too meaty, she'll be constantly tripping over; and that one is too low in girth—touches her belly with her hoof and within a year, if not sooner, she's sure to get a rupture—and that one stamps her foreleg when eating her oats and knocks her knee against the stall," and in this way I found fault with his entire purchase and I was right about everything and it all turned out exactly as I had said it would.

So next day the prince said to me:

"No, Ivan, I can see that I shall never be able to acquire your gift. What about taking a job with me as my 'connoisseur' and choosing the horses yourself and I'll pay you for it?"

I agreed, and for the next three years I lived in peace and contentment, not as a servant or as a hired laborer, but rather as a friend and assistant, and but for my drinking bouts during my days off, I could have saved up a tidy bit, for it is the custom among the army horse buyers that every time a horse breeder arrives on a business visit, he himself goes to spend his time with the army buyer while sending a trustworthy man to get the "connoisseur" on his side by hook or by crook, for the horse breeders know very well that everything depends not on the horse buyer, but on the "connoisseur," if, that is, the horse buyer employs the right man for that job. And being, as I have told you, a born "connoisseur," I performed my duties in the most exemplary way, being deeply conscious of the debt I owed to nature in this respect: I was incapable of deceiving the man I served and the prince knew that I wouldn't deceive him for anything in the world and respected me highly, and indeed we treated each other with the utmost frankness. Sometimes, if he happened to have lost a lot of money at cards the night before, he would come to see me in the stables as soon as he got up in the morning, in the short Oriental coat which he wore instead of a dressing gown, and he'd say:

"Well, my demi-semi-honorable Ivan Severyanych, how are you this morning? Are your affairs prospering?"

He always used to joke like that, calling me his *demi-semi-honorable,* but he respected me highly, as you will see.

I knew very well what it meant if he addressed me in that jocular vein and I'd answer:

"I'm very well, thank you, sir. My affairs, too, thank God, are in excellent order. How are your lordship's affairs?"

"My affairs," he'd reply, "are so bad that I don't think they could be worse."

"Why, what's the matter, sir? Did you lose a fortune last night as usual?"

"You've hit the nail on the head, my demi-semi-honorable sir. I've lost a fortune all right."

"And how much money has your lordship been relieved of?" I'd ask.

He would tell me at once how many thousands he had lost and I'd shake my head and say:

"All you want now, my lord, is a good hiding. What a pity there isn't anyone to give it to you!"

He'd laugh and say:

"That's the trouble, my dear sir. I wish there were!"

"Well," I'd say, "that can be easily remedied, my lord. Just lie down on my bed and I'll put a clean, rolled-up straw mat under your lordship's head and give you a good beating."

Well, so he'd naturally try to make up to me, doing his best to persuade me to lend him some money to try his luck again.

"No, sir," he'd say, "don't flog me, just let me have a little of what's left over from your expenses: my luck's sure to change tonight and I'll clean out the whole lot!"

"No, thank you, my lord," I'd say. "Try your luck by all means, but don't expect it to change."

"What are you thanking me for?" he'd begin with a laugh, and end up by getting really angry. "Don't forget yourself, please," he'd say. "Stop pretending to be my guardian and give me the money!"

We asked Ivan Severyanych if he had ever given any money to his prince to try his luck at cards again.

"Never," he replied. "I'd either tell him a lie, saying that I had spent all the money on oats, or just run away from the house."

"But wasn't he angry with you for letting him down?"

"Yes, he was angry all right. He'd say to me without any further beating about the bush: 'You're fired! You're no longer in my employment, my demi-semi-honorable one!'

"I'd reply, 'Very well, my lord. May I have my passport?'

" 'All right,' he'd say. 'Collect your things, will you? I'll give you your passport tomorrow.'

"But tomorrow he'd forget all about it and we'd never mention the subject again; for barely an hour later he'd come to me in quite a different frame of mind and say:

" 'Thank you, my exceedingly insignificant sir, for being so firm with me and refusing to give me any money to try my luck at cards again.'

"And so well disposed was he to me afterwards that if anything happened to me on my days off he, too, would treat me like a brother."

"And what happened to you?"

"Well, I told you that I used to take days off."

"And what do you mean by *days off?*"

"I used to go out to have a good time. Having acquired a taste for vodka, I didn't drink it every day, nor did I ever drink it in moderation, but if something happened to distress me, I'd get a terrible thirst and I'd immediately take a few days off and disappear. And such moods came upon me without any reason at all; for instance, when we used to send away our horses—and they were not exactly my own flesh and blood, were they?—I'd start drinking, especially if I'd parted from a horse that was very beautiful, for I just couldn't get him out of my head and he'd always be there before my eyes, so much so that I'd try to escape from him as from some ghostly apparition, and I'd take some days off."

"You mean you'd get drunk?"

"Yes, I'd leave the house and start drinking."

"For how long?"

"Well, that depended on the kind of day off it was: sometimes I'd go on drinking till I had spent all the money I had on me and either someone would knock me around or I'd beat someone up myself; another time it wouldn't last so long—I'd spend a night at a police station or have a good sleep in a ditch and everything would be all right again and it would pass off. In such cases I'd stick to a certain rule and whenever I got restless and felt that I had to take a day off, I'd come to the prince and say, 'I'm feeling restless, sir, please take care of my money and I'll make myself scarce.' He wouldn't even try to dissuade me, but just took the money or asked me, 'Does your honor expect to be away long?' And I'd go and he would be left to look after things at home and he would wait patiently for me until my 'day off' came to an end, and everything would turn out all right; but I was beginning to feel deeply disgusted with this weakness of mine and I made up my mind to get rid of it; it was then that I took such a last day off that the memory of it makes my hair stand on end even now."

11.

Needless to say, we did our best to persuade Ivan Severyanych to put the finishing touch to his kindness by giving us a full account of this latest unhappy episode of his life, and he, out of the goodness of his heart, did not refuse our request, and told us the following story about his last day off:

We had a mare by the name of Dido which we had bought from a stud farm, a young, golden bay mare, destined for an officer's saddle. She was a dream of a horse: a lovely head, comely eyes, delicate flaring nostrils that breathed effortlessly, a light mane, a chest set easily between the shoulders like a sailing ship, and her back was slender, her pasterns white, and her feet so light that when she began to fling them about it looked as if she were playing with them. In a word, no lover of horses who had been endowed with an eye for beauty could take his eyes off such an animal and would certainly not easily forget it. I took so great a liking to her that I wouldn't leave the stables while she was there and would stay on caressing her for the sheer joy of it. Sometimes I'd groom her myself and rub her down with a white cloth so that there wasn't a speck of dust left on her coat, and I'd even kiss her on the forehead, on that sweet little curl of hers where her golden coat parted. At that time there were two fairs on at one and the same time, one at L. and the other at K., and the prince and I had parted company—I going to one fair while he was doing business at the other. Suddenly I received a letter from him in which he asked me to send him such and such horses, including Dido. I did not know what he wanted my beauty for, the lovely mare to which I had taken such a fancy. But I naturally surmised that he must have exchanged my favorite for another horse, or sold her, or more likely lost her at a game of cards. . . . So I sent Dido off with some stablemen and, being consumed with a terrible longing for her, a great desire came over me to take a day off.

But my position at the time was rather a peculiar one: as I told you, I had made it a rule that whenever I became obsessed with a desire to take a day off I'd go to the prince, hand him the large sum of money which I always had on me, and say, I'm going to disappear for so-and-so many days, but how was I to arrange things now that the prince was away? So I said to myself, No, sir, this time you're jolly well going to abstain from drink because your prince is away and you can't possibly have your day off as you used to, for you have no one to leave the money with, and you have a considerable sum of money on you, over five thousand. Well, having made up my mind that it just couldn't be done, I stuck to my guns and did not give in to my craving to go out on the town and have a fling. But all the same I could feel no weakening of my desire, which, on the contrary, seemed to grow more and more powerful. At last I could think of nothing else but how to arrange things in such a way that I could both satisfy my passion for drink and assure the safety of the prince's money. With that end in view I began to hide the money, and I hid it in the most unlikely places, where no man would ever dream of putting any money. . . . I thought to myself, What can I do? It is pretty clear that I shan't be able to master my desire, so I must at least—so I thought—put the money away in a safe place where nothing could happen to it, and then I'll give in to my craving and take a day off. But I was greatly perplexed: where could I hide the confounded money? For wherever I put it, the thought would occur to me before I had gone a few steps from the hiding place that someone was sure to steal it. I'd go back, take it out quickly, and again hide it somewhere else. . . . I got sick and tired of hiding it in the haylofts, in the cellars, under the eaves, and in every imaginable unlikely hiding place, for as soon as I went away I'd fancy that someone had seen me hiding it and I'd go back again and once more I'd get it out and carry it about on my person, thinking to myself, No, it just can't be done, it isn't my fate to satisfy my desire this time. Then suddenly a divinely inspired idea occurred to me: Why, I said to myself, who else but the Devil would be tormenting me with such desires, and if so, why not get rid of the scoundrel by throwing myself upon the mercy of the Lord? So I went to early Mass, said my prayers, made sure of my deliverance, and, as I was going out of the church, I saw on the wall a painting of the Last Judgment and on it angels were chastising the Devil in hell with chains. I stopped to have a good look at it, prayed even more fervently to the Holy Angels, and as for the Devil, I just spat at him and, thrusting my fist under his snout, said, "Here's a fig for you, take it and buy yourself anything you like with it!" After that I no longer felt troubled and, having seen to everything at home, went to an inn and ordered tea. . . .

At the inn I noticed standing among the company a sort of tramp, an absolutely contemptible specimen of a man. I had seen him before and I thought of him as just a charlatan or a buffoon, for you could always see him knocking about at fairs, where he annoyed the gentlemen by asking them for help in French. He seemed to belong to the gentry himself and was said to have served as an officer in the army but to have squandered all his money at cards, and he now lived by begging. . . . Here, at the inn where I had come to have my tea, the waiters were trying to throw him out, but he refused to go, and just stood there and said:

"Don't you know who I am? I am not a nobody like you! I used to own serfs myself and I used to flog fellows like you in the stables just for my amusement. It is true I lost my fortune, but it was God's will that I should and I still bear a special mark of His wrath and that's why nobody dares to touch me."

The waiters did not believe him and they laughed at him, but he went on to tell them of the fine style in which he used to live, the fine carriages he used to drive about in, and the way he used to throw the civilian gentlemen out of the public park and how he had once stripped stark naked and paid a visit to the governor's wife, "and now," he said, "I've been cursed for my presumption and my entire nature has been turned to stone and I have to keep on softening it with drink, so come on, give me some vodka! I can't pay for it because I have no money, but I'd be quite willing to eat the glass after I've drunk it."

So one of the gentlemen ordered a glass of vodka to be given to him, for he wanted to see how he would eat the glass. He at once emptied the glass in one gulp and did as he promised and began to crunch the glass with his teeth—fair and square—and ate it in front of everybody, and all the people were amazed at this and burst out laughing. But I was sorry for him, for I thought: here was a well-born man and yet so addicted was he to drink that he didn't mind sacrificing his bowels for a glass of vodka. So I made up my mind at least to let him wash down the broken glass with another drink and I ordered a second glass to be given him at my expense, but I did not insist on his eating the glass. I said, "Don't! Don't eat it!" He was deeply touched by that and gave me his hand.

"I suppose," he said, "you were originally a gentleman's servant."

"I was," I said.

"I could see at once," he said, "that you were not one of those swine. *Grand merci*," he said, "for that."

I said:

"Don't mention it, go in peace!"

"No," said he. "I'm very happy to have a chat with you. Move over a little and I'll sit down beside you."

"All right," I said, "sit down beside me by all means."

So he sat down beside me and began to tell me what a noble family he had sprung from and what a fine education he had had, and again he said:

"What are you drinking? Tea?"

"Yes," I said, "tea. Won't you have some with me?"

"Thank you," he said, "but I'm afraid I can't drink any tea."

"Why not?"

"Because," he said, "my head isn't made for tea, my head's made for desperate things. I'd rather you told them to give me another glass of vodka!"

And in this way he made me treat him to one, then two and three glasses of vodka and I was beginning to get tired of standing him to drinks. But what I disliked most about him was that he told so many lies, showing off all the time and boasting about what an important person he was, and suddenly abasing himself and crying, and all for nothing.

"Do you realize," he said, "what kind of a man I am? Why,"

said he, "I was created by God in the same year as the Emperor and I'm of the same age as he."

"Well, what about it?" I asked.

"What about it? Do you think it's fair that I should have come down in the world as I did in spite of that? Yes, sir, in spite of all that," he said, "I am a man of no consequence and I've turned out to be a nonentity and, as you saw just now, am despised by everybody." And, having said that, he called for more vodka, but this time he asked for a whole decanter of it, and went on to tell me a long story about how the merchants made fun of him in the taverns, and finally he said:

"They're an uneducated lot. They think it's an easy job to go on drinking and eating the glass as a kind of *hors d'œuvre*. But it's a very hard profession, my dear fellow, and I'm quite sure many people wouldn't be able to carry on with it at all. But I've trained myself for it because I realize that a man has to go through everything, and I'm carrying on."

"But why," I argued, "are you so devoted to this habit of yours? Why not give it up?"

"Give it up?" he exclaimed. "Oh, no, my dear fellow, I just can't give it up!"

"Why not?" I said.

"I can't give it up for two reasons," he replied. "In the first place because without drinking I should never go to bed but would go on wandering about the streets, and secondly and principally because my Christian sentiments do not permit me to do so."

"What are you talking about?" I said. "I can well believe that you wouldn't go to bed, for you'd be roaming about the town in search of a drink, but that your Christian sentiments won't allow you to drop such wickedness, that I cannot possibly believe."

"I see," he replied. "So you can't believe it, can't you? Well, everybody else says the same thing. . . . But have you thought what would happen if I ever dropped that drinking habit of mine? Why, somebody else would be sure to pick it up! Now tell me honestly, do you think he'd thank me for it or not?"

"God forbid!" I said. "I certainly don't think so."

"Well, then," he said, "so you see how it is, don't you? And since it's necessary that I should suffer, then you ought to honor me for that at any rate and tell them to bring me another decanter of vodka!"

I banged the table for another decanter and I sat and listened to him, for to tell the truth I found his talk very entertaining, and he went on:

"It is right that I should endure this cross and that it shouldn't fall upon anyone else's shoulders, for," said he, "I am a man of good family and I have received such an excellent education that I could say my prayers in French when I was a little boy, but I was very unkind and I inflicted all sorts of tortures on people, lost my serfs at cards, separated mothers from their children, married a rich woman and made life so unbearable for her that she soon died, and finally, being myself the cause of all my troubles, I even blamed God for having given me such a nature. And that's why he has punished me and given me a different nature, so that I haven't got a vestige of pride left in me: spit in my eyes or slap my face and I don't mind so long as I can get drunk and forget all about myself."

"And now," I said, "don't you ever blame Him for giving you such a character?"

"I do not," he replied, "for although it is worse, yet it is better."

"What do you mean?" I asked. "I don't know what you're talking about—it's worse, yet it's better!"

"That's quite simple," he replied. "For, you see, now I only know one thing and that is that I'm destroying myself, but at least I can no longer destroy others, for everybody turns away from me. I am now," said he, "like unto Job smitten with sore boils and therein," he said, "lies my happiness and my salvation," and with these words he drank up the last glass of vodka and asked for another decanter, saying:

"And you, my dear friend, remember: never scorn any man, for nobody can tell why a man is tormented by any desire, nor why he suffers. We, the possessed, suffer these things so that it shall be easier for the rest. And if you yourself be afflicted by some desire, do not wilfully abandon it lest another man pick it up and be tormented, but rather look for a man who would be willing to take upon himself this wickedness of yours."

"But where can I find such a man?" I asked. "No man will ever agree to do such a thing."

"Do you really think so?" he replied. "Why, you needn't go far to find such a man, for such a man is now before you. I am that man!"

I said:

"Are you joking?"

But he suddenly jumped to his feet and said:

"No, I am not joking, but if you don't believe me, you can test me!"

"But how am I to test you?" I asked.

"That's easy," he said. "Do you want to know what kind of gift I possess? For, my dear fellow, I possess a great gift. As you see, I am drunk now. . . . Am I or am I not drunk?"

I looked at him and I could see that his face was purple and that he was quite fuddled and that he was swaying on his legs, and I said:

"Yes, of course you're drunk."

But he replied:

"Now turn away for a minute to that icon and say the Lord's Prayer to yourself."

I turned away for a minute towards the icon and had just had time to say the Lord's Prayer to myself when that down-at-the-heel gentleman again commanded me:

"Well, have a good look at me now: am I drunk or not?"

I turned round and, indeed, he looked as sober as a judge and there he stood, smiling.

I said:

"What does it mean? What kind of magic is that?"

And he replied:

"That is no magic, but is called magnetism."

"What's that?" I asked.

"It is a kind of will which is given to a man," he said, "and it can neither be lost by drinking nor in sleep, for it is a gift. I have demonstrated it to you," he said, "so that you should understand that if I wanted to I could stop drinking straight away and never taste another drop of liquor in my life, but I don't want any man to start drinking instead of me while I, having mended my ways, should again forget God. But I'm ready and willing to release any man from his desire for drink in one minute!"

"Do me a favor," I said, "and do this for me!"

"But do you drink?" he asked.

"I do indeed," I said, "and there are times when I drink like a fish."

"Well," said he, "do not be downhearted. It is in my power to do it and I shall do it gladly, for I want to repay you for treating me tonight. Yes, I shall release you from your addiction to drink, my dear fellow, and I shall take it upon myself."

"Do me the favor, sir. Please, I pray you, set me free!"

"With pleasure, my dear fellow," he said, "with pleasure," and having said that, he shouted for more vodka and for two glasses.

I said:

"What do you want two glasses for?"

"One," he said, "is for me and the other—for you."

"But I'm not going to drink," I said.

"Whisht! Silence! Not a word! Who are you, tell me? A patient?"

"All right," I said, "have it your own way. I am a patient."

"And I," said he, "am a doctor and you have to carry out my orders and take your medicine," and with that he poured me out a glass and himself a glass and started to wave his hands over my glass like some kind of precentor.

He waved and waved and then ordered:

"Drink!"

I had my misgivings at first but, to be quite frank, I badly wanted a drink of vodka myself and, as he had ordered me to drink, I said to myself, Let's drink it just to see what happens, and I drank.

"Well," said he, "did you like it? Did it taste good or was it bitter?"

"I'm hanged if I know," I said.

"That," he said, "means that you haven't had enough," and he poured me out another glass and again started waving his arms about. He waved and he waved and then, with a final shake, he again made me drink this, the second glass, and again he questioned me: "How was that?"

I pulled his leg. I said:

"This one seemed a bit heavy."

He nodded and at once started waving over the third glass and again commanded, "Drink!" So I drank and said:

"This one was lighter," and thereupon I myself got hold of the decanter and began treating him and pouring one out for myself, and so we went on drinking. He did not try to stop me, but he wouldn't permit me to have a single glass before he'd waved over it, and as soon as I'd get hold of it he'd take it out of my hand and say:

"Whisht! Silence. . . . *Attendez!*" and he would first wave his hand over it and then say, "Now it's ready and *thou canst receive it as it is written.*"

And thus I underwent my cure with the seedy gentleman at that inn till the evening, and I didn't have any qualms of conscience about it, for I knew that I was drinking not for the sake of indulging myself, but for the sake of denying myself. I'd put my hand inside my coat to make sure that the money was still there, and having made sure that everything was in order, I'd go on drinking.

The gentleman who was drinking with me went on telling me all about the life of sin and debauchery he had led and he spoke particularly about love and ended up by trying to pick a quarrel with me on the pretext that I knew nothing about love.

I said.

"It isn't my fault that I don't know anything about all that nonsense, is it? You should be glad that you do know all about it and that that's why you've turned out such a fine specimen!"

But he said:

"Whisht! Silence! Love is a sacred thing!"

"Rubbish," I said.

"You're a yokel," he said, "and a rascal, too, if you dare laugh at one of the most sacred feelings of the human heart and speak of it as rubbish."

"What else is it," said I, "but rubbish?"

"But don't you understand the meaning of 'beauty, nature's perfection' at all?" he said.

"Yes," said I, "I can understand the beauty of a horse."

Whereupon he jumped to his feet and wanted to box my ears.

"Is a horse," he said, "beauty, nature's perfection?"

But as it was getting rather late by that time, he had no time to prove his point to me, for the bartender, seeing that both of us were the worse for drink, winked at the bouncers and all of them, six hefty men, rushed up to us and said, "It's time for you to go, gentlemen," and they took us under the arms and put us out into the street, slamming the doors behind us and locking them for the night.

And then it was that I suffered such bedevilment that although a great many years have passed since that amazing chapter of accidents, I cannot to this day render a clear account to myself of what really took place and by what force it worked upon me, but such temptations and adventures as I underwent that night, I am sure no saint or martyr ever underwent, not, at any rate, one whose life is described in the Book of Saints.

12.

The first thing I did after I had been thrown out of the inn was to feel inside my coat to see if my wallet was still there. Well, it seemed that it was. "Now," thought I, "I must be careful to bring it home."

The night was very dark, as dark as could be. In summer we get such nights near Kursk, you know, pitch dark but very warm and tranquil: in the sky the stars are hung like so many icon lamps and down below the darkness is so dense that you have the impression that someone is feeling you all over, touching you. . . . And during a fair hundreds of wicked people of every description roam about the streets and there are many cases of robbery and murder. In spite of the fact that I knew myself to be a man who was a match for anybody in physical strength, I could not help thinking that in the first place, I was drunk, and secondly, if ten or more men were to attack me, even my powerful physique could not keep me from being robbed, and furthermore, that every time I got up and sat down to pay for the drinks, my companion, that indigent gentleman, could see that I had a lot of money on me. And that was why, you know, it suddenly occurred to me—was he perhaps contemplating some treachery against me that would prove my utter undoing? Where was he, anyway? We had been thrown out of the inn together, hadn't we? So where, in heaven's name, had he disappeared to so quickly?

I was standing there and, peering quietly round me, I called to him softly, not knowing his name, thus:

"Eh, you," I said, "you magnetizer, where are you?"

And he suddenly burst into my sight like some hobgoblin and said:

"Here I am!"

I couldn't recognize his voice and in the pitch darkness even his face did not seem his own.

"Come nearer," I said, and as he did so I took hold of his shoulders and began peering down at him, but I couldn't for the life of me make out whether it was he or not: for as soon as I touched him I suddenly lost my memory, for no reason at all. All I could hear was that he was mumbling something in French: "Dee-ka-tee-lee-ka-tee-pé," and I could not understand a word of it.

"What are you mumbling about?" I said.

But he said again in French:

"Dee-ka-tee-lee-ka-tee-pé."

"Stop it, you fool," I said. "Tell me in Russian who you are, for I've forgotten all about you."

He replied:

"Dee-ka-tee-lee-ka-tee-pé: I'm the magnetizer."

"Oh, to hell with you, you rogue," I said, and for a fleeting moment I seemed to remember who he was, but as soon as I'd begin to look closely at him, I'd see that he had two noses . . .

yes, two noses. And no sooner had I begun to think about it than I'd forget again who he was. . . .

"Oh, damn you!" thought I. "Where could I have picked up a rascal like you?" And once more I asked him, "Who are you?"

He said again:

"The magnetizer."

"Get away from me," I said. "How do I know you're not the Devil?"

"Not exactly," he said, "but not far off, either."

I punched him on the nose and he got cross and said:

"What are you hitting me for? I'm doing you a great favor, curing you of your drinking habits, and you can do nothing better than hit me."

But however hard I tried, I just could not remember him, and I said:

"But who the devil are you?"

He said:

"I'm your faithful friend."

"All right," I said, "supposing you are my friend, would that prevent you from doing me harm?"

"No," he said, "but I'm going to show you such a *petit-comme-peu* that you'll feel like a different man."

"Stop telling lies," I said.

"Truly," he said, "truly, such a *petit-comme-peu* . . ."

"What the devil are you talking French to me for?" I said. "I don't know what your *petit-comme-peu* is!"

"It'll give your life a new meaning," he said.

"All right," I said, "that's different. But what kind of new meaning can it give me?"

"Such a one," he said, "that you'll comprehend beauty, nature's perfection."

"But how am I to comprehend it so suddenly?"

"Come along with me," he said, "and you'll see."

"All right," I said, "let's go!"

So off we went. We walked along, the two of us, unsteadily it is true, but walk along we did. I did not know where we were

going, and then I'd suddenly remember that I did not know who
my companion was and I'd say again:

"Stop! Tell me who you are, or I won't go another step!"

He would tell me and I'd seem to remember it for a little while
and then I'd ask:

"Why do I keep on forgetting who you are?"

And he would reply:

"That," he said, "is due to the action of my magnetism, but
don't be afraid of it, it'll soon pass off, only let me give you another dose of magnetism, a bigger dose this time."

And he suddenly turned me around with my back to him and
started fumbling about with his fingers in the hair on my neck.
. . . Uncanny, that's how it felt: he seemed to rummage about
there as if he wanted to crawl into my head.

I said:

"Look here, whoever you are, what are you burrowing there
for?"

"Wait a minute," he said, "and stand still, will you? I'm intro-
ducing into you the whole force of my magnetism."

"That's right," I said, "let's have the whole of it by all means,
but are you sure that you don't want to rob me of my money?"

He denied it.

"All right," I said, "wait till I find out."

I put my hand inside my coat: the money was safe.

"Now I can see that you are not a thief," I said, but I had
again forgotten who he was and I could not even remember how
to ask him about it, for I was wholly preoccupied with the curious
sensation I had that he had crawled through the back of my neck
right inside me and was looking at the world through my eyes and
that my eyes were just like windows to him.

"Good heavens," I thought, "what a dirty trick to play on me!"
and I asked:

"What's happened to my eyesight?"

"You haven't any left now," he said.

"What are you talking about?" I said. "What do you mean I
haven't any?"

"What I mean," said he, "is that all you'll see with your eyes now is what isn't there."

"What kind of wonder is that?" I said. "Very well, let's try!"

So I opened my eyes wide and peered for all I was worth and I seemed to see all sorts of horrible faces on little legs staring at me from behind dark corners, darting across my path and standing on the crossroads, waiting and saying, "Let's kill him and take away his treasure!" And my little gentleman was there again before me, his hair bristling and his face lit up by some inner light, and behind me I heard an awful din and uproar, voices and twanging instruments and wild shouts and screams and merry laughter. I looked round and I realized that I was standing with my back against a house with open windows inside of which everything was bright, and that it was from there that there came all that noise and the voices and the melancholy strain of a guitar, and in front of me I again saw the gentleman in the tattered clothes and he was waving his hands in front of my face and making passes over my chest, stopping at the heart and pressing against it, and seizing my fingers and giving them a slight shake, and again waving and working away with his hands with such zeal and abandon that I could see that he was all covered with sweat.

But as the light began to shine out of those windows, I felt that I was regaining consciousness. I stopped being afraid and said:

"Listen to me, whoever you are, devil or Satan himself or just a hobgoblin out of hell, do me a favor and either wake me up or vanish out of sight!"

And he said in reply to that:

"Wait, the time hasn't come yet: there's still the danger that you won't be able to stand it."

I said:

"What is it that I won't be able to stand?"

"That," he said, "which is now happening in the heavenly spheres."

"What is happening there?" I asked. "I can't hear anything in particular."

But he insisted that I wasn't listening properly and he spoke to me in the language of Holy Writ.

"To hear it," he said, "thou must imitate the one who playeth the harp, he who inclineth his head towards the heart and straineth his ear to the singing and striketh the strings with his hand."

"Well," I thought, "what's all this about? That isn't at all like the speech of a drunken man, the way he talks now!"

And he went on looking at me and waving his hands over me quietly, while himself continuing to exhort me to do as he wished.

"Hearken unto the strings," he said, "and see how cunningly they are struck one after the other and, as they are struck, the harp bursteth forth into song and the harp player rejoiceth in the honeyed sweetness of its sounds."

I tell you, gentlemen, it was as if I heard no words at all, but as if the waters of a living stream came rippling by my ear, and I said to myself, "Is this a drunkard? See how well he can talk in the tongue of angels!"

In the meantime my gentleman stopped fidgeting about and spoke as follows:

"That'll do for you. Now awaken," he said, "and fortify yourself!"

And with these words he bent down and for a long time he tried to get hold of something in the pocket of his torn trousers and at last he got it out. I looked and saw that it was a little lump of sugar all covered with dirt, apparently from lying so long in his pocket. He removed the dirt with his nails, blew on it, and said:

"Open your mouth!"

I said, "What for?" and just opened my mouth wide. He pushed the lump of sugar into it and said:

"Suck. Suck and fear not: this is a magnetic sugar-mentor and it will fortify you."

I realized, of course, that if he used French words, it was all about magnetism, so I didn't ask him any more questions but was entirely preoccupied with sucking the lump of sugar, and anyway, I could no longer see the man who had given it to me. Whether he went away somewhere and vanished in the dark or whether he just sank through the ground, the Devil alone knew: all I knew was that there I was quite alone and that I was completely restored to my senses. "Well," I thought, "what's the use of waiting for him here? I must go home now." But the trouble was that I didn't know in what street I was and what kind of house it was beside which I was standing. So I said to myself, "Is this a house at all? Maybe I'm just seeing things, maybe it's nothing but a piece of witchcraft. . . . It is night, everybody's asleep, so why's there a light here? But why not try? . . . Let's go in and see what's going on in there: if there are people in this house, real people, I'll ask them the way to my home, and if it is only a delusion and a dream and not living people at all, then what's there to be scared of? All I have to do is say, 'This ground is holy: get thee behind me, Satan!' and everything will vanish. . . ."

13.

Thus fortified in spirit, I walked up the front steps, crossed myself, uttered a short prayer, and—nothing happened! The house remained standing, it didn't even sway, and I saw that the doors were open and that at the end of a very long passage a lantern with a lighted candle hung on a nail in the wall. I looked more closely and I noticed that to the left there were two more doors, both covered with matting, and above them were strange kinds of candlesticks with mirrors in the shape of stars under them. "Well," I thought, "what sort of a house can this be? It doesn't look like an inn, and yet one can see that it is a house of entertainment," but what kind of entertainment I couldn't make out. But as I listened, I heard the strains of a song coming from behind one of the doors covered with matting . . . such a sweet song, too, a song that made your heart stand still, and the voice that sang it was as clear as a bell, a voice that just took your breath away, that bewitched your soul. So I listened and I didn't move from my place, and at that moment a door opened somewhere at the end of the long passage and I saw coming out of it a tall gypsy in wide silken breeches and a velvet cossack coat, showing somebody out of the house through a special door under that distant lantern, a door I hadn't even noticed at first. Although, to be quite frank, I wasn't able to make out the identity of the man he had shown out of the house, I did get the idea that it was none other than my magnetizer, and I heard the gypsy saying to him:

"All right, all right, don't be so angry about the fifty copecks, but stop in again tomorrow and if we get some profit out of *him*, we'll give you more for bringing him to us."

And with those words he bolted the door and rushed towards me, pretending to have just noticed me, and opening the door under one of those curiously wrought mirrors, he said:

"Welcome to our house, sir! Come and hear our songs! We have beautiful singers."

And without giving me time to reply, he quietly flung the door wide open in front of me. . . . I don't know what happened to me at that moment, gentlemen, but everything seemed so familiar to me that I suddenly felt quite at home there. The room was very big but rather low, and the ceiling seemed to sag in the middle, as though thrusting downwards with its belly, and the walls looked dark, as if covered with soot, and the tobacco smoke was so thick that the large chandelier under the ceiling did not shed any light, and but for the fact that it was alight, one would not have noticed that it was there at all. And below in that dense smoke a crowd of people . . . hundreds and hundreds of them, and in front of them a young gypsy girl was singing in that beautiful voice which I had already heard. As I entered, she was just finishing her song and her voice died down on a last note of great tenderness and fell silent. . . . And as that sweet voice of hers fell silent, everything in the room seemed to fall silent too, as if the people there were dead. . . . But in another moment everyone jumped up like mad and began to clap and to shout. But as I looked in sheer bewilderment at those crowds of people I wondered where they had all come from; for as I stood there, more and more faces were constantly appearing through the smoke. "Heavens above," I thought, "are they really human beings or demons in human shape?" But presently I began to recognize among that vast crowd many horse breeders and horse buyers known to me personally, and other well-to-do merchants and landowners whom I knew to be keen horsemen, and among them all a gypsy girl was moving about, such a . . . but it is quite impossible to describe her, she didn't even seem to be a woman, but like some gaily-colored serpent she seemed to be moving about on her tail, her whole slender body bending lithely and a fire blazing in her black eyes. A fascinating figure! She carried a large tray with glasses of champagne round the edge and in the middle a great pile of money. There was no silver in that pile: only gold and bank notes with pictures of blue tits and gray ducks and red heath cocks—everything except the hundred-rouble white swans. Every time she offered a glass to a man, he'd drink the wine and throw some money on the tray, each man indulging his own fancy in this matter and parting either with a gold piece or with a bank note, and then she'd kiss him on the lips and curtsy to him. Well, so she walked round the first row and the second—the people sat in a kind of semi-circle—and then she walked round the last row, behind which I stood, and, having walked round it, she was about to turn back, not wishing to offer me any drink, but an old gypsy who walked behind her suddenly shouted at her, "Grusha!" and he motioned with his eyes in my direction. She just lifted her eyelashes at him . . . Lord, what lovely eyelashes they were! Long and black, and they seemed to be alive and move by themselves like birds. . . . And I saw that, as the old man shouted his order to her, her eyes blazed as if her whole being reared up in anger. She got angry, you see, because she had been ordered to offer me a drink. However, she did as she was told. She went up to me behind the last row, bowed, and said:

"Won't you drink my health, sir?"

I couldn't even reply to her: so instantly did she bewitch me! As soon, that is, as she bowed before me over the tray and I saw how the parting on her head ran between her black hair like a thread of silver and disappeared at the back, I seemed to go stark, raving mad and to lose my reason entirely. I drank the wine she had offered me, while looking at her over the rim of the glass, and I couldn't tell whether her skin was dark or fair, but I could see distinctly how underneath her thin skin the color glowed, as on a cherry in sunlight, and how on her lovely temple a vein was beating. . . . "So that's what real beauty is," thought I, "which is called nature's perfection! The magnetizer spoke the truth: it isn't at all like the beauty of a horse, an animal that is bought and sold."

And so I drained the glass and set it down with a crash on the tray, and she stood waiting to see how much I esteemed her kiss to be worth. I put my hand quickly into my pocket to get some money to put down on the tray, but all I could find there were a few silver coins and other small change. "It isn't enough," I thought. "It won't do to give so paltry a present to so alluring a snake and, besides, I shall lower myself in the estimation of all the people here!"

In the meantime I could hear the gentlemen saying to the old gypsy, without even pretending to lower their voices:

"Really, Vassily Ivanov, why do you order Grusha to treat that lout? We can't help resenting it!"

And he replied:

"We make no distinction between one guest and another, gentlemen. Everybody is welcome and everybody is treated honorably in this house. I'm sorry you should feel resentful, but that's, I suppose, because you fail to realize that even a plain man knows how to value beauty and talent. I've seen many examples of that, gentlemen."

And I, hearing that, thought:

"Oh, to hell with you! Do you think that because you're richer your feelings are more refined than mine? No! What will be, will be. I'll pay the prince back later, but now I shall neither disgrace myself nor cheapen that paragon of beauty by my stinginess."

No sooner said than done: I put my hand inside my coat pocket at once, took out a hundred-rouble swan from my roll of bank notes, and flipped it down on the tray. The gypsy girl immediately took the tray in one hand and with the other wiped my lips with a white handkerchief, and she didn't even kiss me, but just seemed to touch my lips with hers lightly, and as she did so she seemed to smear them with a kind of poison, and then she went away.

She went away and I would have remained standing where I was had not the old gypsy, Grusha's father, and another gypsy taken me under the arms and dragged me forward and made me sit down in the first row next to the captain of police and other gentlemen.

To tell the truth, I did not particularly relish it and I didn't want to stay. I wanted to leave, but they would not let me, entreating me and calling on Grusha:

"Grusha, darling, don't let our dear guest depart!"

And she came forward and . . . the Devil alone, I suppose, could tell what power resided in those eyes of hers: one glance and she seemed to inject some paralyzing venom into my eyes, and she said:

"Do not offend us, sir! Please, stay a little longer in our house!"

"Well," I said, "who would dream of offending you?" and I sat down.

And she kissed me again, and again I had that curious sensation, as if she touched my lips with a poisoned brush and sent a hot stream of blood racing to my heart so that it seemed to be set on fire and to contract with pain.

After that the singing and the dancing began again and once more a gypsy girl went round with the champagne, but this time it was a different girl. She, too, was beautiful, but she couldn't hold a candle to Grusha. She wasn't half as lovely, and to show how little I thought of her as compared with the other, I just grabbed a handful of silver coins from my pocket and sent them rolling on the tray. . . . The gentlemen thought it a great joke and laughed heartily, but I didn't care. All I cared about was keeping my eyes fixed on her, on Grusha, waiting for her to sing alone without the choir. But she did not sing. She was sitting among the other gypsies, joining in the refrain of their song, but she would not sing a solo, and I couldn't hear her voice and only saw her sweet little mouth and her white teeth. . . . "Oh," thought I, "miserable creature that I am! I came in just for a minute and lost a hundred roubles and now I won't even hear her sing again!" But, as luck would have it, I was not the only one among that large company who wanted to hear her sing: the others, too, all the important gentlemen in the room, soon joined in a universal shout:

"Grusha! Grusha! 'The Skiff!' Grusha! 'The Skiff!' "

Well, the gypsies cleared their throats, her young brother touched the guitar, and she began to sing. You know . . . their singing is usually very sensitive and it goes right to your heart, and when I heard her voice, which had sounded so alluring to me even behind the door, I could not help feeling deeply moved. It was lovely! She began, perhaps, a little harshly, a little too boldly, something like this: "The sea's ro—o—o—oaring, the sea's mo—o—o—oaning. . . ." And you could really hear the sea moaning and feel it dashing the little skiff, which was caught up in it, now one way and now another. But when she appealed to the star, there was a sudden change in her voice: "Sweetest, dearest star of morning, twinkling up so high, human sorrow cannot touch me while thou sailest up the sky!" And then a new surprising change, something unexpected. All their songs are full of those appeals: now they weep, sunk in the deepest melancholy, throwing you into such a black dejection of spirits that your soul seems about to part from your body, and then, suddenly, they burst out in quite a different key and your heart feels merry again. . . . So in that song she began by dashing the skiff against the raging waves, and the others suddenly burst out on a high note all together:

> *Ja-la-la, ja-la-la,*
> *Ja-la-la, pringala!*
> *Ja-la-la-pringa-la!*
> *Hey da chepuringala!*
> *Hey hap-hi-ta hara!*
> *Hey hop-hi-ta hara!*

After the song Grusha went round with the tray again, offering wine and kisses, and I gave her another swan from the inside pocket of my coat. . . . People began looking askance at me, for I was lowering my prestige by my extravagance, and they felt ashamed to give anything after me; but I didn't care a fig for my money any longer, for I wanted to show what I felt in my heart; I wanted to fling my soul wide open and I did fling it open. Every time Grusha sang a song I'd give her a swan for it, and I had even stopped counting how many I had given away, just handing them out without a thought, and so when anybody else asked her for a song she would excuse herself, saying that she was feeling "tired," but I had only to wink at the old gypsy—"Can't you make her sing?" so to speak—and he would look at her with such eyes that sing she would. She sang many songs that night, one more enchanting than the last, and I had thrown her without counting I don't know how many swans, until at last—I couldn't tell what hour it was, but the day was beginning to break by then—she was really and truly tired and, looking very wan, she threw a significant glance at me and began to sing, "Go away, look no more, vanish out of my sight." With those words she seemed to beg me to go, but with the other words she seemed to search my mind: "Dost thou want with my brave heart to play, till with my beauty's splendor I thee slay?" And so I thrust another swan upon her! She kissed me again, unwillingly, and I felt as though she had stung me, and her eyes blazed angrily, and the other gypsies, in that evil hour, burst into a farewell refrain:

> *Darling, don't you feel at all,*
> *How much, sweet, I'm in your thrall!*

and all joined in that chorus and looked at Grusha, and I, too, looked at her, humming, "Don't you feel at all?" Then the gypsies burst forth, "Go away, cottage, go away, stove, pity the master, who can't move," and suddenly they all began to dance. . . . The gypsies danced and the gypsy girls danced and the gentlemen danced: they were all caught up in one dance and indeed it did look as though the whole cottage had started to move. The gypsy girls went skipping in front of the gentlemen, who tried to catch up with them and raced after them, the young ones with a wild shout and the older ones with a suppressed groan. . . . I looked round at the seats: there was not a man left there . . . even those among the men who had reached the age of discretion and whom I hardly expected to see indulging in such horseplay, even they had all risen from their seats. One of the more stolid citizens would remain in his seat for a little while, at first clearly ashamed to join in the riot, and either look on or just pull at his mustache, but presently one devil would start jerking his shoulder and another pulling at his leg and, lo and behold, he'd suddenly jump to his feet and start throwing his legs about in a way that was hardly becoming to his station in life. The police captain, a man of immense girth with two married daughters, joined the throng of revellers with his two sons-in-law and went round the room gasping for breath like a sheatfish and lifting his feet heavily, as though he were pulling them out of a bog; and a hussar officer, a rich captain who was a horse buyer for the army, a dashing dancer and a fine, upstanding young fellow, put everybody else in the room to shame: arms akimbo, he sent his heels flying and crashing on the floor—just showing off—and every time he got near to the gypsy girls he'd spread out his arms as if about to enfold them, and every time he got near enough to Grusha, he'd toss his mop of hair, throw his cap at her feet, and shout, "Step on it, crush it, Oh, sweetheart mine!" and she . . . Oh, what a lovely dancer she was! I remember seeing actresses dancing on the stage, but, believe me, compared with her it was just like some army officer's horse without a scrap of imagination cavorting on the parade ground and prancing through the regulation steps just for the sake of show, without a spark of life. But that beauty—no sooner had she joined in the dance than she went sailing off like a swan and she moved with such magnificent ease, her body swaying neither to the right nor the left, that one could almost hear how inside her—inside that serpent—the little bones moved and the marrow passed from one bone to the other, and when she stopped dead, she would arch her back, move a shoulder, and her eyebrow would be in line with the toe of her foot. . . . What a picture! Just to see her dance was enough to turn the head of every man in the room: they were all irresistibly drawn towards her in a headlong rush: some had tears in their eyes, others bared their teeth, and all shouted with one voice, "Take everything we have: just dance!" and they threw their money at her feet, some gold pieces, others bank notes. The dance went on, and the crowd of dancers grew thicker and thicker, only I alone was still sitting down, but even I did not know how long I'd be able to hold out, for I could not bear to see her step on that hussar officer's cap over and over again. . . . Every time she stepped on it the devil would tear at my heart; she'd step again, and again he would grip my heart, and at last I said to myself, "Why go on tormenting yourself for nothing? Why shouldn't your soul rejoice as much as it wishes?" So I jumped up, brushed the hussar out of my way, and began kicking up my heels in front of Grusha. . . . And to make quite sure that she would not step on the hussar's cap again, I thought up a trick: "All of you," I said to myself, "go on yelling that you don't mind giving away all you have, but I am not deceived by that cry of yours, for I shall presently prove to you all by deeds and not by words that I, for one, don't mind giving everything away!" So I bounded in front of her and, taking a swan out of the inside pocket of my coat, I flung it under her feet, shouting, "Crush it! Step on it!" At first she wouldn't . . . notwithstanding that my swan was a damn sight more valuable than the hussar's cap, she wouldn't even look at it and was all for following the hussar, but the old gypsy—good man!—saw it in time and just stamped his foot at her. . . . So she took the hint and followed me. . . . She was sailing after me, her eyes cast on the ground, blazing with anger and almost setting the ground on fire like the dragon in the fable, and I was leaping like a hobgoblin in front of her, and every time I leapt, I flung a swan under her feet. . . . While I worshipped her so that I kept on saying to myself, "Hast thou not, accursed one, created heaven and earth?"—I did not hesitate to shout brazenly at her, "Come on, faster, faster!" and all the while I was flinging swans under her feet, and then I put my hand inside my coat to get another one and I found that there were only about ten of them left. . . . "Well," thought I, "the Devil take you, the lot of you!" and I crumpled them all in my hand and just flung them in one heap under her feet, and having done that I snatched up a bottle of champagne from the table, knocked its neck off, and roared, "Make way, my soul, or I'll drown you!" and I drank it all in one gulp to her health, for after the dance I felt a terrible thirst come over me.

14.

"Well, and what happened after that?" we asked Ivan Severyanych with bated breath.

"After that everything really did happen as *he* had foretold."

"As who had foretold?"

"Why, the magnetizer, of course, who had cast that spell on me: as he had promised to release me from the power of the devil of drink, so he did get rid of him for me and I have not taken another glass since. He did it all right."

"Well, ye-e-es. . . . But how did you settle with your prince for the swans you had set free?"

"That, gentlemen, was settled so simply that I can hardly believe it myself even to this day. How I got back home from those gypsies I couldn't say myself, nor how I went to bed. The first thing I knew was that the prince was knocking at my door and calling to me. I wanted to get up from the wooden chest on which I slept but, try as I might, I couldn't find the edge, so I naturally couldn't get off it. I would crawl to one side of it, then turn to the other, but I just could not find the edge. . . . I seemed to have lost my way on that chest and I could do nothing about it. The prince would shout, 'Ivan Severyanych!' and I would reply, 'One moment, sir!' and just keep on crawling about without being able to find the edge of my bed, and at last I said to myself, 'Well, if I can't get off it, I'd better jump off it!'—but as I took a flying leap, intending to jump as far as possible, something hit me in the face and everything round me began to ring and crash to the ground, and behind me, too, everything rang and crashed to the ground, and I heard the prince's voice saying to his orderly, 'Get a light, quick!' I stood still, not wanting to move, for I didn't know whether all this was really happening or whether I was seeing it in a dream. For I thought I was still lying on the wooden chest, having been unable to reach the edge, but instead, when the orderly had brought in a lighted candle, I saw that I was standing on the floor and that I had crashed through

the glass door of a cupboard and had broken all the china in
it. . . ."

"How did you manage to lose your bearings like that?"

"Quite simply: I thought that I was sleeping as usual on the
wooden chest, but on returning home from the gypsies I must
have fallen asleep on the floor and I kept on crawling about
looking for the edge of the chest and then I took that flying leap
and crashed through the china cabinet. I was wandering about
all over the room because he—the magnetizer, that is—had removed the devil of drink from me, but had left the roaming devil
with me. . . . I at once remembered the words he had said to
me, 'Mind, you may find things much worse if you leave off
drink!' and I went in search of him, for I wanted to ask him to
demagnetize me to my old state, but I couldn't find him. It
seemed he had taken too much upon himself and he couldn't
stand it, poor man, so he drank so much at the inn opposite the
gypsies' house that he died."

"So you remained magnetized like that?"

"Yes, so I remained."

"But did that magnetism work on you for a long time?"

"Why only for a long time? It's probably still working today."

"But how did you settle with the prince? Didn't you have to
give him some explanation about those swans?"

Why, of course I had to give him an account of what I did with
them, only it didn't matter one way or the other. You see, the
prince himself came back without a penny, having lost everything
at cards. He began asking me for some money to try his luck
again, but I said:

"You're wasting your time, sir, I have no money."

He thought that I was joking, but I said:

"No, sir, I'm telling you the truth. While you were away I had
an expensive day off."

He asked, "How could you possibly have spent five thousand in
one day off?"

I said, "I gave them all to a gypsy girl. . . ."

He didn't believe me.

I said, "All right, don't believe me, but I'm telling you the truth."

He lost his temper and said:

"Shut the door and I'll show you how to waste government money," but then he suddenly changed his mind and said, "Never mind, I'm as big a wastrel as you."

So he lay down in the room to finish his night's sleep and I, too, went to sleep in the hayloft. When I came to, I found that I was in a hospital and I was told that I had had an attack of d.t.'s and had tried to hang myself, but, thank God, they put me into a strait-jacket. Later, when I got better, I went to see the prince on his estate, for he had resigned his commission in the meantime, and I said:

"I want to work for you, sir, until I've paid you the money I owe you."

But he said, "Go to hell."

Well, I could see that he was very cross with me, so I went up to him and bowed my head before him.

"What are you up to now?" he asked.

"Give me a good beating, at any rate, sir," I said.

But he said:

"Why do you assume that I'm angry with you? Perhaps I don't even consider you to have been at fault."

"Good heavens, sir," I said, "how can I not be at fault if I have wasted such a vast amount of money? I know very well, sir, that hanging is too good for a villain like me!"

He, however, replied:

"But my dear fellow, what could you do about it if you are an artist?"

"How do you mean, sir?" I said.

"I mean just what I say," he replied, "my dear Severyanych, my semi-honorable one—an artist."

"I'm afraid, sir," I said, "I don't understand."

"Don't think it is anything bad," he said, "for I, too, am an artist."

"Well," I thought to myself, "I can see that all right: it isn't only I who got d.t.'s."

But he got up, knocked out his pipe, and said:

"I don't wonder that you should have flung all the money you had on you before her, when I, my dear fellow, gave for her more than I have and more than I have ever had."

I just glared at him.

"For pity's sake, sir," I said, "what are you saying? Just to hear you talk like that, sir, frightens me!"

"There's no need to be frightened," he said, "for the Lord is merciful and I may be able to extricate myself somehow or other, but the fact is that I've paid fifty thousand to the gypsy camp for Grusha."

I gasped.

"Do you really mean it, sir?" I said. "Fifty thousand for a gypsy girl! But the little tramp isn't worth it, sir!"

"Now," he replied, "my semi-honorable friend, you're talking like a fool and not at all like an artist. Not worth it? Why, a woman is worth everything one has in the world, for she puts such a curse on you that you can't get rid of it for a whole kingdom, but she can rid you of it in a second."

Well, I couldn't help thinking that that was true enough, but all the same I went on shaking my head and said:

"Such a lot of money! Fifty thousand!"

"Yes, sir," he said, "and, please don't rub it in, for I was damned glad they accepted that much for her, or I should have had to give them more. . . . I'd have given them anything in the world for her!"

"You should have just spat, sir."

"I couldn't do that, my dear fellow," he said. "I couldn't just spit."

"Why not?"

"Because she had stung me with her beauty and her talent and I had to get cured or I'd have gone mad. But, tell me the truth, she is beautiful, isn't she? Eh? It's true, isn't it? She has something that drives a man mad, hasn't she?"

I bit my lips and nodded silently: "It's true, all right," was what I implied.

"You know," the prince said, "I shouldn't hesitate for a minute to die for a woman. Can you understand that? Can you understand how one wouldn't mind dying for a woman?"

"Well," I said, "there's nothing incomprehensible about it: beauty is nature's perfection."

"What do you mean by that?"

"I mean," I said, "that beauty is nature's perfection and to a man who falls under its spell death itself may be happiness!"

"You're a fine fellow, my demi-semi-honorable and all-too-insignificant Ivan Severyanych!" my prince exclaimed. "Yes, yes, one may even be happy to die and that's why I'm so glad to have turned my life upside down for her: I've resigned my commission and mortgaged my estate and I shall be living here from now on and see no one, but just keep on looking at her!"

Here I lowered my voice even more and said in a whisper:

"What do you mean by . . . looking at her, sir? Is she here?"

And he replied:

"What else do you think? Of course she's here."

"Is that possible?"

"You wait here," he said, "and I'll bring her at once. You are an artist and I shouldn't dream of hiding her from you."

And with these words he left me and went out. I stood there waiting and thinking to myself:

"That's bad! To say that you don't want to look at any face but hers is a bad sign: it means that you'll soon get tired of her!" But I didn't enter into all the implications of the prince's words, for as soon as I remembered that she was there, I felt hot all over and my head began to swim, for I couldn't help thinking, "Shall I really see her now?" And then both of them suddenly came in, the prince walking ahead of her, carrying a guitar with a wide scarlet ribbon in one hand and dragging poor Grusha with the other, clasping both her hands in his, and she was walking with her head cast down, resisting him and not looking, with only those long, black eyelashes of hers fluttering like the wings of a bird.

The prince brought her into the room, picked her up in his arms, and set her down like a child on a wide, soft sofa with her feet in one corner, put a velvet cushion under her back and another under her right arm; then he put the ribbon of the guitar across her shoulder and placed her fingers on the strings, and sitting down on the floor beside the sofa, he leaned his head against her scarlet morocco-leather shoe and nodded to me: "Sit down, too," so to speak.

So I, too, crossed my legs and let myself down quietly on the floor by the door and there I remained sitting, looking at her. There was an uncanny stillness in the room. I sat there for a long time, till my knees began to ache, but every time I looked up at her she was sitting in the same position and when I happened to look up at the prince I saw that he had almost gnawed through his mustache from sheer agony of soul, but he spoke no word to her.

So I nodded to him: "Ask her to sing!" so to speak. And he, too, gave me to understand in pantomime that, so to speak, she wouldn't listen to him.

So the two of us went on sitting on the floor and waiting, and then suddenly she started to sigh and to sob, but she seemed to be doing it in a kind of delirium, and a tear rolled down her cheek and her fingers began to move over the strings of the guitar like wasps and to hum. . . . And all at once she began to sing in a very soft voice and it sounded as if she were crying, "Good people, hear my sorrow and my heartache. . . ."

The prince whispered to me, "Well?"

And I replied to him in French, also in a whisper:

"*Petit comme peu,*" I said, and I could say no more for at that moment she suddenly cried out, "But for my beauty they'll sell me, they'll sell me . . ." and she hurled the guitar from her lap, far into the room, and tore her kerchief from her head and, throwing herself down on the sofa, she buried her face in her hands and began to sob, and I, too, looking at her, began to cry, and the prince . . . he, too, began to cry and, picking up the guitar, he did not seem to sing so much as to chant, as though intoning a verse at divine service, and to moan, "If only thou'dst see my heart's on fire, my soul's consumed with longing for thee . . ." and the rest was drowned in his tears. So he went on singing and crying, "Comfort me, the comfortless one, bestow

the happiness of thy love upon me, the unhappy one. . . ."
So great was the wretchedness of his spirit that she, I saw, was
beginning to notice his tears and his mournful singing and was
growing more composed and resigned, and then suddenly she
withdrew her hand from her face and put her arm round his head
with great tenderness, like a mother. . . .

Well, of course, I realized that she must be very sorry for him
at that moment and that she would comfort him and gladden his
soul, so consumed with longing. So I got up and left the room
unobserved.

"Was it then that you entered the monastery?" one of the
passengers asked.

"No, sir, not then, but much later," Ivan Severyanych replied,
adding that while still in the world of men, he was first of all
destined to see a great deal of that woman and to be with her
until everything fate held in store for her came to pass and his
own destiny, too, was fulfilled.

The passengers naturally urged him to tell them the story of
Grusha, even if only in bare outline, and Ivan Severyanych did as
they asked him.

15.

You see, gentlemen (Ivan Severyanych began), my
prince was a good man, but his character was very unstable. If he
wanted a thing, he had to have it at any price, you just had to give
it to him or he'd go off his head, and at that particular time he
would not hesitate to give anything in the world so long as he got
it, but when he got it, he did not appreciate his good fortune. That
was exactly what happened between him and the gypsy girl, and
her father (Grusha's father, that is) and the rest of the gypsies
belonging to his camp had a pretty shrewd idea about the prince's
character and that was why they had asked such a great price for
her, more than his property warranted, for although his estate
was quite big, it was burdened with debt. Such a sum as the gypsy

camp had asked for Grusha was more than the prince had in cash at the time and he had to raise it as a loan and resign his commission.

Knowing all his weaknesses, I did not expect him to make Grusha happy and my expectations were fully justified. For a time he waited on her hand and foot and would not let her out of his sight, unable, it seemed, to draw his breath without her, but suddenly he fell to yawning in her presence and he began asking me to share their company.

"Sit down," he used to say, "and listen."

I would take a chair, sit down somewhere near the door, and listen. But it frequently happened that when he asked her to sing, she would say:

"Who shall I sing to? You," she would say, "have grown cold and I must have someone whose soul will be set ablaze and be tormented by my song."

So the prince would at once send for me, and he and I would listen to her together; and after a time Grusha herself began to remind him to send for me, and we grew very friendly and after her singing I would frequently have tea with the prince in her rooms, but, of course, either at a separate table or somewhere by the window, except when she was alone, in which case she would always insist that I sit beside her. Many days passed like that and the prince was getting more and more worried, and one day he said to me:

"Do you know, Ivan Severyanych, things are not going well with me, my affairs are in a very bad state."

I said:

"They couldn't be as bad as all that, sir. Thank God, you live as a gentleman of your position should and you have everything you want."

Well, he just got angry with me.

"What a blithering idiot you are, my semi-honorable one," he said, "I have everything indeed! What is it that I *have*?"

"Everything you want," I said.

"It isn't true," he said. "I'm as poor as a church mouse. Why, I have to think twice before I can treat myself to a bottle of wine for dinner. Is that life? Is that life, I ask you?"

"Good heavens," I said to myself, "so that's what is worrying you, is it?" and I said aloud, "Well, sir," I said, "even if you can't afford a bottle of wine occasionally, it's nothing to make a fuss about, for after all, sir, you've something much sweeter than wine or honey."

He understood that I was referring to Grusha and he looked a little ashamed and began to pace the room and wave his arms about, saying:

"Of course . . . of course . . . naturally . . . but only . . . you see, I've spent the last six months here and I haven't seen a living soul. . . ."

"But what do you want to see people for, sir, if you've got someone you desire more than anyone in the world?"

The prince reddened.

"You don't understand anything, my dear fellow," he said. "One thing's only good if one has the other."

"Aha," I thought, "so you've changed your tune, have you?" and I said, "What do you intend to do now, sir?"

"Let's start dealing in horses," he said, "I'd like to see horse breeders and army buyers in my house again."

Horse dealing is an unprofitable business at the best of times and it is certainly not a fit occupation for a gentleman, but I thought, "Anything for a quiet life," and I said, "By all means, sir, let's."

So we opened up stables and began to keep all sorts of horses which we were supposed to get in good shape for the fairs. But no sooner had we started than the prince got completely carried away by that new passion of his: he would raise some money and immediately spend it all on the purchase of horses, buying any horse that caught his fancy without listening to my advice. So we bought a whole multitude of horses, but when it came to selling them we just couldn't find any purchasers. . . . The prince soon got tired of it, anyway, and dropped his horses and began to do anything that came into his head: one day he'd get all excited about some new and wonderful flour mill which he would start building immediately, next day he'd open a saddler's shop, and the outcome of all his activities would be more losses and greater debts and, what was much more serious, there was a change for the worse in his character. He never stayed at home for any length of time now, but kept rushing off to one place or another, always on the lookout for something, while Grusha was left alone, and in such a condition, too, for the poor girl was with child. Time would hang heavily on her hands. "I don't see much of him now," she used to say, but she went on showing a bold front to the world and in her relations with the prince in particular she'd try to be as inexacting in her demands as possible: as soon as she noticed that he was beginning to get tired of staying at home after a day or two, she'd immediately say:

"Why don't you go somewhere, my precious jewel? Go out and enjoy yourself. Don't sit about with me: I'm such an ordinary uneducated woman."

The prince would be full of contrition at those words of hers, and he'd kiss her hands and hold out for another two or three days, but when he kicked over the traces after that, there'd be no holding him; but he'd leave her under my personal supervision.

"Take good care of her, my semi-honorable Ivan Severyanych," he'd say. "You're an artist, not a good-for-nothing wastrel like me, an artist of the first water, and that's why it seems you know how to talk to her and why you find each other such congenial company. As for me, I'm getting sick and tired of her 'precious jewels.'"

I said:

"Why should you, sir? It's just a word of endearment."

"It may be a word of endearment," he said, "but it's stupid and tiresome all the same."

I said nothing, but after that I went to see her as a matter of course: whenever the prince was away I'd visit her twice a day in her rooms, just for a cup of tea, and I'd try to cheer her up as much as possible. And I felt she needed cheering up, for every time she started talking to me, she'd begin to complain bitterly.

"My dearest friend, Ivan Severyanych," she would say, "the green monster, jealousy, is eating me up."

I, of course, did my best to comfort her.

"Why be so eaten up by jealousy," I'd say, "if wherever he goes he always comes back to you?"

But she'd start crying and she'd beat her breast and say:

"Please, tell me the truth, my dear friend, don't hide it from me: where does he spend all his time?"

"Why," I'd say, "with his friends in the country and in town."

"But are you sure," she'd say, "that he hasn't got anyone, some woman who keeps him away from me? Tell me, wasn't he in love with some woman before he met me and has he now gone back to her, or does he intend to marry her perhaps, the wretch?" And her eyes, as she said that, would blaze with such hatred that I felt afraid of what might happen if her suspicions were justified.

I comforted her as best I could, but I could not help thinking, "Who can tell what his lordship may not be up to?" For it was very rarely that we saw him at all at that time.

Well, when the thought that the prince might be contemplating marriage occurred to her, she began plaguing me to find out what he was doing in town.

"Please," she said, "my dear, dear friend, Ivan Severyanych, go to town and find out everything for certain and come back and tell me about it without concealing anything from me."

She kept on plaguing me more and more persistently and in the end made me feel so sorry for her that I thought, "Come what may, I'll go and find out, although if I do discover that the prince is unfaithful to her, I shan't tell her everything, but at least I'll have a look and clear the matter up one way or the other."

I thought of a good excuse for going to town: I said that I had to buy various medicaments for the horses from the herb dealers. So early one morning I set off, but I didn't set off just any old way—oh, no!—I devised a cunning plan of my own.

Grusha did not know, and the servants had been strictly forbidden to tell her, that before he met her the prince had had another mistress in town, a woman of good family, Yevgenia

Semyonovna, the daughter of a secretary in some government department. She was well known throughout the town as a fine pianist and was altogether a very kind-hearted lady, good-looking, too, and she had had a daughter by the prince, but she grew rather fat and it was said that the prince had left her because of that. However, being still very rich at the time, he had bought a house for the lady and her daughter and they lived on the income the house brought in. After rewarding her in that way, the prince never visited Yevgenia Semyonovna again, but our servants, for old times' sake, remembered her for her kindness and every time they happened to go to town, they'd stop at her place, both because they loved her and she was very nice to them and because she loved to find out about our prince from them.

So on my arrival in town I went straight to her, to this kind-hearted lady, and I said:

"I'd like to stay at your house, if I may, madam."

She replied:

"Yes, of course, but why don't you stop at the prince's flat?"

"Has he a flat in town?" I asked.

"Yes," she replied. "He's been staying there for more than a week. He's starting some new business, I believe."

"What kind of business?" I asked.

"A cotton mill," she said. "I understand he's taking it on a lease."

"Good heavens, madam," I exclaimed, "what has he thought up now?"

"Why?" she said. "Is there anything wrong?"

"Not that I know of," I said, "except that I'm rather surprised at his doing that."

She smiled.

"That's nothing," she said. "There's something you really ought to be surprised at: I've received a letter from the prince in which he writes to say that he intends to pay me a call today. It seems he's longing to see my daughter."

"And did you give him your permission, ma'am?" I asked.

She shrugged her shoulders and said:

"Why shouldn't I? Let him come and have a look at his

daughter," and, having said that, the poor lady sighed and fell into thought and so she sat with head bowed, still so young and fair and robust-looking and, besides, her manners were so different from Grusha's. . . . Grusha knew nothing better than her "precious jewel," but this one, this one was quite different. . . . So I grew quite jealous of her on Grusha's account.

"Oh," I thought to myself, "I only hope that when he looks at that child of his, he won't cast a glance at you, too, with that insatiable heart of his, for if he does, nothing good will come of it for my dear Grusha."

Turning these thoughts over in my mind, I was sitting in the nursery, where Yevgenia Semyonovna had asked the old nurse, Tatyana Yakovlevna, a very talkative old lady who was a native of Moscow, to treat me to a cup of tea, when suddenly I heard a ring at the front door and presently the parlor maid rushed in and said to the nurse:

"The prince has just arrived!"

I was about to get up to go to the kitchen, but Tatyana Yakovlevna, who had a real passion for gossiping and hated to be deprived of a listener, said to me:

"Don't go, Ivan Gologanych, we can both retire to the dressing room and sit down behind the wardrobe. She'd never bring him in there and we shall be able to have a cosy little chat together."

I gladly agreed to her suggestion, for I hoped to learn something useful for Grusha from Tatyana Yakovlevna, who, once she started talking, would never stop; and as Yevgenia Semyonovna had sent me a little eau-de-Cologne bottle filled with rum for my tea, I decided, being already a strict teetotaler myself at the time, to pour it into nurse's tea; for I was anxious to do everything possible to encourage her natural talkativeness in the hope that the dear old lady—bless her heart!—would tell me something which she would not otherwise have told me.

We left the nursery and ensconced ourselves behind the cupboards in the dressing room, which was very narrow, more like a passage than a room, with a door at one end. As luck would have it, that door led straight into the room where Yevgenia Semyonovna had received the prince, and the couch on which they had sat down was standing against that door. In a word, only that door, hung with a curtain on the other side, separated me from them, but it was really as if I were in the same room with them, for I could hear every word they said.

As soon as he entered the room, the prince said:

"How do you do, my dear and trusted friend?"

And she replied:

"How do you do, Prince? To what do I owe the pleasure of your visit?"

And he said:

"We shall talk about it later. Let me have a look at you first, let me kiss your sweet head, my dear," and I could hear how he gave her a smacking kiss on the head and then asked about his daughter.

Yevgenia Semyonovna replied that she was at home.

"How is she?"

"She's quite all right, thank you," she said.

"She must have grown, eh?"

Yevgenia Semyonovna laughed.

"Of course," she said, "she's grown."

The prince said:

"You don't mind my seeing her, do you?"

"Of course not," she said, "I'd be delighted!" and she got up, went into the nursery, and called the nurse, Tatyana Yakovlevna, who was having such a grand old time with me.

"Please, nurse," she said, "bring darling little Lyuda to the prince."

Tatyana Yakovlevna was fed up. She put her saucer of tea down on the table and said:

"What a nuisance they are, to be sure! A body can't sit down to have a nice talk with a man without them starting to shout for her and spoil all her pleasure!" She then covered me up quickly with her mistress' skirts which hung on the wall and said, "Wait for me here," and went to fetch the little girl.

I stayed behind the cupboards and I could hear how the prince kissed the child twice and dandled her on his knees and said:

"Would you like, *mon enfant*, to go for a ride in my carriage?"

The little girl said nothing, whereupon the prince said to Yevgenia Semyonovna:

"*Je vous prie*, please, let her have a ride in my carriage with the nurse. I'm sure she'll enjoy it."

Yevgenia Semyonovna started objecting in French, why and *pourquoi* and so on, but he too said something in French, something to the effect that it was "absolutely necessary," and after they had exchanged a few words in this way, she at last very reluctantly agreed to fall in with his suggestion and said to the nurse:

"Dress her and go for a ride with her."

So off they went for a ride and those two remained together and I eavesdropped on them, for I could not possibly leave my hiding place behind the cupboards and besides, I said to myself, "Now is my chance to find out the truth and know for sure whether either of them plans any harm to Grusha."

16.

Having made up my mind to eavesdrop, I did not content myself with that but also wanted to see what I could with my own eyes, and I worked things out so that my wish was fulfilled to my entire satisfaction: I climbed very quietly up on a stool and I soon discovered a chink in a groove above the door and pressed my eye eagerly to it. I saw that the prince was sitting on the sofa and that Yevgenia Semyonovna was standing by the window and . . . yes . . . watching her little darling being put into the carriage.

After the carriage had driven off, she turned to the prince and said:

"Well, prince, I did all you wanted me to do: tell me now what business brings you here."

And he answered:

"Damn the business! . . . There's plenty of time to discuss my business: it isn't a bear, it won't run off into the forest. First of all, come here, darling, sit down beside me and let's have a good talk, as we used to, you and I, in the old days."

Yevgenia Semyonovna, however, did not budge from her place by the window, leaning against it with her hands behind her back. She was silent, knitting her brows. The prince implored her:

"What's the matter, darling? Won't you sit down beside me? I want to talk to you!"

She obeyed him and came over; seeing that, his lordship at once began again jokingly:

"That's right," he said, "let's sit down as we used to, darling," and he wanted to embrace her, but she pushed him away and said:

"Tell me your business, Prince! What is your business? What can I do for you?"

"Good heavens," said the prince, "do you want me to put all my cards on the table without any preliminaries?"

"Of course," she said, "tell me straight out what you want. We're old friends, aren't we? So why stand on ceremony?"

"I want money," said the prince.

Yevgenia Semyonovna just looked at him and said nothing.

"Not a lot of money," said the prince.

"How much?"

"At the moment, only twenty thousand."

Yevgenia Semyonovna again said nothing and the prince went on to describe in very eloquent language how he was buying a cotton mill and how he hadn't a penny to bless himself with, "but," said he, "if I manage to buy it, I shall be a millionaire, for," he said, "I intend to modernize the whole works, get rid of the old machinery and everything, and start manufacturing beautifully colored cloth and sell it to the Asiatics in Nizhny. I'll make it all out of rubbish and dye it in bright colors and it'll sell like hot cakes and I'll make a lot of money, but right now I need twenty thousand which I have to pay as a deposit for the factory."

Yevgenia Semyonovna said:

"But where can you get all that money?"

And the prince replied:

"I'm damned if I know, but I must get it, for I've thought everything out most beautifully. You see, I have a man, Ivan

Golovan, an army horse buyer, not very bright, but a fine fellow, as honest as they make them and very dependable, and he was for many years a prisoner among the Asiatics and knows all their tastes well. There's a fair in Nizhny now, so I'll send Golovan down there to get me contracts and take samples of the sort of stuff they want and I'm quite sure there'll be plenty of orders. . . . Well, then . . . first of all I'll immediately repay that twenty thousand. . . ."

Here he stopped and Yevgenia Semyonovna, too, was silent for a moment, then she just sighed and said:

"Your plan, Prince, is excellent."

"Yes, isn't it?"

"It certainly is excellent," she said. "You will do just that. You'll pay the deposit on the factory, then everybody will look on you as a manufacturer, they'll start saying in society that your affairs have improved . . ."

"Yes, yes!"

"Yes, and then . . ."

". . . Golovan will get hundreds of orders and deposits in Nizhny and I'll repay my debt and be a rich man!"

"Please, don't interrupt me: you first of all throw dust in the eyes of the President of the Noblemen's Chamber, and while he regards you as a rich man you'll marry his daughter, and then, having made sure of her dowry, you will indeed be a rich man!"

"So that's what you think, darling?" said the prince.

And Yevgenia Semyonovna replied:

"Why? Don't you think so, too?"

"Well," said he, "if you can see through it all, then may the Lord hearken unto your words and bring us joy everlasting."

"Us?"

"Of course," his lordship said, "for then we shall all be in clover: you'll mortgage your house for me and I'll pay your daughter ten thousand interest for the twenty thousand!"

Yevgenia Semyonovna said in reply:

"The house is yours. You gave it to her and you can take it back, if you want to."

He began to object. "No, no," he exclaimed, "the house isn't mine, but as you are her mother I ask you . . . I mean, of course, if you trust me . . ."

But she said:

"Really, Prince, is that all I have trusted you with? Haven't I trusted you with my honor and my life?"

"Oh, I see," he said, "you mean . . . Well, thank you, thank you . . . You're such a darling . . . So I may send the mortgage to you for your signature tomorrow, may I not?"

"Yes," she said, "send it and I'll sign it."

"But aren't you afraid?"

"No," she said, "after what I've lost already, I've nothing to be afraid of any more."

"But aren't you sorry? Tell me, aren't you sorry? I presume you still love me a little, don't you? Or do you just pity me? Eh?"

But she merely laughed at his words and said:

"Stop talking nonsense, Prince! Won't you have some stewed cloudberries with sugar? They're delicious just now!"

Well, the prince seemed hurt by that offer of hers, doubtless having expected something quite different, so he got up and smiled.

"No, thank you, my dear," he said, "you can eat your cloudberries yourself; I don't feel like indulging in a sweet just now. Good-bye, darling, and thank you," and he began kissing her hand and meanwhile the carriage returned.

Yevgenia Semyonovna got up and gave him her hand as a farewell gesture and said:

"But what are you going to do with that black-eyed gypsy girl of yours?"

Well, the prince just struck his forehead and said:

"Good heavens, I'd forgotten all about her! What a clever woman you are, darling! Believe it or not, but I cannot ever forget how clever you are and thank you for having reminded me of that precious jewel of mine!"

"Had you really forgotten all about her?" she said.

"On my word of honor, I had," he said. "It just slipped my mind, but, of course, I shall have to do something for the silly fool."

"Do something by all means," said Yevgenia Semyonovna, "only let it be something good: remember, she isn't a Russian girl, a mixture of tepid blood and new milk. She won't take things lying down; she'll never forgive you for old times' sake."

"Don't you worry," he said, "she will."

"Is she in love with you, Prince? I'm told she's terribly in love with you."

"Oh, I'm sick and tired of her, but, thank God, she seems to be very fond of Golovan."

"How will that help you?" Yevgenia Semyonovna asked.

"Well, I'll buy them a house, register Ivan as a merchant, and they'll get married and live happily ever after."

But Yevgenia Semyonovna shook her head and said, smiling:

"Oh, my poor prince, what a silly man you are! Where's your conscience?"

And the prince said:

"Leave my conscience alone, please. I've no time for it just now: I have to send for Golovan to come to town today, if possible."

So of course Yevgenia Semyonovna told him that I was in town already, and she said, "He's staying at my house." The prince was very glad to hear that and asked her to send me to him as soon as possible, and he himself left immediately.

After that things began to move fast, just as in a fairy tale. The prince loaded me with all the necessary legal documents to show that I had complete power to act for him and that he was the owner of a cotton mill and he taught me to say what kind of cloth his factory was manufacturing and he sent me straight from town to the Nizhny fair, so that I had no time even to see Grusha, but all the time I was very annoyed with the prince, for how could he have said that she would be my wife? At the Nizhny fair I ran into luck. I got hundreds of orders and samples as well as money from the Asiatics, and the money I sent to the prince and I myself went back to the estate and I just didn't recognize it. . . . Everything seemed to have changed as if by magic: it had all been redecorated like a peasant's cottage before the holidays and not a trace of the wing where Grusha had had her apartments could be seen: it had been levelled to the ground and where it had stood a new building had been erected. I just gasped with astonishment and rushed to see where Grusha was, but not a soul could tell me anything about her; the servants were all new, all of them had been hired and were not the prince's own, and all of them gave themselves such airs and they wouldn't even let me get near the prince. Before this the prince and I had just been pals, like two army men, but now everything was done in a grand style and if there was anything I wanted to tell the prince I had to do it through his valet.

I never could stand that sort of thing and I shouldn't have stayed there another minute if I hadn't felt so sorry for Grusha. But, try as I might, I couldn't find out what had happened to her. When I tried to question some of the old servants, they shut up and I could see that they had received strict orders not to tell me anything. It was only with the greatest difficulty that I at last succeeded in persuading an old maidservant to tell me that Grusha had left only a short while ago. "It's only a matter of some ten days," she told me, "since she left in a carriage with the prince and did not come back." So I went straight to the coachmen and tried to find out from them where the prince had taken her, but they wouldn't tell me anything. All they would say was that the prince had changed his horses at the first stage of the journey and had sent them back, leaving with Grusha for some unknown destination on hired horses. No matter where I turned, I could pick up no trace of the poor gypsy girl and that was that: whether the villain had stuck a knife into her or shot her with a pistol and had thrown her body into a ditch in a wood and covered it up with dry leaves, or whether he drowned her in a pond or a river, it was impossible to say, but all that might easily have happened, seeing what a slave he was to his passions; for she certainly stood in the way of his marriage, as Yevgenia Semyonovna quite rightly warned him, because Grusha loved him, villain that he was, with all the passion of her unrestrained gypsy heart and it was not like her to put up with his foul treachery and meekly to bear her burden like Yevgenia Semyonovna, who was indeed a true Christian lady, sacrificing her life for him as she did, just letting it burn out like a lamp before an icon. I fancied that when the prince told Grusha about his intended marriage, the gypsy blood in her must have blazed up like a flame through the smoke of a campfire and she must have uttered God knows what threats and so he had murdered her.

So the more I considered it, the more convinced did I become that that must actually have happened, and I just could not bring myself to watch all the preparations for the prince's forthcoming marriage to the daughter of the President of the Noblemen's Chamber. And when the day of the marriage came and the maidservants were given brightly colored kerchiefs to wear and the menservants were all dressed up in new liveries, each according to his duties, I refused to put on my new suit of clothes, but took everything to my little storeroom in the stables and left it there, and from early morning I took to the woods, where I wandered about till evening, not knowing myself for what purpose, hoping against hope to stumble upon her dead body. When evening came I left the woods and sat down on the steep bank of the little river, and beyond the river I could see the prince's mansion glittering with lights and I could hear the noise of merriment coming from there. The guests were enjoying themselves and the band was playing and the music and the sounds of revelry could be heard a long way off. I sat there, no longer even looking at the mansion but with my eyes fixed on the water, where the lights were reflected in the rippling waves and the columns of the house were swaying to and fro like the columns of some watery palace. And I felt so miserable, so sick at heart, that I did what I had never done before, not even in the days of my captivity: I began to talk to the unseen powers and, as in the fairy tale of that Sister Alyonushka whose brother kept on calling her, I called to my poor Grusha, that dear sister of mine, in a grief-stricken voice:

"Oh, my dear sister," I said, "my poor little Grusha, answer me, speak to me, say just one word to me, appear to me just for a minute!"

And imagine my surprise, gentlemen, when after calling her three times like that in a mournful voice, it seemed to me that someone was running towards me and I felt terrified, for I could hear clearly that someone had run past me once, then had begun to circle round me, whispered in my ear, peered into my face over my shoulder, and, all at once, rushed at me out of the darkness of the night! . . . and hung round my neck, trembling convulsively. . . .

17.

I was frightened out of my wits and nearly collapsed on the ground, but I did not lose consciousness, and I felt that somebody—alive and light—was fluttering on the ground like a wounded crane, sighing, but uttering no word.

I said a silent prayer and looked up: and there before me was poor Grusha's face.

"My dear," I said, "my poor, poor darling! Are you alive or have you come to me from the next world? Don't be afraid to tell me the truth," I said, "for I won't be afraid of you, my poor little thing, even if you are dead!"

And she heaved a deep sigh—it seemed to come from her very heart—and said:

"I am alive."

"Well," said I, "thank God for that."

"But," said she, "I have come here to die."

"Good heavens, my dear Grusha," I said, "what are you saying? Why should you die? Let us live together happily: I'll work for you, I'll build a little house for you, my poor little one, and you'll live with me like my own dear sister."

But she answered:

"No, Ivan Severyanych, no, my dear one, my dearest friend, thank you very much for your great kindness to me, a poor, unhappy creature, but I, miserable gypsy girl that I am, cannot go on living, for if I do I might bring death and ruin to an innocent soul."

I questioned her:

"Who are you talking about? Whose soul are you so sorry for?"

And she answered:

"I'm sorry for her, the young wife of my seducer, for she is so young and innocent, poor dear, and my jealous heart will never reconcile itself to her happiness and I shall kill both her and myself."

"You mustn't talk like that," I said. "Cross yourself, do! You were baptized, weren't you? Think what will happen to your soul!"

"No," she said, "I'm not even sorry for my own soul: let it go to hell, for here it is worse than hell!"

I could see that the poor girl was beside herself and that she did not know what she was saying, so I took her by the hands and held them tight and looked at her. I was amazed to see how terribly changed she was and I could not help wondering where her beauty had gone to. Even her body seemed to have shrunk to a shadow and only her eyes were blazing in her dark face, like the eyes of a wolf at night, and they seemed to me to be twice as large as before, and her belly bulged terribly, for her pregnancy was drawing to an end, and her poor little face was no bigger than a fist and her black locks fell over her cheeks. I looked at the dress she was wearing and I saw that it was a cheap cotton one, of a dark color and all in holes, and she wore her shoes on bare feet.

"Tell me," I said, "where have you come from? Where have you been and why have you lost all your looks?"

She smiled suddenly and said:

"Why? Am I not beautiful? Beautiful? This is what my sweetheart has done to me for the great love I bore him, for giving up my lover for him, for giving myself entirely to him, body and soul! He locked me up in a safe place and he set guards on me and he commanded them to keep a good watch over my beauty . . ." And then she burst out laughing suddenly and said wrathfully:

"Oh, you stupid fool of a prince! Is a gypsy girl one of your young ladies that she can be kept under lock and key? Why, if I felt like it I could go straight to your young wife and bite her throat out!"

I saw that she was all convulsed by her jealous fit and I

thought, "Let me try to distract her thoughts not by the fear of hell, but by sweet memories," and I said:

"But think how dearly he loved you, Grusha, how he loved you! How he used to kiss your feet . . . do you remember how he used to kneel in front of the couch while you were singing and kiss your scarlet slipper all over, top and bottom? . . ."

She began to take notice of my words and her long black eyelashes fluttered over her dry cheeks and, looking down at the water, she said in a hollow voice:

"Yes, he loved me, the villain, he loved me, he didn't begrudge me anything while I didn't care for his love, but as soon as I fell in love with him, he left me. And who did he leave me for? Is she, my rival, better than I, or will she love him more than I? . . . Oh, he is so foolish, so foolish! The sun in winter doesn't warm like the summer sun, and he'll never again taste love like mine. You'd better tell him that. Tell him: before her death Grusha made this prophecy about you and said that this would be your destiny!"

I was glad that at last she had become so talkative and I started questioning her and said:

"What did happen between you and the prince and why did it all happen?"

She threw up her hands and said:

"Oh, it didn't happen for any reason at all, except for his treachery. . . . He got tired of me, that is the only reason," and while saying this, she began crying bitter tears. "He bought me dresses according to his taste," she said, "dresses which were no good to a pregnant woman, dresses with narrow waists. I would put them on to please him, but he'd get angry and say, 'Take it off: it doesn't suit you!' But if I didn't put them on and came out to him in a loose dress, he'd get angrier . . . he'd say, 'What an awful sight you are!' It was then that I understood that I had lost him for good, that I had become odious to him. . . ."

She began to sob now and she looked straight ahead and whispered:

"I had felt it coming for a long time," she said, "I knew that he wasn't fond of me any more, but I wanted to see what kind of conscience he had. I thought: I mustn't plague him, I must make him pity me, but he had no pity for me. . . ."

Then she told me such a strange, stupid story about her last parting from the prince that I couldn't understand and I still cannot understand how a little thing like that could make even a wicked man betray and ruin a woman forever.

18.

Grusha told me everything. "After you," she said, "had gone away and disappeared"—that was when I had gone off to the Nizhny fair—"the prince did not return home for a long time and I heard rumors that he was going to be married. . . . I cried a lot because of that and lost my good looks. . . . My heart ached and I felt how my child pressed against it. . . . I thought: it will die in my womb. Then, suddenly, I heard them say, 'He's coming!' I trembled all over and I rushed to my rooms to get myself up as nicely as possible for him. I put on my emerald earrings and I took down from the wall, from behind a sheet, a dress trimmed with lace and with a low bodice, which he liked better than any of my other dresses . . . I was in such a hurry to put it on that I couldn't get the back fastened, so I left it unfastened and just threw a red scarf over it, so that he wouldn't notice that it wasn't fastened, and I rushed out to meet him on the steps . . . I was trembling all over and before I knew what I was doing I had exclaimed, 'Oh, my darling, oh, my sweet, my fair, my precious jewel!' and I threw my arms round his neck and fainted. . . ."

The poor thing nearly fainted again as she told me of it.

"When I came to," she went on, "I was in my room . . . lying on a sofa and trying to remember whether I had really embraced him or whether I had only dreamt about it. . . . I felt awfully weak," she said, "and did not see him for a long time. . . . I kept on sending for him, but he wouldn't come. . . ."

At last he did put in an appearance and she said to him:

"Have you thrown me over altogether? Have you forgotten me?"

And he said:

"I am very busy."

She said:

"What are you so busy with now? Why weren't you so busy before, my precious jewel?"

And she stretched out her arms again to embrace him, but he made a wry face and pulled with all his might at the silken ribbon round her neck.

"Luckily," she said to me, "that silk ribbon round my neck wasn't very strong, it had become frayed and it broke, for I had been wearing an amulet on it for many years, or he would have strangled me, and I think that was what he had intended to do, for he got quite white in the face and he hissed out at me:

" 'Why are you wearing such a dirty ribbon?' "

"I said, 'Why are you so concerned about my ribbon? It was clean, it has gotten dirty now because I worry such a lot, it has gotten dirty from the heavy sweat on my body.'

"But he just spat and went out and late in the afternoon he came back, looking angry, and said:

" 'Let's go for a ride in my carriage!' and he pretended to be nice to me and he kissed me on the head and I, suspecting nothing, sat down in the carriage with him and we drove away. We drove a long time, changing horses twice. He would not tell me where we were going, but I saw that we reached some woods, it was a marshy, wild, and dreadful place. And in that forest we soon came to some beehives and behind those beehives was a cottage and there three strong, young girls in madder-red dresses met us and they addressed me as 'madam.' As soon as I got out of the carriage, they took me under the arms and dragged me into a room which was all ready for me.

"All that troubled me greatly and my heart contracted with pain, but I was particularly frightened of those young girls.

" 'What kind of an inn is this?' I asked the prince.

"But he replied:

*" 'It isn't an inn. This is where you are going to live from now on.'

"I began to cry and to kiss his hands, imploring him not to leave me there, but he showed no pity: he pushed me away from him and went away. . . ."

Here poor Grusha fell silent and bowed her head, then she sighed and said:

"I wanted to run away. I tried a hundred times to escape, but I couldn't, for those girls kept watch over me and didn't let me out of their sight. . . . I felt so wretched there and finally I made up my mind to trick them and I pretended to be carefree and happy and told them that I wanted to go for a walk in the woods. They took me for a walk, but they wouldn't take their eyes off me. I kept on looking at the trees, at the top branches and the bark, to find out which way the sun was shining at noon, and all the time I was trying to think of a way of giving those girls the slip, and yesterday I carried it out. After dinner I went out with them to a clearing in the wood and I said:

" 'Come on, sweethearts, let's play blindman's buff in this clearing!'

"They agreed.

" 'But instead of binding our eyes,' I said, 'let's tie our hands and tag each other with our behinds.'

"They did not object to that, either.

"So we did. I tied the hands of one of them very tightly behind her back and rushed off with another behind a bush and tied her up there and the third I just overcame by sheer force in the sight of the other two; they screamed for help, but I ran away faster than a racehorse, pregnant as I am, keeping to the woods all the time, and so I ran for a whole night and in the morning I collapsed by some old beehives in a thick part of the wood. Here an old man approached me and started talking to me, but I could hardly make out what he was saying with those toothless gums of his. He seemed all covered with beeswax and he smelled of honey and in his yellow eyebrows bees were swarming. I told him that I wanted to see you, Ivan Severyanych, and he said to me:

" 'Call him, my pretty maid, once with the wind and once

against the wind, and then he'll feel a longing for you and he'll start looking for you and you'll meet.'

"He gave me some water to drink and some honey and cucumber to strengthen myself with. I drank the water and ate the cucumber with the honey and went on my way again, calling you all the time, once with the wind and once against the wind, and so we met. Thank you," she said, and she embraced me and kissed me and said, "You're like a dear brother to me!"

I said:

"And you're like a dear sister to me," and, overcome by my feelings, I began to shed tears.

And she, too, wept and said:

"I know, Ivan Severyanych, I know everything and I realize that you alone really loved me, my dear, dear friend. Prove to me that you still love me and do what I shall ask you in this fateful hour."

"Tell me what you want me to do," I said.

"No," said she, "you must first swear to me by all that you hold sacred in the world that you will do what I ask of you."

So I swore to her by the salvation of my soul, but she said:

"That's not enough: for my sake you might even break that oath. No," she said, "swear to me by something which is even more sacred."

"But," I said, "I can't think of any more terrible oath than that."

"Well," she said, "I've thought of something for you and you say it quickly after me and don't try to think about it at all."

I promised her that, fool that I was, and she said:

"Damn my soul as you have damned yours if you do not do as I tell you."

"All right," I said, and right then and there I damned her soul.

"Well, listen to me now," she said, "for now you can become the real savior of my soul. I have no more strength," she said, "to go on living and tormenting myself, seeing how shamelessly he has treated me and how he has heaped dishonor upon me. If I live for one more day, I shall surely kill *him* and *her* and if I take pity on them, I shall kill myself and damn my soul forever.

. . . So do take pity upon me, my dear, dear brother—thrust a knife into my heart!"

I started back from her and began making the sign of the cross over her, trying to get as far away from her as possible, but she threw her arms round my knees, and she wept and prostrated herself before me, saying:

"You will live and obtain forgiveness from God for my soul and for yours, but if you force me to lay hands on myself, you'll condemn me to eternal damnation. Won't you do it? . . ."

Ivan Severyanych knit his brows in his great distress at the recollection of that scene and, biting his mustache, he seemed to bring the words out from the bottom of his tortured heart, and he sighed rather than spoke:

"She took my knife out of my pocket . . . opened it . . . straightened the blade . . . and put it into my hands . . . and she carried on in a way that I could not bear to see.

" 'If you don't kill me,' she said, 'I shall repay you all by becoming a harlot!'

"I trembled all over at those words of hers and told her to say her prayers, but I did not stab her: I just threw her over the steep bank into the river. . . ."

Hearing this last confession of Ivan Severyanych, all of us for the first time began to doubt the truth of his story and there was a great silence for a time, but at last somebody cleared his throat and said:

"Did she drown?"

"The water swallowed her up," replied Ivan Sveryanych.

"And what did you do after that?"

"What do you mean, sir?"

"I suppose you must have suffered a lot."

"Of course I did."

19.

I ran from that place without thinking and without figuring out what I was doing or where I was going, and all I remember is that someone seemed to be running after me, someone who was terribly tall and big and shameless and naked; his whole body was black and his head was small as an onion, and he was all covered with hair, and I guessed that if it was not Cain, it was Satan himself, the foul fiend of hell, and I kept on running away from him and called upon my guardian angel for help. When I came to myself I was already on the highway, sitting under a willow tree. It was a dry autumn day, the sun shone, but it was cold and the wind raised clouds of dust and yellow leaves were tossed about in it. I did not know what hour of the day it was or what place it was or where the road led to, and there was a horrid emptiness in my soul: not an inkling of an idea what I should do. All I was thinking about was that poor Grusha's soul was doomed now and that it was my duty to suffer for her and to save her from everlasting hell. But how I was to do it I didn't know and that filled my mind with distress and anguish, but, suddenly, something touched me on the shoulder: I looked up and I saw that it was a dead twig that had fallen from the willow tree and was being carried far away by the wind, and I followed it with my eyes and then suddenly I saw Grusha walking, only she was very small and looked no more than six or seven years old, and behind her shoulders there sprouted little wings. As soon as I saw her, she flew away from me like a bullet and there was only a swirl of dust and dry leaves left behind her.

I thought: That must certainly be her soul following after me and she has gone ahead to show me the way. So I went. I walked for a whole day without any idea of where I was going, and I was dead tired, and then some people overtook me, an old man and an old woman travelling in a cart together, and they said:

"Sit down in our cart, stranger, and we'll take you on your way."

I sat down in the cart and they went on and I could see that they were greatly distressed.

"We are in great trouble," they said. "Our only son is being taken away into the army and we have no money and cannot hire another man in his place."

I was very sorry for the old couple and I said:

"I'd gladly oblige you and go instead of your son, but I have no papers."

But they said:

"That's nothing: leave that to us. All we want you to do is to take our son's name and to call yourself Peter Serdyukov."

"All right," I said, "that suits me. I shall continue to pray to my own saint, St. John, and I don't mind what I call myself."

So we agreed on that and they took me to another town and enlisted me in the army there in place of their son and gave me twenty-five roubles in silver and promised to help me while they lived. I gave away the money they had given me, the twenty-five roubles, to a poor monastery to offer prayers for Grusha's soul and I petitioned the army authorities to send me to the Caucasus where I could die for my faith as soon as possible. So it was done, and I spent more than fifteen years in the Caucasus and revealed my real name and occupation to no one but was known as Peter Serdyukov, and only on St. John's Day did I pray for myself to God through the intermediary of the Saint, the blessed Evangelist. And I had almost forgotten my past life and occupation and was serving my last year in the army in this manner when, as it came to pass, on that very day, St. John's Day, we were in pursuit of the Tartars, who had given us a lot of trouble and had gone beyond the river Koys. There are several rivers of that name in those parts: one of them flows along the Andian Valley and is known as the Andian Koys, a second flows along the Avarian Valley and is known as the Avarian Koys, and a third and fourth are known as the Korikumuyskaya and Kuzikumuyskaya, and all of them meet and where they meet the river Sulak starts. But all four of them are very rapid and cold, and especially the Andian one, behind which the Tartars had fled. We had killed a great number of those Tartars there, so many that we couldn't even count them, but some of them succeeded in crossing the Koys River and they hid themselves on the other side behind boulders and as soon as we exposed ourselves they started firing at us. But there was great cunning in the way they fired, for they did not waste a single shot but kept back their fire until they were certain that each bullet would find its mark, for they knew that we had a lot more ammunition than they, and they were so set on inflicting casualties on us that although we were all in full view of them, those devils would not fire in our direction even once. Our colonel was a man of great courage who liked to fancy himself another Suvorov, and he always said "Bless my soul," and taught us to be brave by his own example. So he just sat down on the bank, bared his legs and put them into the ice-cold water up to his knees, and began praising it to the skies.

"Bless my soul," he said, "how warm this water is! Just like new milk in a pail under the cow! Will any of you lads volunteer to swim to the other side with a rope so that we can put a bridge across?"

While our colonel sat there chatting like that to us, the Tartars stuck the barrels of two rifles through a slit between two boulders, but did not shoot. As soon as two soldiers had volunteered and began to swim across, however, they began firing at them and those poor devils just disappeared under the waves. We pulled out the rope and another pair took to the water while we opened a murderous fire upon those boulders behind which the Tartars were hiding, but we couldn't do them any harm, for our bullets hit the stones and those confounded devils just let go at the swimmers and the water became red with blood and the soldiers again disappeared. A third pair followed, but they did not reach the middle of the Koys either, the Tartars sending them to the bottom of the river. Well, after the third pair there were no more volunteers, for everybody could see that this was no longer war but just plain murder. But as the murderers had to be punished, the colonel said:

"Listen to me, lads, isn't there one among you who has committed a mortal sin and who would like to expiate his crime for his soul's sake? Bless my soul, what a splendid chance he has now of washing away his offense with his blood!"

"Well," I thought to myself, "What better chance can I have of ending my life?" and I stepped forward and took off my clothes. I said the Lord's Prayer, prostrated myself on every side before my comrades and my superiors, said to myself, "Well, Grusha, dear sister of my heart, may my blood expiate your sin," and then took in my mouth the string which was tied to the rope by one end and, taking a flying leap from the bank, plunged into the river.

The water was terribly cold: I had shooting pains under my armpits and my chest contracted painfully and I got a cramp in my legs, but I carried on. . . . Above me our bullets were whizzing past and round me. Tartar bullets went plopping into the water, but they did not hit me. I did not know, however, whether I was wounded or not, but I did reach the other bank. . . . There the Tartars could no longer fire at me, for I was separated from them by one side of a ravine and to shoot at me they would have had to show themselves under the hail of bullets which our soldiers kept up from the other bank. So there I was standing under the rocks and pulling away at the rope. I pulled it across and then we threw a bridge over the river and our men were soon on the other side, but I was still standing there, hardly realizing what was happening under my very eyes, for I was thinking all the time: did anybody see what I saw? For, as I swam, I saw Grusha flying above me and she was now a girl in her teens, just about sixteen, I should say, and she had large wings already, bright wings, spanning the whole river, and she protected me with them. . . . However, as nobody said a word about it to me, I said to myself, "It seems I shall have to tell about it myself." So when the colonel started embracing me, kissing me and extolling me to the skies, saying:

"Bless my soul, what a gallant fellow you are, Peter Serdyukov!" I replied:

"I am not a gallant fellow, sir, but a great sinner, and neither the earth nor the water will receive me!"

He began to question me:

"What sin did you commit?"

And I replied:

"I have sent many innocent souls to their doom in my time," and that very night in his tent I told him what I have just told you, gentlemen.

He listened to me very attentively, then he sank into thought and, finally, he said:

"Bless my soul, the things you have gone through! But all the same, my dear fellow, whatever you may say, I am going to recommend you for a commission. I shall send in my report about it right away."

I said:

"Just as you please, sir, but won't you also send an inquiry to that town I told you of to find out whether or not it is true that I killed a gypsy girl?"

"All right," he said, "I shall make that inquiry."

And so he did, but the inquiry the colonel sent out went from one town to another and came back with the answer that my whole story was a lie. The police authorities where the prince's estate was situated declared that "we know nothing about any gypsy girl" and that Ivan Severyanych, "of whom we do know that he was employed by the prince, was freed from serfdom a long time ago and later died at the house of the state-owned peasants, the Serdyukovs."

Well, what more could I do to prove my guilt?

The colonel said to me:

"Don't you dare tell any more lies about yourself, my dear fellow. You must have got a bit touched in the head as you swam across the river. You are suffering from the aftereffects of the cold water and fright. For my part," he said, "I'm glad that what you've told me is just a pack of lies. Now there's nothing to prevent you from becoming an officer. Bless my soul, that's capital!"

Well, I don't mind confessing that I myself got a bit muddled at that point. Did I really push Grusha into the water or had I imagined everything that night, overcome as I was by so strong a longing to see her?

So they made me an officer for my bravery, but as I insisted on telling all and sundry the whole truth about myself, they discharged me from the army with a George Cross, so that I should no longer worry myself over the whole business.

"Accept our congratulations," the colonel said, "you are now a member of the nobility and you can get a job in the Civil Service. Bless my soul, what a glorious life you're going to have," and he gave me a letter to an important man in St. Petersburg. "Go and see him," he said. "He'll help you with your career and see that you're taken care of."

So I eventually got to St. Petersburg with this letter, but I had no luck with my career.

"Why not?"

"You see, I couldn't get a job for a long time and then I got mixed up with Theta and that brought me more troubles."

"What do you mean by 'getting mixed up with Theta'? What is Theta, anyway?"

"The man to whom I was sent about my career got me a job at the Noblemen's Registration Office as an information clerk, and at that office each clerk is given his own letter and all persons whose names begin with that letter have to go to him for information. Now, some letters are very good letters: for instance, the letters B or P or K, for a great many family names begin with those letters and the clerk makes a good income, for the inquirers are naturally anxious to reward him for his zeal on their behalf. But I was given the last and most insignificant letter of the Russian alphabet, the letter Theta, which is pronounced the same as the letter F, and there are very few people whose names begin with it, and even those whose names rightly should begin with it try their best to wriggle out of it and to disown it and any one of them wishing to take out a registration of nobility pretends that his name really begins with an F. While you're wasting your time looking for his name under Theta, the rogue goes and registers himself under F. So, naturally, there's very little profit in such work, while, of course, it means that you have to be at the office all the time. Well, I saw that things couldn't be much worse and I tried to get another job, and what better job could I wish for than that of a coachman? But nobody would employ me. 'You're an officer,' they said to me, 'and you have a military order and we can't very well swear at you or knock you about!' I was in such a terrible fix that I almost thought of hanging myself, but, thank God, I always stopped short of committing such a folly, desperate though I was. But to save myself from death or starvation, I took on a job as an artist."

"What kind of an artist were you?"

"I mean, I was an actor."

"Oh? At what theatre?"

"At a side show on Admiralty Square. There they did not scorn the nobility but accepted everybody: there were army officers there and heads of civil service departments and students, but especially former officials of the High Court of Justice."

"And did you like that life?"

"No, not very much."

"Why not?"

"Well, in the first place, you see, we had to rehearse and learn our parts during Holy Week or during Shrovetide when they sing in the churches: 'Open, ye gates of repentance,' and, secondly, my part was a very difficult one."

"Oh?"

"Yes. I had to play Satan."

"Why was it so difficult?"

"Well, just imagine, gentlemen, I had to dance during two intervals and turn somersaults, and the turning of somersaults was a particularly tricky business, for I was covered from head to toe with the shaggy coat of a gray goat and I had a long tail on a wire, which would always get between my legs, and the horns on my head would get mixed up with every blessed bit of property on the stage, and, besides, I was getting on in years, I was no longer young and I had lost my youthful lightness, and, to make things worse, I had, according to the script, to be beaten all through the play. Well, all that is awfully tiresome, gentlemen. I admit the sticks they beat me with weren't real sticks but were made of canvas and were hollow inside with some cotton wool in the middle, but, all the same, I got tired of being constantly knocked around, and some whose business it was to beat me, whether because of the cold or just for fun, got very clever at beating me quite hard. They were mostly former High Court officials who seemed to have developed quite a knack for delivering a succession of heavy blows. You see, they were a terribly clannish bunch and when they got a chance to play tricks on an army man they would let themselves go and be awfully unpleasant, for they had to beat me in front of the public from noon, as soon as the police flag was hoisted, to midnight, and all that time the man whose turn it was to beat me rained hard blows on me to amuse the public. There was not much fun for me there. And on top of it all a rather unpleasant incident occurred after which I was forced to give up my part."

"What happened?"

"I boxed a prince's ears."

"Which prince?"

"I don't mean a real prince, of course, but a theatrical one. He was one of those former High Court officials, but he played the part of the prince at our theatre."

"What did you box his ears for?"

"Because he deserved it. He was an incorrigible buffoon, always up to all sorts of silly tricks, liked to play practical jokes on everyone."

"On you as well?"

"Yes, on me too. He was an awful nuisance, played the devil with my costume, in the rehearsal room where we used to sit over a coal fire and drink tea he'd steal behind me and fasten my tail to my horns or do something else to raise a laugh and I wouldn't discover it till I had run out in front of the public, and our manager would be cross with me. However, I let him alone as long as it was only me that he annoyed, but he soon began to molest one of our fairies. She was a very young girl who belonged to an impoverished nobleman's family, and she played the goddess Fortune, who had to save the prince from my hands. She had to appear in a dress of glittering tulle material with wings and we had very hard frosts at the time and her hands, poor thing, used to get quite blue, pinched, and he would keep on bothering her, thrusting his attentions on her, and once at the climax of our show, after the three of us had fallen through a trap door into a cellar, he began to pinch her. Well, I naturally felt very sorry for the poor thing and I gave him a thrashing."

"And how did it all end?"

"Oh, the whole thing blew over. You see, there were no witnesses in the cellar except the little fairy, so he couldn't very well bring an action against me, but our High Court mob went on strike and demanded that I be dismissed and, as they were the chief actors there, the manager, to please them, fired me."

"And where did you go after that?"

"Well, for a while I had nothing to eat and no roof over my head, but that little fairy was so grateful to me that she used to give me food; but of course my conscience wouldn't let me be fed by a poor girl who had hardly enough to eat herself, so I kept on racking my brains for a way to get out of this situation. I did not want to go back to that Theta business and, besides, the poor thing already had to provide for another man who was also down on his luck, so I decided to enter a monastery."

"Was there nothing else you could do?"

"What could I have done? I had nowhere to go and life in a monastery appealed to me."

"So you got to like life in a monastery?"

"Yes, very much. Everything was quiet there, just like in my old regiment. You'd be surprised how much life in a monastery resembles life in the army. Everything's provided, clothes, footwear, food, and the authorities look after you and demand strict obedience."

"But don't you find this obedience a bit irksome?"

"Not at all. Why should I? The more obedient a man is, the easier everything in life is for him. No, I have nothing to find fault with in my present position as novice at a monastery: I am not forced to attend divine service unless I want to and I perform my duties as in the old days. If they tell me, 'Harness the horses, Father Ishmael' (they call me Ishmael now), I harness the horses, and if they tell me 'Unharness the horses, Father Ishmael,' I unharness them."

"So," said we, "it seems that in the monastery you got your old job back?"

"Yes, I was given the job of coachman from the start. You see, in the monastery they don't mind my officer's rank, for although I'm not a full-fledged monk yet, not having taken my monastic vows, I am treated as if I were a real monk."

"And when do you intend to take your monastic vows?"

"I won't take them at all."

"Oh? Why not?"

"Well, I don't consider myself worthy."

"Because of your old sins and transgressions, you mean?"

"Yes, I suppose so. But why should I, in any case? I feel very happy in my present position and I live in peace."

"But have you ever told the whole story of your life as you've told it to us to anybody else?"

"Why, yes. I've told it to many people, but what's the use if I have no documents to prove it? They just don't believe me, and so, it seems, I've brought the worldly lies with me into the monastery, where, incidentally, they are convinced that I must be of noble birth. It doesn't make much difference, one way or another, for I am getting old now and it's only a question of how much longer I have to live."

The story of the enchanted wanderer was evidently drawing to a close now. All that was left for us to find out was how he had fared at the monastery.

20.

As our wanderer had reached his journey's end—namely, the monastery, to which he, being of so sincere and religious a cast of mind, seemed to have been destined from birth—and as everything seemed to go so well with him there, we were at first inclined to think that Ivan Severyanych had had no further misfortunes; but in that we were mistaken. One of our passengers remembered that, according to legends, novices were in constant trouble because of the unending machinations of the Devil, and he asked:

"Didn't the Devil try to tempt you in the monastery? I'm told that he is very fond of tempting monks!"

Ivan Severyanych looked calmly at the questioner from under his eyebrows and replied:

"Tempt me? Of course he did. Why, if St. Paul the Apostle himself could not escape from him—for doesn't he write in his Epistle to the Romans that 'there was given me a thorn in the flesh, the messenger of Satan to buffet me'—then how could I, poor and miserable sinner that I am, hope not to be tormented by him?"

"What particular torments did he inflict on you?"

"Oh, all sorts."

"But what?"

"Various abominations and, at first—before, that is, I got the better of him—he even tried to lead me into temptation."

"But you got the better of *him*, the Devil himself?"

"Of course, what else did you expect? It is our special calling in a monastery to frustrate the Devil and his works, but, to be quite frank with you, gentlemen, I don't think I would have been able to do it unaided—without the help, that is, of an old hermit who had had great experience in that line and who knew a remedy for every temptation under the sun. As soon as I told him that Grusha appeared to me so vividly all the time that the air round me seemed to be full of her, he at once thought it over and said to me, 'James the Apostle saith, *Resist the Devil and he will flee from thee*, so all you have to do,' he said, 'is to resist.' And he also told me how to do it, saying, 'As soon as you feel that your heart begins to burn within you and you remember her, you must understand that it is Satan who is drawing nigh unto you and you must immediately gird up your loins and be ready to do battle with him. First of all fall down on your knees, for,' he said, 'a man's knees are the first instruments against the Devil, since as you kneel your soul immediately flies upwards. Being thus exalted in spirit, you keep on prostrating yourself with all the strength in your body, and, indeed, carry on with it until you are worn out, and, furthermore,' he said, 'wear yourself out with fasting even unto starvation, for the Devil, when he sees that you are ready to win a martyr's crown to defeat his knavish tricks, will never let you go as far as that, but will run off at once, because what he fears most is to bring a man by his machinations to the bosom of Christ sooner than necessary, and he usually says to himself, *I'd better leave him alone and tempt him no more, for he will be more likely to stumble that way.*' And I did as he told me and so indeed it came to pass."

"Did you have to torment yourself like that for long before the Devil finally left you alone?"

"Yes, a very long time, and it was by starvation alone that I conquered the fiend, for, it seems, he fears nothing else: I used to abstain from food and drink for four days on end, and it was only then that *he* realized that I was a match for him and he lost heart and weakened. As soon as he saw me throwing out my little bowl of food through the window and taking up my beads to count the number of genuflections, he understood that I was in deadly earnest and ready to win a martyr's crown, if need be, and he ran away, for he is terribly afraid of bringing a man to the point where he begins to partake of the consolations of joy everlasting."

"Well, yes . . . er . . . *he* would hardly . . . But even if you did conquer him, you had to suffer a great deal at his hands, didn't you?"

"Yes, but after all it was I who was oppressing the oppressor and I did it without suffering any particular inconvenience."

"And have you gotten rid of him completely now?"

"Yes, completely."

"And he no longer appears to you at all?"

"No, he never appears to me any more in the seductive shape of a female, and if he does now occasionally appear somewhere in a corner of my cell, he looks a pitiful sight: squeaking just like a little pig who is being slaughtered. I have even stopped tormenting the rascal. I just cross myself and prostrate myself once, and he stops squealing."

"Well, thank God you managed it so well."

"Yes, indeed. Still, while it is true that I've conquered the temptations of the big Devil, I must confess to you, gentlemen, although it is strictly against the rules, that I'm getting sick of the silly tricks the little devils are playing upon me."

"Oh? Have the little devils also been annoying you?"

"Of course . . . I admit that according to their rank they're rather an insignificant lot, but they don't give me any rest all the same. . . ."

"What exactly do they do to you?"

"Well, they're only children, of course, and, besides, there are so many of them in hell and, not having to worry about board and lodgings, they've nothing much to do, so they're constantly asking for permission to visit the earth and create confusion and, having obtained that permission, they just enjoy themselves: the more important the position of a man, the more they annoy him."

"But what, for instance . . . How do they annoy people?"

"Well, they shove something in your hand or put something in your way and you knock it down and break it and thereby annoy or anger someone: this they consider a great prank and it makes them very happy and, indeed, so pleased are they that they start clapping their hands and rush off to their superior, 'Look,' they say, 'we have made a Christian lose his temper, give us a penny for it!' That's really all they're after . . . Just a lot of kids . . ."

"But what, for instance, did they do to you to annoy you?"

"Well, there was one instance when a Jew hanged himself in a wood near our monastery and all our monks began to say that it was really Judas Iscariot and that he walked about our monastery at night and groaned, and there were many who had seen him with their own eyes. I didn't give a hang about him, for I said to myself, 'Haven't we enough Jews left?' But one night as I was asleep in the stables, I suddenly heard someone walking past and he put his head through the door over the crossbeam and began to groan. I immediately said a prayer, but he remained standing there. So I made the sign of the cross, but still he stood there groaning. 'Well,' I said to myself, 'what can I do for you? I can't possibly pray for you, for you are a Jew, and, besides, I have no special dispensation to say prayers for suicides. Get out of here,' I said, 'back to your forest or the desert!' And I put such a curse on him that he trotted off and I fell asleep again, but the next night the rascal was there again and again he started groaning. . . . Wouldn't let me go to sleep, confound him! I did my best to pay no attention, but I couldn't. 'What a nuisance,' I said to myself. 'Isn't there enough room for him in the woods or on the steps of the church that he must come crashing into my stables? Well, it seems it can't be helped, I shall have to devise some effective means of getting rid of you!' So next morning I drew a large cross on the door, trusting that he wouldn't come again now, but no sooner had I fallen asleep than there he was again: standing by the door, if you please, *and* groaning! 'Hang thee for a jailbird,' I said to myself. 'Will nothing avail thee?' So he kept me in a sweat all through the night and in the morning, as soon as the bell began to toll for morning Mass, I jumped up and rushed off to lodge a complaint with the abbot, but on the way I met brother Diomedes, our bellringer, and he said to me:

" 'What do you look so scared for?' "

"So I told him all about it. 'That's what I had to put up with last night,' I said, 'and I'm going to the abbot to complain about it.'

"But brother Diomedes said:

" 'Don't waste your time going to the abbot, for he has been putting leeches to his nose all night and is now in *a very bad temper* and will do nothing for you in this matter, but, if you want me to, I shall be able to be of greater help to you than he.'

" 'It makes no difference to me,' I said. 'I'll be very glad indeed if you can help me and I'll give you my old warm mittens for that: you'll find them a great comfort when you have to ring your bells in winter.'

" 'All right,' he said.

"So I gave him my mittens and he brought me from the belfry a door from an old church on which was painted the Apostle Peter with the keys to the heavenly gates in his hands.

" 'That,' brother Diomedes said, 'is the most important part of it, the *keys*, I mean. All you have to do is put this door against the door of the stables. Nobody can pass through that.'

"I was so overjoyed that I nearly fell at his feet and I thought, 'Why put this door in front of the stable doors and then have to remove it again when I can fasten it there so that it can always serve me as a barrier?' And so I did. I hung this door on strong hinges and to make doubly sure I attached a heavy block to it with a big stone on a rope. All this I managed very quietly during the day and by the evening it was all ready and when night came I lay down to sleep. Well, what do you think happened? That night I woke up again and blessed if somebody wasn't breathing there! I couldn't believe my own ears. But, no! I wasn't imagining it: there it stood and breathed! And that wasn't all, gentlemen. Not by a long shot! For not only did it breathe, but it was also trying to burst the door open! My old door had a lock on the inside, but that one I didn't provide with a lock, for I depended entirely on its sacred nature to keep the fiend out, and, anyway, I had hardly had time for it. So he went on pushing it more and more till I could distinctly see his snout coming through it, but the door, being wide open now, suddenly slammed shut because of the block. . . . He jumped back and I thought I could hear him scratching himself, but after a little time he began pushing the door open again, more vigorously this time, and again I just caught a glimpse of his snout before the block once more slammed the door shut with a bigger bang than ever. I suppose he must have gotten a good bang on the head that time, for he quieted down and stopped pushing the door open and I fell asleep again, but after a little while I woke up and I saw that he had resumed his work, the rascal, and with greater vigor than ever. This time he didn't just butt the door with his horns to try to push it open, but he went about his task with great deliberation, pushing the door slowly with his horns. . . . So I covered my head with my sheepskin, for I was properly scared by that time, but he just tore the coat off me and licked me on the ear. . . . Well, I couldn't put up with such impudence any longer, so I put my hand down under my bed, got hold of an axe, and—smack!—

I just heard him utter one bellow and then he collapsed on the floor. 'Serves you right!' I thought. But imagine my surprise, gentlemen, when next morning instead of the Jew I beheld our monastery cow, which those little devils had put there in his place, the confounded imps!"

"Did you hurt it?"

"Hurt it? I killed it with my axe. There was a terrible to-do in our monastery about it, I can tell you!"

"You must have had a lot of unpleasantness because of it!"

"I should think so. The abbot said that I had just imagined it all and he thought that was because I didn't go to church frequently enough, so he gave me his blessing and told me to stand by the screen where the candles are lit every evening after I had finished with the horses. But they, those mischievous little devils, did something to me which brought utter disgrace on me. On the night of Shrove Tuesday during the service of Holy Communion when the father abbot and the dean stood, as behooved their respective ranks, in the center of the church, an old lady of the congregation gave me a candle and said to me, 'Put it up for me, Father, and may the Lord bless you!' I went up to the lectern where the Saviour of the Waters icon was hanging and began to fix the candle, but I brushed against another and it dropped to the floor. I bent down to pick it up and was about to fix it when I brushed against two more and they immediately dropped to the ground. I started fixing them and, lo! four fell down! I just shook my head at that, thinking, 'Well, that's those little brats again playing their tricks on me and tearing the candles out of my hands! . . .' I bent down again to pick them up, but as I raised myself quickly with the fallen candles I got a terrible blow on the back of my head against the candlestick and . . . the candles just showered down on the floor! Well, I got mad and knocked the remaining candles off with my own hand. 'If they are *that* impudent,' I thought, 'then I'd better knock them all down myself as quickly as possible!' "

"And what happened to you then?"

"They wanted to put me on trial for that, but our hermit, the blind old monk Syssoy, who lives in our monastery in strict seclusion from the rest of the monks, interceded for me. 'Why are you going to put *him* on trial,' he said, 'when it is Satan and his attendants who brought about his downfall?' The abbot listened to him and he gave me his blessing and ordered that I should be lowered into a pit and that I should stay there, and this he did without any trial."

"Did they keep you in that pit for long?"

"When he had blessed me, the old abbot did not say how long I was to remain there. All he said was, 'Let him be put there,' so I was kept there the whole summer until the first autumn frosts set in."

"Didn't you find it even drearier and more heartbreaking in that pit than on the steppe?"

"No. You can't even compare the two. Here I could hear the church bells and some of my friends among the monks would come and see me. They would come and stand over the pit and we would talk to each other, and the father treasurer ordered a hand mill to be lowered to me on a rope to grind salt for the kitchen. How can you compare it with the steppe or indeed any other place?"

"But why did they take you out? Was it because the frosts came and it got too cold?"

"No, not for that reason at all, but for quite a different reason, for, you see, I began to prophesy. . . ."

"Prophesy?"

"Yes. While I sat in that pit I fell into thought and I kept thinking what a paltry spirit I had and how much I had had to suffer on account of it and how I seemed incapable of improving myself, and I sent one of our novices to the old man, the hermit, to ask him to pray to God to grant me a more accommodating spirit. And the hermit sent me back an answer, saying, 'Let him pray well and then wait for what he has no right to expect.' So I did as I was bid: three nights I knelt in my pit on those excellent instruments of penitence, my knees, and I prayed most fervently and I began to await a sign of grace which should work a miraculous change in my soul. And we had another novice by the name of Gerontius, a man who had read a prodigious number of books and subscribed to newspapers, and he gave me the life of the Very Reverend Tikhon Zadonsky to read, and whenever he happened to pass my pit he would always take a newspaper from under his cassock and throw it down to me. 'Read it,' he used to say, 'and perhaps you may find something in it that may be of use to you and, anyway, it will help to while away your time in the pit.' So while waiting for the unlikely realization of my prayer, I began in the meantime to occupy myself with reading: as soon as I had finished grinding the salt which had been given to me for my day's task, I would begin to read, and I usually began with the life of the Very Reverend Tikhon and there I read how the Holy Mother of God, accompanied by St. Peter and St. Paul, had visited him in his cell one day. It is written that the saint asked the Holy Virgin to prolong peace on earth, but St. Paul said to him in a loud voice, 'This sign I give thee when peace shall come to an end: when,' said he, 'everybody will be saying, It is peace, and confirm it, then suddenly dire ruin will befall them.' And I began to reflect on those apostolic words and at first I couldn't understand the meaning of the revelation the apostle had given to the saint. But then I read in the papers that in our own country and in foreign parts people kept on saying that an era of eternal peace was being established throughout the world, whereupon my prayer was granted to me and I suddenly understood that what had been said was about to be fulfilled, namely, 'When everybody will be saying, It is peace, then suddenly ruin will befall them,' and I was filled with fear and trembling for my Russian nation and I began to pray and whoever came to visit me I implored with tears in my eyes, saying, 'Pray that under the rule of our Czar every enemy and evildoer may be vanquished, for the day of dire ruin is nigh!' And it was granted to me that the tears I shed were wonderfully prolific . . . for it was for my country that I wept. So they went and told the abbot, saying, 'Our Ishmael is shedding many tears in his pit and he is prophesying war.' The abbot then gave me his blessing and ordered that I should be transferred to the empty hut behind the kitchen gardens and that they should put therein the Sacred Silence icon on which the Saviour is presented in the shape of an angel with gently folded wings, not with His crown of thorns, but as the Lord of Hosts, with His hands crossed serenely over His breast. And I was bidden to prostrate myself daily before that icon until I lost my spirit of prophecy. So they shut me up in that hut and I remained locked up there until spring, praying all the time to Sacred Silence, but as soon as I beheld a man the spirit of prophecy would again descend upon me and I would start prophesying again. It was at that time that the abbot sent a doctor to have a look at me to see whether I was quite right in the head. The doctor spent a long time with me in my hut and, having listened to my story just as you are doing now, gentlemen, he just spat and said, 'What a drum you are, my dear fellow: they beat you and beat you and they can't finish you off!' So I said, 'What can I do about it? I suppose it has been ordained that way.' But the doctor, having heard all I had to tell him, said to the abbot, 'I can't make out what's the matter with him. Is he just a harmless, good-natured soul, or is he a lunatic, or, maybe, really a prophet? That, however,' he said, 'is for you to say, for I know nothing about prophecies, but my advice to you is to send him away: let him go and visit remote places, perhaps he's been too long in one place.' So they let me go and now I am on my way to the Solovky Monastery to pray at the tombs of St. Zossima and St. Sabbatai, for which I have obtained the blessing of the abbot, for I want to kneel to them before I die."

"But why before you die? Are you ill?"

"No, I am not ill, but just in case it becomes necessary to fight again."

"Are you again talking about war?"

"Yes, I am."

"So Sacred Silence didn't do much good?"

"I can't say; I am doing all I can to keep silent, but the spirit overcomes me."

"What exactly does he tell you?"

"He's always saying to me, 'Take up arms!' "

"But why? You aren't going to fight, too, are you?"

"Of course I am! What else would you have me do? I want to die for my people."

"But not in your cowl and cassock?"

"Why, no. I shall take off my cowl and cassock and put on my old uniform again."

Having said that, the enchanted wanderer seemed again to feel the spirit of prophecy coming upon him and he fell into a quiet meditation which none of his fellow passengers dared to interrupt with any more questions. And, indeed, what more could we have asked him? He had told us the adventures of his past life with all the frankness of his simple soul, and his prophecies remain for the time being in the hands of Him Who conceals the future from both the wise and the foolish and reveals it only now and then unto babes.

The Left-handed Craftsman

*A Tale of the Cross-eyed, Left-handed Crafts-
man of Tula and the Steel Flea*

1.

When the Emperor Alexander Pavlovich wound up
the Congress of Vienna, he decided to take a trip across Europe
to see what the different countries could show him in the way of
wonders. He went and paid a visit to every country and, being a
very easygoing sort of man, he had friendly chats with all sorts of
people, and everyone he spoke to tried his best to astonish him
with some new kind of invention, for all of them wanted to get
him on their side. The Emperor had with him a Don Cossack—
Platov his name was—and that Cossack just hated to see his
sovereign admiring anything foreign and, being terribly homesick,
he kept on badgering his Majesty to return to Russia. Every time
Platov saw the Emperor showing too great an interest in some
foreign invention he would say, while the rest of his Majesty's

suite kept a diplomatic silence, "If it please your Majesty, we have much better things at home," and one way or another he would manage to distract the Emperor's attention.

Now the English knew that and they had thought up all kinds of cunning tricks for the Emperor's arrival; for they had made up their minds that they would extort from the Emperor the admission that everything foreign was much superior to everything Russian, and they very often succeeded, especially at large assemblies where Platov found it a bit hard to say what he wanted to say in French, because, to tell the truth, Platov wasn't much interested in French and, being a married man, he thought all French talk silly and hardly worth while. But when the English began to invite the Emperor to come and see all their arsenals and sawmills and soap factories and what not, being anxious to show him how much better they did things than the Russians, Platov said to himself:

"This has jolly well got to stop. I've put up with it so far, but I'm not going to let it go any farther. I may or may not be able to say it, but I'm hanged if I'm going to let our side down."

No sooner had he said this to himself than the Emperor turned to him and said:

"Now then, my dear fellow, you and I are going to have a lovely time tomorrow, for we're going to have a look at one of their military exhibitions. They've got wonderful things there," he said, "and when you see them you'll have to admit that, however much we may think of ourselves, we Russians are no good at all."

Platov did not say a word in reply to the Emperor, but just buried his big, broken nose in his shaggy coat. When he came back to his lodgings, however, he told his orderly to fetch him a bottle of strong Caucasian vodka from his trunk and, filling a large glass to the brim, he swallowed it at one gulp. Then he said his prayers in front of his folding travelling shrine, covered himself up with his shaggy coat, and started to snore so loudly that the English in the house couldn't sleep a wink that night.

"Let's sleep on it," he thought to himself.

2.

Next day the Emperor and Platov went to visit the museums in London. The reason his Majesty took no other Russian with him was because the carriage they had been given only had room for two.

They arrived at a building which did not look particularly large from the outside, but which had a beautiful entrance and miles and miles of corridors and one room more wonderful than another, and, after they had been taken through them all, they were brought to the main room, which had enormous statues in it and right in the middle a statue of Apollo Belvebeery under a big canopy.

The Emperor was watching Platov all this time, for he wanted to see whether anything would surprise him at all and also what he would look at, but the Cossack did not look at anything. He walked with his eyes fixed on the ground and all he did was twist his long mustache round and round his finger.

The English at once began to show them all the marvellous things they had in that room and they explained which of them they found most useful in their wars, such as storm gauges, camel's-hair coats for their infantry, and raincoats treated with pitch for their cavalry. The Emperor looked highly pleased with everything, but Platov was not a bit impressed and, in fact, took pains to show quite plainly that it meant nothing to him.

The Emperor said:

"Really, my dear fellow, I can't understand how you can be so indifferent. Doesn't anything here impress you at all?"

But Platov replied:

"The only thing that impresses me, your Majesty, is that my gallant Cossacks won so many battles and routed thousands of your enemies without any of the things here."

The Emperor said:

"You're talking through your hat, my dear fellow."

But Platov replied:

"That is as it may be, your Majesty, but I'm afraid I can't argue the point with you, for it is my duty not to reason why, but to do and die."

The Englishmen, noticing that the Emperor and his Cossack officer were having some argument, at once took them to the statue of Apollo Belvebeery and, taking a musket from one of his hands and a pistol from the other, said:

"See the sort of thing we produce in this country," and they gave him the musket.

The Emperor looked at the musket without batting an eyelid, for he had many similar muskets in his own palace in Tsarskoye Selo, but when they gave him the pistol and said, "This pistol is of an unknown and quite incomparable make, your Majesty. One of our admirals snatched it from the belt of a pirate chief in Kandelabria," the Emperor took one look at the pistol and couldn't take his eyes off it. He sighed and sighed, poor man, and very pitiful sighs they were, and he said:

"Indeed, it is wonderful! What perfect workmanship!" And, turning to Platov, he said in Russian, "If only I had such a fine craftsman in Russia, I'd be the happiest man in the world and I'd be so proud of him that I'd make him a nobleman on the spot."

As soon as he heard the Emperor talk that way, Platov put his hand in the pocket of his wide breeches and took out a pistol-opener. The Englishmen were quite shocked to see him do that and they said, "You will never be able to open it," but Platov paid no attention to them and began to pick the lock of the pistol. He tried it once and he tried it twice and the third time he opened it and, taking the lock out completely, he asked the Emperor to have a look at the trigger, just inside the bend. The Emperor looked and there he saw an inscription in Russian, "Ivan Moskvin of the town of Tula."

The Englishmen looked very astonished and they kept on nudging each other, as if to say:

"Dear, dear, we've put our foot in it this time and no mistake!"

But the Emperor said to Platov crossly:

"You shouldn't have made them look so foolish. Now I can't help feeling sorry for them. Come on, let's go."

So they went back to their carriage, and the Emperor went to a ball that night, but Platov downed an even larger glass of strong Caucasian vodka and slept soundly, like a real Cossack.

He was glad to have made the English look foolish and to have done justice to the Tula craftsman, but he could not help feeling vexed with the Emperor for being so sorry for the English in such a situation.

"Why was the Emperor so cross?" thought Platov. "Damned if I can make it out at all!" and, worried by such thoughts, he got up twice, crossed himself, and drank so much vodka that in the end he fell fast asleep.

But the Englishmen could not sleep that night, for they were greatly worried, too. While the Emperor was having a good time at the ball, they thought up such a new wonder for him that it took the wind out of Platov's sails completely.

3.

The next morning, when Platov came to bid the Emperor good morning, his Majesty said to him:

"Tell 'em to get the carriage ready for two immediately and let's go and see their other museums."

Platov plucked up enough courage to drop a hint to his Majesty that it was about time they packed up and stopped looking at foreign products and began thinking of returning to Russia, but the Emperor said:

"No, no, my dear fellow, there's a lot more I'd very much like to see. They told me last night that the sugar they manufacture here is first-class."

So off they went.

The English showed everything they had to the Emperor, all their first-class products, but Platov just looked and looked and then he said suddenly:

"Can you take us to the factory where they make the sugar *Molvo*?"

Well, the Englishmen had never heard of *Molvo* sugar and they kept on whispering to each other, winking at each other, repeating to each other, "*Molvo, Molvo*," without, of course, realizing that it was the sugar we manufactured in our own country, and, at last, they just had to admit that although they had every kind of sugar under the sun, they had no "*Molvo*."

Platov said:

"So you haven't got it, have you? Well, what are you bragging about then? Come to our country and we'll give you tea with real *Molvo* sugar from the Bobrinsk factory."

But the Emperor tugged him by the sleeve and said softly:

"Look here, don't you go interfering with my politics!"

Then the English asked the Emperor to come and see their very last museum where they promised to show him mineral stones and Infusoria they had collected from all over the world, beginning with the largest pyramid from Egypt and ending with fleas which could not be seen with the naked eye and which lived under the skin of animals.

The Emperor went.

They looked at the pyramids and the mummies and all sorts of scarecrows besides, and as they left Platov said to himself:

"Thank goodness, everything has gone off well: the Emperor did not seem to be impressed by anything."

But when they came to the last room, there were English workmen all drawn up in a row in their clean jackets and aprons and one of them held a tray on which there was nothing to be seen.

So the Emperor looked very surprised, for he did not expect to be given an empty tray.

"What does it mean?" he asked, but the English craftsmen answered, "This is our humble present to your Majesty."

"What is it?"

"Well, Sir," they said, "can you see this speck of dust?"

The Emperor looked and, indeed, there was a tiny speck of dust on the silver tray.

The workmen said:

"May it please your Majesty to wet your finger and put it on your hand."

"But what am I to do with this speck of dust?"

"It isn't a speck of dust," they said. "It is a flea."

"Is it alive?"

"Why no, your Majesty," they replied, "of course it isn't alive. We made it out of our best English steel and in its middle there is a spring and there's a hole through which you wind it up. If it please your Majesty to turn the key, it will at once begin to dance."

The Emperor became very curious and he asked:

"But where's the key?"

And the Englishmen replied:

"The key is just in front of your eyes, your Majesty."

So they brought a microscope and the Emperor saw that indeed there was a key beside the flea on the tray.

"May it please your Majesty to put the flea on your hand," they said. "There's a little hole in the middle of the flea's tummy and as soon as you turn the key seven times the flea will start to dance."

It was with great difficulty that the Emperor managed to get hold of the key and only with even greater difficulty that he could keep it between his finger and thumb. However, after taking the flea in his other hand, also between finger and thumb, he put the key in and as soon as he began to wind it he felt how the steel flea's feelers began to move, then its tiny legs began to stir and, at last, it gave a jump, cutting a caper in one movement, and next it skipped to one side and went through two variations and to the other side and went through two more variations, and so it danced through a whole quadrille in three turns.

The Emperor immediately commanded that the English should be given a million for the flea in whatever kind of money they wished, whether in silver or in small bank notes.

The English asked to be paid in silver because they didn't know much about paper money, and then they immediately played another of their tricks: they presented the flea to the Emperor, but they didn't give him a case in which to put the flea, and without a case it was quite impossible to keep either the flea or its key, for they could easily get mislaid and thrown out with the rubbish. The case for the flea was made out of a whole diamond nut in the middle of which a place had been bored for it. The diamond, however, they would not give to the Emperor because, they said, it really belonged to the Treasury and whatever belongs to the Treasury no Englishman dares to touch, not even for the Emperor himself.

Platov nearly lost his temper over that, for, said he:

"What's the meaning of all this humbug? They give your Majesty a present and take a cool million for it, but it seems that isn't enough for them! The case," said he, "always goes with a thing like that!"

But the Emperor said:

"Let it be, my dear fellow. Mind your own business and don't go interfering with my politics: they have their own way of doing things." And he asked them, "How much do you want for the diamond in which the steel flea has to be kept?"

The Englishmen asked five thousand for it.

The Emperor Alexander Pavlovich said, "Pay them!" and he himself put the flea into its diamond case along with the key, and to make quite sure that he wouldn't lose it, he put it into his golden snuffbox which he ordered to be put into his travelling case which was inlaid with mother-of-pearl and whalebone.

The Emperor took leave of the English craftsmen very graciously and said to them, "You're the best craftsmen in the world and I'm quite satisfied that my own people can't stand up to you!"

Well, the Englishmen were naturally very pleased about it and Platov could say nothing to contradict the Emperor's words, so he just grabbed the microscope and, without saying anything about it, put it in his pocket, "For," he said to himself, "it belongs with the rest and you've gotten a lot of money for it as it is."

The Emperor knew nothing about that—not until they arrived in Russia, anyway—and they had left England soon after, for his Majesty was getting very depressed because of the military situation and wanted to go to confession to the priest Fedot in

Taganrog. On their way to Russia there wasn't much of a pleasant nature that the Emperor had to say to Platov, for they had disagreed violently with one another: the Emperor was of the opinion that the English had no equals in craftsmanship, while Platov maintained that our men could make anything they saw, but that all they lacked was good education and proper training, and he put it to his Majesty that the English craftsmen had quite different rules so far as their everyday life was concerned, and that every man Jack of them enjoyed full opportunity to manage his private affairs as he liked and that consequently everything had quite a different meaning for him.

The Emperor refused to listen to such talk and Platov left their carriage at every stop and downed a large glass of vodka to drown his vexation and chewed a piece of salted biscuit and then he'd light his enormous pipe made out of a large tree root, in which he'd put a whole pound of Zhukov tobacco, and he'd sit down beside the Emperor in the carriage and they would travel on in silence. The Emperor looked one way and Platov looked another, sticking his pipe out of the window and letting the wind carry the smoke away. In this way they travelled together till they arrived in Petersburg, and the Emperor did not even ask Platov to accompany him to his priest Fedot.

"You're not fit for any religious conversation," his Majesty said, "and, besides, you go on smoking like a chimney and my head is covered with soot from that pipe of yours."

Platov was thus left behind to nurse his grievance, and he lay down on his couch and sulked and all the while he lay on his couch he went on smoking Zhukov tobacco without stopping.

4.

The wonderful flea of the best English steel remained in Alexander Pavlovich's whalebone case until his death in Taganrog. The Emperor gave it to the priest Fedot, whom he asked to hand it to the Empress when she had sufficiently recovered from her grief. The Empress Yelisaveta Alexeyevna took one look at the flea's capers and just smiled, but she was not interested in it and did not look at it again.

"I am a dowager now," she said, "and I don't care for any amusements any more," and on her return to Petersburg she gave this curiosity, together with all the other jewels, to the new Emperor as an heirloom.

The Emperor Nikolai Pavlovich at first paid no attention to the steel flea either, for when he ascended the throne there were all kinds of disturbances and he was too preoccupied to think of it, but one day later on he began to examine the case left to him by his brother and he took out the snuffbox and from it he produced the diamond nut and in it he found the steel flea, which had not been wound up for a long time and was lying there quietly, just as if it had gone stiff in all its joints.

The Emperor looked at the steel flea and was surprised.

"What a silly thing it is and why has my brother taken such great care of it?"

The courtiers wanted to throw it out, but the Emperor said: "No, this must mean something."

So they called in the druggist who owned the pharmacy opposite Anichkin Bridge, who was used to weighing poisons in very small scales, and they showed it to him. He immediately took the flea and put it on his tongue and said, "I can feel a chill on my tongue as if it were made of some strong metal," and he bit on it a little with his teeth and said, "If it please your Majesty it isn't a real flea, but a flea made out of some metal, and it isn't our work; it hasn't been made in Russia."

The Emperor ordered his courtiers to find out immediately where it came from and what was the meaning of it.

The courtiers started looking through all the state papers and letters, but they could find no mention of the steel flea in them. So they began making inquiries here and there, but nobody knew anything about it. Luckily, however, the Don Cossack Platov was still alive and was, as a matter of fact, still sulking on his couch and smoking his pipe. As soon as he heard of the commotion at the palace, he got up from his couch, threw away his pipe, pinned on his medals, and went to see the Emperor.

The Emperor said:

"What can I do for you, gallant old man?"

And Platov replied:

"I don't want anything for myself, your Majesty, for I have plenty of drink and food and I'm quite satisfied, thank you. I have come," he said, "to tell you all about that steel flea which I understand has been found," and he told the Emperor all about it, saying, "It all happened in England before my very eyes. There's a key beside it and I've got the microscope through which you can see it and with that key you can wind up the flea through a tiny hole in her tummy and she'll start skipping about all over the place and cut capers as she turns from one side to the other."

So they wound up the steel flea and she began to skip about and Platov said:

"It is true, your Majesty, that it is quite delicate workmanship, quite a beautiful piece of work altogether, but it isn't right to admire it and let your feelings run away with you. It should be given to our craftsmen in Tula or Sesterbek (in those days Sestroretsk was still called Sesterbek) to be examined in order to see if they could not do something more wonderful so that the English should not think that they are in any way superior to the Russians."

Now the Emperor Nikolai Pavlovich had great confidence in his Russian subjects and he did not like to have to admit the superiority of any foreigner and he answered Platov and said:

"You spoke well, my gallant old fellow. Take it and see what you can do about it. I don't want this box now, anyway, for I have plenty of troubles as it is. Take it and don't go back to sulking on your couch, but go straight to the gentle Don and have a heart-to-heart talk there with my Don Cossacks about their life and their loyalty to me and ask them what they would like me to do for them, and when you pass through Tula show this steel flea to my Tula craftsmen and let them see what they can do about it. Tell them from me that my brother was very impressed with this thing and praised the foreign craftsmen who made it highly, but that I have great confidence in my people and I hope and trust that they are not a whit worse than anybody else. I know they will not disappoint me and will do something about it."

5.

Platov took the steel flea and, passing through Tula on his way to the Don, he showed it to the Tula master gunsmiths and told them what the Emperor had said and then asked them:

"What are we going to do about it?"

The master gunsmiths replied:

"We are greatly honored by his Majesty's gracious words, sir, and we shall always be bound to his Majesty because he has confidence in his own people, but we cannot possibly tell you offhand what we'd better do about this business. We have to consider it very carefully, for the English aren't fools but a very clever people and their craftsmanship has a good deal of sound common sense behind it. One can do nothing against the English," they said, "without careful consideration, but with the Lord's blessing we may be able to do something. If your honor, like our lord and master the Emperor, has confidence in us, then we should advise you to carry on with your journey to the gentle Don and to leave this flea with us, just as it is in its case and in the Tsar's golden snuffbox. Have a good time on the Don and give the wounds you have received in defending your country a chance to heal and when on your way back you're passing through Tula again stop here and send for us: with God's help we should have thought of something by that time."

Platov did not conceal his disappointment with the Tula craftsmen that they should be asking for so much time and that they should not tell him plainly what they intended to do. He questioned them closely about it and he spoke to them with great cunning as the people of the Don know how to do, but the Tula craftsmen were no less cunning than he, for, as a matter of fact, they had already thought of something, but they were afraid that if they told it to Platov he would not believe them capable of accomplishing such a thing and for that reason they wished to put their plan into execution at once and reveal it later.

They said:

"We hardly know ourselves yet what we shall do, but we shall put ourselves into the hands of the Lord and maybe the Tsar's words will not have been spoken in vain and to our shame."

So the more Platov tried to match his wits against theirs, the more the Tula craftsmen outwitted him.

Platov wriggled and wriggled, but he couldn't wriggle into their minds and in the end he realized that he would have to do as they wished. So he gave them the golden snuffbox with the steel flea and said:

"Well, have it your own way, but, mind, I know the sort of people you are, but since I can't do anything about it, I shall have to trust you. All the same I think I'd better warn you not to try any monkey business with me, such as stealing the diamond and putting some worthless stone in its place, and, above all, the Lord help you if you should do anything to the delicate English workmanship, and, last but not least, don't take too much time over it, for I'm a fast traveller; before two weeks have passed I shall be on my way back from the gentle Don to Petersburg and I'd better have something to take with me to show to the Emperor."

The gunsmiths did their best to reassure him.

"We shall not spoil the delicate workmanship," they said, "and we shall not change the diamond for some worthless stone, and two weeks is more than enough, and be assured that by the time you go back to the Emperor, you will have *something* to show to his Majesty which will be worthy of his greatness."

But what that *something* was they did not say.

6.

Platov left Tula, and the gunsmiths—three men who were the greatest craftsmen of them all, including one who was cross-eyed and left-handed, with a birthmark on his cheek and his hair above the temples pulled out during his studies—took leave of their friends and their families, packed their bags, taking some food with them, and disappeared from the town.

All that was known about them was that they did not leave the town through the Moscow tollgate, but went in the opposite direction, and it was surmised that they had gone to Kiev to offer up prayers to the saints and to ask advice from the holy men of whom there were always a great abundance in Kiev.

But while that was near enough to the truth, it was not the whole truth by any means. Neither the time nor the distance permitted the craftsmen to go to Kiev, for it would have taken them three weeks and, besides, that would hardly have given them sufficient time to do something that would put the English nation to shame. They could have gone to Moscow instead, which was only "twice ninety miles" away and where there are also plenty of saints. And in the opposite direction there were also "twice ninety miles" to Oryol and from Oryol to Kiev another good five hundred miles. You cannot make such a journey in a few days and, when done, it would take you more than a few days to rest your tired limbs, for it would be some time before your feet lost their numbness and your hands stopped shaking.

There were even people who thought that the Tula craftsmen had just been bragging to Platov and, having thought it over afterwards, had gotten properly scared and fled, taking with them the Tsar's golden snuffbox with the diamond and the steel flea which had caused so much trouble. However, such a supposition was also quite without foundation and quite unworthy of the great craftsmen upon whom the hope of the nation now rested.

7.

Tula craftsmen are famous for their skill in metal work, but they are also known far and wide as experts in the field of religion. Nor is it their native country alone that resounds to their glory. No, the fame of their great piety has reached as far as Mount Athos, where it is well known that natives of Tula are not only past masters at church singing, excelling in tremolo parts, but also expert painters of the picture *Eternal Ringing*. It is a no-less-known fact that those of them who dedicate themselves to the service of the Lord by entering a monastery become excellent stewards and excel as collectors of monastery funds. At Mount Athos they know that Tula men are a very resourceful people and that but for them the remote corners of Russia would assuredly never have seen many of the sacred objects from the faraway Orient, and Mount Athos would have had to do without many useful gifts which are such a shining example of Russian piety and generosity. Today the Mount Athos Tula monks carry the sacred objects all over our country and are real adepts at collecting funds even where there is nothing to collect. A Tula native is full of devotion to the Church and is a great practitioner of pious deeds, and for that reason the three Tula craftsmen who had taken upon themselves the burden of justifying Platov's faith in his country and upon whom the good name of their country now depended made no mistake in failing to take the road to Moscow but in going southward instead. They never thought of going to Kiev, the town of their pilgrimage being Mtsensk, a district town in the province of Oryol where the ancient image of St. Nicholas, "graven out of stone," is kept, an icon which in ancient times had sailed down the river Zusha on a large stone cross. This icon of a "stern and most terrifying" aspect shows the full-sized figure of the saint clad in garments of silver, with a rather dark visage, holding a church in one hand and the sword "Victory in Battle" in the other. It is in this "victory" that the whole meaning of the icon lies, St. Nicholas—and the Mtsensk St. Nicholas in particular—being the generally acknowledged patron saint of trade and warfare, and it was to him that the Tula craftsmen had gone to pray. They held a special divine service in front of this icon and another in front of the stone cross, then they returned home at night and, without saying a word to anyone, started on their work in dead secret. They gathered, all three of them, in the house of the left-handed craftsman, locked the doors, closed the shutters, lit the lamp in front of the icon of St. Nicholas, and set to work.

They stayed there one day, two days, three days, without going out, just hammering away at something, forging something, but what it was they were forging nobody knew.

Everyone in Tula was very curious about it, but nobody could discover anything of what the three craftsmen were doing, for they had said nothing to anyone and they did not show themselves in the streets. . . . Many people went to the little house and knocked at the door under any pretext they could think of, either to ask for a light or for a pinch of salt, but the three craftsmen would not open the door for any reason whatsoever and it was not even known what they did about food. Some people even tried to frighten them by shouting that the house next door was on fire, hoping that they might run out in a panic and that it might then be seen what they had been forging, but nothing would deceive those cunning craftsmen: only once did the left-handed one stick his head out of the window and shout:

"Let the whole town burn down for all we care: we're busy!" and his head with the pulled-out hair disappeared, the shutter was closed with a terrific bang, and the hammering was resumed, the mystery remaining as dark as ever.

Only through some minute chinks in the shutters could people see a fire burning and hear the hammers striking ceaselessly on the anvils.

In short, the whole thing was kept such a terrible secret that nothing of what was going on in that little house could be discovered, and so it went on until the return of the Cossack Platov from the gentle Don on his way back to the Emperor, and all during that time the three Tula craftsmen did not see or talk to anybody.

8.

Platov travelled in a great hurry and with some ceremony: he himself sat in the carriage and on either side of the coachman sat a Cossack with a cat-o'-nine-tails in his hand and they kept after the coachman unmercifully to make sure that he

kept the horses going at full gallop. And should either of the
Cossacks doze off, Platov himself would dig him in the ribs with a
foot, and they'd drive away at an even smarter pace. Such minis-
trations had an excellent effect and it was quite impossible to rein
in the horses at any station, for they always overshot their mark by
a hundred lengths. Then the Cossacks would wield their cats-o'-
nine-tails in an opposite direction and the coachman would turn
around and drive up to the inn.

In this way they came flying into Tula, at first rushing a hundred lengths beyond the Moscow tollgate; then the Cossacks applied their whips to the coachman in an opposite direction and,
turning around, they stopped at the steps of the inn, where new
horses were ordered to be harnessed to the carriage. Platov himself did not leave the carriage, but merely ordered one of the
Cossacks to bring him the craftsmen with whom he had left the
steel flea and not to take too much time over it, either.

Off ran the Cossack to tell the three craftsmen to make haste
and bring their work which was to put the English to shame, but
he had gone only a short distance when Platov sent more and
more Cossacks after him to hurry them up.

Having sent off all his Cossacks, he began to pick out some onlookers from the crowd of people that had by that time gathered
around the carriage, and nearly put a foot out of the carriage himself, too impatient to wait any longer and wishing to run there
himself, grinding his teeth in a most ferocious way: for it seemed
to him that they were not quick enough.

In those days everything had to be done efficiently and expeditiously like that, so that not a single moment should be lost
where the welfare or glory of the Russian people was at stake.

9.

The Tula craftsmen who were engaged on that marvellous piece of work were just then putting the finishing touches
to it. The Cossacks were quite out of breath when they arrived
at the house and the onlookers from among the public whom

Platov had picked out as messengers had not arrived at all, for, being out of practice, their legs just refused to function on the way and the poor men collapsed in the roadway and, fearing what Platov might do to them, they all ran to their own homes, where they immediately hid themselves where no one could find them.

But as soon as the Cossacks reached the house after their breathless sprint they gave a mighty shout and, finding that the craftsmen took no notice and refused to open the door to them, they unceremoniously tried to pull the shutters off the windows, but the bolts were so strong that they did not budge; then they tried to open the door, but it was barred from the inside with a huge oak beam. Then the Cossacks picked up a big tree trunk which they found lying in the street, put it, firemen's fashion, against the eaves of the roof, and in the twinkling of an eye took the roof off the little house. But having pulled the roof off, they themselves were knocked down by a spiral of foul air, for the atmosphere inside the little room where the craftsmen had been working ceaselessly for so many days had grown so thick that when it rushed out through the roof, every man in the street was nearly suffocated by it.

The messengers raised a clamor:

"Hey, you there, you dirty so-and so's, how dare you knock us down with your spray of stinking air? Don't you believe in God at all?"

But the craftsmen replied:

"We are just driving in the last nail and, as soon as we're finished, we shall bring the work out."

The messengers, however, shouted back:

"He'll eat us up alive if we wait as long as that and he won't leave anything over to remember us by."

But still the craftsmen replied:

"He won't have a chance to eat you up, for even as you were speaking, we were driving the last nail in. Run and tell him that we're bringing it this minute."

The Cossacks ran off to tell Platov what the craftsmen had said, but they were not too confident, for they thought that the Tula craftsmen would deceive them; so they'd run and stop and run and stop, always looking round to see if the three craftsmen were coming after them. However, their suspicions were not justified, for the craftsmen did come after them, and so fast, too, that they had had no time to dress properly as they should have done in presenting themselves before so important a personage as the Emperor's representative, but were fastening the hooks on their coats even while running through the streets. Two of them had nothing in their hands and the third one, the left-handed one, carried the Tsar's case with the English steel flea wrapped in a green cloth cover.

10.

The Cossacks ran up to Platov and said:

"Here they come."

Platov at once said to the craftsmen:

"Is it ready?"

"Everything's ready," they replied.

"Give it to me!"

They gave it to him.

The carriage was waiting with the coachman and the outriders in their places. The Cossacks immediately sat down on the box on either side of the coachman and raised their cats-o'-nine-tails over his head and held them like that.

Platov said:

"What's all this? Where's your work with which you were going to gladden the Emperor's heart?"

The gunsmiths replied:

"Our work is in that case."

Platov asked:

"Will you kindly explain what you're talking about?"

But the gunsmiths said:

"What's there to explain? It's in front of your eyes: just take a good look."

Platov shrugged his shoulders and roared:

"'Where's the flea's key?"

"Just in front of you," they replied. "Where the flea is, there the key is, too: in the diamond nut."

Platov wanted to take hold of the key, but his fingers were so short and stubby that, try as he might, he could not grasp either the key or the flea and he lost his temper completely and started cursing like a real Cossack.

He roared:

"Damned cheats, that's what you are. You haven't done a damn thing and I wouldn't be surprised if you damaged the thing into the bargain. I'll knock your heads off!"

But the Tula craftsmen said to him:

"You have no right to insult us like that, but we have to put up with your insults because you are the Emperor's representative. Since, however, you don't trust us and even think that we're likely to be disloyal to the Emperor's command, we shan't tell you the secret of our work. Take it to the Emperor—he will see the kind of master craftsmen we are and whether or not he has any reason to be ashamed of us!"

But Platov just roared at them again:

"You're damned liars, the lot of you! Just catch me trusting you or letting you off that easily! One of you is coming with me to Petersburg and I'll make him talk there! He'll tell me your secret all right!"

And, having said that, he stretched out his hand, caught the left-handed craftsman by the scruff of the neck with his stubby fingers so that all the hooks of his coat flew off, and flung him at his feet in the carriage.

"Sit there," said he, "like a damned poodle until we get to Petersburg. I'll hold you responsible for all of them. And you," he said to his Cossacks, "off you go, and look sharp, for I must be at the Emperor's palace in Petersburg the day after tomorrow!"

All the craftsmen dared to do for their colleague was point out to Platov that it was hardly right for him to carry off one of their fellow craftsmen without giving him a chance to obtain an official document, and they also wanted to know whether he would be allowed to come back. But instead of a reply Platov showed them his fist—a terrible, scarred, red fist—and shaking it at them, he said, "Here's your official document!" And to the Cossacks he said, "Off with you, boys!"

The Cossacks, the coachman, and the horses all started working at one and the same time and carried off the left-handed craftsman without a document, and in a day, as Platov had ordered, they drove up to the Emperor's palace and, having driven up at a gallop, they even drove past the columns.

Platov got out, pinned on his medals, and went to see the Emperor, telling the Cossacks to mount guard over the cross-eyed, left-handed craftsman at the entrance to the palace.

11.

Platov was afraid to show his face to the Emperor, for Nikolai Pavlovich had a terribly good memory, quite a remarkable memory, in fact, and he never forgot anything. Platov knew that he would most certainly ask him about the flea and he, who had never feared an enemy in his life, got so frightened that as soon as he entered the palace with the case, he quietly hid it in one of the rooms behind the stove. Having hidden it, Platov presented himself to the Emperor in his study and quickly began to give his report about the talks he had had with the Cossacks on the banks of the gently flowing Don. He told himself that he would do his best to interest the Emperor in his report about the Don Cossacks and that if the Emperor himself remembered the flea and began to ask questions about it, he would give him the case and accept full responsibility for the failure of his mission, but that if the Emperor did not mention it, he (Platov) would not say a word about it either, and would give the case to the Emperor's valet with instructions to put it away safely; in the meantime he would put the Tula craftsman into a fortress where he would remain indefinitely until he was needed.

But the Emperor Nikolai Pavlovich never forgot anything and as soon as Platov had finished his report about his talks with the Don Cossacks, he asked him:

"Well, how did my Tula craftsmen make out in the matter of the English steel flea?"

Platov explained the position just as it appeared to him.

"Your Majesty," he said, "the flea is still in the same place and I have brought it back, but I'm sorry to have to report, sir, that the Tula craftsmen were quite unable to do anything more wonderful."

To which the Emperor replied:

"I know that you are a gallant old soldier, but what you are telling me can't possibly be true."

Platov began to assure him that he was telling the truth and he described everything exactly as it had happened, adding that the Tula craftsmen had asked him to show the flea to the Emperor.

Nikolai Pavlovich patted his back and said:

"Let me see it. I know that my people will never let me down. There must be something about the thing that surpasses understanding."

12.

So they produced the case from behind the stove, took off the cotton cover, opened the golden snuffbox and the diamond nut—and there was the flea lying as it had been lying before.

The Emperor looked at it and said:

"What the devil? . . ." but his faith in the Russian craftsmen was not in the least shaken and he ordered his favorite daughter, Alexandra Nikolayevna, to be summoned to his study, and when she came, he said to her:

"You have such slender fingers, my dear, take the little key, put it in the flea's tummy, and wind up the spring."

The princess began to turn the key and the flea immediately began to move her feelers, but that was all she did: her feet did not move! Alexandra Nikolayevna wound the spring up as far as it would go, but the flea did not even attempt to cut any capers or dance the quadrille as before.

Platov turned green in the face and roared:

"Oh, the dirty dogs, now I can understand why they didn't want to show anything to me. It's a good thing I brought one of those fools with me!"

Having said that, he rushed out of the palace, caught the left-handed craftsman by the hair, and began to tug at it so hard that tufts of hair began flying about all over the place. But when Platov stopped beating him, the Tula craftsman smoothed the remaining strands of hair on his head and said:

"All my hair was pulled out by my schoolmaster, as it is, and I really don't think there was any need for you to go through the same operation again."

"No need?" Platov roared. "Why, didn't I rely on you and vouch for you and now you've gone and damaged a work of such rare craftsmanship!"

The left-handed one replied:

"We are very grateful to you for having vouched for us, but we didn't damage anything: just look at the steel flea through the strongest microscope."

Platov ran back to tell the Emperor about the microscope, just saying to the left-handed craftsman:

"You wait, I'm not finished with you yet!"

And he ordered the Cossacks to tie the Tula craftsman's elbows more tightly behind his back, while he himself mounted the steps at a run, panting and uttering a prayer under his breath. "The Lord and the Holy Virgin have mercy upon me," and so on. And the courtiers who were standing on the steps pretended not to see him, thinking, "Poor old Platov, he's got himself into a real mess now and he's sure to be kicked out of the palace," for they just couldn't stand him because he was so brave.

13.

As soon as Platov reported to the Emperor what the left-handed craftsman had said, his Majesty looked greatly gratified and he exclaimed:

"I knew that my Russians would never let me down," and he

commanded that a microscope be brought to him on a cushion immediately.

When the microscope had been brought, the Emperor took the flea and put it under the glass, at first upside down, then sideways, and then with its tummy downwards—in a word, he turned it every way, but he could not see anything. Still he did not lose his faith in the Russian craftsmen, but merely said:

"Bring me at once the gunsmith who is downstairs."

"Your Majesty, he ought to be tidied up a little. I brought him with me just as he was and I'm afraid he's been knocked about a bit."

But the Emperor replied:

"Never mind, let him be brought as he is."

So Platov went and said to the gunsmith:

"Come along, you so-and-so, to his Majesty himself."

And the left-handed craftsman replied:

"All right, I'm sure I don't mind."

So he went just as he was dressed at the time: in his torn boots, one of his trouser legs stuck inside his boot and the other dangling outside, all the hooks torn off his threadbare coat and his collar all in shreds; but he did not seem in the least put out by his tattered appearance.

"Well," he thought, "if the Emperor wants to see me, I must go, and if I have no official document on me, nobody can blame me for that. All I have to do is tell him how it happened."

As soon as the left-handed craftsman came in and bowed, the Emperor said to him:

"What does it all mean, my dear fellow? We looked and looked at the flea and put it under a microscope, but we can't find anything remarkable about it."

And the left-handed one replied:

"Are you quite sure, your Majesty, that you looked carefully?"

The lords in attendance on his Majesty began winking at the Tula craftsman, as if to say, "That's not the way to talk to the Emperor! You ought to follow the example of us courtiers: let your speech be full of cunning and flattery. Nobody talks in plain language here."

But the Emperor said to them:

"Just leave him alone, will you? It's you who are the fools, not he. Let him explain in his own way."

And he at once explained the situation to the Tula craftsman, saying:

"We put the flea under the microscope this way," and he put it under the microscope. "Look for yourself," he said, "you can't see anything there!"

The left-handed craftsman replied:

"You can't see anything there, your Majesty, because our work is so fine that you will never see what we did if you put it under the microscope that way."

The Emperor asked:

"Which way should we put it?"

"You have to examine each foot separately under the microscope and then each heel separately to see how the flea walks," said the left-handed craftsman.

"Good heavens," said the Emperor, "is it really as detailed as all that?"

"I'm afraid it is, your Majesty," said the Tula craftsman. "That is the only way to see our work, if, that is, you really want to admire it."

So they put the flea under the microscope as the left-handed craftsman had directed, and no sooner had the Emperor taken a look at it through the glass than a smile broke out on his face and he took the Tula craftsman just as he was, unkempt and covered with dust, and embraced and kissed him, and then he turned to all his courtiers and said:

"You see, I knew better than any of you that my Russians would never let me down. Why, the fellows have shod the flea's feet."

14.

Everybody now walked up to the miscroscope and had a look at the flea, and, indeed, each of the flea's feet had been shod with real horseshoes. The left-handed craftsman, however, pointed out that even that was not the most remarkable thing about the Tula craftsmen's achievement.

"If you had a better microscope which magnified five million times," he said, "you'd have been able to read on each of the horseshoes the name of the craftsman who made it, for each of them bears a name."

"Is your name there, too?" asked the Emperor.

"No, Sire," replied the left-handed craftsman. "I made the nails with which the horseshoes were fastened and you couldn't see those under any microscope."

The Emperor asked:

"Where is the microscope with which you were able to do such wonderful work?"

But the left-handed craftsman replied:

"We are very poor, your Majesty, and we can't afford a microscope, but our eyes are sharp enough."

Seeing that the left-handed craftsman had come through his ordeal with flying colors, all the courtiers began to congratulate him, each embracing and kissing him in turn, and Platov gave him a hundred roubles and said:

"I hope you won't bear me a grudge, my dear fellow, for having torn your hair out."

But the Tula craftsman replied:

"Why, of course not: we're used to having our heads bitten off."

And he said no more, in fact he hardly had time to say anything, for the Emperor immediately ordered the shod flea to be wrapped in a package and sent back to England as a present, in order to show the English that we did not think it so wonderful after all. And the Emperor commanded that a special courier should take the flea, one who could speak foreign languages, and that the left-handed craftsman should accompany him, so that he himself could show the English what the Russian craftsmen had done and, generally, what fine craftsmen they were in Tula.

Platov made the sign of the cross over him:

"May the Lord's blessing accompany you on your journey," he said, "and I'll give you some of my own Caucasian vodka to comfort you on the way. Don't drink too much and don't drink too little, just take it steadily."

And he did so: the vodka was delivered.

And Count Kisselvrode gave orders that the left-handed craftsman should be taken to the Tulyakovsky public baths and given a good wash, that his hair should be cut at a hairdresser's, and that he should be dressed in the clothes of a court choirboy, so that it should appear that he was a man of some rank.

So they clothed him in this fashion, gave him plenty of tea with Caucasian vodka to drink, drew in his belt very tightly so that his bowels would not be shaken up during the journey, and sent him off to London. Thus it was that the left-handed craftsman started on his foreign adventures.

15.

The Emperor's courier and the left-handed craftsman travelled very fast and they did not stop for a rest anywhere between Petersburg and London. All they did was tighten their belts a notch at every station so that their bowels wouldn't get tangled up with their lungs; but after his presentation to the Emperor, the left-handed craftsman, according to a special order issued by Platov, could have as much vodka as he liked at the government's expense, and so he just kept himself going on vodka alone and tasted no food, and while travelling across Europe he sang songs, always adding a foreign refrain:

> Sing merrily, sing merrily,
> C'est très joli!

On their arrival in London, the courier immediately went to deliver the package to the right people, leaving the left-handed craftsman in a private room at an inn. But the Tula gunsmith soon got tired of waiting in that room by himself. Besides, he also got hungry. So he knocked at the door and asked the waiter for food by pointing to his mouth, and the waiter at once took him downstairs to the dining room.

The left-handed craftsman sat down at a table, but he did not know what to do next, for he could not ask for anything in English, but he soon found a way out of that difficulty. He just knocked on the table with a finger and pointed to his mouth and the English at once guessed that he was asking for some food and they brought him some; only they did not always bring him what he wanted, but he would not eat anything that was unsuitable. So when they brought him a blazing plum pudding, he just said, "No, thank you, I don't know anything about such things and I'm not sure that I could eat it without burning myself," and they took the plum pudding away and gave him something else. Neither would he drink their vodka, for it was green, just as if it had been mixed with green vitriol. In short, he chose everything that appeared natural to him, and so he spent his time waiting for the courier in a cool place and helping himself from a bottle.

Meanwhile the people to whom the courier had brought the flea immediately examined it under the most powerful microscope and at once sent a full description of it to the police headquarters so that a public announcement could be published about it the next day for everybody's information.

"And," said they, "we'd like to see the master craftsman himself right away."

The courier took them to the left-handed craftsman's room and, not finding him there, to the dining room, where our Tula gunsmith had not been wasting his time and had by that time managed to get quite flushed, and he said:

"There he is!"

So the Englishmen at once started patting the Tula craftsman on the back, just as if he were their equal; and they shook his hands and said, "Good lad, good lad, a splendid craftsman! We shall discuss everything with you in good time, but now let's drink your health!"

They ordered a lot of wine and offered the first glass to the left-handed craftsman, but he very civilly refused to drink the first glass, for he said to himself, "Who knows, maybe they want to poison me out of jealousy."

"Thank you," he said, "but it's the host who should drink the first toast, so please drink first yourselves!"

The Englishmen tasted the different kinds of wine before him and then they began to fill his glass, and he got up, crossed himself with his left hand, and drank their health.

They noticed that he had crossed himself with the left hand and they asked the courier:

"Is he a Lutheran or a Protestant?"

The courier replied:

"No, he is neither a Lutheran nor a Protestant, but he is of the Russian Orthodox faith."

"Then why does he cross himself with his left hand?"

The courier said:

"Because he's left-handed. He does everything with his left hand."

The English marvelled even more and they began treating both the courier and the left-handed craftsman very liberally to drinks, and for three days they entertained them in this manner and then they said, "That'll do." So they each drank a whole bottle of soda water and, feeling refreshed, they began to question the left-handed craftsman about where he had been taught his trade and where he had studied and how much arithmetic he knew.

The left-handed craftsman replied:

"Our studies, gentlemen, are really quite a simple matter: we know our psalm book and the *Book of Half-dreams*, but we don't know much arithmetic."

The Englishmen exchanged glances and said:

"That's just marvellous!"

But the left-handed craftsman said to them:

"That's how it is in our country."

"And what kind of a book is the Russian *Book of Half-dreams?*" they asked.

"Oh," he said, "you see, it is a book in which, for anything in the psalm book that King David may have left unexplained, you can find a number of additional explanations."

"That's a great pity, for it would have been much better if you knew at least the four rules of arithmetic. That would have been much more useful to you than the whole *Book of Half-dreams*, because then you would have understood that each engine is so constructed that it can perform only certain tasks according to its power and, although you're certainly very clever with your hands, you don't seem to have realized that an engine such as the one inside the steel flea was made according to the most exact specifications and cannot possibly carry the weight of horseshoes. That's why the steel flea cannot skip and dance any more."

The left-handed craftsman agreed entirely.

"We needn't argue about that," he said. "It is quite true that we haven't advanced far in science, but we've always been loyal sons of our motherland."

And the Englishmen said to him:

"Stay with us; we'll make a highly educated man of you and you will become quite an accomplished craftsman."

But the Tula craftsman would not agree to their proposal.

"I'm very sorry, gentlemen," he said, "but I have parents at home."

The Englishmen offered to send money to his parents, but the left-handed craftsman refused to accept their offer.

"We are devoted to our country," he said, "and, besides, my dear father is a very old man now and my mother is an old lady and they are used to going to church in their own parish and I'd feel very lonely here by myself, for I am still a bachelor."

"You'll get used to it," they said, "and once you accept our faith we'll marry you off."

"That," the left-handed one replied, "is quite out of the question."

"Why?"

"Because," he replied, "our Russian faith is the true faith and as our forefathers worshipped God, so must their descendants do, too."

"But you don't know anything about our religion," said the Englishmen. "We also are Christians and we have the same Bible as you."

"The Bible," the Tula craftsman replied, "is the same for everybody. That's true enough. But our books are much thicker and our religion, too, has more in it."

"Why do you think so?"

"We have ample proof of that," he replied.

"What, for instance?"

"Well," he said, "we have miracle-working icons and relics of saints and you have nothing at all and you haven't even any extra holidays except Sunday and, secondly, even if I were lawfully wedded to an Englishwoman, I would find it embarrassing to live with her."

"Why should you?" they asked. "Don't belittle our womenfolk —our girls, too, dress very neatly and they're good housewives."

But the left-handed craftsman said:

"I don't know them."

The Englishmen replied:

"That doesn't matter. The important thing is that you could get to know them. Would you like us to arrange to present them to you at a special coming-out ball?"

The left-handed craftsman blushed.

"Why trouble the girls?" he said, and refused even to hear of it. "A coming-out ball," he said, "is a gentleman's affair and does not suit the likes of us. Besides, if they ever heard of it back home in Tula, they'd just laugh at me."

The Englishmen got rather curious and asked:

"But if you have no coming-out parties, how do you arrange such matters at home in order to be quite sure you make a good choice?"

So the left-handed craftsman explained to them how things were done in his country.

"In our country," he said, "if a man has honorable intentions about a young lady, he sends an old woman who is an expert in such affairs and she makes an offer and then he pays a visit to the young lady's house and everything is done very properly and he never sees the girl by herself, but always in the presence of all her relatives."

They understood, but they said that they had no such old

women and no such customs, and then the Tula craftsman said:

"That seems all for the best then, for if I were to undertake any such business my intentions would have to be honorable and I'm afraid I do not feel so disposed to a foreign nation, so why trouble the girls?"

The Englishmen liked him for the sincerity of his opinions, so they began slapping his back and patting his knees in a very pleasant and civil fashion and they said:

"We're rather curious about one more thing, though: have you noticed any disagreeable features about our girls that make you so anxious to avoid them?"

But the left-handed craftsman said very candidly to them:

"I'm not finding fault with your girls, but I don't mind admitting that I dislike the way their dresses seem to flare out all around them so that it is hard to say what they are wearing and what occasion they are wearing it for: underneath it there's one thing pinned on here and another thing there and on their hands they wear some sort of stockings, just like monkeys—sapajous—and on top of it all they wear velvet capes."

The Englishmen laughed and said:

"Why should that bother you so much?"

"It doesn't bother me," he replied, "and I daresay there's nothing wrong with it, only I'm afraid I would feel ashamed to look on and wait till she got out of it all."

"But are your fashions better?"

"Our women's fashions in Tula are simple enough," he said. "Each girl wears her own lace and even our great ladies wear lace."

They invited him to their homes and introduced him to their ladies and served him tea and asked him:

"What are you making such faces for?"

And he replied:

"We're not used to drinking such sweet tea."

So they let him have a lump of sugar to suck according to the Russian custom. They seemed to think that holding a lump of sugar in his mouth would make his tea even sweeter, but he said:

"No, it doesn't, for we like it better that way."

The English could do nothing to change his mind and make him like the English way of life and they only succeeded in persuading him to stay a short time as their guest, promising to take him through their factories and show him how everything was done in England.

"And then," they said, "we shall take you back in one of our own ships and *bring you alive to Petersburg.*"

And he gladly agreed to that.

16.

The Englishmen took the left-handed craftsman under their protection, but sent the Russian courier back to Russia. Although the courier was a person of rank and knew foreign languages, they did not seem to be interested in him, but they certainly were very interested in the left-handed craftsman, and they began to take him around and showed him everything. He saw all their factories, their machine shops and their soap factories and their sawmills, and he liked the way they did things very much, but especially he liked the way their workers lived. Every one of their workers had enough to eat, and he was not dressed in rags, but wore a good jacket and thick leather, iron-shod boots, so as not to injure his foot if he stepped on a nail or anything; he did not do his work because somebody stood over him with a whip, but because he had been taught his trade and knew what he was doing. In the factories a multiplication table hung in front of every worker, who also had a slate by his side, so that whatever his master did, he immediately looked at the table and checked it with understanding, then he wrote something on his slate, wiped something else off it, and thus got everything right: what was written down in the figures was later to be seen in the work. And whenever a holiday came, they'd gather in twos, take a walking stick in their hands, and go out for a walk, doing everything with great decorum and showing the utmost politeness to each other, just as it should be.

The left-handed craftsman observed their life and watched

them at work, but he showed the greatest interest in something that used to astonish the English. He'd go through their arms factories, but he didn't seem to be interested in the manufacture of new guns so much as in the way the old guns were kept. He'd praise everything, but whenever he was shown any new guns, he'd say:

"We can do that as well."

But whenever he saw an old musket, he'd put his finger in the barrel, then take it out and rub it on the wall and sigh:

"That," he'd say, "certainly beats ours hollow."

The Englishmen were quite at a loss to understand what he meant, but he would ask:

"Could you tell me, please, if our generals ever saw your old guns?"

He was told:

"Those who have been here probably saw them."

"Do you know if they had their gloves on at the time?"

"Your generals," they said, "always wear full dress uniforms when they come here and they always go around in their gloves, so they must have had their gloves on at the time."

The left-handed craftsman said nothing, but he suddenly became very homesick and he said to the English:

"Thank you very much for your kind hospitality and I'm very pleased with everything, but I've seen all I wanted to see, and now I would like to go back home as soon as possible."

They could do nothing to keep him any longer. He could not be sent back by land because he didn't know any foreign languages and to send him back by sea was also inadvisable, because it was autumn and strong gales were blowing, but he kept on begging them, "Let me go home!"

"We have looked at the barometer," they said, "and we can see that a big gale is blowing up and you might get drowned, for this isn't your Gulf of Finland, but the rough, stormy sea."

"I don't care," he replied. "It makes no difference where a man dies, since we all walk under God, but I must go home, for otherwise I may go out of my mind."

As they did not want to keep him against his will by force,

they fed him, showered money on him, gave him a farewell present of a gold repeater, and to shield him from the cold weather during his sea voyage, they gave him a woolen overcoat and a cap which could be pulled down over his head to protect him against the boisterous sea breezes. So they clothed him very warmly and took him aboard a sailing vessel which was bound for Russia. There he was put, dressed up like a real gentleman, but he did not like staying below deck with the other gentlemen, because he did not feel comfortable in their company, and he'd go on deck and take shelter under a tarpaulin and ask:

"Which way is Russia?"

The Englishman to whom he would address the question would point with his hand or jerk his head, and he would turn his face in that direction and look yearningly towards his native land.

As soon as they left the harbor and got onto the open sea, his longing for Russia grew and grew, so that it was quite impossible to comfort him. A strong gale was blowing, but the left-handed craftsman refused to go down to his cabin, but sat on deck under the tarpaulin with his cap pulled down over his eyes, gazing constantly towards his native land.

Again and again the Englishmen would go up to him and ask him to go below deck where it was warm, but he kept refusing and, at last, beginning to get annoyed with them, he started telling them lies.

"No, thank you," he'd say. "I feel much better here. I'm afraid I shall be seasick below deck."

So he just stayed there all the time, except when he had to go down for some special reason, and because of that an English sailor, who to the left-handed craftsman's misfortune knew Russian, took a fancy to him. The sailor could not help admiring him for putting up with such stormy weather, although he was a Russian landlubber.

"You're a fine fellow," he'd say. "Come on, let's have a drink!"

So the left-handed craftsman had a drink.

And the jovial English sailor said:

"Have another!"

So the left-handed craftsman had another, and both of them got drunk.

The sailor asked him:

"Tell me, what is the secret you're carrying away from our country to Russia?"

The left-handed craftsman replied:

"That's my business."

"Well, if that's how it is," the lively sailor said, "then let's make an English bet."

The left-handed craftsman asked:

"What kind of a bet is that?"

"Let's agree never to drink by ourselves, but always together and always the same amount. What I drink, you drink, and what you drink, I drink, and he who can drink more wins the bet."

The left-handed craftsman thought: "The sky's cloudy, my belly's rowdy, and my poor heart craves for the sight of my home beyond the waves, so why not make the bet and at least have something to cheer me up?"

"All right," he said, "I agree."

"But, mind, no tricks!"

"Don't you worry about that," the left-handed craftsman said.

So they agreed and shook hands on it.

17.

Their contest started while they were still on the open sea and they went on drinking until they reached the estuary of the Dvina at Riga, and all this time both of them drank the same amount of liquor and neither of them was able to drink more than the other, and so perfectly matched were they that when one of them took a look at the sea and saw a devil jumping out of the waves, the other one would immediately see a devil too, except that the jovial sailor would see a ginger devil, while the left-handed craftsman would maintain that the devil he saw was as black as a Negro.

The left-handed craftsman said:

"Cross yourself and turn away, for it is the devil of the deep."

But the Englishman did not agree.

"No, sir," said he, "it isn't a devil you're seeing at all: it's a deep-sea diver. If you like I'll throw you into the sea and you needn't be afraid, for that deep-sea diver will hand you back to me at once."

And the left-handed one replied:

"All right. In that case, you can throw me into the sea."

So the mariner picked him up by the seat of his trousers and carried him to the rail intending to dump him into the sea, but the other sailors saw them in time and informed the captain, who ordered that both of them should be locked up below deck and given wines and rum and cold food, so that they should have plenty to eat and drink and be able to carry on with their bet, but he would not send them down any blazing plum pudding, for he was afraid that the liquor inside them might catch fire.

So they were safely locked up until the ship berthed in Petersburg and neither of them won the bet and they were placed in different carriages, the Englishman being taken to the English Embassy on the English Quay and the left-handed craftsman to the nearest police station.

18.

As soon as the sailor was brought to the English Embassy, a doctor and a pharmacist were brought to see him. The doctor ordered that the sailor be put right into a hot bath, and the pharmacist at once rolled a pill of gutta-percha and stuck it into the sailor's mouth, and then both of them took him out of the bath, put him on a featherbed, and covered him up with a fur coat and left him there to have a good sweat and, to prevent any interference with his rest, an order was given that no one in the Embassy should sneeze. The doctor and the chemist waited until the sailor was asleep and then they prepared another gutta-percha pill for him, put it on a table near the head of his bed, and went away.

But the left-handed craftsman was taken to the police station, thrown on the floor, and asked:

"Who are you and where do you come from and have you got a passport or any other document?"

Weakened by illness, drink, and seasickness, the left-handed craftsman could not say a word in reply, but just kept on moaning. So they searched him, took off his good clothes, confiscated his gold repeater and his money, and the police captain ordered him to be taken in a sleigh to the nearest hospital and he told the policeman not to bother to pay his fare.

The policeman took the left-handed craftsman and was going to put him in a sleigh, but it took him a long time to find one, because the cabbies usually drive by as fast as they can when they catch sight of a policeman. All this time the left-handed craftsman lay on the cold pavement. Then the policeman caught a cabby at last, but there was no warm fur rug on the sleigh, for whenever a cabby sees a policeman and cannot get away, he hides the warm fur rug under him on purpose to make quite sure that the policeman's feet get frostbitten. So the left-handed craftsman was taken in an open sleigh, and whenever they had to change over from one sleigh to another they just dropped him in the road, and when they lifted him up again, they'd yank his ears, for by then he was unconscious and they wanted to make sure he was not dead. At the first hospital they would not admit him without a document, and when they took him to a second hospital he was again refused admission for the same reason, and the same thing happened at a third and at a fourth, and by daybreak they had dragged him all over Petersburg, through narrow byways and alleys, and every time a hospital refused to admit him, the policeman would have to get another sleigh, so by this time he was all black and blue from all that knocking around. Then some assistant doctor told the policeman to take him to the Obukhvinskaya Public Infirmary, where poor people with no known address were usually taken to die.

There the policeman demanded a receipt and the left-handed craftsman was left lying on the floor in a passage until a bed could be found for him.

The English sailor got up the next morning at the very time that the Tula gunsmith was being brought to the infirmary, swallowed the second gutta-percha pill, had a quick breakfast of roast chicken, washed it down with soda water, and said:

"Where's my Russian pal? I'm going to look for him."

So he dressed and set off.

19.

By some miracle the English sailor found the left-handed craftsman in less than no time, even before he had been put to bed and while he was still lying on the floor in the passage.

"I must give the Emperor a message," said the left-handed craftsman to the mariner. "Just a few words, but it is most urgent."

The Englishman ran off to see Count Kleinmichel and he made an awful fuss, saying to the Count:

"How can you allow a man to be treated like that? He may only wear a sheepskin, but he has a human soul, hasn't he?"

The Englishman was immediately kicked out for daring to mention the human soul. Then somebody tipped him off, "You'd better go and see the Cossack Platov: he's a man of warm human feelings."

The Englishman found Platov sulking on his couch. Platov listened to his story and he remembered the left-handed craftsman.

"Why, of course, I know him well," he said. "I've even pulled him by the hair, but I'm afraid I don't know what I can do to help him in his present trouble, for, you see, I've left the army for good and am just a private individual and nobody pays any attention to me any more. But you'd better run quickly to Commandant Skobelev, who has had experience in such matters and can do something, and, in fact, I am almost certain he will do something."

So the sailor went to see Skobelev and he told him everything, how it all happened and what the left-handed craftsman was suffering from, and Skobelev said:

"Yes, yes, I know of such an illness, but I'm afraid that not even the Germans can cure it. What you want is a doctor whose father was a Russian priest, for such doctors are acquainted with such cases from early childhood and they know what to do. I'll send the Russian doctor Martyn-Solsky to that hospital and let him have a look at your friend."

But when Martyn-Solsky arrived at the infirmary, the left-handed craftsman was already drawing his last breath, for the back of his head had been split open when they threw him down on the pavement, and all he could say before he died was:

"Tell the Emperor that the English don't clean their muskets with bath brick and that we shouldn't clean them with bath brick either, or God help us if there is another war, for they won't shoot properly."

And having given that loyal message to the Emperor, the left-handed craftsman crossed himself and died.

Martyn-Solsky wasted no time, but went straight to Count Chernishev and asked him to give the message to the Emperor, but Count Chernishev just scoffed at him and said:

"You'd better stick to your emetics and your purges and don't interfere in a matter that doesn't concern you: in Russia we have generals for that kind of thing."

So the Emperor was not told and the guns continued to be cleaned with bath brick until the Crimean war, and when, during that war, the Russians loaded their guns, the bullets just rattled about, because the barrels had been cleaned with crushed brick. It was then that Martyn-Solsky reminded Count Chernishev about the left-handed craftsman, but Chernishev said:

"Clear out of here, you pill merchant, and mind your own business, or I'll deny you ever told me anything about it and then you'll be in real trouble!"

And Martyn-Solsky thought: "He most likely will deny having ever heard anything about it from me"—and he kept silent.

But if they had brought the left-handed craftsman's message to the Emperor in time, there would have been quite a different story to tell about the Crimean war.

20.

But all this is now a tale of "old, unhappy, far-off things and battles long ago," and even if it didn't belong to days that are very "far off" there would be no need to forget it in a hurry, in spite of the fairy-tale character of this legend and the epic nature of its hero. The name of the left-handed craftsman, like the names of many other great geniuses, has been lost forever to posterity; but even as a myth created by the popular imagination, it is interesting; and his adventures can serve as a chronicle of an epoch the general spirit of which has been truly and faithfully rendered.

Such craftsmen as the fabulous left-handed craftsman are no longer to be found in Tula; the machine has made the inequalities between natural talents and endowments less obvious, and genius can hardly be expected to compete with application and mere accuracy. While favoring an increase in wages, the machines do not encourage the artistic boldness which sometimes broke through all the barriers of the merely possible and inspired popular imagination to create similar fairy-tale legends of this sort.

The workers, no doubt, know how to value the practical devices put at their disposal by science, but they will remember the old days with pride and affection. That was their epic story, and one with a very "human soul," too.

The Sentry

1839

1.

The incident the story of which is offered to the reader's attention below is both moving and terrible in its significance for the heroic character who played the chief part in it, and the denouement of the affair is so singular that hardly anywhere except in Russia could anything like it have happened.

It is partly an affair of court intrigue and partly a historic event that characterizes fairly well the manners and the spirit of a very interesting but extremely poorly chronicled period of the thirties of this nineteenth century.

There is nothing fictional in the following story.

2.

During the winter of 1839, shortly before the Festival of the Epiphany, there was a great thaw in Petersburg. The weather was so warm and wet that it looked as though spring had come in earnest: the snow melted, water dripped from the roofs, and the ice on the rivers turned blue and water appeared on its surface. Deep, unfrozen pools of water could be seen here and there on the Neva right in front of the Winter Palace. The wind was warm and westerly, but very strong; the water was driven in from the sea, and guns were continually fired as a warning against floods.

The guard at the palace was made up of a company of the Iz-maylovsky regiment under the command of a very brilliant and well-educated young officer by the name of Nikolai Ivanovich Miller, who was well received in the highest social circles (subsequently a full general and the director of the Lycée, the highest educational establishment for the sons of the nobility). He was a man of so-called "humane" ideas, which had been observed in him for a long time and which, in the view of his superiors, interfered a little with his advancement in the service.

In fact, however, Miller was a most conscientious and trustworthy officer and, in any case, at that particular time the duty of the guard at the palace involved no danger of any kind. It was a most peaceful and tranquil time. All that was required of the palace sentries was to stand at their posts according to regulations. And yet it was during Captain Miller's turn of duty at the palace that a most extraordinary and alarming event took place, an event which the few of his contemporaries who are still with us probably scarcely remember.

3.

At first everything went well with the guard: the posts were assigned, the sentries were placed, and everything was in perfect order. The Emperor Nikolai Pavlovich was in excellent health, he had gone for a drive in the evening, had returned home and gone to bed. The palace, too, slept. The night was very quiet. In the guardroom all was still. Captain Miller pinned his white handkerchief to the traditionally greasy high back of the officer's chair and sat down, intending to while away the time by reading.

Captain Miller had always been a passionate reader and for that reason he was never bored, for he read his book and did not notice how the night slipped away. But suddenly at about three o'clock he was to experience a terrible shock: the sergeant on duty stood before him and, looking pale and trembling with fear, stammered in a thick voice:

"Trouble, sir, trouble!"

"What's the matter?"

"A terrible calamity, sir!"

Captain Miller jumped up in indescribable alarm and was only with difficulty able to ascertain what the nature of the "trouble" and the "terrible calamity" was.

4.

What had happened was that the sentry, a private of the Izmaylovsky regiment by the name of Postnikov, who was standing guard outside the palace at what is today known as the "Jordan" gate, had heard desperate cries for help from a man who was drowning in one of the pools over the ice of the Neva just opposite his post.

Private Postnikov, a former house serf, was a highly impressionable and very sensitive man. He listened for a long time to the distant cries and groans of the drowning man and he was paralyzed with horror. Terrified, he peered in every direction, but as though by design, there was not a living soul to be seen anywhere on the whole visible expanse of the quays and the Neva.

There was nobody who could give help to the drowning man, who was sure to sink. . . .

Meanwhile the man was struggling long and stubbornly.

There seemed to be only one thing left for him to do: to sink to the bottom without further struggle, but no! His exhausted groans and cries for help would suddenly stop, then they would start again, always getting nearer and nearer to the palace quay. It was obvious that the man had not given up hope and was moving in the right direction, making straight for the lights of the street lamps, but of course he would not be saved after all, for if he kept coming that way he was quite sure to fall in the "Jordan" pool, a hole cut into the ice of the river for the consecration of the water on the morning of the festival of Epiphany. For once he got as far as the hole, he would fall in, be drawn under the ice, and —that would be the end of him. . . . Now he was quiet again, but a minute later he could again be heard splashing through the water and moaning: "Help! Help!" He was now so near that one could even hear the splashing of the water as he struggled along. . . .

It occurred to Private Postnikov that it would be quite easy to save this man. All he had to do was run on to the ice and the drowning man would be sure to be within reach. He had only to throw him a rope or hold out a stick or his gun and the man would be saved. The man was so near that he could take hold of it and save himself. But Postnikov remembered the duties of his service and his oath; he knew that he was the sentry, and that a sentry must not leave his sentry box under any pretext whatsoever.

On the other hand, Postnikov's heart was very troubled: it ached, it throbbed, it sank. . . . He would gladly have torn it out and thrown it at his own feet—so much did those groans and cries for help distress him. It was awful to hear another man perishing and not be able to stretch out a helping hand to save him when, as a matter of fact, it was quite possible to do so, for the sentry box would not run away and nothing untoward could possibly happen. "Shall I run down? Shall I? Will anybody see me? Oh, dear, whatever happens I can bear it no longer! There he is groaning again. . . ."

For the entire half-hour during which this was going on Private Postnikov's heart was so lacerated with suffering that he began to fear for his reason. He was an intelligent and conscientious soldier with clear judgment and he realized perfectly well that for a sentry to leave his post was so great a crime that he would be court-martialed at once, sentenced to run the gauntlet between two lines of soldiers armed with sticks, sent to a Siberian convict prison, or perhaps even be shot. But from the direction of the swollen river the groans were coming nearer and nearer and he could already hear the sounds of mumbling and desperate floundering.

"I'm drowning! Help! Drowning!"

Another step and he would fall into the "Jordan" hole and then —the end!

Postnikov looked round once or twice on all sides. There was not a soul to be seen anywhere, only the lanterns shook and flickered and now and then that cry for help was borne on the wind—perhaps the last cry . . .

Another splash, another short cry for help, and there was a gurgling sound in the water.

The sentry could bear it no longer and—he deserted his post.

5.

Postnikov rushed to the pier, ran onto the ice with his heart beating violently, then into the pool of water that had risen about it, and, having in no time discerned the spot where the drowning man was struggling for his life, he held out the stock of his rifle to him.

The drowning man caught hold of the butt-end and Postnikov pulled him by the bayonet and dragged him out on the bank.

Both the man who had been saved and his rescuer were drenched to the skin, and as the man who had been saved was in a state of complete exhaustion and kept shivering and falling down, his rescuer, Private Postnikov, could not bring himself to abandon him on the ice. He therefore led him out onto the embankment and began looking around for somebody he could hand him over to. While all this was taking place, there had appeared on the embankment a sleigh in which sat an officer who was in command of the Palace Veterans' Company (which has since been disbanded).

This gentleman, who had made an appearance at such an inopportune moment for Postnikov, was, it would seem, a man of a rather frivolous character and, besides, a little muddleheaded as well and extremely impudent. He jumped out of his sleigh and began inquiring:

"Who is this man? Who are these people?"

"He was drowning, sir," Postnikov began to explain. "Sinking."

"Who was drowning? Who? You were? Why are you here?"

But the man just spluttered and mumbled, and Postnikov was no longer there: he had shouldered his rifle and gone back to his sentry box.

The officer may or may not have realized what had happened, but he made no further inquiries and at once put the man who had been rescued from the river into his sleigh and drove with him to the Admiralty Police Station on Morskaya Street.

There the officer made a statement to the inspector to the effect that the man in the wet clothes whom he had brought with him had been on the point of drowning in the pool on the river opposite the palace and that he, the officer, had saved him at the risk of his own life.

The man who had been saved was wet to the skin, exhausted and shivering with cold. His fright and the terrible efforts he had made to save himself had made him lose consciousness and he did not care who had saved him.

The sleepy medical attendant at the police station bustled around him and an official statement was drawn up from the officer's verbal deposition, though the police, being naturally of a suspicious nature, could not help wondering how the officer had managed to emerge from the water quite dry. The officer, who was anxious to get the lifesaving medal, explained it by some happy concurrence of circumstances, but his explanation sounded incoherent and improbable. They went to wake the superintendent and sent to make inquiries.

Meanwhile, at the palace this incident gave rise to quite a different and very rapid sequence of events.

6.

In the palace guardroom the different turns the affair had taken after the officer had put the man who had been saved from drowning into his sleigh were unknown. There all the Izmaylovsky officer and the soldiers knew was that Postnikov, a private of their regiment, had left his sentry box and rushed off to save a man. This being a great breach of military discipline, Private Postnikov was certain to be court-martialed and sentenced to be flogged, while all his superior officers, beginning with the commander of the company down to the colonel of the regiment, would have to put up with all sorts of unpleasantness against which they could neither defend themselves nor offer any excuses.

The wet and shivering soldier Postnikov was of course immediately relieved from his post and, brought to the guardroom, candidly related to Captain Miller all that we already know, with all the details up to the moment when the officer of the Veterans' Company put the man he, Postnikov, had saved into the sleigh and told his driver to drive as fast as he could to the Admiralty Police Station.

The danger grew greater and more unavoidable. The officer of the Veterans' Company would, of course, tell everything to the police superintendent and the superintendent would report it to Chief of Police Kokoshkin, who would in his turn report it to the Emperor, and then they would all be in for it.

There was no time to be lost: the superior officers had to be informed.

Captain Miller at once dispatched an alarming note to the commander of his battalion, Lieutenant-Colonel Svinin, in which he begged him to come to the palace guardroom as soon as possible so as to take all the necessary measures to avert the terrible calamity that was threatening them.

That was about three o'clock, and Kokoshkin usually presented his report to the Emperor fairly early in the morning, so that very little time remained for considering what action had to be taken.

7.

Lieutenant-Colonel Svinin did not possess that compassion and that kindness of heart for which Captain Miller had always been distinguished. Svinin was not a heartless man, but first and foremost he was a stickler for strict discipline (a type of military martinet that is now remembered with regret). Svinin was well known for his severity and he even liked to show off as an exacting disciplinarian. He had no taste for evil and he did not try to cause anyone any unjustly inflicted suffering; but when a man violated any of the rules of the service, Svinin was inexorable. He considered it inappropriate to go into the motives that guided the action of the culprit in any given case, adhering to the principle that in the service any misdemeanor must be severely punished. For that reason everyone in the company of the guard knew that Private Postnikov would have to suffer severely for having left his post and that nothing in the world could save him from punishment, and that Svinin would not regret it in the least.

Such was the reputation this army officer enjoyed among his superiors and his comrades, among whom were men who did not sympathize with Svinin, for at that time "humanism" and other similar delusions had not entirely died out. Svinin was quite indifferent to the praise or censure of the "humanists." It was absolutely useless to beg or entreat Svinin or even to attempt to move him to pity. To all this he was hardened, with the rigorous tenacity of those who in that time were out to make a public career for themselves; but even he, like Achilles, had a weak spot.

Svinin's career in the army had begun well and he quite naturally watched his step and made sure that, just as with a full dress uniform, not a single speck of dust should settle on it; and yet this unhappy escapade of one of the men of the battalion entrusted to him would most certainly cast a shadow on the discipline of his entire battalion. Whether the battalion commander was guilty or not guilty of what one of his men had done while carried away by the most honorable feelings of compassion was something that those on whom Svinin's well founded and carefully maintained military career depended would not stop to inquire. Indeed, many of them would be only too pleased to bar his path in order to provide an opening for a relative of theirs or for some fine young fellow who enjoyed the patronage of highly placed persons, should the Emperor, who could be expected to be angry, say to the commander of the regiment that he had "weak officers" and that their men were "undisciplined." And who was the cause of it all? Why, Svinin! And so they would go on repeating that Svinin was "weak" and in this way the reproach of weakness would stick to his reputation like an indelible stain. Then he would never stand out among his contemporaries nor leave his portrait in the national gallery of the historical personages of the Russian Empire.

Though in those days very few people devoted their time to the study of history, they nevertheless believed in it and were particularly anxious to take part in its making.

8.

As soon as Svinin, at about three o'clock in the morning, received Captain Miller's alarming note, he jumped out of bed, put on his uniform, and, angry and apprehensive, arrived at the guardroom of the Winter Palace. There he immediately questioned Private Postnikov and satisfied himself that the incredible occurrence had really taken place. Private Postnikov candidly repeated his statement to his battalion commander, telling him exactly what had happened while he was on guard duty and what he, Postnikov, had already related to his company commander, Captain Miller. The soldier said that he was guilty before God and the Emperor and that he could not expect mercy; that

262 » NIKOLAI LESKOV: Selected Tales

while standing guard, hearing the groans of a man who was drowning in the pool of water on the river, he had suffered a long time, he had struggled with himself, torn between his sense of military duty and his feelings of compassion, and that at last he had yielded to temptation and given up the struggle: he had left his sentry box, jumped onto the ice, and dragged the drowning man onto the bank, and, as ill luck would have it, had run into the officer in command of the Palace Veterans' Company.

Lieutenant-Colonel Svinin was in despair; he gave himself the only possible satisfaction of venting his anger on Postnikov, whom he at once had put under arrest and placed in the regimental lockup, and then made some biting remarks to Miller, whom he reproached for his "humane notions," which were of no use at all in the army. But all that was not enough to put the matter right. It was quite impossible to find, if not a justification, then at least an excuse, for such an action as the leaving of his post by a sentry, and there remained only one way out of the difficulty—to conceal the whole affair from the Emperor.

But was it possible to conceal such an occurrence?

Apparently the whole thing was quite impossible, for the rescue of the drowning man was known not only to the whole of the guard, but also to that detestable officer of the Veterans' Company, who no doubt had by this time reported the whole matter to General Kokoshkin.

Where was he to go now? To whom could he turn? To whom could he look for help and protection?

Svinin wanted to call on the Grand Duke Mikhail Pavlovich at once and make a clean breast of everything to him. Such a devious approach was quite customary in those days. The Grand Duke, whose hot temper was well known, would storm and rage, but his character and habits were such that the sharper the words he used at first—even going so far as to cut the man before him to the quick—the sooner he would forgive him and himself take up his defense. There were not a few such instances, sometimes even brought about on purpose. Words never hurt anyone, and Svinin was very anxious to bring the matter to a favorable conclusion. But

was it possible to obtain entrance to the palace at night and disturb
the Grand Duke? On the other hand, if he waited till morning before going to see the Grand Duke, it would be too late, for by then
General Kokoshkin would already have reported to the Emperor.
And while Svinin agitatedly went over these difficulties in his mind,
he looked at the matter and realized that there was another solu-
tion which had hitherto been hidden from him as though in a mist.

9.

Among well-known military tactics is one according
to which at the moment when the greatest danger threatens from
the walls of a beleaguered fortress the thing to do is not to re-
treat but to advance straight under its walls. Svinin decided not
to do any of the things that had occurred to him at first, but to
go and see General Kokoshkin at once.

All sorts of terrifying and absurd stories were current at the time
about Chief of Police Kokoshkin, but among other things it was
asserted that he was endowed with a tactfulness so versatile that
it enabled him "not only to make a mountain out of a molehill,
but also to make a molehill out of a mountain."

Kokoshkin was indeed very stern and menacing and he inspired
great fear in everybody, but occasionally he would shut his eyes to
the escapades of some gay young scamps among the army officers,
and there were many such young scamps in those days and very
often they found in him a powerful and zealous protector. Generally speaking, he was able to do much, and he knew how to do it,
too, if only he chose. Both Svinin and Captain Miller knew this
side of his character. Indeed, it was Captain Miller who had
strengthened his battalion commander's decision to go and see
General Kokoshkin immediately and put his trust in the general's
magnanimity and in the "versatile tact" which would probably
suggest to him the means of getting out of this unpleasant predicament without arousing the Emperor's wrath, which Kokoshkin
(to his honor be it said) always did his best to avoid.

Svinin put on his overcoat, raised his eyes aloft, and muttering, "Lord, Lord!" a few times, drove off to Kokoshkin.

It was already past four o'clock in the morning.

10.

Chief of Police Kokoshkin was awakened and told of the arrival of Svinin, who had come on important business that would brook no delay.

The general at once got up and, with a short quilted robe thrown over his shoulders, rubbing his forehead, yawning and shivering, came out to receive Svinin. Kokoshkin listened with great attention, but with the utmost calm, to all that Svinin had to tell him. To all these explanations and requests for indulgence he merely said:

"The soldier left the sentry box and saved a man's life?"

"Yes, sir," answered Svinin.

"And the sentry box?"

"Remained empty during that time."

"I see. I knew that it remained empty. I'm very glad to hear it was not stolen."

This brief comment convinced Svinin more strongly than ever that the general knew everything already and that he had of course already made up his mind in what manner he would lay the facts before the Emperor in his morning's report, and, moreover, that he would not change his decision. Otherwise such an event as a soldier of the palace guard leaving his post would without a doubt have caused great alarm to the energetic chief of police.

But Kokoshkin did not know anything about it. The superintendent of police to whom the officer in command of the Palace Veterans' Company had brought the man he had allegedly saved did not consider it a matter of any particular importance. As he saw it, it was most certainly not a case that would justify him in disturbing a tired chief of police in the middle of the night, and, besides, the whole thing seemed extremely suspicious to him because the officer of the Veterans' Company was quite dry, which would certainly not have been the case if he had saved a man from drowning at the risk of his own life. The superintendent regarded the officer as an ambitious liar who wanted to have another medal on his chest, and that was why he kept him waiting while the clerk on duty was drawing up an official report of the alleged occurrence and trying to find out the truth from him by cross-examining him about minute details.

The superintendent, too, felt aggrieved that such a thing should have happened in his district and that the man had been saved not by a policeman but by an officer of the palace guard.

Kokoshkin's calm, on the other hand, was explained simply: first, by the fact that he was terribly tired after a day of hard work requiring him to be constantly on his feet and his having taken part in the extinguishing of two fires that night; and, secondly, because the act committed by Private Postnikov was no direct concern of his as chief of police.

Still, Kokoshkin at once gave the necessary instructions.

He sent for the superintendent of the Admiralty Police Station, ordering him to come at once and to bring the officer in charge of the Veterans' Company and the man saved from drowning, and asked Svinin to wait in the small reception room adjoining his office. Then Kokoshkin retired to his office and, without closing the door, sat down at the desk and began signing papers; but almost immediately he dropped his head on his arm and fell asleep in his chair at the desk.

11.

In those days there were neither telegraphs nor telephones, and in order to transmit the orders of the authorities as expeditiously as possible, the "forty thousand couriers" immortalized by Gogol in his *Government Inspector* used to gallop headlong in all directions.

This, of course, was not as quick as the telegraph or the telephone, but at least it lent considerable animation to the town and bore witness to the unremitting vigilance of the authorities.

By the time the panting superintendent, the lifesaving army officer, and the man saved from drowning had arrived from the Admiralty Police Station, the nervous and energetic General Kokoshkin had had a doze and refreshed himself. That was evident from the expression on his face and the manifestation of his mental faculties.

Kokoshkin ordered all who had arrived to come to his office and also asked Svinin to come in.

"The official report?" Kokoshkin demanded laconically of the superintendent in a recovered voice.

The superintendent handed him a folded piece of paper in silence and then whispered in a low voice:

"I must beg leave to say a few words to you in private, sir."

"Very well."

Kokoshkin went towards the bay window followed by the superintendent.

The indistinct whisperings of the superintendent could be heard, as well as the much more distinct, though abrupt, interjections of the general.

"I see . . . Yes . . . Well, what about it? It might have happened . . . They always manage to come out dry. Nothing more?"

"Nothing, sir."

The general came away from the bay window, sat down at his desk, and began to read. He read the report in silence without showing any signs of uneasiness or suspicion and then addressed the man who had been saved in a loud voice.

"How did you happen to get into the pool of water in the river opposite the palace, my good man?"

"I'm sorry, sir."

"I see! Drunk?"

"Sorry, sir. I wasn't drunk. Just had a drop or two."

"Why did you go in the water?"

"I wanted to cross the river the nearest way across the ice, sir, but I lost my way and got into the water."

"So it was dark before your eyes, was it?"

"Yes, sir. It was dark all round, sir."

"So you couldn't see who pulled you out, could you?"

"Afraid not, sir. I believe it was him." He pointed to the officer and added: "I couldn't make out who it was, sir. I was too scared, sir."

"Yes, that's what comes of gadding about when you should be asleep. Have a good look at this gentleman now and don't you ever forget who was your benefactor. An honorable man risked his life to save you."

"I shall always remember him, sir."

"What's your name, sir?" Kokoshkin asked the officer.

The officer gave his name.

"Do you hear?" Kokoshkin asked the man saved from drowning.

"Yes, sir."

"Are you of the Orthodox faith?"

"Yes, sir."

"Mention his name when offering up a prayer in church."

"I will, sir."

"Yes, pray to God for him, and now you can go. You're no longer needed."

The man bowed to the ground and rushed out of the office, greatly pleased to have been let off so easily.

Svinin stood there nonplussed, unable to understand how by God's grace things were taking such a turn.

12.

Kokoshkin turned to the officer of the Veterans' Company.

"You saved this man at the risk of your own life?"

"Yes, sir."

"You have no witnesses to prove it, have you? But then, it being so late, I don't suppose there could have been any witnesses."

"No, sir. It was dark and there was nobody on the embankment except the sentry."

"There's no need to mention the sentry: a sentry has to stand at his post and he has no right to allow himself to be distracted by anything else. I believe what is written in this report. It was taken down from your own words, wasn't it?"

This Kokoshkin uttered with special emphasis, and there was a note of suppressed menace in his raised voice.

But the officer was not in the least put off and, opening his eyes wide and throwing out his chest, he replied:

"It was taken down from my own words, sir, and it is absolutely correct."

"Your action deserves a reward."

"Thank you, sir," the officer said, bowing gratefully.

"There's nothing to thank me for," went on Kokoshkin. "I shall report your self-sacrificing act to the Emperor and I expect your chest may be decorated with a medal this very day. Now, sir, you may go home. Have a warm drink and don't leave the house as perhaps you may be needed."

The officer of the Veterans' Company beamed with pleasure, bowed, and went out.

Kokoshkin gazed after him and said:

"It is possible that the Emperor may wish to see him."

"Yes, sir," replied the superintendent, catching on.

"I do not require you any more."

The superintendent went out and, as he closed the door behind him, he crossed himself piously.

The officer of the Veterans' Company was waiting for the superintendent downstairs and they went away together, feeling much more amicably disposed towards one another than when they had come.

Only Svinin remained in the office of the chief of police. Kokoshkin looked at him long and piercingly at first and then he asked:

"You didn't go to see the Grand Duke, did you?"

In those days when the Grand Duke was mentioned everybody knew that it referred to the Grand Duke Mikhail Pavlovich.

"I came straight to you," replied Svinin.

"Who is the officer on guard?"

"Captain Miller."

Kokoshkin again looked at Svinin in silence, then he said:

"I think you told me something different before."

Svinin did not even realize at first what the general was driving at and he said nothing. Kokoshkin added:

"Oh, never mind. Go and have a good sleep."

The interview was at an end.

13.

At one o'clock the officer of the Veterans' Company was in fact sent for again by Kokoshkin, who informed him most amiably that the Emperor was highly pleased that among the officers of the Veterans' Company of his palace there were such conscientious and self-sacrificing men and that he had bestowed on him a medal for lifesaving. Then General Kokoshkin handed the hero the medal with his own hands, and the officer went away to show it off and boast about it. The affair was therefore completely at an end, but Lieutenant-Colonel Svinin could not help feeling that somehow or other it was unfinished, and he considered himself called upon to dot the "i's."

He was so troubled that he was ill for three days, and on the fourth he drove to St. Peter's Church, had a service of thanksgiving celebrated before the Saviour's icon, and, returning home in a more composed frame of mind, sent to ask Captain Miller to call on him.

"Well, thank God, my dear fellow," he said to Captain Miller, "the storm that was hanging over us has blown over and the unfortunate incident with the sentry has been completely settled. I think we can now breathe freely. We owe it all without a doubt first to the mercy of God and secondly to General Kokoshkin. People may say he is unkind and heartless, but I am filled with gratitude for his magnanimity and with respect for his resourcefulness and tact. He took advantage in quite a marvellously masterly way of the boastfulness of that rogue of an officer, who should really have received a thorough thrashing in the stable instead of a decoration. But there was nothing else to be done: he had to be made use of so that many should be saved, and Kokoshkin gave such a clever turn to the affair that nobody suffered the slightest unpleasantness—on the contrary, everyone is very pleased and satisfied. Incidentally, I am informed by a reliable person that Kokoshkin himself is highly satisfied with me. He was pleased that I had not gone anywhere else but come straight to him and that I did not argue with that rogue who was given the medal. In short, no one has suffered and everything has been done with so much tact that there is nothing to be afraid of in future. All the same, there is a little thing we have overlooked on our side. You see, we must tactfully follow Kokoshkin's example and wind up the affair on our side in such a way as to protect ourselves against the recurrence of such an incident. There is still one person whose position has not been formally settled. I speak of Private Postnikov. He is still under arrest in solitary confinement and I suppose he must be very worried about what is going to happen to him. We must put an end to his worries."

"Yes," cried Miller, looking delighted, "it is high time."

"Why, of course, and you're the person best qualified to do so. Please go at once to the barracks, call your company together, bring Private Postnikov out of his cell, and see that he gets his two hundred strokes of the birch before the whole company."

14.

Captain Miller was astonished and made an attempt to persuade Svinin, in view of the general rejoicing, to spare and pardon Private Postnikov, who had suffered so much already while waiting in his cell for a decision on what was going to happen to him. But Svinin flared up and did not even permit Miller to continue.

"No," he said, "don't even suggest it to me. I've just been talking to you about tact and you're already beginning to act tactlessly. Don't speak of it!"

Svinin changed his tone to a drier and more official one and added firmly:

"And as in this affair you, too, are not quite in the right, and, indeed, are very much to blame because of a soft streak in your nature unbecoming to an army man, which deficiency of your character is reflected in the discipline of your subordinates, I order you to be present personally at the execution of the sentence of flogging so as to make sure that it is carried out properly—and as severely as possible. For this purpose be so good as to see that the flogging is done by the young soldiers who have just arrived from the army, for in this respect our old soldiers are all infected with the liberalism of the guards: they do not flog a comrade as they should, but merely scare the fleas off his back. I shall myself come to see how the culprit is handled."

There could be no question of any evasion of the orders given by a superior officer and the soft-hearted Captain Miller had to carry out strictly the orders given him by the commander of his battalion.

The company was drawn up in the courtyard of the Izmaylov-sky barracks, the rods were fetched in sufficient quantity from the stores, and Private Postnikov, brought out of his cell, was "handled" with the zealous participation of his young comrades, newly arrived from the army. These fellows, unspoiled by the "liberalism" of the guards, dotted the "i's" on his back in full measure, as ordered by the commander of the battalion. Then Postnikov, having been properly punished, was lifted up from the overcoat on which he had been flogged and carried to the regimental hospital.

15.

Battalion Commander Svinin, notified that the flogging of Private Postnikov had been carried out, at once paid a paternal visit to the hospital in person and was highly gratified at seeing unmistakable evidence that his orders had been carried out without stint or favor. The compassionate and nervous Postnikov had been "handled" soundly. Svinin was satisfied and ordered that Postnikov be given, on his behalf, a pound of sugar and a quarter of a pound of tea, so that he could enjoy himself while recovering. Lying on his hospital bed, Postnikov heard this order and said:

"I am quite content, sir. Thank you very much for your fatherly kindness."

And, in fact, he *was* "content," because, while languishing in solitary confinement for three days, he had come to expect something much worse. Two hundred strokes of the birch, according to the strict ideas of those days, did not amount to much when compared with the punishments meted out by the military courts; and Postnikov would have been sentenced to such a punishment if all those bold tactical evolutions related above had not—luckily for him—taken place.

But the number of persons pleased at the incident just described was not limited to these.

16.

The story of the heroic exploit of Private Postnikov soon spread via the grapevine "telegraph" throughout the capital, which in those days, with the voice of the press silenced, lived in an atmosphere of endless gossip. In passing from mouth to mouth the name of the real hero, Private Postnikov, was lost, but the epic story itself was blown up until it assumed a highly interesting romantic character.

It was said that a most extraordinary swimmer had swum from the side of the Peter and Paul Fortress and had been fired on and wounded by one of the sentries at the palace and that an officer of the Veterans' Company, who happened to pass by, plunged into the water and saved him from drowning, for which the one received the reward he merited and the other the punishment he deserved. This preposterous rumor even reached the cloisters of the church, where at that time there lived a bishop who was a very careful man and far from indifferent to worldly affairs, and who was kindly disposed to the devout Moscow family of the Svinins.

The perspicacious bishop found the story of the shooting a little obscure. What nocturnal swimmer could it have been? If he was a runaway convict, then why was the sentry, who was merely doing his duty, punished for shooting at him as he swam across the

Neva from the fortress? If, however, he was not a convict, but a mystery man who had to be saved from the waves of the Neva, then how could a sentry be expected to know anything about it? It just could not have happened in the way the town gossips said. Many things are accepted in the "world" in a rather thoughtless and flippant manner, whereas those who live in monasteries and in the cloisters in town look at things much more seriously and know the real truth about what is happening in the world outside.

17.

One day when Svinin happened to come to church to receive the Bishop's blessing, His Eminence mentioned to him, "incidentally," the story about "the shooting." Svinin told him the whole truth, which, as we know, was nothing like the story about "the shooting."

The Bishop listened to the real story in silence, gently fingering his white rosary and never taking his eyes off the narrator. When Svinin had finished, the Bishop said quietly:

"Wherefore we must conclude that in this affair not everything has been told and not everywhere have the facts been stated strictly in accordance with the truth."

Svinin stammered and then said evasively that it was not he but General Kokoshkin who had made the report.

The Bishop passed his rosary through his waxen fingers in silence a few times and then said:

"One must distinguish between what is a lie and what is not wholly true."

Again the rosary, again silence, and, at last, the quiet murmur:

"What is not wholly true is not a lie. But the less said about it the better."

"Yes, that is really so," Svinin said, thus encouraged. "What troubles me most of all, however, is that I had to mete out punishment to that soldier who, though he had neglected his duty. . . ."

The rosary again and then a quiet interruption:

"The duties of service must never be neglected."

"Well, yes, but he had done it through magnanimity, through compassion, and after such a struggle and at such a risk. He realized that in saving the life of another he was destroying himself. . . . It is a high, a holy feeling!"

"Holiness is known only to God. Corporal punishment is not destructive to a common man, nor is it contrary to the customs of the nations, nor to the spirit of the Scriptures. The rod is easier to bear by the coarse body than light suffering by the soul. In this case justice has not suffered in the least."

"But he was deprived of the reward for saving a man's life."

"The saving of a man's life is not a merit, but a duty. He who could save a life and does not save it is liable to the punishment of the laws, but he who saves does his duty."

A pause, the rosary, and quiet murmuring.

"For a soldier to suffer degradation and wounds for a heroic action may prove far more profitable than for him to become overbearing because of a mark of distinction. But what is most important in this matter is to take care never to mention anywhere what anyone said about it and on what occasion."

It was quite evident that the bishop too was satisfied.

18.

If I possessed the temerity of the happy chosen ones of Heaven to whom, through their great faith, it is given to penetrate the secret of God's will, then I too would perhaps have dared to permit myself the supposition that God himself was probably satisfied with the conduct of Postnikov's humble soul which He had created. But my faith is small; it does not permit my mind to behold anything so high: I am of the earth, earthy. I am thinking of those mortals who love goodness simply for the sake of goodness and do not expect any rewards for it from any quarter. These straightforward and reliable people, it seems to me, should also be fully satisfied with this holy impulse of love and with the no-less-holy endurance of the humble hero of my true and artless tale.

The White Eagle

(A Ghost Story)

Of meat the dog dreams, and of fish, the fisherman. [THEOCRITUS (*Idyll*)]

1.

꙳꙳꙳꙳꙳
꙳꙳꙳꙳꙳ There are more things in heaven and earth. . . . This is how we usually begin such stories as this, for we are anxious to shield ourselves with a Shakespearean quotation from the arrows of those wits among our critics by whom nothing remains unexplored. However, I still maintain that "things" take place which are certainly very queer and inexplicable and which are sometimes called supernatural, and for this reason I, for my part, am always ready to listen to such stories. It was also for this reason that two or three years ago when, behaving like children again, we began to play at spiritualism, I gladly joined one such circle. The rules of this circle required that at our evening séances not a word should be spoken about politics or religion, but that our conversation should be confined strictly to the realm of spirits, their appearances and the part they have played in the lives of living men. The rules even

prohibited the discussion of "ways of preserving and saving Russia," for in such a discussion many people, "starting with protestations of loyalty to our government, ended up with prayers for its demise."

For this reason, too, any taking of "famous names" in vain was strictly forbidden, except, of course, the name of the Creator, which, as is well known, is used merely as a rhetorical flourish. Breaches of these rules of course occurred, but even then those who were guilty of breaking them exercised the utmost circumspection. It did sometimes happen that two inveterate politicians would retire to a window or the fireplace and begin whispering to one another, but even then one of them was sure to caution his friend by a *pas si haut*, and our host for the evening would keep an eye on them and jokingly threaten them with a fine.

Each of us in turn had to tell some fastastic story *from his own life*, and as not everybody has the knack for telling a story, no criticisms were made as regards its artistic excellence, nor were any proofs of authenticity demanded. If a man said that the event he was telling us about really took place, we all believed him or, at any rate, pretended to believe him. Such was the convention which we faithfully observed.

I confess that I was chiefly interested in the psychological aspect of the proceedings. I never doubted the wisdom of Hamlet's remark that "there are more things in heaven and earth than are dreamt of in your philosophy," but what interested me most of all was what things happened to whom. And indeed, here the psychological aspect was of the utmost importance, for however much the teller of the story tried to assume an impartiality in keeping with the higher sphere of disembodied spirits, you could not help noticing that the apparition from the grave took on a certain nonspectral coloring on revisiting our earth, just as a sunbeam on passing through stained glass takes on a tint not its own. Here it was quite impossible to make out what was truth and what was untruth, while to watch this blending of reality and unreality was an occupation that I, for one, found most fascinating. I want to tell you of just such a case.

2.

The "martyr on duty," that is to say, the man whose turn it was to tell the ghost story, occupied a rather important position in the Civil Service and was, besides, a highly original character. His name was Galaktion Ilyich and he was nicknamed in jest "the moth-eaten aristocrat." There was a kind of pun about his nickname, for he was, in fact, a nobleman of sorts, and he did seem somewhat moth-eaten, both literally and metaphorically, being terribly emaciated and also of rather low origin. Galaktion Ilyich's father was a serf who was employed as a butler at a famous house; later he became a tax farmer and ended up as a famous philanthropist who had distributed thousands to charities and built numerous churches, for which he was given an order in this world of transient things and in the world to come was no doubt allotted an honored place among the heavenly hosts. He sent his son to a university to make a man of him, but the prayer beseeching the Almighty to keep his memory alive among men forever which was sung over his grave in the Nevsky monastery weighed rather heavily on the shoulders of his heir. The son of a "servant," he reached a certain high position in society and was admitted to the best houses, but in spite of this the jocular nickname given to him fixed the title of "moth-eaten" to him for good.

No one really had any clear idea of Galaktion Ilyich's real abilities or whether in fact he did possess a first-class brain. There was nothing mysterious about his career, though: when he entered the Civil Service he was, thanks to his father's influence, attached to the department headed by Count Victor Nikitich Panin, who had a great regard for his father because of certain qualities evident only to himself, and having taken the son under his wing, he quite soon pushed him over the line where "promotion" becomes automatic.

It would be safe to assume, at any rate, that Galaktion Ilyich did have certain merits which made it easy for Victor Nikitich to help him along with his promotions. But so far as society was concerned, Galaktion Ilyich was a complete failure, nor was he generally favored by fate as regards worldly joys. His health had always been delicate and his appearance was most unprepossessing. Tall and lanky like his late patron, Count Victor Nikitich, he lacked the count's outward stateliness. Unlike the count, Galaktion Ilyich did not inspire respect, but only fear mingled with some disgust. His yellowish skin was stretched tightly over a long, lean trunk; his unusually high forehead was dry and unnaturally yellow; his temples had a pale greenish tint, the color of a corpse; his nose was short and broad, just like the nose on a skull; he had no trace of eyebrows; his mouth was always slightly open, revealing his long teeth; and his eyes were dark, discolored, and sunk in deep, black caverns. In short, he was at one and the same time a typical country footman and the spitting image of a living corpse.

You could not help feeling shocked when meeting him for the first time.

The remarkable fact about Galaktion Ilyich's appearance was that he looked much more repulsive when he was younger and that the older he became, the less unprepossessing did he become, so that one was no longer shocked by his presence.

He had a most gentle disposition and a kindly, sympathetic, and—as we shall soon see—even a sentimental nature. He was a dreamer and, like most men of low origin, he kept his dreams locked up in his breast. At heart he was a poet rather than a civil servant and he loved life passionately, but he never enjoyed life to the full. He bore his misfortune stoically and he knew quite well that he was doomed to die an unhappy man. Even his promotions in the service failed to sweeten his existence, for he had reason to suspect that Count Victor Nikitich kept him as his private secretary chiefly because his very presence exercised a depressing effect on people. Galaktion Ilyich could see very plainly that when the people who were waiting for an interview with the count had to tell him their business, their eyes became dulled and their knees began to knock together. By producing this lamentable effect upon the count's petitioners, Galaktion Ilyich helped to increase his patron's popularity, for each visitor afterwards felt that his talk with the count himself had a very pleasant and even invigorating effect upon him.

As the year passed Galaktion Ilyich grew from a civil servant who submitted reports into one who had reports submitted to him, and he was entrusted with a very important and highly delicate mission in a remote part of the country, where the supernatural event in which he had played so prominent a part took place. The story of that eerie experience is told below in his own words.

3.

About twenty-five years ago (began the moth-eaten aristocrat) rumors began to reach the authorities in Petersburg about most flagrant abuses of his powers by the provincial governor P———v. These abuses seemed to have affected almost every department of the provincial government. The authorities in Petersburg were thus informed that the governor himself took part in floggings, that he together with the president of the Noblemen's Chamber confiscated all the local supplies of spirits for his own factories; that he helped himself quite arbitrarily to loans from the government funds; that he demanded that the entire postal correspondence be submitted to him so that he could send on only those letters he approved of and tear up those he disapproved of, which he did, revenging himself on the people whose letters contained disparaging remarks about him; and that, finally, he had no scruples about keeping people imprisoned without trial for as long as he pleased. He was despite all this, however, an artist, kept a large and excellent orchestra, was a lover of classical music, and was himself a fine performer on the cello.

For a long time only rumors of his high-handed actions reached the capital, but later on a minor official arrived and on his own initiative wrote a most detailed and damning report of the wretched business and submitted it to the proper authorities. The whole affair now assumed such serious proportions that it seemed that the only thing to do was to send a High Court Commission. That was what should have been done, but as both the governor and the president of the Nobleman's Chamber were highly thought of by the Emperor, it was not so easy to call them to account for their misdeeds as one would have wished. Victor Nikitich wanted first of all to obtain incontestable evidence of all the crimes of which the governor was accused and decided to send one of his own men to that province to obtain this evidence, and his choice fell on me.

He called me in and told me that he had had such and such reports of the unhappy state of affairs in that province and that unfortunately there seemed to be some basis for those reports. But before letting the affair take its usual course, he wished to make certain that the facts were indeed as stated and he had therefore decided to send me there to investigate the matter.

"I shall be happy to do what I can, sir," I said with a bow.

"I'm quite convinced you're the man for this job," he said, "and I want you to understand that I rely on you completely. You have such a way with you that people would never attempt to put you off with a lot of nonsense, but will tell you the whole truth."

This appearance of mine (Galaktion Ilyich explained with a gentle smile) is due simply to my melancholy appearance, which usually spreads depression all over the place. However, a man has to make the best of whatever talent he may possess.

"All the papers are ready for you," the count said, "but remember, officially you're going there to deal only with the affairs of your department. Just that and nothing else; you understand?"

"I quite understand, sir," I said.

"Officially," the count repeated, "you have nothing at all to do with any abuses in any other department, but that is only officially, for actually your duty is to get to know *everything*. You will be accompanied by two officials who have been specially trained for that kind of work. When you get there, you will start immediately on your mission and appear to concentrate on questions of office routine and court procedure, while unofficially you'll examine everything thoroughly. You will summon the local officials for examination and you are to deal with them as severely as possible. Don't be in a hurry to come back; I'll let you know when I want you to return. What was the last decoration you received?"

"The Vladimir, second class, with a coronet, sir," I replied.

The count removed his famous paperweight—"the shot bird" —with one hand, produced his personal notebook from under it, with his right hand seized a huge ebony pencil, and, without even attempting to conceal it from me, wrote down my name and jotted down next to it three words: "The White Eagle."

Thus I even knew the reward I was to get after accomplishing my mission—namely, the Order of the White Eagle—and the next day I left Petersburg without further ado.

I was accompanied on my mission by my personal valet Yegor and two High Court officials, both of them very adroit men of the world.

4.

Our journey, I need hardly tell you, was uneventful, and, on our arrival in the town, we rented an apartment and settled down—myself, the two officials, and my valet.

Our flat was so comfortable that I did not find it difficult to refuse the most comfortable accommodations very kindly offered to me by the governor. For I naturally did not want to be under any obligation to him whatever, although I could not help, of course, exchanging official visits with him and, as a matter of fact, I was present at his concerts of Haydn quartets once or twice. However, I am not a lover of music—indeed my knowledge of classical music is very scant—so I did my best, as you can imagine, not to get on too friendly a footing with him, for what I was interested in was not his fine manners, but his evil deeds. Still, the governor was a very clever and perspicacious man and he did not bother me with his attentions. He seemed to have given me full liberty to deal with all the incoming and outgoing registers and protocols, but in spite of that I had a queer feeling that something was going on all around me, that people were trying to find out how they could compromise me and then, I suppose, get me mixed up in their own illegal transactions.

I am afraid I am obliged to mention here the distressing fact that members of the fair sex were not altogether unconcerned in these dark goings on. Various ladies began to honor me with their visits, pressing numerous complaints and petitions upon me, but invariably ending up by making certain suggestions to me which left me staring at them dumbfounded. But I remembered Victor Nikitich's advice and dealt with them "as severely as possible," and these phantoms of delight vanished from my unworthy sight. My two officials, on the other hand, were more susceptible to female charms, and although I knew of their successes, I did not interfere with their private affairs, nor did I prevent them from pretending to be the important men for whom they were so readily mistaken. Indeed, I found it very useful that they were visiting people and were successful with the ladies. All I asked of them was that there should be no public scandal and that I should be apprised of which of their social activities attracted the greatest attention on the part of the local politicians. They were very conscientious fellows and they kept nothing back from me. What everybody seemed anxious to find out from them was what my weaknesses were and what I liked best.

As a matter of fact, they would have had trouble discovering it, for, thank heavens, I have no particular foibles and even my tastes have, as far as I can remember, always been very simple. All my life I have been used to simple fare, I drink only one glass of cheap sherry a day, and even the sweets I was so very fond of as a young man, all sorts of fine jellies and pineapples, no longer make my mouth water: I'd a hundred times rather have an Astrakhan watermelon, a Kursk pear, or a honey cake, tastes which I acquired as a child. I did not envy anyone his riches or fame or beauty, and if I did envy a man anything, it was only his health. But the word "envy" hardly describes my feeling. The sight of a man glowing with health did not arouse in me the spiteful thought of why he should be like that while I was just the opposite. When I looked at such a man I felt pleased that he at least should be able to enjoy life to the full and drain the cup of happiness to its very dregs, though I must confess that there have been times when I could not help feeling a twinge of regret that I should not be able to enjoy the sweets of life that only good health enables a man to enjoy, the good health that I have never possessed.

The pleasure that the sight of a hale and hearty man gave me accounted for the eccentricity in my aesthetic tastes: I never ran after a Taglioni or a Boziot and was left entirely cold by opera and ballet, where everything is so artificial; what I liked most of all was to listen to the songs and watch the dances of the gypsies in Krestovsky Lane; for their fire and abandon, the passionate force of their movements, excited me tremendously. Some of those gypsies were not even handsome, but once they began to dance, it seemed as if Satan himself were leading them on. They'd dance with their feet, wave their arms about, turn their heads this way and that, twist their trunks, their bodies caught up in a whirling tornado of movement. Looking at them I felt weak and helpless, but I couldn't take my eyes off them, and I'd abandon myself to idle dreams of how different my life would have been if I had been robust and healthy. For what delights could one not snatch from life's banquet if only one enjoyed good health?

That was why I said to one of the two officials attached to me, "Look here, my friend, if they should ask you what it is I like best in the world, tell them that the thing I admire most is good health and that what I enjoy most is to be in the company of gay, cheerful, happy men."

"I didn't commit any indiscretion there, did I?" Galaktion Ilyich asked, interrupting his story.

The listeners thought it over for a moment and replied:

"Of course not!"

"I'm glad you think so," Galaktion Ilyich said, "for that happens to be my opinion, too. However, listen to what happened later."

5.

As soon as I settled down to the daily grind of my new job (Galaktion Ilyich went on), an official of the local high court was sent to me as my private secretary. He introduced the various visitors who came to see me and, whenever necessary, supplied me with the addresses of people I wanted to see myself or went round to the different government departments to make the inquiries I wanted made. The official detailed for that duty was in many ways rather like myself. He was a melancholy specimen of a man, a middle-aged, dry-as-dust civil servant. The impression he produced was not a particularly cheerful one, but I did not pay much attention to him anyway. His name, I think, was Ornatsky, an excellent name on the whole, a name that seemed to have been taken out of the pages of an old-fashioned novel. One day, however, I was told that Ornatsky had been taken ill and that the administrative clerk had sent me another official.

"Who is he?" I asked, and I added: "Wouldn't it have been just as well to wait until Ornatsky was well again?"

"No, sir," replied the administrative clerk. "Ornatsky, I'm sorry to say, has taken to drink, and it usually takes him a long time to recover from his drinking bouts. I'm afraid we shall have to wait until Ivan Petrovich's mother cures him of it. But you needn't worry about the new man, sir, for it is Ivan Petrovich himself who has been appointed in Ornatsky's place."

I looked at him a little bewildered: who was Ivan Petrovich *himself* and why mention him twice in as many sentences?

"What kind of a man is this . . . Ivan Petrovich?" I asked.

"Ivan Petrovich, sir? Why, he's an official in the registrar's office —assistant director. I thought you had noticed him, sir. A very handsome man. Everybody notices him."

"No," I said, "I'm afraid I haven't noticed him. What did you say his name was?"

"Ivan Petrovich, sir."

"And surname?"

"His surname is . . ." the administrative clerk stopped short, looking a little embarrassed. He pressed three fingers against his brow, trying to remember the surname, but, evidently failing to do so, added with an ingratiating smile, "Excuse me, sir, but I just can't recall his surname. It's gone clean out of my head. Oh, yes, yes, I've got it now, sir. His surname is Aquilalbov, but we just call him Ivan Petrovich or sometimes, as a joke, 'White Eagle,' he being such a handsome fellow. Yes, sir, he's a first-rate man, enjoys an excellent reputation with his superiors, his salary as assistant director is fourteen roubles fifteen copecks a month, and he lives with his mother, who dabbles in fortune-telling and is also quite good at healing people of all sorts of . . . er . . . infirmities. Shall I introduce him to you, sir? Ivan Petrovich is waiting in the next room."

"Well, I suppose you might as well ask—er—Ivan Petrovich to come in," I said.

"White Eagle!" I thought. "What a queer coincidence! But it was the Order of the White Eagle that I was promised and not Ivan Petrovich."

The administrative clerk in the meantime opened the door and shouted, "Ivan Petrovich, come in, please."

I am afraid I cannot describe him to you without using some well-worn clichés and making comparisons which you may think rather exaggerated, but I give you my word of honor that however much I tried to describe Ivan Petrovich to you, my description of him would not convey a picture half as beautiful as the original. There stood in front of me a real "white eagle," an unmistakable *aquila alba*, as he is pictured at the official receptions given by Zeus on Olympus. A tall, large, and exceptionally well-proportioned man, he looked such a picture of health that one couldn't help feeling that he had never had a day's illness in his life and that he did not know the meaning of boredom or fatigue. Health exuded from him, but not in a crude way, no! It poured out of him in a way that was both attractive and serene. It didn't bowl you over, you understand. It soothed you. It made you feel at peace with yourself, happy. His complexion was of a most delicate pink, spreading imperceptibly to a fine, healthy redness, his cheeks were framed by a fringe of fair down which, however, was already showing signs of a maturer growth. He was exactly twenty-five years old. His hair was fair, slightly wavy, and his beard was of the same color, with a most charming part in the middle; his eyes were blue and his eyebrows and eyelashes dark. In short, no Russian legendary hero could have been handsomer. But add to that a spirited, highly intelligent, cheerful and frank expression and you get all the attributes of a really handsome man. He was dressed in a civil servant's uniform which fitted him like a glove, and across one shoulder he wore a sash of a dark red with a magnificent bow. In those days such sashes were still fashionable.

I could not take my eyes off Ivan Petrovich and, knowing the rather unfortunate effect my own appearance had on people who saw me for the first time, I said simply, "How do you do, Ivan Petrovich."

"How do you do, sir," he replied in a very cordial voice, which also produced an exceedingly good impression on me.

His answer, though strictly within the limits of social convention, had a curious intimacy about it which, while not overstepping the line our respective positions had drawn between us, yet at once lent our conversation a character of friendly familiarity.

I began to understand why people could not help liking this man.

Seeing no reason why I should take exception to his tone, I said to Ivan Petrovich that I was very pleased indeed to make his acquaintance.

"For my part, too, sir," he replied, "I regard it as both an honor and a pleasure."

We took leave of each other, the administrative clerk going back to his office and Ivan Petrovich remaining in my reception room. In about an hour I summoned him to my room.

"How's your handwriting?" I asked him.

"I have quite a firm hand," he replied, and immediately added, 'Do you want me to write something for you, sir?"

"Yes, please," I replied.

He sat down at my writing table and, after a minute, handed me a sheet of paper in the middle of which was written in a legible firm hand:

"Life is here to be enjoyed. Ivan Petrovich Aquilalbov."

I read it and burst out laughing: he could not have described himself better than in the words he had written—"Life is here to be enjoyed!" Life was nothing but happiness to him.

The man was certainly to my liking. I asked him to copy out

a rather important document and he did it at my table with exemplary speed and without making a single mistake.

Later we parted. Ivan Petrovich went away and I remained at home alone and gave myself up to my morbid thoughts, and, I confess, in my thoughts I was, goodness knows why, transported to *him*, that is to say, to Ivan Petrovich. He, I thought, was not moaning and groaning, he was not suffering from fits of depression, life was given to him so that he could be happy. . . . And how could he manage to live such a happy life on his fourteen roubles? . . . Must be lucky at cards, or perhaps he, too, was not above accepting a bribe here and there, or rich widows, maybe . . . Why else did he wear that lovely red sash? . . .

I was sitting before a pile of official documents and my head was full of such idle thoughts about things which were no concern of mine anyway. Just then my valet announced the arrival of the governor.

I asked him to come in.

6.

"I'm giving a chamber concert the day after tomorrow," said the governor, "a quintet, and I've every reason to expect that the performance will be good. There'll be a few ladies among my guests. I understand you've fallen prey to melancholy in this provincial hole of ours and I've come to ask you to honor me with your presence at the concert, if not to enjoy the music, then for a cup of tea. I daresay a little distraction will do you a world of good."

"Thank you very much," I said, "but who told you that I'd fallen prey to melancholy?"

"Ivan Petrovich said something about it."

"Oh, Ivan Petrovich? That's the fellow who's on duty here, isn't it? Do you know him?"

"Of course I know him. He's our student, artist, singer—does everything in fact except cheat."

"So he is no cheat, is he?"

"No, sir, he's as happy as Policrates and there's no reason in the world why he should be a cheat. He's a general favorite in our town and takes an active part in all our festivities."

"Is he a musician?"

"He's good at everything; he can sing, act, dance, organize gay parties, parlor games. . . . Yes, sir, Ivan Petrovich can do all that and more. Where there's a feast, there is Ivan Petrovich; a raffle or theatricals for charitable purposes—Ivan Petrovich is there, too; he distributes the prizes, arranges them most beautifully, paints the scenery, and then transforms himself from a scene painter into an actor, ready to take on any part. You can't imagine what a fine actor he is! Kings, benevolent old uncles, passionate lovers —it's all grist for his mill, but best of all he acts old women."

"Old women, did you say?"

"Yes, he's quite wonderful in such parts. Now I'm going to let you in on a secret. I'm preparing a little surprise for that party of mine with the help of Ivan Petrovich. *Tableaux vivants!* Ivan Petrovich will be responsible for producing them. Now one or two of them will be the usual kind for the dear ladies who like a little self-display, but three will be real works of art."

"And Ivan Petrovich will be responsible for them?"

"Yes, Ivan Petrovich. The *tableaux* will represent Saul's visit to the witch of Endor. A rather hackneyed biblical subject, you say? Ah, but that's where Ivan Petrovich comes in! Everybody's gaze will be fixed on him, especially when at the opening of the second *tableau* our real surprise of the evening is revealed. To you, I think, I can safely reveal this great secret of ours. The curtains are drawn and you see Saul, a king from head to foot. He will be dressed just like the rest, there won't be the slightest difference between his costume and those of his companions, for, as you will remember, Saul goes to the witch in disguise so that she will not recognize him, *but it is impossible not to recognize him.* He is a king and, moreover, a real biblical shepherd-king. The curtain descends, the king's figure in the *tableau* quickly changes its position: Saul lies prostrate before Samuel's ghost; Saul cannot be seen any more, it is as if he were not there at all, but instead you will see Samuel in his mantle, and what a Samuel! An inspired prophet, whose face is full of strength, majesty, and wisdom. This one could well 'command the king to appear in Beth-el and Gilgal!' "

"And that will again be Ivan Petrovich?"

"Yes, Ivan Petrovich. But that's not all. If there's a demand for an encore, and I'm quite sure there will be, in fact I shall see to it that there is, we shan't bore you with a repetition of the same scenes, no, sir! You will see the continuation of the epic. The new scene from the life of Saul won't have Saul in it. The ghost has disappeared, the king and his servants have gone, in the doorway one can just see the robe of the last retreating figure, and on the stage only the witch is left. . . ."

"And the witch, too, is Ivan Petrovich?"

"Of course! But what you'll see isn't just a witch from *Macbeth*, no cheap effects to make your flesh creep, no horror, no grimacing. No! What you'll see is a face which knows what even the wise have never dreamed of. Yes, by looking at this face you will realize how terrible it must be to talk to spirits dragged from their graves."

"I can imagine it," I said, little dreaming that within three days I should not only imagine, but personally experience the horror of talking to a spirit dragged from his grave—but that happened later. For the time being all my thoughts seemed to revolve around Ivan Petrovich, that gay living man who had popped out of the ground so suddenly, just like a mushroom in a field after a shower: it is still very small, but you can see it from anywhere; everybody looks at it and admires it: "What a lovely, firm mushroom!"

7.

I told you what the administrative clerk and the governor had said about Ivan Petrovich. When I asked my own officials whether they had heard of him, both of them promptly replied that they had met him many times at the different social functions at which they themselves had shone so conspicuously and that he was really a very nice fellow and sang charmingly to the accompaniment of a guitar or piano. There could be no doubt that they, too, liked him. Next day the archpriest paid me a visit. After I had been to his church, he used to come to see me regularly and bring me the consecrated bread every holy day and gossip sanctimoniously about everybody in town. I never heard him utter a good word about any man or woman and he made no exception so far as Ivan Petrovich was concerned. Still, pious dabbler in local scandal though he was, I found him very useful, for he not only knew everything that was going on in the town, but also the origin and nature of every intrigue, new and old. It was he who brought up the subject of Ivan Petrovich.

"I see you've got a new assistant," he remarked cryptically, and he added, "All this is done with a purpose, you know. . . ."

"Yes," I said, "they sent me a fellow by the name of Ivan Petrovich."

"He's not unknown to me," said the archpriest. "In fact, I know him quite well. My brother-in-law, whose incumbency I'm now occupying with the added duties of supervising the education of orphans, baptized him. His father was the son of a priest . . . became a government clerk; and his mother . . . Kyra Hippolitovna . . . curious name she's got . . . was greatly in love with his father, ran away from her parents to marry him . . . but she soon tasted the bitter dregs of the love potion and . . . luckily, she soon became a widow."

"Did she educate her son herself?"

"I'm afraid his education's nothing to boast of. He didn't finish his secondary school, stayed till the third form and then got himself a job as a clerk at the criminal court. A very lucky fellow, though: last year he won a horse and a saddle in a lottery. Went hunting hares with the governor the other day, I believe. He also won a piano which the officers of some regiment had put up as the prize in a raffle before leaving our town. I took five tickets and didn't win it, but he had only one ticket and he got it. Plays it himself and teaches Tatyana. . . ."

"Who's Tatyana?"

"An orphan girl they've adopted . . . not bad looking, dark-skinned. He teaches her."

I spent the whole day talking about Ivan Petrovich and in the evening I heard a curious kind of buzzing in my valet's room. I called him in and asked him what he was doing in his room.

"Doing some fretwork, sir," he replied.

"What kind of fretwork?"

It seemed that Ivan Petrovich, seeing that Yegor was at loose ends in the evenings, had brought him a fret saw and some blades and pieces of wood from cigar boxes with patterns pasted on them and taught him to saw out little trays which he intended to put up as prizes in a raffle.

8.

On the morning of the day of the governor's party, at which Ivan Petrovich was to surprise us all by his acting in the *tableaux vivants*, I did not want to detain him, but he insisted on staying with me until lunch and he even succeeded in making me laugh. I said as a joke that he ought to get married, but he replied that he preferred to remain "an old maid." I invited him to go back with me to Petersburg.

"No thank you, sir," he said. "I'd rather stay here, for here everybody likes me, and besides, there's my mother and Tanya, the orphan girl we've adopted; I'm very attached to them and I'm afraid Petersburg is hardly the place for them."

What an amazingly amiable young man! I even embraced him, so touched was I by his love for his mother and that orphan girl. We took leave of each other three hours before the *tableaux vivants* were due to start.

My last words to him were, "I can hardly wait to see you in the different parts tonight."

"I'm afraid I shall bore you," replied Ivan Petrovich.

He went away and after lunch I tried to take a nap in my armchair, for I was anxious to feel as fresh as possible at the party. But Ivan Petrovich would not let me sleep: no sooner had I shut my eyes than he disturbed me in rather a curious way. He suddenly walked into my room as if he were in a great hurry, pushed the chairs in the middle of the room out of his way noisily, and said, "Well, here I am! Thank you very much for casting an evil spell on me. I shall pay you back for that!"

I woke up, rang for my valet, and told him to help me dress, but I could not get that dream of mine out of my head: so uncannily clear had Ivan Petrovich appeared to me!

I arrived at the governor's house. The brightly lit rooms were crowded with people, but the governor himself, in greeting me, whispered, "Afraid the main part of the program will have to be scrapped: there won't be any *tableaux*."

"What's happened?"

"Sh-sh. . . . Don't want to speak in a loud voice for fear of spoiling the party. Ivan Petrovich is dead."

"Ivan Petrovich?"

"Dead."

"Are you sure?"

"Positive. The poor fellow's dead."

"But that's impossible! Only about three hours ago he was in my office and there was nothing the matter with him. He looked the picture of health."

"Well, he got home from your office, lay down on a couch, and died. . . . And you know . . . I think I'd better warn you in case his mother . . . She's quite beside herself with grief and she might come to see you. The poor woman is convinced that you are responsible for her son's death."

"Me? Why me? He wasn't poisioned at my place, was he?"

"She doesn't accuse you of that."

"What is she accusing me of?"

"She accuses you of having cast a spell on Ivan Petrovich, or, more specifically, of having *given him the evil eye*."

"But really," I said, "that's pure nonsense!"

"Of course it's nonsense," replied the governor, "but don't forget that you're in a remote provincial town now where people believe in nonsense. Still, if I were you, I shouldn't worry about it."

Just then the governor's wife invited me to join her in a game of cards.

I sat down at the card table. Oh, I can't tell you what torture I went through during that frightful game of cards! In the first place, I felt terribly oppressed by the thought of the nice young man I had admired so much now lying dead on a slab, and, secondly, I became obsessed by a strange feeling that everybody in the room was whispering about him and pointing at me. "Gave him the evil eye!" I could even hear those stupid words, "Evil eye, evil eye, evil eye . . ." Thirdly, let me be quite truthful with you, gentlemen, every time I looked up from my cards I could *see* Ivan Petrovich himself. I don't know what kind of strange illusion it was, but wherever I chanced to look, there was Ivan Petrovich. . . . Sometimes I saw him walking slowly across an empty room, the doors of which were open; sometimes I saw him joining two people who were discussing something and listening to their conversation; then, suddenly, he'd appear beside me and look at my cards. . . . Whenever that happened, well . . . I'd just slam down my cards and my partner would be annoyed with me. At last even the other people in the room began to notice that something was wrong with me and the governor whispered in my ear:

"It isn't Ivan Petrovich interfering with your enjoyment of the evening, is it? He must be revenging himself on you!"

"Well," I said, "as a matter of fact I am feeling a little indisposed. With your permission, ladies and gentlemen, I think I'll go home."

They were good enough not to raise any objections and I immediately drove home.

As I sat down in the sleigh, I noticed that Ivan Petrovich was sitting beside me; then, after a little while, he sat down on the driver's box with his face turned towards me. I was wondering whether I was coming down with a fever, but when I arrived home, things became even worse. The moment I got into bed and extinguished my bedside lamp, I saw Ivan Petrovich sitting on the edge of the bed, and he even began talking to me.

"You really did give me the evil eye, you know," he said, "and it is your fault entirely that I'm dead. There is no other explanation for my death. That's what proves your guilt so conclusively, you see. Everybody loved me—my mother and little Tanya. Poor little Tanya, nobody will help her to complete her education. Oh, what a terrible blow my death has been to them!"

I rang for my valet and, however much I disliked doing it, I asked him to make himself a bed on the carpet and spend the night in my room. But Ivan Petrovich was not in the least discomfited by Yegor's presence in the room. On the contrary, wherever I looked I was sure to see him standing in front of me. I could do nothing to get rid of him.

It seemed ages to me before morning came. The first thing I did was to send one of my officials to the mother of Ivan Petrovich with three hundred roubles for the funeral expenses. I told him to use the utmost tact in handing the money to her. But my messenger came back with the money. They refused to accept it, he told me.

"What did they say?" I asked.

"They said, 'We don't want it: there are lots of good people in the town who'll be glad to pay for his funeral.' "

I was therefore to be counted among the *bad* people.

And every time I thought of Ivan Petrovich, he'd immediately appear before me.

When dusk fell I just could not stay at home. I took a cab and went there myself to have a look at Ivan Petrovich and take leave of him. That was the custom, after all, and I hardly expected to be in anybody's way. I put as much money as I could lay my hands on in my pocket, seven hundred roubles in all, intending to persuade them to take it for Tanya's education.

9.

I had a look at Ivan Petrovich: the "White Eagle" lay there as if he had been shot on the wing.

Tanya was walking about in the room. She was rather dark-skinned, about fifteen years old, in a black calico dress. She kept on walking up to the dead man and putting something right. She'd smooth his hair and kiss him.

Oh, what torment it was for me to see it!

I asked her whether I could have a few words with Ivan Petrovich's mother. The girl said, "I'll ask her," and went into the other room. In another minute she opened the door and asked me to come in, but no sooner did I enter the room where Ivan Petrovich's mother was sitting, than the old woman got up and excused herself.

"I'm sorry," she said, "I thought I might be able to see you, but I was mistaken: I cannot see you!" and she walked out of the room.

I felt neither hurt nor embarrassed—just crushed.

"Perhaps you, my dear, who are so young, will be kinder to me," I said to Tanya. "Please believe me, I did not wish, nor did I have any cause to wish, Ivan Petrovich any harm, let alone his death."

"I believe you, sir," she murmured. "No one ever wished him any harm. Everybody loved him."

"I hope you'll believe me," I said, "when I tell you that during the few days I knew him, I, too, came to love him."

"Yes, yes," she said. "Oh, those terrible 'few days'! Why did they have to be? Auntie's so upset, sir. That's why she did not want to see you, but I . . . I am sorry for you."

She stretched out her two small hands to me.

"Thank you, thank you, my dear child," I said, grasping her hands, "for your kind feelings. They do honor to your heart and to your head. What utter nonsense indeed it is to say that I gave him the evil eye!"

"Yes, of course it is," she said.

"In that case," I said, "will you be so kind as to do me a favor *for his sake?*"

"What kind of favor?"

"Take this envelope, please . . . there's some money in it . . . just for any household expenses . . . for your aunt."

"She won't accept it."

"Very well, for you, then . . . for your education, which Ivan Petrovich had set his heart on. I'm sure he would have approved of it."

"No thank you, sir. I can't possibly accept it. He never took anything from anybody. He was a very, very honorable man."

"But do you think you're being fair to me in refusing to accept it? It means that you're blaming me, doesn't it?"

"No, I'm not blaming you. I'll prove it to you."

She opened Ollendorf's French primer, which lay on the table, took a photograph of Ivan Petrovich from it, and gave it to me.

"He put it there himself," she said. "We got as far as that in our lesson yesterday. Take it as a keepsake from me."

That was the end of our interview. Ivan Petrovich was buried the next day and I remained for another eight days in that town, and every minute I spent there was a nightmare to me. I couldn't sleep at night and I used to lie awake listening to any noise, opening the window just to hear some human voice, but there was little comfort in that. Two men would walk past and I'd strain my ears to catch their words. As a rule, they would be discussing Ivan Petrovich and me.

"That's where the devil who gave Ivan Petrovich the evil eye lives," one of them would be sure to say.

A man would be returning home late at night. He would be singing. I could hear the snow crunching under his feet and I could make out the words of his song. "Oh, what a gay lad I was. . . ." I waited for him to come up to my window, but when he did, it was Ivan Petrovich I saw!

On top of that the archpriest came to see me.

"Evil spells no doubt exist," he said, "but I've never heard of grown people being affected by them. Ivan Petrovich was poisoned!"

I winced. "Why should he be poisoned and by whom?"

"They were afraid that he might tell you things. There should have been a post-mortem. A pity. They'd have discovered the poison."

Lord, deliver me at least from such suspicions!

Then I suddenly received a confidential communication from the head of the department saying that the count desired me to confine my mission to what I had already found out and return to Petersburg at once.

I was very glad and in two days I finished my packing and left for St. Petersburg.

During the journey Ivan Petrovich never left me alone. He'd appear before me at any time of the day or night, but whether it was because of the change of place or because one can get used to anything, I was no longer terrified of him and I even got used to his company. He kept on popping up before my eyes, but I wasn't even interested any longer: sometimes when I would doze off—why, we'd even crack jokes together! He'd boast, "Taught you a lesson, didn't I?" and I'd reply, "Ah, but you had no time to learn French, did you?" He'd say, "What does that matter? I don't need to learn French now: I've taught myself the lingo and I can speak it like a native!"

10.

On my arrival in Petersburg I felt that my superiors were not so much dissatisfied with me as that they looked at me rather strangely, as if they were sorry for me. Count Victor Niki-tich himself saw me for only a minute. He didn't say anything to me, but to the head of the department, who was married to a sister of mine, he said that it seemed to him that I was *ill*. . . .

No explanations of any kind were asked for. In another week it was Christmas, then the New Year came. There was the usual kind of New Year's excitement; everybody was waiting with impatience for the publication of the New Year's Honor List. I was not particularly worried about it, since I knew the honor I could expect—the "White Eagle." My sister had sent me the order and ribbon as a present on New Year's Eve and I put it in my desk together with an envelope with one hundred roubles for the messengers who were to bring me the official command.

But that night Ivan Petrovich nudged me as I lay in bed and thumbed his nose right in my face. He had been much more courteous when alive and, besides, this behavior hardly suited his amiable character. Still, there he was, thumbing his nose at me just like any street urchin.

"That'll do for you for now," he said. "Now I must hurry to poor Tanya."

Having said that, he vanished.

I got up next morning, but there were no messengers with the official confirmation of my new honor. I hastened to my brother-in-law to find out what had happened.

"Can't understand it at all," he said. "It was there in the Honor List, but it seems to have dropped out of the printed page. You see, the count himself crossed it out. Said he'd submit your name personally. I understand something's happened that's making things a bit awkward for you at present. A civil servant seems to have died in suspicious circumstances after leaving your office. . . . What exactly did happen?"

"Oh, never mind," I said. "Please, don't ask me."

"No, really. . . . The count, you know, has asked me several times whether you weren't indisposed. He's received many letters from there from all sorts of people, including one from the local archpriest. . . . How did you get yourself mixed up in such an unsavory business?"

I listened to him and I felt like sticking out my tongue at him or thumbing my nose, just like Ivan Petrovich's spirit.

Ivan Petrovich, on the other hand, having rewarded me with that rude gesture of his instead of the "White Eagle," vanished and did not appear to me again for another three years, at the end of which time he paid me a last visit, one that was the most palpable of all his spectral appearances.

11.

It was Christmas again and then New Year's Day and the same excitement about the New Year's Honors. I had been passed over so many times already that I had stopped worrying about it. If they did not want to give me a decoration, I might as well make the best of it. I saw in the new year at a party given by my sister. It was a very gay party, lots of people. Dinner was served and they were all filing into the dining room, while I was trying to get out unobserved and moving towards the door, when I heard above the hum of conversation the following words:

"Now the days of my wandering are over. My mother is with me. Dear Tanya's married to a good man. Let me perform my last trick and *je m'en vais*." And then somebody began to sing in a drawling kind of voice:

> Good-bye, my sweetheart,
> Farewell, my native land.

"Aha," thought I, "so he's appeared again, has he? Seems to be talking French, too. I'd better wait for someone. Damned if I'm going to walk up the staircase by myself!"

And then he brushed past me, still wearing the same civil service uniform with the lovely deep-red sash, and no sooner did he pass me than the front door slammed with such force that it made the whole house shake. . . .

My brother-in-law and the servants rushed out to make sure that nobody had helped himself to the guests' fur coats, but everything was in order. The queer thing, however, was that the front door was locked and bolted! I didn't utter a word for fear of being accused again of being subject to hallucinations and being pestered with inquiries about my "health." The door had slammed and that was the end of it as far as I was concerned. There might have been hundreds of reasons for its slamming.

I waited until I found somebody who was going my way and I reached home without further incident. I had a different valet now, not the one who had accompanied me on my confidential mission, to whom Ivan Petrovich had given fret saws and cigar boxes. He met me, looking a little sleepy, and lighted me to my bedroom. As we passed my little study, I noticed something on my desk, a parcel wrapped in white paper. I took a look at it: it was my Order of the White Eagle, which, as you'll remember, my sister had given me three years ago. I always kept it under lock and key. How could it have gotten there? I know it might be said that I had put it there myself and then forgotten all about it. Well, I won't argue about it, but how will you explain this? On the bedside table at the head of my bed I found a small envelope with my name written on it and I seemed to recognize the handwriting. Yes, it was the same "firm hand" that had written, "Life is there to be enjoyed!"

"Who brought this?" I asked.

My valet pointed to the photograph of Ivan Petrovich on the wall of my bedroom (I kept it in memory of dear little Tanya) and said:

"This gentleman brought it, sir."

"You must be mistaken," I said.

"No, sir," he replied. "I recognized him at once!"

In the envelope I found a copy of the official New Year's Honors List: I was given the "White Eagle." But what was even more welcome to me was that I slept through the whole night without waking, although I did hear some distant singing in my sleep and was able to make out the most stupid refrain imaginable: "Good-bye-ee, good-bye-ee, *au contradance je aller-ee!*"

From my experience of the spirit world which I had gained from Ivan Petrovich, I realized that it must have been Ivan Petrovich himself, who had taught himself "the lingo" and spoke it "like a native" and who was now serenading me for the last time. And so it was: he had paid me back and he had also forgiven me. So far, so good. But what I can't understand is why everything is so mixed up in the spirit world that a human life, than which nothing, surely, can be more valuable, is revenged by some silly spook stuff and a decoration, and the arrival or departure of a spirit is accompanied by the singing of such a silly refrain as: "Good-bye-ee, good-bye-ee, *au contradance je aller-ee!*" That, gentlemen, is something I shall never understand.